The Witch of Kelvert

By

Ben Jamar Billups

To the family,

thank you for the love

and inspiration.

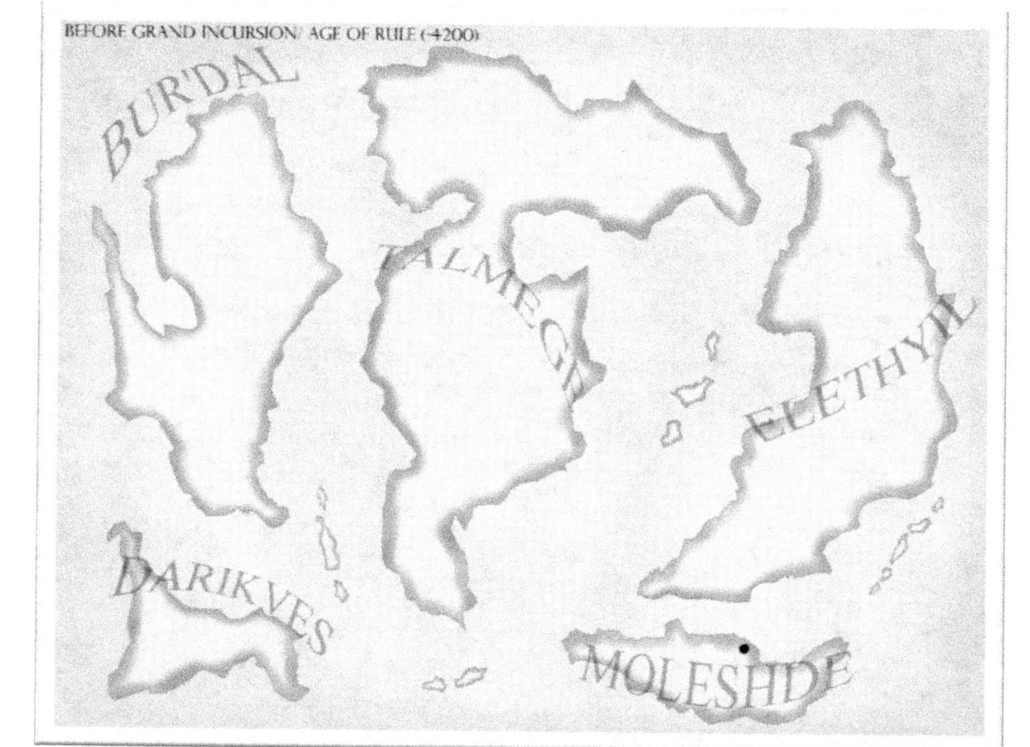

BEFORE GRAND INCURSION: AGE OF RULE (-4200)
BUR'DAL
TALMEGA
ELETHYIL
DARIKVES
MOLESHDE

MOLESHDE BGI -912

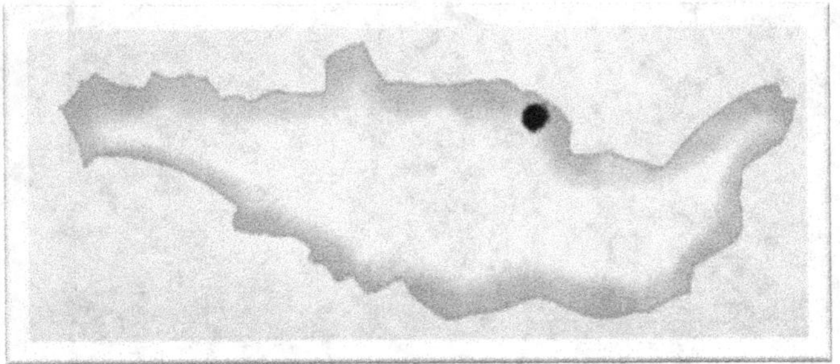

KELVERT DRYLANDS OF MOLESHDE -912 BEFORE GRAND INCURSION

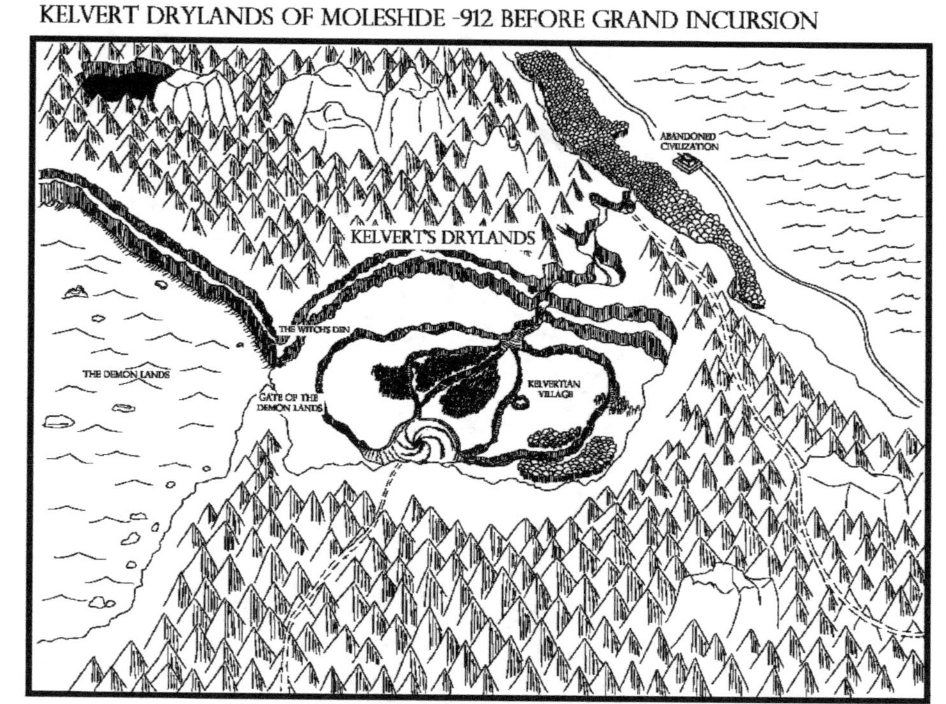

Table of Contests

Chapters:

Part 1:
Howls Through the Night

Ch. 1

Run from Death

The wind howled, coursing through a large opening in the cavern ceiling, stirring dust and bringing little reprieve to the night's humid air. Nuyani turned in her bedroll, but sleep remained elusive as a constant throb pulsed from the center of her body.

'By Lord Kelvert's will, what is happening?" she asked, invoking the name of her deity for guidance. She sat up and placed a hand over her stomach. A festive drum beat away within her stomach at a rapid pace, too fast and constant for a heartbeat. Yet, none of the resonance could be felt by her hand. No pain or sound rose from the strange pulses as they passed through her and out. The ghostly pulses strengthened as she dwelled on the sensation, becoming deeper. Only adding to the confusion was the soft throb of her heart, a handspan higher.

"What is this?" Nuyani asked. Licking her lips, she found her tongue dry and rose to fetch water. She became sensitive to the condition of every muscle stiffening despite her bedroll and the humid draft carrying specks of sand pelting her face.

It did not help she remained dressed in runner's wear as her leather-wrapped hand brushed against the hide clothing. A single article made of red leather covered her torso with short sleeves, and wooden buttons fastened shut to keep the clothing tight and harder to snag on brush. A hood was stitched to the top with a fitted brim to remain secure on her brow and prevent wind from blowing it back. On each of her limbs, she wore leather bindings and cords all the way down until they laced between her fingers and toes. The tough material protected against brush and beast but could do little to resist the annual sandstorms capable of stripping flesh from bone. The winds were powerful enough to carry man, woman, or child miles away in its gale lasting for days. Through the darkness, Nuyani sauntered a few paces away with closed eyes. She knelt low and reached past a rock ledge and into the confines of a basket.

'Where are you?' she thought while grumbling unintelligibly. Her fingers then ran over a clay bowl. She removed the dish from the basket before searching with her other hand for a jar lid. Finding the small nob, Nuyani lifted the top and plunged the bowl into the cool water.

"By his shine, what is this?" Nuyani groaned. The rapid beat grew stronger and harsh, calling her attention as it echoed out into the area surrounding her. As if her hands became the air itself, she could feel the worn stone floor, circulating dust and course surface of the basket and jar with every wave passing through a small radius around her. Yet, some of the waves were uneven, becoming distorted toward her front. A resistance pushing against the beat felt as if someone repeatedly jammed a finger into her stomach. Nuyani opened her ember glowing eyes as a sudden blue light filled the large cavern walls. Darkness faded, revealing dozens of dust-ridden huts casting long shadows against the cavern walls. She froze with her mouth agape as she looked upon the visage of a woman slowly rising above the ground. Her entire decrepit body was made of light, with the details of the stone wall showing through her form. Her visitor's sparse hair cascaded about in the air as if it were submerged in water.

'What is that thing?' Nuyani asked, looking at the lower legs gradually disappearing with their feet gone altogether, every finger nearly three times the natural length and thinned to the tip as claws. Even from the backside, the figure's drooping jaw passed her shoulder and collar bone.

Nuyani could not speak. A strange cold passed through her garments and nipped at her skin. The light figure flew about the cavern, passing through the rooves of each hut. Its body rippling like a ribbon in each pass. As the light died and reemerged, Nuyani stayed still. Her body trembled as she released the bowl, letting it sink.

'Is this a spirit? What are you? Please. You aren't a demon, are you?' she wanted to ask, only to find her voice stolen. 'Lord Kelvert, I beg you. Please guide me,' she prayed.

"Run," a sharp whisper sounded in her voice. Nuyani blinked, finding herself exposed but unnoticed by the apparition.

She stayed low, moving toward her stone ax, knives, and pouches bearing smaller tools, poisons, and herbs. Nuyani turned toward a shadowed path cutting through the stone wall, making her way for the exit. As she inched near the tunnel, the throbbing in her stomach shifted in the direction of the disturbance growing in pressure, stifling the beat further, but at her flank. Nuyani turned about, finding the apparition's head peeking out of the stone floor only a few paces away. She looked into the voided eyes bearing a small iridescent glint at their center.

The cold enwrapped Nuyani as the specter's jaw descended to mid-chest. A blood-turning lament filled the area and echoed from the stone walls around them. Pain filled Nuyani's ears as she knelt before the invader. The pulse dulled, and her vision grew dark with light draining into the specter's eyes.

'Great Lord, am I to be taken now? After all these years, is it time? Do you blame me? Please. I only want to live,' Nuyani thought. The growing chill penetrated through her body, sending a shiver down her spine and limbs. Her visitor reeled an arm back, claw-like fingers extended.

"Run," the whisper snapped once more as the pulse returned, repelling the cold and trembling. Every muscle was filled with renewed strength as the woman leaned back, dodging the swipe. Nuyani turned toward her exit and sprinted down the narrow path. Her arms and knees grazed the stone walls as she followed the soft silver glow overhead from flowers growing on vines clinging to the ceiling.

'Thank you, Great Lord,' Nuyani prayed with tears streaming across her cheeks. She reached the end of the silver path. Wind swept into her face as the curling silhouette of the cliff entrance and stone ceiling stood before her against the night sky. She immediately broke toward the east, running down a slope until the rocky floor turned to dirt. With a clear path, Nuyani cut through the land at full speed, leaving dust trails taller than herself, and charging through the brush and shrubs with abandon. The wind stung her eyes, but Nuyani did not slow for such discomfort as the distorted resonance warned her of the specter's presence. Death echoed in her thoughts.

She did not stop until a branch slid beneath her arm and side, cutting the exposed skin through a frayed hole in her suit. Nuyani cried out as she slid to a stop, burying her feet in the dirt as she reached to clutch the wound. The woman then knelt below one of the taller bushes growing out of a small dune and looked to the sky for passing shadows of blood-manes. Only the stars laid bare surrounding the two moons of Kelvert in crescent. Nuyani leaned forward, trying to catch her breath as she inspected her wound. Blood covered her hand as a sting rose from a short gale revealing the cut was only skin deep. Nuyani gritted her teeth as she looked back toward her home. The cliffs were a thin line of shadow against the night sky, with only a single gap.

Breathing rapidly, she leaned back against the small dune and looked toward the moons. One was larger and held a green tint, while the other held a soft blue. Such a night for her people was considered a sign to reflect and rest but, if she remained asleep, Nuyani shivered at the thought of the apparition's presence. Not even the beasts of the land disturbed her home yet, another threat arrived. Nuyani's heart continued hammering away above the rapid drumming radiating from her stomach. She compared both beats with a second look. Her heart felt tangible with short, strong palpations and subtle shaking of her chest she could barely notice. The ethereal drum was different. It held sway over her senses, making her acutely aware of her body and surroundings.

'I don't know what this is, but Lord Kelvert has granted me a chance,' Nuyani thought as she focused on the ebb. The rapid waves kept a strong tempo within her, only to reach a fraction of the strength as they emitted from her and coursed through the air. She could feel the breeze passing by on her arms and legs as if the leather binds were never there. Small grains and pebbles pricked at her skin beneath the thick crimson leather. Slowly she could feel the world around her.

'Great Lord, what is this you've given me?' the runner wondered as she tried to decipher the resonant sensation.

The waves became thinner the further they reached, growing contorted and shifting at her right.

'What is…' her thoughts ceased as the loud cries of an animal broke the night's silence. Nuyani looked toward the south, peeking only slightly over her shrub as two more blue lights pierced through the brush. Nuyani could hear the stomp of hooves and final groans of life from the animals. The thinner waves reaching the area became even more skewed around the beasts only to ease in their distortion once more as lights shot skyward before arching toward the west.

"No," she muttered while covering her lips. 'They're death. There's more. They must be from the demon lands. They must have passed the gate,' she concluded. The animal cries ended, followed by a moment of silence. The disturbance of the pulses shifted, growing stiffer. Nuyani shot to her feet as the blue lights revealed their approach. The waves dulled in a small portion at her side. Looking to the west, she found the previous apparition approaching. Nuyani raced on, heading toward the east with her pursuers close behind. Both fists were clenched tight, threatening to snap the binds covering them. Despite the night heat, a chill crawled up her back as the subtle creaking of bone echoed clearly in her ears despite the rushing wind. Nuyani did not dare turn and see their faces, but the voided eyes' visage was clear in her mind. Leaning forward, Nuyani ran harder, pulling away from the specters in gradual inches. A line of shadow appeared on the ground before her and closed in. The runner leaped forth, crossing over a wide gap as the moon glows glimmered on the water surface of a river filled with water bites eager for a meal. Nuyani landed on the other side, crushing a small dune robbing her of some speed. A swipe whistled past her ear, spurring Nuyani on.

'Lord Kelvert, what must I do? How will I escape?' the runner questioned as she looked about the drylands. Her foe could skulk through any barrier and was nearly as fast. Another line of shadow grew closer. Nuyani could feel the weights against the rear of her core. The sources mixed and surged like rapid waters containing small beads, each threatening to spill and topple her. Nuyani landed on the other side of the river and entered a field of tall grass. Ear-piercing howls rose from the apparitions engulfing her.

Her mind dulled. Numbness encased her. Her body grew limp, causing her to roll across the ground until she reached a clearing. A herd of tall horns awoke and rose to escape. Each beast had thick red coats and small tails. Their faces were long with white fur and two twisting horns growing from the top of their brow pointing toward the sky. Despite their large size, the creatures jumped high into the air and raced off with speed and grace. The specters stopped. The tall blades of grass-covered Nuyani; their attention turned to the animals. Awaking to the sound of groaning beasts once more, Nuyani's eyes shifted about. She lay in a twisted heap, unable to move. The numb sensation holding her slowly faded, replaced by burning pain and violent shaking. Once again, the cold crept through her back just beneath the skin.

'Why can't I move?' she thought as more cries and hard thuds sounded.

Her heartbeat echoed in her ears as she remembered the pulse from her stomach. Placing her attention on the core, it remained in a soft murmur compared to its prior hum.

'What is this sense? C…can this help me?' Nuyani questioned as flashes of blue passed through the blades of grass. 'Focus.'

Her gaze remained anchored to one spot on the ground. Her thoughts ceased. The small vibrations grew stronger, passing through every limb. Their waves were chaotic and uneven as different portions varied from weak to strong. Nuyani kept her mind clear. The pulses grew more robust and balanced. Each raced on until the small quantities grew distorted. Keeping her focus, the vibrations stayed strong as the shallow beads returned; passing waves showed the spirits shifting around her. Smaller beads appeared in the resonating sense only to disappear seconds later. A moment later, another thud signaled a beast falling to the earth.

'Are they taking life?' Nuyani questioned, seeing how easily death occurred from their touch.

Her fingers twitched as the echo coursed through her. She struggled, clawing at the ground, moving slowly through the grass. The specters claimed more victims in their wake. New pressures rose then dispersed. Nuyani kept focused, strengthening the ring of each pulse, and the chill melted away.

Nuyani then felt one of the beads of water sway her way. She turned to her side. One of the specters charged forth, reaching out to grab her. Nuyani lifted her arm in defense. The two collided as the specter twisted in the air, stunned. Nuyani rolled a few more times in the grass.

'I blocked it!' Nuyani stopped and jumped to her feet. She looked with wide eyes at the twisting figure adrift in the air. The specter stopped turning only to right itself. It then released a cry before its body faded from sight. Silence followed. Nuyani kept low in a stance and reached for her knife. No blue lights shined but, she was aware of the beads shifting on the surface of her core encircling her.

'I can stop them. Just nee…'

One of the specters revealed themselves with a flash of light, nearly forcing Nuyani to close her eyes. The runner took a blind swipe at her foe only to pass through the apparition. The spirit did the same. Nuyani's reflexes allowed her to dodge a fatal blow, but the claws passed through her forearm's leather bindings and raked down her left.

Nuyani screamed as she tore away. A single pulse erupted from her body with an orange aura. The specter retreated as well, cloaking itself in the night. Nuyani looked around. Her foes stayed at bay covered in an unseen veil, yet they weighed against her core all the same.

'Why did it pass through?'

Nuyani studied the resonance. The beats were slower and softer than before, giving her enough sense to locate the apparitions, but paled in the strength needed to harm them. Nuyani gritted her teeth. Her arm was numb once more, with only the sensation of warm blood trickling through the wraps as her only feeling. Under the grip, the bindings were loose. She stole a glance at her hand. The fingers were shriveled around the handle of the stone knife with wrinkled skin. Nuyani looked forward and retrieved her other blade. The vibrations grew. A bead swayed, growing distinct. Nuyani waited as the press increased. The very air at her right flank grew cold. Nuyani sliced at the air. Blue flames burst forth, revealing the apparition as its arm was cut through at the elbow with ease. Slicing through her pursuer felt like cutting a thin wet cloth.

Her foe wailed, staggered from the blow. Nuyani leaped forth and struck again, stabbing into the spirit's chest. A final cry rose as the spirit burst into countless blue embers, slowly descending and dying out. Ignoring the sight, Nuyani turned to another bead fast approaching and ducked as the spirit revealed themselves. Claws sliced through the air. Nuyani turned about, ready to retaliate, only for the third apparition to release another howl. The sound grew muffled from the blood turning cry. Nuyani glared at the howling spirit as a small portion of cold formed, but none hindered her movements. The runner lunged at the specter. Its ally could not stop her as she closed the distance and gave a horizontal slash through the neck. A final wail was released from the head, flipping in the air before bursting into the same embers.

'They can't move if they scream,' Nuyani concluded. She could feel her left arm returning to life with the pulses dispersing the cold.

Her remaining foe did not wait, turning in the air to fly west. Its body rippled, trailing behind the head. Nuyani's brow furrowed before she sped off after the specter. She could not allow such an elusive foe to go free. Pain ran through her body. Her forearm stung with every foot strike but, she could not give in. The specter dived into the dirt as the two raced toward the west. Nuyani paid little mind to its trick following the slosh and sway of its presence only a few feet below. The line of shadow appeared once more. Nuyani leaped over. The apparition emerged from the steep riverbank and into the opposite side. The two continued cutting through the land. Nuyani narrowed her eyes to the horizon. She could see the river fast approaching. Careful to align herself with the specter, she slowly inched forward until she nearly passed the apparition. The river grew near, and Nuyani lunged in a shallow arch. The apparition emerged just below her, close enough for a wild swipe to sheer through the specter's back. Another cascade of embers rained over the water. The water bites clamored for an empty feast.

Nuyani twisted in the air, attempting to roll off her back, but found her course careening into the edge. The soft dirt did little to cushion the impact as she whipped forward. Both knives flew from her grasp, sending her tumbling on and stopping beneath another shrub bearing small violet flowers. Nuyani wheezed. Her lungs burned from the sudden impact and constant running. Dirt soiled her clothing and face as she held a dazed stare into the night sky. A knife fell beside her. The pulses dulled, leaving her limbs heavy and unbearable.

'Great Lord, I live. Thank you. What power have you given me? Why do I have this? Am I supposed to fight these things? Please, tell me. Were they right about me? I can touch spirits. I guess it is true now,' the woman thought.

"I guess I am the witch," Nuyani rasped. A sudden white glow then emerged from Nuyani's side. The woman sat up, prepared for another attack, wincing in pain.

"Admitting it doesn't absolve your crimes, witch," a man's voice echoed. Nuyani shot him a glare and looked toward her left to find a skull half-buried in the dirt. The bush grew out of the left eye socket. The man before her was tall and well-toned. Like her, he had dark brown skin. He glared at her with black eyes and scratched his head through a short afro. His bush-like goatee emphasized his frown, showing his disappointment in her survival. From his neck down to mid-chest were bloody claw marks symbolizing his death. Bloodstains remained on his shredded light brown tunic. Many of those who perished with great want, their spirits never pass, lingering and haunting the lands in a familiar vessel from their bodies to small trinkets or personal items and take years to accept their death before passing.

'At least you are a spirit I know,' Nuyani thought before she retorted. "And what crime is that, hunter? Not dying to murderers?" Her voice grew weak. Waves of fatigue dampened what little strength remained.

"Existing witch. How many deaths are piled on your shoulders? By the Great Lord, you should be…"

"I am living thanks to his will! You linger here because of your own fault, To'anu!"

"Don't use my name," the man demanded. His half-empty quiver swayed in his movements. The man kept his glare before he turned away.

Nuyani smirked. "What? You agree, then? You're only dead for trying to kill me. You aren't on my shoulders. Realize that and be free." Her fists clenched in the dirt. It did little to comfort having any death related to her.

The man turned to her narrowing his eyes, and tilted his chin to the woman. "Seems visitors have come to take your corrupted spirit, witch. I wonder why they fled toward the demon lands. Clearly, they want you home."

Nuyani narrowed her own eyes at the spirit. She swayed side to side, her vision doubling. "I'd take them for your friends first. Stalking someone never a bother to others. The Great Lord watches over me and leads me with this g-gift to defeat them. I li-ive thanks to his will."

The man chuckled. "Finding comfort in delusion?"

"…In my survival."

"Keep your comfort then. At least be of some use, witch." The man's words were suddenly missing their spiteful edge as his gaze fell to the cliff gap. Nuyani looked at him, pondering his thoughts. His hatred dimmed. "They must be yours, Nuyani. They must be after us." A tremble rose in the man's voice.

The words grew muffled in her ears. Her head lowered further and further with strength seeping away. "I h-have nothing to do with th-them and don't use m…" She collapsed in the dirt. Nuyani's senses dulled with only the small press of a bead near her core remaining. Its weight then faded once she became unconscious.

To'anu shook his head. "Tell me you lie, witch. Tell me your end removes those things. Aren't the beasts enough? Aren't the storms? Please tell me you lie. If not… Lord Kelvert, I plead to you. Guide her in any way to protect them. If her words are true, please lead her to protect them. May she forgive us." The spirit shrank into a small white wisp and receded into the skull.

Ch. 2

Run For Life

As heat waves shimmered off the red ground, a boy clad in runner's wear peered at the dirt following the tracks of game. He stalked along a trail littered with hoof tracks weaving through the dirt mounds. He wiped away the beads of sweat on his brow with a leather-wrapped hand. Several soft grunts sounded off in the distance. He gave pause, looking about before crawling beneath a bush. The thorns scratching against his attire went ignored as he moved further, hidden from the world.

'Found you,' the boy thought as his heart hammered away. His black eyes fell upon a group of charge-horns lumbering about. Each one had flat snouts with three pairs of protruding tusks along with two pairs of eyes. Their lumbering pink and red mass was wider than three men and longer than two lying on the ground. The beasts were only a head taller than the average man thanks to their large hump sitting between their shoulders.

The boy glanced over at the scene, counting the number of animals present. As four of them slept lying on their sides, two more grazed further away on some of the brush, while the last pair grazed on the remains of a recently killed animal. Too little remained to recognize what.

'Focus, Cuganwa. You are faster. Just follow the plan,' The boy reminded himself. His eyes skirted back toward the dirt path before he wiped his brow once more. 'Lord Kelvert, may your light shine on my efforts,' Cuganwa prayed as he retrieved a small stone fitting perfectly in his palm.

The boy crept to the blind side of the closest beast as its side rose and fell steadily. The others were out of sight as Cuganwa held his breath and wound his arm back.

'Follow the path,' the boy told himself as he pitched the stone.

The rock sailed forth and struck the beast with a soft plop sound, shaking its back. The charge-horn let out a low growl. It twisted around and fixed an eye on the boy waving his hands about. The beast's eyes contracted, glaring at the boy as it rose to its hooves. The charge-horn released a heavy squeal calling the other's attention. Cuganwa sped down the same tracks as heavy trampling echoed behind him. The bow peered back as he saw the towering brutes race after him.

'Good. They've followed,' he thought while measuring the distance. Their heavy gait did little for them in speed as they jostled about. The boy looked back, confident in his lessons.

Cuganwa rounded several brushes, listening to their charge. Yet, the sound grew softer. The boy's eyes widened as he looked back, wondering if he had lost his pursuers. Behind him, five of the charge-horns remained trotting along.

"Are they…" Cuganwa first questioned only for one of the beasts to let out a thunderous squeal. Its lament preceded the loud trampling once more, but from the boy's right. Three beasts stormed through the brush, causing the boy to veer left in a desperate lean. The charge-horn's tusks grazed against Cuganwa's side, threatening to pierce his garment. The runner regained his footing and was forced to turn the path as the other charge-horns tried to head him off. He looked into the maddened gaze of a beast, failing to notice his approach to a riverbank with rounded gray stones. The boy looked ahead, realizing his folly.

"No!" he rasped. Before him, the embankment rose steadily and was crowned with vegetation. Green stalks were covered with red berries and topped with yellow bulbs amongst the vibrant green leaves wide enough for fanning. Their alluring colors invited any unwary picker to a plentiful harvest but, Cuganwa knew the truth. It was a death snare with every fruit filled with poisons and toxins.

He glanced at the wide yawning river housing the countless water bites. Their silver scales and violet bellies glistened in the noon sun. Their heads were angled with unblinking black eyes trained on him.

'Faster,' Cuganwa urged as he veered toward the right, trying to return to the dirt. The charge-horns were too close, cutting him off and forcing the boy into the greenery.

With no other choice, Cuganwa took a deep breath and crossed his arms before pulling on the extra slack of his hood down, ensuring his fingers were not exposed. Plowing through the stocks, the watery outer membranes of the red berries like dew broke on contact. Wooden barbs shot from the vibrant red cores and stuck to the leather draining the clear liquid layer. The yellow fruit atop burst immediately, scattering clouds of white powder from a few. The boy ignored them all as he rushed on. The charge-horns did the same as three of the beasts followed. Cuganwa pushed through each stalk, losing more speed, and strained his breath. The charge-horns slowed in their pursuit, losing the child within the green curtain. One of the charge-horns caught sight of Cuganwa and ran forth to bite at his leg. It missed and chomped into a stalk base. Dozens of the small berries were stuck inside the animal's mouth as barbs shot toxins into the gums, killing it mid-step. Its body continued and careened over the embankment and fell into the river. Scaled tails and fins flickered in the air as the water bites took on their meal.

The next charge-horn followed after Cuganwa as more powder descended on them. The beast took a breath. Toxins coursed through the creature, causing every muscle to spasm. Each limb locked out, sending the beast into a roll and toppling more of the stalks. Within the snare, another stalk arose, coiling like a serpent. The enormous bulb rose from the center, peeling back the sepals and revealing hundreds of thorns. It darted forth, sinking its bite into the leg of the beast. With ease, dragging the creature deeper into the thick center of the snare and out of sight.

Cuganwa staggered, brushing past the stalks. His head became muddled from the lack of air. His grip grew painful to maintain. His lungs burned and ached, threatening to force his breath. Each press grew slower. In the rise of his rear foot, he struck under the chin of the remaining charge-horn. Fear spurred him on as he pressed harder, increasing his speed. His heart hammered along with something else. Another beat coursed through him just a bit lower. His lungs eased in their burn. His thoughts grew clearer.

'Great Lord, please guide me,' Cuganwa thought followed the strongest direction of the radiating pulses. He started toward the left. A moment later, he no longer felt the bombardment of stalks on his arms. Cuganwa kept his head low and released the grip of his hood. He remained cautious of his sweat filled with the powder and kept it from entering his mouth. Layers of powder were caked onto his brow and cheeks. He slowly breathed through gritted teeth, relieving the burn in his chest.

'I can make it.' He cut through two dunes as the remaining charge-horns funneled through.

"Duck, boy!" someone shouted.

Cuganwa dived to the dirt as several twangs sounded. He heard the coursing arrows strike with sharp thuds. The missiles fired true, burying in the eyes and necks of each beast. The animals fell to the floor. Blood trailed from their wounds into the dirt.

"Recover!" someone commanded.

Eight men stood from a nearby brush line and stepped forward. Each was wearing a red shawl matching the land around them and covering their light brown tunics tucked into their trousers of the same color and held in place by red sashes. Slung across their chests were tools of sheathed knives, axes, pickaxes, waterskins, and extra pouches. At their sides sat quivers of arrows. Each hunter also wore an ivory knife sheathed in their sash marking their hunter status in the village.

"Secure the area," a large man with a short afro and wider face than most ordered. They encircled the game, and Cuganwa removed their shawls to the contrast with the red land as a warning with arrows notched and ready for the pull.

Cuganwa breathed slowly as he turned his head to the sky, sitting back on his heels. He kept his eyes closed, fearful of the powder on his face.

"Hold on, Cuganwa! Pull back your hood, boy," the larger man ordered as he and another hunter approached with a large sack and water skin. The child did so, revealing his matted wet hair. "Don't move, boy. By the Great Lord, why did you run through the snare?" Cuganwa remained silent as the cool water trickled down his face, washing away the powder.

"You act too much like the charge-horns themselves," the other hunter stated. "Although, I can't say your effort did not bring results. Six grown monsters. A good hall."

"Must be a mating party. It is that time of year, after all. Not bad for a first run, Cuganwa. But let's see what your father has to say about it." The man pushed a rag into the boy's hand, letting him wipe away the rest. The child opened his eyes, seeing a cheerful smile. "Welcome back, Little Charge-horn. Care to tell us what happened?"

A sheepish smile crossed over Cuganwa's face. "I…thought I ran too fast. They tried to ambush me," he admitted.

Many of the others laughed. "Well, now you know better."

"Oh, don't worry. Many of us have learned things the hard way. Now change into your clothes."

As the boy dressed, Odaru let out a sharp whistle.

The hunter then left to instruct the other hunters as several whip-necks rose above the shrub and dunes. The animals had narrow snouts with wide amber eyes at the sides and triangular ears flickering at gnats. Layers of bone covered the crests and sides of their large heads, with small horns protruding from the bone. Their long thin necks did well to support their large heads. Each of them had two water humps aligned with their spines and thin tails ending with brush-like coarse fur. Each of their long legs had knotted muscles and had wide hooved toes and flat feet that could cover a man's face. The beasts stood nearly three times a man's height making them one of the tallest creatures in the drylands. Their enormous backs bared saddles made from leather, wood, and bone fitted with two seats facing the front and flank. Long bones jutted out from the sides of the saddles to the rear with tightly woven tarps attached for cargo.

The animals moved in a line following the pull of their reins as another man rose from the other side of the dunes. He had a thick salt and peppered beard bound in a knot that reached down to mid-chest. Below were necklaces of wooden beads painted in a dark blue, each representing a successful hunt. Unlike the others, he wore a red tunic, marking his position as the party leader. With broad shoulders and a stern glare, Cuganwa kept his eyes turned away as he glanced at the runner's garment covered in powder and dotted with viper kiss berries. The man stalked forwards, leading four of the whip-necks as another hunter following did the same. The two led the animals in a small circle within the ring of hunters.

"Ah, Sutama. A good hall for today," Odaru called as he strolled forward.

He gave a stern look to the charge-horn covered in the white powder and back to the boy. In a deep tone, he replied, "And what is this?"

Odaru sighed. "A lesson learned." Both hunters looked at the boy as he finished dressing.

Sutama handed his reins to Odaru and walked toward Cuganwa. "Well," the man barked. Cuganwa stood straight and turned to him immediately. "What reason are you, or the prey, covered in that mess?".

Cuganwa stood straight as he blurted out, "I was tricked! I thought I lost them!" Odaru looked at Cuganwa with a cautious stare as the man motioned for him to lower his voice. In a softer but clear tone, he continued, "They slowed their pace and cut me off from the path."

The man's brow furrowed. Sutama then continued, "We've lost runners for that foolishness, and we've warned you ahead of time. How did you get into the snare?"

"When they cut me off, I was too close to the river…"

"And you ran through it?" Sutama's eyes went wide. The hunting leader scratched his beard, allowing Cuganwa's silence to answer the question. He then turned toward the game as two hunters retrieved the arrows.

"What say you, boys! Is Cuganwa worthy of keeping in the party?"

"I say he is," Odaru answered first. "He knows what to expect now. I doubt any game will touch him after this."

"I agree. Bait is hard to come by. We may need to keep one that works well," another hunter teased.

All around the circle, most agreed to keep him in with only two of the hunters disagreeing. Both were sixteen and would be the youngest if not for Cuganwa, only a few years younger. The boy's heart pounded fiercely, rivaling its echo within the snare.

Sutama crossed his arms as he looked silently into the distance. When his eyes shifted to the child, he uncrossed his arms, revealing an ivory knife in his hands.

"Seems you may be ready, Cuganwa," Sutama said.

He extended the weapon out to him. Cuganwa's eyes widened as he retrieved the knife and pulled it out of the sheath. It was an entire single piece from the tip to the hilt. A polished sheen glistened in the sun covered the weapon. The blade was carved into a natural claw-like shape following the tusks of heavy-horns and massive animals in the northern region of the drylands. Cuganwa ran a finger over the indented designs of a charge-horn's head beneath Kelvert's star. The boy looked up to see his father wearing a smirk.

"Good work. You've passed the initiation. Just don't mention the snare around your mother."

"Yes, father. Thank you," the boy said.

"Sutama! Blood-manes are gathering in the north," another hunter said. Those on the same side looked as the remaining hunters toward the south kept their wary eyes forward for more danger.

The man then moved on as he took command of the group. "We have our new runner!" Now let's get the sleds built and mount up for home!"

"Yes, sir," the others sounded in unison. Cuganwa eagerly took the twine at the back of his sheath and fastened it to his sash before turning to help the others. Six hunters removed supplies from the saddles and laid them on the ground. Three sleds were fastened together with quick work using pairs of large femur bones covered in resin and several other bones, leather, tarps, and twine. Each sled had enough room to carry two of the beasts. With some digging and maneuvering, the group soon had the charge-horns bound to the sleds. Each sled had two whip-necks towing them with a rope fastened to the rear saddle horns. Despite the extra weight, the whip-necks pulled the animals with ease. Sutama drove the lead steed as another hunter sat facing the opposite direction with their bow in hand. The whip-neck beside them had the same. The second pair of whip-necks was unmanned but, their reins tied to the sled before them as they dragged their own. Cuganwa and Odaru sat a pair in the rear alongside the younger hunters and the last sled. The remaining two whip-necks were driven by hunters unburdened by any load as free-riders.

As the group rode off at a slower pace, loud grinding filled the air. Cuganwa looked out into the horizon, remembering the strange buzz in his stomach

before he ran on. The boy pulled out the knife, admiring
his prize. He now had a purpose in the village. Even for
running, many sought after hunting positions in the
territories of the drylands. Cuganwa outraced the others.
"Thank you, Lord Kelvert. I will do what I can," Cuganwa
prayed.

Ch. 3

Dangers of the Land

"By the Great Lord…" Nuyani groaned. She rose from the ground as small twigs brushed against her hood. She lurched forward and twisted about with eyes wide open only to find To'anu's skull. It was daytime, and she was on the ground instead of the cave in her bedroll. She found her knife lying by her side and returned the blade to its sheath. The sun sat at its peak.

With a dry throat, Nuyani whispered, "Why am I…"

She grew silent. Memories of the night's chase returned with the images of pale blue, decaying women of light, and dark eyes. Nuyani leaned forward and unraveled the leather binds of her left forearm in haste.

'That couldn't have happened,' she thought. A hard thud struck her chest. Four lines of dried blood trailed down her arm from elbow to wrist. Some of the blood caked the underside of her bindings.

"Great Lord, what has happened? What came for me?" The visage of her pursuers remained fresh in her memory. Their loud, despairing cries as if murdered rang in her ears. Her body trembled. Cold traveled through her spine. "What were those things?"

Loud squealing rose, breaking her trance. 'I'm outside!' she remembered. Nuyani jumped to her feet, expecting a charge-horn to barrel through the brush toward her at any moment. She turned to the noise only to find a figure fleeing between the dirt mounds and brush. Three of the beasts were closing in. Nuyani sprinted forth, stalking over dirt mounds for a clearer view as she drew near. She slid to a stop, burying her feet in the dirt. Before her, a dozen men in wait behind a line of brush. Their whip-necks laid their heads down on the floor. Their arrows were notched. Nuyani stood frozen as they watched their new runner. Her eyes fell on Sutama. Her fists shook from tightening as a vein bulged in her brow. She lifted her foot, motioning to step forward.

"Murderer,' she thought.

She turned and dropped below the small mound watching as the others did. Her eyes widened when she saw spurts of white powder fire into the air.

'Did the fool go into the snare? This must be a new runner,' she concluded. One of the hunters then called out to the runner as the group swiftly rose from hiding, pulled, and released their arrows, dropping the beasts. Nuyani flinched upon hearing the twang of their strings. She waited, hearing the others discuss their new runner's performance.

'You should take that fool back and put him in a gatherer's party. He'll be killed or get someone killed,' Nuyani thought. Her fists remained clenched only to loosen once she gazed at her home in the cliffs. 'I want my real home,' Nuyani whined as the images of fire, and the faces of enraged villagers rose in memory.

"Sorry," the woman whispered as she buried her head in her arms.

She listened as the others conversed about the efforts before moving to construct their sleds and leave toward the east. Nuyani did not move until the loud grinding was unnoticeable. She rose to her feet, watching the figures become distorted in the heat waves rising from the horizon.

'I don't belong there. Demons don't belong in the village. Witches don't belong in the village,' Nuyani told herself and turned to the mountain gap.

"Follow," her mind echoed.

Nuyani froze. 'What is this?' she thought. The questions she was certain were her own thoughts did not echo like before. Yet, the command used her voice. No answer. Only a growing hum rose within her body. 'Just like last night,' Nuyani summarized.

Once again, the feeling of distortion in the pulses rose, yet it was tame compared to the specters. The stronger distortion came in the direction of the hunters. Nuyani hesitated. No chill rose.

'Is this all right?' she questioned while studying the disturbance and headed toward the east. Nuyani checked her tools, finding only one knife and her small pouch of tools remained. Her ax, spare knife, and water skin were gone.

"Great Lord, please guide me," she grieved with a sigh. She ran in a wide arch toward the south and crouched below the dunes and shrubs, cautious of being spotted by the free riders. Once she was parallel to the caravan, she walked to match their pace. The group was a great distance away at a size smaller than her thumb on the horizon. 'They shouldn't see me here.'

As she walked along, her mind returned to the apparitions and their strange nature. Remembering their slaughter of the tall horns and the last fleeing to the demon lands.

'A demon if I ever knew one. But I am not like them. I'm not dead yet, but…' Her thoughts dwelled on their nature. Each time she saw their face, a tremor crawled through her body. Death described everything about them: malnourished figures, claws like beasts, unnatural drooping jaws, and spirited figures with missing legs. A cold dominated the air just in their presence.

"Howlers. Great Lord, may I never meet another," Nuyani wished as hidden bruises on her legs, arms, and back ached with every step. 'Are they the ones taking villagers? Am I blamed for those missing at night? Is this the reason for their hatred in blaming me?" Nuyani scowled. The possibilities fit all too well. Blood-manes sailed through the sky night and day, competing with blade-jaws for food. Yet neither would truly bother going to the village. For both predators were not impervious to the arrows nor the storms. Her clenched fists pained from growing tension until she sighed.

"Guide me with your shine. I don't know what I need to do."

After an hour passed, the hunter started their small talk about their experiences. Cuganwa learned about many of the trials some had to endure in their time and mistakes that cost others.

"Why were you two against me joining?" Cuganwa questioned the other hunters, Iogda and Selsaj.

Iogda looked at him with narrowed eyes before he spewed, "You aren't even strong enough to draw a bow that can kill the charge-horns."

Selsaj added, "We may need a runner, but a hunter with a bow can cover our backs better."

Cuganwa looked forward, understanding their reasons. Though, he could hear some contempt in their voices.

"So, Little Charge-horn…" Odaru teased. Cuganwa groaned upon hearing his new nickname. "I will tell you of an old teammate whom I took over for as second for when he made his mistake." Cuganwa turned in his seat, looking at the older hunter's back. "He was ambitious and constantly tried to outdo everyone in skill. He showed off far too much but, he was always a good man. Whether he wanted to lead the group or become chief, I don't remember but, he lost his life chasing after the witch." The boy's ears perked up. The tales of stolen children and seduced hunters meeting their end were passed through stories warning them to never venture outside at night or follow the lights of dying fire when seen out of place. They were the eyes of the witch, and she only came to take those out of spite. It was ludicrous to imagine taking someone on alone who could live out in the wild amongst the beasts. "His name was To'anu. We don't know where he is or if his soul is free but, he wanted to kill her for fame and tried chasing after her on a whip-neck. "Odaru sighed, changing the cheerful air he held around him. "Just an ambitious fool. A good hunter but too bold."

The seasoned hunters grew silent. Cuganwa understood the drive. Many stronger families were from those who contributed more and earned powerful stations. Hunters were the most renowned, for their ventures brought them the closest to danger. The boy looked at his knife, knowing it was the same reason he wanted to join and ran every day growing up, even when blisters formed under his feet or his leather sandals grew worn. The witch was known to steal villagers away, a spirit reborn corrupted, passing through a water bite. Their people believed in reincarnation as the cremated bodies were poured into the same river that allowed them to live; the same portion of the river Lord Kelvert kept them safe in before he disappeared.

"The witch killed him?" Cuganwa asked.

"We don't know, but I would not be surprised." The man chuckled, trying to lighten his dower tone. "Now, I almost lost my life too being careless. I was lucky. Guided."

"Wait. What did you do?"

"You like flat-bellied lizards, yes?" The man turned to glance at Cuganwa, who nodded and held a strong stare at the man. His tongue brushed against the inside of his teeth as memories of a pudgy brown lizard shaded like a whip-neck's hoof scurried about the ground. He first tasted the lizard after his mother roasted one with a few spices and salts. The meat was succulent as the scales held the flavor with a soft but satisfying crunch.

"Y-yeah," the boy replied after a short pause. Odaru chuckled.

"Well, I found one wandering further from the river while we were on break. I chased it into the brush, but I got separated when a blade-jaw came by." The man's tone grew stern and forward. "When those things come by, you flee. You run. You hide. Not even our good friends here can fend off such beasts." The man patted his whip-neck's shoulder as a smile came over his face. "They will kill many of us before we can get just one of them." Cuganwa's heartbeat grew stronger as he listened. Odaru turned around to see the boy still staring at him, petrified.

"Keep your eyes to the rear, Cuganwa." The boy turned to face the horizon as the older hunter continued, "There is a reason we are to help one another and not act too bold. The others had to leave, and I was stranded in the bushes. Now, the blade-jaw. Oh, it growled as it came closer. It found me easily. But, by the Great Lord's light, it turned to face something else and ran off."

Cuganwa blinked as his heart throbbed harder. "What did it go for?"

"I can't say. Probably something with a little more meat than my scrawny self." Odaru gave another chuckle as his tone lightened up. The hunter stared off into the sky. "Thank Lord Kelvert's will, my trek back was not so dangerous. I was surprised to make it back. I had nothing but a knife and arrows. My bow was gone too. Still had my waterskin, though, so it wasn't the worst. The night out here is beautiful, but every beauty seems to come with its dangers."

"So, you're the one that walked back!" Cuganwa looked at him once more before remembering his task. All the villagers knew guards spotted someone outside and sent men to retrieve them. "That would scare me. Being out of the village at night. Were you?"

"Of course. Don't let your pride overtake you. Some have been out before. That used to be a rite of passage in my grandfather's time, but they stopped that."

"They had people out during the night!"

"Stay focused, Cuganwa. Yes. Didn't the elders teach you this story?"

"No," Cuganwa replied. There were many stories, but never one about men staying out in Elder Yanuma's tales. Most of their history was told by the elder accounting for trials hunters faced, bad decisions met with swift consequences, their birth from the rivers, and the demons that try to taint their spirits. A few folk tales of towering huts made of stone were told sometimes. They sat beside endless waters stretching further than the eye could see, but Cuganwa always found it was silly.

"Hm. Well, they don't want to encourage pointless risks. It would spur the restless to do something foolish."

"So, I will keep quiet about that too."

"Good, Little Charge-horn. We all have our secrets. Always keep them unless it is important."

Cuganwa glanced back at the hunters, who grew silent. Cuganwa returned his gaze to the rear, looking over the land. The cliffs were small but, the gap was easy to spot as a golden glimmer shined from the land beyond. The hunters named the gap as the demon gate where blood-manes and blade-jaws were teeming. Their stories and rumors about the witch came to the boy's mind. All the beasts, deadly plants, and the vicious storms that occurred every year had one person thriving. Here he was in a hunting party facing those dangers as one born of sin waited to hunt them when or if she could. Cuganwa pulled out his knife, wondering if he would ever need to use it. The ivory was too soft to use for real need, aside from a desperate situation, more of an ornament and marker.

'Lord Kelvert, guide me with your shine. If I am in danger, give me the strength to fight. I will fight and protect the village from all threats if need be,' the boy declared in an oath. He tightened his grip and put the blade away.

Just as he looked up, a shadowed figure appeared in the distance. Cuganwa narrowed his eyes, studying what it was, realizing he was staring at a blood-mane looking back at them as it glided through the air headed north. The beast had the head of a bird sticking out of a large plume of feathers covering the neck. It had a sharp hooked beak, and large dark brown eyes focused on him. Both of its wings were large enough to blanket the rest of its body, which had four limbs. The front pair resembled bird talons and the rear resembling a feline with smaller claws. It had a long brush-ended tail trailing behind its entire body. Both fur and feather were blood red.

"There's a blood-mane watching us."

"And that's why you keep an eye out. Worry not, Cuganwa. They're not foolish enough to attack us."

Cuganwa kept a wary eye on the beast, "Why's that?"

"Unlike most animals in Kelvert's land. They do not have thick hides protecting them from the storms, so they hide in caves deep in the cliffs. Our arrows would kill them as easily as their talons would do to us."

"Why'd it come so close?"

"A test. If we aren't ready, they will be." The boy looked to the other hunter, Selsaj, facing toward the rear. His gaze, too, was fixed on the predator. Fingers curled around the string with an arrow sitting between the second and first. His grip of the bow had tensed.

'Everyone is prepared,' Cuganwa thought. As he watched the animal soar on, he noticed a dull hum rising in his stomach. He brought a hand to his abdomen, wondering if something was wrong. Despite the disturbance, none of the pulses radiated to his palm as his heart would. The waves ended the moment they reached the surface of the skin and were much faster than his heart. Cuganwa wanted to call on Odaru for help but, the hum stopped. He paused for a moment to study the sensation. 'Must be my nerves,' he thought and took a swig of water.

Lulled by a silent hour following the caravan, Nuyani strolled on, standing straight, confident the others could not see her. Her thoughts dwelled on the constant hum rising from her core. As she breathed slowly, her senses with the pulse grew distinct. Stronger, solid waves echoed forth. All around her, the drumming ball allowed her to recognize the countless distortion as light pressures weighed on its surface.

'This has to be life,' she concluded as one moving pressure slowly grew lighter from her right. Nuyani looked to her side, finding a small shrew running away from her. She smiled softly. Her joy faded when she looked at the hunters in their small form. 'To survive, you protect and aid one another,' the woman recited from old lessons as she felt their light presence. Her eyes narrowed as a disturbance rang back. Palpations collided and receded amongst the ethereal waves. Nuyani's body then lurched forward, nearly felling her. She looked down at her foot. What seemed to be roots and blades of grass were crawling up the limb—a small, misplaced death snare.

"What?" Nuyani questioned before hacking at the vegetation. The plants moved faster, desperate, slithering around her other leg as well. A subtle pressure too weak for her to notice rose from the grass beneath the soft echo. "By the Great Lord… To the winds!" Nuyani cursed while the vegetation nearly reached her knee. Then, a pressure rose from the north, rivaling the same weight and flow as the howlers. Nuyani glanced toward the northwest. A lumbering mass sped on, heading for the hunter. The woman hacked at her legs carelessly, unconcerned if the blade slipped through her wrappings. Her green binds were cut down until she thrashed about, tearing away with a final vicious kick. Nuyani turned and bolted toward the hunting party.

Cugnawa rubbed his stomach, trying to soothe away the mysterious drumming. He drank his water skin near dry and chewed on spare jerky, which neither satiated the disturbance. In the distance, he noticed some movement. It was heading their way.

"Something's coming from the rear!" one of the archers shouted.

The words reached the free-riders, who, in turn, passed the message on to the others. Cuganwa watched as the drivers looked to his father, who held his hand up, signaling the entire group to halt. There was little reason to try and outpace the beast with their mounts weighed down. Sutama held his glare until he gave several twists of his hand. Both free-riders rode toward the beast as the drivers turned their whip-necks around to face the threat and had the animals stretch their legs outward for stability with simple commands. Odaru and the others let out several calls as the whip-necks groaned and rose their heads to the sky before crashing them down. Clouds of dust cascaded under their collision as Cuganwa felt the shock of every blow. The group continued their clamor as the mass drew near. The creature was an enormous charge-horn, double the size of any they had killed before. Its hump was a sagging mass of decay, and yellow puss dangled over the side of one shoulder. In its heavy press shaking the earth, some fluid seeped out from the rot and fell to the floor. Its yawning jaws released a deep unearthly squeal.

"Lord Kelvert, protect us," the boy whispered as he watched arrow after arrow bounce off its hide. A few managed to stick in its skin around the neck but, this had not deterred the beast. Both free-riders rode parallel to the charge-horn firing into its neck and eyes. The charge-horn shook its head and veered to both sides, attempting to down the riders. With both drivers moving further away, it ran toward the first whip-neck. The group themselves released careful shots toward the threat. One of the arrows then struck the beast's leg and passed through. The charge-horn veered to its right with a wounded limb refusing to open, heading toward Odaru's sled. The whip-. neck circled its head through the air and hammered into the beast's side with a loud thud but, the beast crashed into the sled. Its full weight pulled the slings on the saddleback before they snapped. Odaru and Cuganwa were launched into the air their whip-neck lost balance.

The ropes held the smaller charge-horns, sending their game rolling through the sand. The larger beast tumbled as well, with dust obscuring everything. Blue sky and red ground spun around him before he landed stomach first on a charge-horn's carcass knocking the wind from his lungs and falling unconscious. Momentum carried the boy over as he fell to the dirt. The whip-neck, Muga, to the side groaned. Screams of pain erupted in the dust.

"Surround it! Find the men first! Kill the thing!" Sutama barked. The others did as ordered.

Cuganwa awoke wheezing heavily as he rose to his feet within the dust. A haze of red and brown surrounded him with little sunlight appearing overhead. The shouts of the others were muffled.

'What happened?' the boy questioned as he struggled to stand. Deep grunts and rustling sounded at his left, and Cuganwa looked through the dust to find a large shadow moving. The words grew clearer as cries of pain filled the air.

'The charge-horn!' the boy remembered as he saw the animal stand. Each of its eyes was glazed over, three had been destroyed by arrows. Nearly a dozen arrow shafts littered its neck from the side, and every wound had blood and puss trailing down to the earth. The charge-horn turned toward the shouting.

'Odaru!' Cuganwa realized, recognizing the voice. The humming grew rapid yet, he barely noticed. All the pain and burning in his chest were alleviated. The boy leaped over a dead charge-horn's head and cut the monstrous beast off before it could get closer to the fallen hunter.

The animal stopped once it caught sight of the child. Cuganwa drew his knife as he looked into its remaining dead, glazed-over eye. It did not move, yet the beast's reaction told the boy that it was aware of his presence. The wind picked up, carrying away much of the dust.

Sutama went wide-eyed at the reveal of his son facing down the beast. "Move, boy!" Cuganwa only stepped toward the side away from Odaru, who lay pinned beneath the unconscious whip-neck's shoulder. The animal followed. The other hunters continued firing, their arrows firing at the beast's side as one of the free-riders came closer to attack with their mounts. The charge-horn released a growl as it lowered its body, ready to strike. Cuganwa reeled his knife back.

'Fight!' the boy ordered himself. A blur of red burst from his right, causing the boy to freeze as it collided with the beast. The charge-horn's head jerked in the opposite direction from where it was struck as its body tilted over, falling on its side. Everyone stared at the figure motionless.

Nuyani stood before them. Her knife plunged into the animal's neck further than any arrow. The animal lay still with a new trickle of blood trailing to the dirt. She did not bother to look at them.

'You're welcome,' Nuyani thought as she jumped down from the beast, aggressively yanking the knife free. The others did nothing as they maneuvered to help the downed hunter. Cuganwa looked stunned. As she worked to retrieve a tool from her last pouch, Nuyani failed to notice the boy approaching.

"By the Great Lord, thank you," Cuganwa said.

Nuyani stiffened. 'Thank you?' She then turned. "What did you say?"

The boy's eyes widened as a look of awe was replaced by horror. The glow of her eyes gleamed in his. Cuganwa realized the witch had appeared and lunged at Nuyani. She retaliated with a swift kick in the boy's chest, pushing him away more than striking. The boy fell back as she gave him an unimpressed glare.

"No!" Sutama shouted as an arrow struck the ground between them. The woman dropped low, covering her kill with one hand and pointing her knife at the hunting leader. Another arrow was already notched as the large man stepped toward his son's left. "Take your kill and leave. You've done enough." Nuyani's eyes narrowed at the hunter as she fumbled with the bag while she held her knife toward Sutama. Revealing a clear jagged stone, the woman hovered it over the charge-horn and tightened her grip. Cuganwa shivered, watching light shimmer from the stone like the reflection of a river surface. The light streamed over the charge-horn's head. Its body stretched to a fine point before the point twisted upward and drained into the stone. The hulking beast receded into the crystal with only the pool of blood and arrows remaining on the ground.

"What?" the boy rasped. Rumors had prepared him for a hideous person deformed by their soul. Only a woman furrowing her brow in rage stood before them.

"Now go!" Sutama bellowed.

Nuyani raised her chin in defiance, but took a few steps back. 'You don't command me,' She thought as she waved her hand over another charge-horn gripping the stone. Light shined again, pilfering a second.

"Getaway!" Iogda said as he and Selsaj released their arrows. A blur of red showed her speed as Nuyani dodged the first missile and parried the second with ease.

"Do not fire!" the hunting leader bellowed.

Nuyani turned and darted off toward the west, taking only seconds to cross the land with nothing but a dust cloud left in her wake. Cuganwa was in awe of the display, watching until he saw a massive fist reaching for his tunic. With ease, Sutama yanked the boy to his feet with rage burning in his eyes. Cuganwa's heart raced again, and he could not control his fidgeting as his free hand opened and closed.

"What were you thinking!" Sutama said.

Cuganwa started, "She is the witch. I thought I had to…"

"You never go for a life unless yours, or another's, is threatened! We have laws and rules to keep us alive! Never raise a hand unless absolutely needed. She could've taken you," the man said and gave a soft shove releasing the boy's clothing. His father then snatched away the ivory knife from the boy's hand. "You aren't ready."

Sutama walked off to help the others as they splashed water onto the whip-neck, waking it. The stead quickly rose off Odaru and proceeded to lick the man's face in guilt as he sat up.

"Calm now. I live, and I don't blame you," the man said as he scratched the whip-neck under the chin. Cuganwa was amazed at the man's cheerful nature with a broken shin.

'I messed up,' the boy thought as the group moved about resetting the sled. The boy bit his lip as he aided the others. Aside from Sutama scolding Iogda and Selsaj, the group remained silent. Worse, the boy found everyone avoiding eye contact with him. In moments, the hunters remounted and left. Cuganwa kept his eyes on the western cliffs, wondering what his actions may bring in attacking someone they all feared.

"You're a fool! You're a damn fool," Nuyani said. Her voice echoed in the cavern. She tossed the crystal across the floor, making it skid until it hit the baskets before walking in circles around the firepit and bedroll. "Of course, they'd fire at you. You had the biggest kill and took one of theirs. You can't even eat all that before it goes bad." Nuyani stopped as she tapped her foot on the ground and chewed on her thumbnail. She winced and stopped when turning her wrist reminded her of the new scars and scratches adorning her.

"What kind of night was that?" Nuyani started rubbing her legs, hoping some pressure would alleviate the pain. Before her lay the rest of the empty village, with the afternoon sun streaming through the ceiling port. 'It's no longer morning,' Nuyani thought as she knelt to the floor. She placed both hands over her heart, closed her eyes, and lowered her head. "As I gaze upon the dawn, may your light guide me. Under your glow, I am protected. Under your glow, I will protect. I will aid my kin. I will aid my home. As day ends, I follow the will of your gleam even through night," Nuyani prayed. She raised one of her hands with a palm to the ceiling, gesturing to the morning sun. She then lowered her arms and stared at her bed. Her eyes burned, causing her to wipe at one.

'I am protected?' Nuyani thought. She sat on her heels, pausing for an answer, hoping even the strange buzz would chime in. Aside from a brief sensation of

weightlessness, nothing stirred within her. The woman
then sighed before crawling to her bedroll and lying down.
Fatigue overtook her as she went to sleep.

45

Ch. 4

The Dead Remain

A passing hour loosened the lips of the group, though none addressed Cuganwa aside from Odaru. The hunter hummed gleefully with a festive smile. His left leg stuck out further thanks to a tourniquet. Cuganwa occupied himself with thoughts of the day's events. It all ended in the burning eyes of the witch. Aside from their strange glow, she seemed no monster to him. The charge-horns and death snare were after them. Yet, he attacked the "vengeful witch" who could've waited for the beast to take one or two lives before killing it. His father stayed his hand only until she struck him.

"Protector. Protector. How you may shine," Odaru sang allowed. "Great you. Great one. For guarding this life of mine." Cuganwa looked back, finding the veteran hunter half turned with a large grin expressed on his face. Odaru turned back, facing forward.

"You're welcome," Cuganwa whispered as he turned back as well. "I've tried to do something worthwhile." The boy looked down at his hand, thinking of his attempt to stab the charge-horn. Nothing about his effort would've been fruitful, yet he fought on. The strange pulse had calmed, leaving him with little clues to its nature.

"She had to be controlling it," Selsaj stated. His tone grew louder, catching the boy's attention. "Every time we see her, she's doing something we don't understand and leaving something we can use. She must be trying to buy her way back in."

Iogda replied, "How could she control one of those things? They aren't the brightest and quite unruly. Seems like a hassle to me."

"I think she's trying to work on Sutama and control the beast. She may be taking it back to some pets."

"What? No."

The sleds soon came to the rough ground once more. The grinding noise was loud and filled the air quieting the young hunters. They traveled on a worn path through the brush before reaching a bone, wood, and mortar bridge. One of the free-riders rode ahead, ensuring the path was clear as the other followed in the rear of the caravan. With the bridge just wide enough for the whip-necks to move side by side, they all crossed with ease. Cuganwa looked at the structures as small stones fell into the water, calling the water bites' attention. He remembered stories from his father taking masonry workers from the craft hut to fix the bridge on occasion, a task that often kept him from returning until the sun was nearly set. Everyone halted just beyond the bridge. Cuganwa looked toward his father. One of the free-riders pointed to the south as he conversed with Sutama. Cuganwa peered over finding parts of the tall grass parsed and matted to the floor. Two tall horns lay on the ground beyond the grass.

Cuganwa looked back at his father. The man gestured toward the grass just before the free-rider scouted the area. The ride at their rear joined him. Odaru then sat sideways in his seat as he removed his bow from a side quiver and notched an arrow.

"Keep your eyes on the rear, Cuganwa," Odaru instructed. The boy did so.

'What's happening? We don't hunt tall horns,' the boy thought.

Moments passed before the group was ordered to dismount. Six of the men climbed down and moved to join Sutama standing beside the grass. Cuganwa did the same.

Sutama then looked at all of them. "We have an entire herd of tall horns slain here." Selsaj's eyes widened. "I am uncertain why but, they need to be dropped into the river before any beasts think they have a new spot to hunt near the path."

"How does an entire herd get killed?" one of the hunters questioned. Sutama shook his head.

"Either way, we take one with us. The elders will have to hear about this," Sutama added.

Selsaj then asked, "Why not take more?"

Sutama turned to the hunter. "If we don't know why they are dead or what killed them, we invite dangers to the village. We've never had this game before. Let's learn what is safe or dangerous. Then we will choose."

The group moved on, searching the area for each of the animals. Cuganwa and the others had difficulty dragging the beasts to the river. Each one had claw marks cutting through their sides, some were shallow, and even in places around the hind legs. The group tossed a sixth tall horn over the edge. Cuganwa followed the others only for his foot to strike something, nearly causing him to trip. The boy looked down and found an ax. 'Did someone drop their ax?' the boy then looked around and found a patch of dirt bare of earth. A clump of dirt had gathered with thin drag marks trailing to the center.

Cuganwa turned to the group before he announced, "I found an ax! Did someone drop theirs?"

The others stopped and inspected themselves. Only two hunters carried such a tool on them as the others preferred to leave them strung to the saddles. The men looked at each other shaking their heads and back at the boy. Curious eyes then scanned the floor, finding several of the same marks along a bare trail. Once the group was done with the herd, and the last was tied to the rear sled, they presented the ax to Sutama. As the older hunters discussed the meaning, Cuganwa climbed back onto his whip-neck. Selsaj then climbed on his own, continuing their conversation.

"She had to have done it," Selsaj declared. He kept an arrow notched, but did little to keep guard.

"How? She had to tackle the charge-horn just to kill it. No way she could do that to the tall horns or with that many close together. They're too fast, and arrows bounce off them too. Why bother?" Iogda continued.

"For us, they are difficult."

"And? How would she have done it?"

"Blade-jaws."

"No," Iogda said, annoyed.

"What else? They are the only ones who hunt everything. I don't think even blood-manes bother with them, but they were all cut."

"Where were the prints, tracks, or blood from them fighting back?" Iogda turned to face his partner. "There weren't any. Not even hoof prints, but we found bodies. Only the ax and signs like the witch was crawling through there."

"If she was crawling, then how would she be attacking them with blade-jaws?"

"I don't know. But why did she take two charge-horns? One makes sense but, that second was not her s" Selsaj's tone grew aggressive. Cuganwa wondered if he were still mad at it being taken, he could not blame the hunter. "It just seems like something she could do. That stone can hold things larger than her, the ax left out here and the animal coming from where we were, but was bigger than any charge-horn we've caught. I bet even larger than Odaru or Sutama have seen."

"Then why leave the bodies?" Selsaj shrugged.

"Remember the tale of the first sinner? He took the chief's wife and family controlling blade-jaws to kill them because he did not become chief himself. She must be trying to learn the same."

"But, why leave them?"

"I'm not certain and….I hope you're wrong."

50

"That is not a strength we can deal with on our own. If anything, we would have to deal with using every party in the village."

"True but, that is why I think this is a test, and the meat or animals she leaves is just a way of trying to buy herself back in. She kicked Cuganwa away, but only a warning shot? We ignore each other, but what'll happen if this continues? We'd be blindsided."

"What about the charge-horn? Why take it for food if she could control it?"

"No. I think her spells don't work on them like blade-jaws or blood-manes."

"If she controls them."

"Yes, if. But those are demons. Charge-horns are game. Her spells deform it, and she sends it after us, or it gets loose. Then takes it back as food and win favor."

Iogda sighed and shook his head. "We should tell the others. That would be best."

"Oh! We hear you fine, boys! You've been loud enough!" the two looked toward the front, finding all eyes on them. "Your concern is valid! We will take your thoughts to the elders. Let's continue!" Sutama said. The group continued with the final stretch of their trip, closing with the sun close to setting.

A long white wall protruded over the land above the dirt mounds and brush as the sun brought an orange sky. Sutama retrieved a horn from his sash and released a long call ringing through the air. A torch strung to a pole jutted up from the wall swung back and forth, signaling their call was received. The group then rounded the area toward the southern portion, where much of the land was flattened and bare. Sutama circled the whip-necks fitting closely to the outer wall and away from the brush line. The hunters then waited, standing in a perimeter facing the drylands. Cuganwa stood further back, watching as Odaru remained in his saddle. An arm then came around the boy's side pushing something into his hand. The boy looked down to find his father handing off the knife silently. Cuganwa took up the blade and looked to his father with wide eyes.

The man's expression was softer than before as he nodded and walked toward the wall. Shifting sand rustled behind them as the white wall was picked apart. Countless bones, all standing at half the height of the whip-necks, were removed as villagers opened the path. Each had pointed ends that were thin and flexible to withstand the strong winds. Soon, a space just wide enough for the whip-necks to pass was made. Sutama called for the drivers of the animals in as village guards poured out to cover their rear. The hunters then led their mounts into the village as dozens of onlookers watched them bring their game. Those working on the gate raced to replant the defenses. Many pointed to the tall horn lying on the last sled.

"Hah!" He's alive!" Cuganwa heard. Many of the children were watching as he descended with the others. The boy smirked at his friends as he held up the knife to prove his new station. Some clapped and cheered as others looked away with disdain, old rivals with remaining prayers to be hunters. Each one was beaten in a foot race. As Odaru took the lead of the animals, the whip-necks were driven further into the village. Many started to comment on his wrapped leg.

"Sutama, your group has come late," a voice almost as commanding rang out.

The village chief approached with a broad smile, slightly obscured by his mustache curled upward on opposite ends. He was well toned and in his late thirties. His sign as chief was displayed by his full red attire and a bracelet holding a clear stone.

"Hello, Gamaunda. We had a bit of an issue along the way and other concerns," Sutama replied. Gamaunda nodded his head.

"By the Great Lord's shine, you still return with all your men and more game than expected. No better a trade wanted but, let's speak more over here."

The man nudged his head to the side, away from most of the others. The rest of the hunters returned to their families. Cuganwa watched as they spoke to one another. He looked around the village as everyone spoke to others. Feeling as if he were being watched, Cuganwa turned around, finding a woman leering at him with a smirk. He blinked and gave a nervous laugh. She wore a thin green shawl over her head and a long dress dyed blue and white. Around her neck, she wore a wooden medallion engraved with the symbols of Kelvert. Spiked rays of light rose upward from a center piercing just beyond a wide crescent arch above them.

"Hello, mother," the boy said as he approached and gave a hug.

"Hello, hunter. Did you enjoy your first trip?" the woman asked.

Cuganwa paused, looking to the ground. "…Yes." His mother tilted her head to the side, studying the boy's reply.

With quick hands and the return of her smirk, she grabbed the knife from its sheath. Cuganwa failed to block her as she stepped away and turned the blade in her hands, inspecting the ornament. "Sweet enough of you to bring me a gift, dear."

"Mom, please," Cuganwa started as he glanced at the other children. "I've passed."

"Well, I don't think you should be one." Her smirk turned into a scowl. "How did Odaru hurt his leg?"

"He fell when the whip-neck lost balance," Cuganwa answered.

Her brow arched upward. She blinked several times, trying to decipher his words. "A whip-neck lost its balance?" She narrowed her eyes. "What happened?"

'Please don't ask more. I can't mention the witch,' the boy thought. "It's true. Another charge-horn came out of the brush and almost ran into Muga. Then we fell."

"Who's Muga?"

This time, the boy blinked. "Is that important? The whip-neck we were riding?"

"You fell with him? Why didn't you mention that first?"

"A lot more was happening beside us falling."

"He could've cut the ropes before you two fell. What happened to the charge-horn? Who missed that last one?"

"I did," the boy admitted. "When I was running, I never saw it."

The woman chuckled. She then handed the knife back. "It will be troublesome if you make mistakes like that too often. Be careful."

The boy smiled back. "Yes, mother." He returned the blade to its sheath.

"Hi, Cuganwa!" a voice shrilled. Small arms then wrapped around his waist. A small figure tackled into his side.

Looking down, Cuganwa was greeted with a large grin and eager brown eyes from a young girl. "Hey, Caluu," Cuganwa greeted as he hugged her back.

"Did you make it! Are you a hunter!" she shouted.

"Yes. Yes. I made it. I will be going with them from now on."

"And soon, he will start his bow training," Sutama added, gaining everyone's attention. Gamaunda was with him. Caluu clung onto the boy's arm as the three listened. "You won't be going out every time but, there isn't a hunter who doesn't know how to shoot a bow."

Cuganwa smiled. "But first, you must make yours," the chief reminded him. He kept his usual smile as he nodded to the others before turning back to Cuganwa. "You will appreciate it more when it is done by your own hands. Remember, your aim will be the thing that both protects you and others."

"Yes, Chief Gamaunda," the boy replied.

The man smirked before turning to Sutama. "So, a meeting tonight to discuss more."

"We will be there, chief," Sutama assured. Gamaunda placed a hand on the boy's back and nodded before leaving.

"How will Odaru fair with a bad leg?" his mother asked.

"Oh no, Jogia. Cuganwa will join me tonight." The woman blinked several times and fixed her body to face him completely. "Odaru is being seen by the elders now. I am sure they will ask him as many questions as they will us."

Jogia's brow furrowed. "I don't like him being there."

"No. He's a hunter and will be treated as such." Sutama grew a smile. "Remember, three more years, and he could marry."

"Five," the woman declared.

Cuganwa narrowed his eyes, "I'm just thinking of hunting right now."

"Can I be a hunter next?"

"Caluu, not for a while, my love."

"I can run too!" she protested.

"Oh. Then run home with Mother." The two turned to head further into the village, but not before Jogia kissed Sutama and raced with the young girl. Both laughed as they sped off.

Sutama smiled at them. Cuganwa looked at his father, noticing a sense of fatigue.

"Did you tell her?" the man asked.

"No. I've said nothing about it," Cuganwa replied.

Sutama sighed. "Good. I am proud of you. Just remember to cherish life. It can be gone in only a moment."

"Father, why am I joining you at the meeting?"

The man turned to Cuganwa, his expression hardened. "Today's events need all witnesses. You of most. Twice danger came to you, then…other matters."

Sutama continued, "After supper, we leave for the meeting and see what the elders have to say. Let's go home."

Night came with its usual howl of the wind. Nuyani's core hummed rapidly, radiating through her body in a single breath. Her eyes shot open as a sudden pressure was clear and grew heavier upon the internal drum. Nuyani pushed away, rolling to her side as long blue claws shot from the floor, proceeding the same grotesque figure.

'By the Great Lord, why have you come?" she thought. Nuyani gritted her teeth, staring at the specters as she reached for her knife. Without hesitation, she leaped toward the apparition and sliced at its limb. The blade passed through the specter, leaving it unharmed as it reeled back.

"What!" she questioned after landing on the floor with new bruises to add on her legs.

The howler then attacked once more, reaching for her with a swipe. Nuyani rolled to her feet, holding her blade at the ready, and her arm chambered to her side. She held a maddened glare and subtle smirk. The specter waited for an arm's length away, watching with voided eyes. Nuyani chuckled. 'I don't think they will like your eyes any more than mine, howler. Why didn't I cut you?" She fixed her smirk into a growl, ready to defend her home.

"Focus on the beat. No words."

Her attention remained on her foe. Her thoughts grew silent. She was ready to strike, ready to react. The ringing pulses echoed through her, and each muscle grew lighter. The apparition's presence became a solid sloshing bead sitting at the front of her core. The howler shifted, moving toward the domed huts, continuing to face her as it fled. Nuyani darted forth without a moment's wait. The apparition whipped through the air passing through a hut wall. She stopped before striking the stone surface. Its glow shifted while shining through the small round window. The pressure became heavy. Nuyani stepped back as the claws glided through the stone, almost striking her stomach.

'Not so feral after all,' Nuyani thought. The howler drifted forth, peeking out of the wall. Nuyani stared back, slowly inching toward her foe. The vibrant energy grew stronger. Nuyani noticed her body was fine. The sense of cold plaguing her the night prior did not emerge. She inched closer to the small doorway, ready to attack once more. Going for another lunge, she broke off midway to reach the door and tried to stab the specter through the opening.

Her foe whipped into a circle evading the attack before swinging at Nuyani's arm. The claws passed through the leather once more but only managed to knock away her arm. Her forearm struck the doorway's edge causing the woman's knife to drop to the floor beneath her. The apparition paused, looking between Nuyani and the knife. The specter retracted its arms and hid beneath the floor as Nuyani retrieved her knife. Nuyani tested her grip. Aside from the old scars she had yet treated, the apparition's blow did nothing.

'Praise to the Great Lord,' Nuyani thought as she crouched low and faced the direction of the pressure.

"You will not have me," the woman stated as she stared at the ground. "You have failed to catch me. You run only to attack again. Why are you still here?"

The hum of her core strengthened, leaving soft vibrations in her ears. Nuyani cleared the hut as the shifting weight stayed in the same place. The cavern's draft brushed against the blade's surface. The brisk wind passed through her mind. She sat still, waiting for the howlers to move. Waves shifted at her core, instantly growing heavy. Nuyani lifted her foot as the claws rose from the floor, bringing its blue glow. She dodged the howler's attempt to grab for it. Nuyani stabbed at the limb but, it sank into the floor, leaving a loud tap as stone struck stone.

"Damn it." The apparition's presence shook and grew lighter. "Is it backing away?" As her blade hovered a few inches over the ground, she could feel the small granules of dust pressing against her fingers. 'This drum. By the Great Lord, what is it?'

Nuyani dropped her thoughts as the waves grew stronger and shifted, becoming lighter again. Light burst from the ground as the howler revealed its head inside the hut. Nuyani leaped for her foe as its jaw descended. Her orange eyes widened as an ear-piercing scream bombarded her. Nuyani froze for a moment, maintaining her glare at the apparition. Moments passed as the stabbing throb radiated through her mind. Her hearing grew muffled. Nuyani drudged through the onslaught, swinging at its head. The howl ended as the apparition backtracked, rising from the ground and passing through the wall. Its hand was missing. Nuyani dashed forth as her foe passed through the stone. She struck the wall with all her might.

A sense of cold ran over the tip of the blade. Her thoughts dwelled on the internal drum's presence. A shriek rang through the cavern, barely audible to Nuyani. A sinister smile appeared on her face as she felt the weight against her core disperse. Blue embers glowed then died out beyond the hut's small window.

She laughed to herself, letting it echo in the dark of the cavern. "Thank you, Great Lord. Can I sleep now?" Nuyani sat with her back against the wall. Her arms and legs lost all strength. No other pressure or distortion lingered. "Please be the last." A scowl came over her face. She brought both hands over her ears. All she could hear was her heartbeat amongst a constant headache. She mumbled several prayers to herself. The words came in muffled sounds.

Nuyani rested, continuing to test her hearing until the words were clear. Halting as she noticed the dark shift. A dim silver haze formed into thin, sparse paths outlining the simple details in the stone. After three or four beats rose, a sharper, stronger pulse would rise. The more the rhythm repeated, the brighter the silver lines became. A strain rose in her eyes as if she were staring for too long. Nuyani laughed. 'Now I can see in the dark?' She moved to retrieve her blade. The haze outlined the weapon's edges as the center remained pitch black. When she picked up her weapon, the tip fell off. Nuyani felt an urge to throw the blade but stopped. She sighed while inspecting it. 'I'm awake anyways. I should gather some more supplies.' She stalked off to the cavern front and rummaged through her baskets for another waterskin, herbs, and rags. Retrieving some small pieces of wood, Nuyani placed them into the fire pit. She retrieved the same small stone and gripped it in her hand. Before her, lights shimmered and danced over the back wall proceeding the charge-horns before they poured out piling atop of one another. Nuyani covered her nose and mouth. Her eyes stung from a rancid odor emitted by the larger beast, then fell onto the gray and yellow lump of flesh in the middle of the charge-horn's back.

"I don't think I should eat this one," Nuyani mumbled.

Lights danced over the larger charge-horn before it drained into the small crystal. Nuyani took a deep breath, relieved of its stench. Leaving to retrieve another ax, Nuyani hacked at the charge-horn's spine, taking several hits concentrated on one area to break through the hide. A trail of coarse fur lined the beast's back and was great for kindling. Nuyani cut some off using it, and flint, to burn in the fire pit. She then removed the hide and several portions of muscle from around the smaller charge-horn's belly before placing it on a tarp. Nuyani glanced at the larger beast, biting her lips before deciding to return the festering creature to the stone.

With wood stocked, a strong flame soon started the front of the cavern and quelled the pulse. Nuyani moved to retrieve the ax, only for a twinge of pain to emerge, reminding her of her scars.

Rummaging through her supplies, Nuyani took the time to clean her wounds. She washed out the blood and grounded down several herbs with some water before wetting them and wrapping the pulp around her forearm. Nuyani sucked in a sharp breath at the sting. As she waited, she looked at the cavern entrance. Only the silver glow shined through the dark. Yet, she never wanted to find a beast ready to take her. Not once in her years alone had a single animal dare to venture inside the cavern, leaving her with questions as she turned toward the abandoned huts. The dead village was not common knowledge. Nuyani wondered if anything that happened in the cavern was something the animals feared. 'No matter, all the better for me,' Nuyani concluded as she returned to her tools.

Keeping mental notes, she prepared her tool strap for the venture bringing her spare ax in place of the knives and ax she lost. Nuyani stored away her bags of nuts and berries within the closest hut. Many of the drylands' regions were picked by the village parties leaving late afternoon as the safest time to avoid encountering any of the others, though some sighted her easily. She made her way through the tunnel and into the night, concerned only for the predators that stalked the dark. She stood at the slope with new vigor, focusing her mind on the hum. A moment passed as a simple pulse rang from her core.

'Yes. I don't need those demons to reach it,' Nuyani cheered.

She concentrated on the sensation until the beat was rapid. With her sense under control, Nuyani darted off toward the south, heading a little toward the east to avoid any blade-jaws or blood-manes. All around her, life scurried and moved beneath the blanket of darkness. Yet, she could feel the presence as if they leaned against her. The pulse maintained its usual ebb as the blue lines did not appear.

Nuyani chuckled, still holding a new awareness with wind sailing past her. 'I can feel them. I wonder if that is how these howlers see as well,' Nuyani thought. Her smile disappeared as she remembered To'anu's words stating they were taking her home. She kept silent, letting the warm winds of the night carry away her thoughts. The land slumbered even in her race. Larger pressures rose and fell in her passing, and the crescent moons remained in their sapphire and emerald glow; only another night or so before new moons took their place. Slowing in her steps, Nuyani reached a dry riverbed where countless rocks lingered close by. Aside from a lone bush to her left, the remaining pressure was before her, leading to a stone no taller than her knee. When she stepped forward, a small lizard scurried out. Nuyani sighed and glanced at the looming shadow of the cliffs only a few dozen meters away.

Even with her speed, an ambush by any beast was not something she would risk without reason. Nuyani squatted before the stones and picked out a few slightly larger than her hand. Untying one of her sacks, she placed three stones within it just as a pressure appeared and shifted against the drum. Nuyani rose as the bushes rustled behind her. The woman sprinted forward and bound over the smooth stones. Behind her, heavy panting and stones tossed about sounded off. Once on the other side, Nuyani sprinted on, only to look back at a prominent figure in the dark with glowing eyes. It gave up and watched as she moved away. With the release of a sigh, Nuyani told herself, 'Not even the blade-jaws will scare me. I might get stubborn and caught if I'm not careful.' Thoughts of To'anu's wounds came to mind. 'No. I must not be careless.'

She made her way toward the lower center of the drylands seeing small lights dance in the air, followed by the soft trickle of water. The humid breeze whipping past her face became brisk. She stopped when another dark line appeared on the earth. The water before her was merely a stream with the moon's light revealing the stones at the bottom. The riverbank edge on both sides was filled with wildflowers but, she did not linger and stepped into the water crossing through the gentle cool. Her body eased, letting the tension of her muscles dissipate. Before she could leave the water, Nuyani looked to the moons. With soft sounds, no predators to be found, peace came to her mind. The face of the apparition returned, and Nuyani's ease faded. She made her way toward several clusters of flax flowers and porcupine grass, gathering several clumps within another sack. Nuyani looked at both bags wondering how cumbersome the return trip would be. Unlike game, she could never use the crystals to carry supplies and ease her burden.

"Another down. I just need wood and wax," she stated before continuing to the east.

The moons sat high as she neared a small forest at the southeastern corner of the drylands.

Towering cliffs stood in the distance. She arrived at a small forest with trees that grew sideways. Often called lizard bark, each trunk had branches that kept it elevated in the air as if they were short legs buried in the ground as the sky-bound branches left short canopies at the top. Nuyani hid between two trees before checking the pulse and surveying the area. Only the still presence of the trees remained. In the distance, she could see another pair of glowing eyes looking up from another small stream passing through the area. It was a fox. The animal proved to be just as cautious, turning away and darting into the night.

'Stay vigilant, little friend,' Nuyani focused on her core once more, wondering why she had not noticed the animal. 'Can you hide from me?' she wondered.

Nuyani dropped the idea and kept her core's pulse strong as she neared one of the trees. The trunk stood at shoulder height, giving enough distance for her to hack at the branch bases. Nuyani retrieved her ax and swung at the branch, splitting several short inches. The sound thundered against the cliffs. She rushed, knowing the noise would alert anything nearby. With a few more hacks, she severed the first branch. Nuyani then stared at the piece seeing if she could use her core to make the silver lines appear once more. After a moment passed with no luck, Nuyani sighed and judged the shape with what sparse light there was and felt it was a good piece for another ax. She then started on another branch. Nuyani took several breaths. Chopping echoed in the dark. With her ax raised, she dived beneath the tree. A crash shook the tree as Nuyani curled into a ball with her ax held close. A loud screech filled the air with the shadowed claws raking at the dirt. Remaining rapid, the rhythm returned as the blue haze formed the outlines of the tree, branches, and claws closest to her. A blood-mane pushed against the tree. Its strength made the lumber creek as it shifted outward. Her heart pounded away as she slid further from the animal's grasp.

Nuyani breathed slowly, carefully reading the animal's movement. The presence shifted as the tree eased. Trouncing shook the tree as a snap sounded off. The branch she worked on broke off as the beast climbed over. With a roll and swift hands, Nuyani was out from beneath the tree as the beast tried to reach her, flapping wings sending gusts of wind all around. Nuyani paid no mind as the looming shadow in the sky faded into the distance. After an hour of scavenging, she returned home, dropping her supplies on the floor before the firepit still burning. She severed another portion of the charge-horn's fur and hide before placing it in the flame.

The flames rose, giving a stronger light. Nuyani then retrieved a lone basket, small clay pot, and string. After several trips, she left for the river and lowered the basket and pot within the water. A cautious eye scanned the area on occasion, fearful of another beast.

'All right, charger horn. Your turn has come. Or howlers. Great Lord, please let them rest,' she thought.

To her benefit, the trip proved silent as she returned to the cavern. Hours passed as she went to work. As daytime broke, Nuyani had a new ax and knives flinted from the stones and stopped making the lacquer she needed for the leather hide. Without any hornet's wax, she would need to retrieve the ingredients again. Nuyani released the larger charge-horn beside its smaller counterpart. As the light faded, its odor rushed through the area. She heaved and pressed her mouth and nose into her arm.

'Can't waste this,' she reminded herself. The beast could be used for many tools, from water skins made from gutting the humps, stomach, or bladder into other leather pieces. Nuyani studied her attire, finding several frayed sections chipping away. She paused, noticing the stream of light peering through the eastern hole within the ceiling. Unlike the other, it was smaller and without any means to reach it, making her wonder how it had formed.

Dropping her tasks, she knelt. She started her prayer once more and finished with the rising gesture of her hand. Her thoughts flashed to the apparitions and then to the grass that bound her for a moment.

'Great Lord, please reveal some answer. What is happening in your lands? Are the spirits corrupted? Why?' She turned back to look at the growth on the charge-horn, her face twisted in a scowl. Returning to her work, Nuyani avoided it. She cut off smaller hide sections and let the coagulated blood drain slowly into another urn thanks to an indented line carved through the rock floor and leading to a small lip over the edge. Nuyani did not bother with its hump but used the other sections of the beast. Its bladder and stomach could still make great water skins, and she only thought to use the rest of the meat and bones for hunting other game. Gathering meat from the other charge-horn along with the larger one's hide, she climbed the indented ladder leading to the ceiling exit. A cross-hatched barrier of rib bones from heavy-horns barred any animal from getting through. Each bone flexed like a bow with ends anchored into small stone divots lining the rim.

She laid down on the floor before placing several slabs of meat and the hide on the ground for drying. She peered out to an endless desert of golden sand as the mountain chain continued to the west. It was a completely different world from her own. Nuyani let go of her collection of questions and turned to head back down. She forgot the salt to preserve the meat. A soft distortion riled the drum's pulse at her flank in mid-step. Nuyani spun around, brandishing her new knife. Her ember eyes widened as she looked at a figure standing just beyond the barrier.

"Mother?" Nuyani whispered.

"Hello, Nuyani," the woman smiled. Nuyani looked much like her, aside from the small wrinkles framing her face. The woman wore a simple brown dress. A small trail of blood fell from a gash on her right temple.

"This…this can't be. How…"

"Relax, Nuyani," her mother chuckled. "You've changed so much. So strong. Even his strength grows within you," Tears swelled in her eyes.

Nuyani rushed to the bone gate. "By the Great Lord, how are you here? Have you been alone all this time? Why haven't you passed on?"

The woman shook her head. "I can't answer, Nuyani. There isn't time. Tonight, there will be danger in the village. You have gifts from the Great Lord. Use them to protect them." A soft echo followed her mother's words. Nuyani could feel her presence grow light as the rhythm became stable. The woman had passed through the barrier and was placed on Nuyani's cheek. More tears streamed from the lone daughter as she felt a familiar warmth. "You've grown stronger. Use this strength to help others."

'I…" Nuyani felt mixed. All she could see were the maddened glares and arrows sent her way.

"A difficult life? I am sure. But don't give up. You can survive. Teach them the same. I love you, Nuyani." Her presence faded faster as the light of the sun peeked over the cliff growing brighter.

"I love…" The barrier shook violently, hitting Nuyani's hand, forcing her to step back. Her attention called to a blood-mane trying to force its way through to the meat on display. The cage ends jostled in their anchor points. Nuyani turned back to find her mother gone, her core's beat unhindered.

Nuyani gritted her teeth and turned to the beast, still snapping and clawing through the barrier. Grabbing her knife, she lunged at the animal, cutting at anything poking through. The blood-mane cawed at her in protest but gave up, releasing a beat of its wings and flying away.

Nuyani released her weapon and fell to the floor, burying her face in her hands.

"Great Lord, she's still here. She's trapped. Where is she? How can I fight for them when she is out there?" Nuyani looked out into the demon lands.

"By Lord Kelvert, I will do as you ask. But I will see you free, mother. Whatever is out there, I will free you from its grasp," she mumbled.

Ch. 5

Disturbed

Supper was short as Cuganwa followed his father through the tents. The party leaders' meeting was taking place, and the boy took Odaru's place, leaving his heart pounding away. In all his life, Cuganwa had never stepped inside the main tent. Few without the true need ever did if they were not village servers or guards. The tents closer to the village center were shorter than the others allowing Cuganwa to see many of the long torches carried by the night guard. As the two made their way toward the chief's tent, other hunters and their seconds came into view. Everyone walked through a large clearing before reaching the tent's front entrance. An enormous totem engraved with figures and symbols of their history sat at the entrance's left, along with two spear-wielding guards allowing them to pass. They watched everyone, ensuring no weapons had entered aside from the ivory knives. They passed through the entrance flaps and down the mortared stairs before entering the tent's largest section.

The boy said nothing as he followed his father's lead. The others remained silent as they funneled through and began to sit down on a larger carpet, forming a crescent with its open side facing toward the four wooden seats. Others began to talk in low roars. Cuganwa looked at some of their ivory knives. The engravings were easy to see even as they were sheathed. Each held the same symbol of Kelvert's light, but with different animals on items marking their territory. The boy caught sight of a woman staring back at him with a smirk. Her knife held the design of heavy-horns. It was Lamoy. She had a thin, slender build, still showing a strong frame. She always wore two feathers of a blood-mane in the front of her hair. She earned her position taking out the beast with an ax after it tried to attack their caravan.

Lamoy leaned back on her hands as she kept her legs crossed, like everyone else. She looked toward the far-off tent wall. Unlike the rest, her attire had green trousers instead of the normal light brown. Cuganwa looked away, not wanting to be rude. He saw another hunter staring at him with a fierce gaze as he turned. He wore a necklace of different colored beads like the other leaders along with the usual red and light brown for hunters. The man was well built. He had a short beard of full black and wore a red head wrap. On his knife was the silhouette of a blood-mane often in wait by salt deposits near the cliff bases. Cuganwa slowly reeled back, wondering if he had offended the man in any way. The boy motioned for his father but, everyone's attention then turned toward the front after two drumbeats. Another villager, a young boy only a year or two older than Cuganwa, stood before them. He wore a light brown tunic, trousers, sash and had the small drum tucked under his right arm.

Behind the aid were four separate curtains covering rooms built into the larger tent. Gamaunda passed through the closest curtains to the exit before standing by the nearest chair. He still wore the same full red attire making him almost blend entirely with the rest of the tent aside from the seats and carpet they sat on.

More guards and village aids entered the tent as the drumming continued. Each of the guards wore red tunics and dark blue trousers easily contrasting the dirt. A white sash adorned their waists, and their straps hanging across their torso had a few knives, extra cords tied around the strap knots in a way to quickly pull off for binding, waterskins, and their quiver of arrows. Cuganwa often looked away from the guard. The memory of a thief killed on the spot after the guards caught him in the act was fresh in the boy's mind. To aid and protect others was a law that the village held dearly.

As the village aid continued the drumbeat, the other curtains opened as the three elders stepped into the open space and took their seats. Each had different roles in guiding the village, while their matching attire to the stones in their rings granted power from the Great Lord. Elder Belractu wore the violet gem allowing him to heal most wounds unless too grave. Despite his age at seventy-two, he still maintained a lean build. His violet tunic was sleeveless. A pair of stern eyes scanned the area through a gray cloud of hair, beard, and mustache as he sat down.

The next elder was Elder Yanuma wearing a simple green dress with her gem, allowing her to recall all the knowledge and memories she was given. Few understood how it worked but, she recited stories and told the village lessons and history as if she were there to see it. Cuganwa remembered her lessons and her smile and gentle demeanor to be a deception of her strict teachings of the village. She had wiry gray hair loosely bound into a single, thick braid reaching midback and was quite thin.

Last was Elder Moyaud. Unlike the others, he rarely wore a tunic showing his thin frame one could confuse for withering away. The elder maintained a shaved head and short beard as he looked about the tent ceiling. 'Why are you looking up?' the boy questioned. The man's eyes were now on him for a moment.

The boy leaned back, surprised by the sudden attention. The elders then turned away and gazed into the air, watching something Cuganwa could not. The blue gem he wore was often said to allow the elder to see spirits and the will of others. He often instructed the village when the storm would arrive and barely spoke or ate with anyone.

"Evening, dear hunters. I hope Lord Kelvert has guided you well," Gamaunda started. "Tonight, let us discuss our situation before the storm comes once more. That and a few other matters." The chief wore a soft grin. "First, let us hear your ventures and exchange needs." Another village aid then stepped forth with several strands of beads draped over their arm. It was an elderly man with a studious eye. "Please, Cumaul. Tell us how the harvest goes."

The first party leader on the opposite end of the crescent started with their supplies and the number of baskets they filled with grasses and herbs along with rabbits and hens they caught. As they spoke, the village aid slid several beads from one end of the strands to the other. The elder then took three strands of beads from one end to the other. The elder then took three strands of beads with separate counts on both ends and tied knots in the middle to keep count. With the number known, Gamaunda then requested the party leader and repeated the same for supplies and stock required. Cuganwa listened attentively. He never realized how much the village needed every day. A single basket usually had enough meat, spices, and water to feed a family of five in proper portions for twenty days. There were just over a thousand people throughout the village, and they all relied on the hunters for survival. Cuganwa looked down in awe. He imagined the countless trips for supplies and game, the resources to create bows and other weapons. The sheer numbers were exhausting to think about for a day, yet the village survived day in and out.

'I will do my best, Lord Kelvert,' the boy assured himself before looking back up and finding Elder Moyaud peering at him for a second time. Cuganwa held eye contact, wondering what reason the man had. 'Is it that strange for me to be here?' The elder's stare seemed neutral of any emotion, giving a little hint to the man's thoughts.

When the man turned back to gazing at the empty air, Cuganwa, once again, noticed a strange buzz at his core. 'Are we about to be attacked?' the boy wondered as he looked around. The sensation then ceased, leaving him with more questions. Moyaud narrowed his eyes as he looked toward space and took a deep breath. Sutama then started to speak, recalling their game and the number of arrows they needed for the next venture. Cuganwa's attention returned to the conversation, ignoring the buzz.

"We have brought in five today but, they are starting to gather in larger groups for the mating seasons and storms. The winds have been stronger as of late," Sutama said.

Gamaunda sat down and leaned forward in his seat, resting both of his elbows on his legs as he stared at the party hunter. The elders also stared at him aside from Elder Moyaud. "But we have another situation to consider," the chief said. Sutama nodded. "The witch came by once more and took one, yes?"

The other party leaders looked toward the seasoned hunter with a mixture of anger and confusion. The huntress, Lamoy, however, wore a wry smile, and the hunter who glared at Cuganwa hardened his stare as if ready to fight.

"Yes, she has," Sutama answered.

"She lingers in your region still. She should've been dead already!" the leering hunter said.

"Deyunca, let them explain before making such judgments. You've protested her death for the last three years. Let it rest. I trust Sutama's word as much as I do yours, but that can be lost," the chief said. He turned to Sutama and waved to his father for him to continue.

"No. We haven't tried to kill her. We know better. Since she escaped, she has done nothing against us to warrant an attack," Sutama explained. "Today, she appeared after the largest charge-horn I'd ever seen, rammed into one of our sleds. My men couldn't kill it despite their shots hitting their target." The man held a hand up, gesturing to his own neck and eyes. "Six or more through here and three eyes gone, but it did not die. One of my men shot through its leg, making it go off to the side. Odaru and Cuganwa fell along with the whip-neck." Dust was everywhere but, in it, Cuganwa and the beast rose while Odaru was pinned under the whip-neck." The man placed a hand on Cuganwa's shoulder. "This one jumped in front of it since my second was in pain and tried to protect him." Sutama looked the others each in their eyes as he lowered his hand. "That was when the witch came out and attacked the charge-horn."

"How'd she kill it if arrows didn't work?" one of the hunters questioned.

"She ran it through with a knife. Her speed makes her capable and difficult," Sutama answered.

"You had six, but a seventh just appeared, and now only five?" Elder Belractu questioned.

Sutama exhaled deeply. "Yes, she took two in anger. She was provoked, elder," Sutama crossed his arms. Others looked to each other in bewilderment. Though they knew Nuyani's abilities, even her crystal, it was still hard to imagine a small woman carrying away such large creatures on her own. Few even cared to believe it, thinking Sutama merely lost his game. "My boy first thanked her, forgetting about the witch, and attacked when she turned. The witch kicked him away and took the seventh and another that fell from the sled. I believe in spite."

"You know her so well," Deyunca chided.

"Deyunca! Show some restraint. There are more important matters to this problem," the chief shouted. "Leader Sutama, why would she need so much food? Surely, she couldn't eat it all, even cured and dried. Does she not linger near the cliffs?"

"I don't know if what some of my men fear is true, and she is taking the extras to feed pets. That would be a reason. I don't agree because of what we've seen in our return home," Sutama continued. Gamaunda waved to a village aid who disappeared inside Moyaud's space only to return with three other men carrying the dead tall horn. Eyes fell on the animal as it was placed at the center between the elders and party leaders, the claw marks on full display near the rear. Bloodied as the wounds were, none would believe them to be so fatal. "There was at least a dozen in all with claw marks like this in one area. I doubt even her speed would allow her to cause such wounds alone but, they were also intact. Her controlling or having pets that could hunt them makes no sense."

"Blade-jaws?" another hunter questioned.

"I would think so but, I don't think the witch is the culprit," Sutama said. Cuganwa then caught Deyunca making a face in anger as he looked at the ground. 'Who is she? Why is she so angry?' the boy questioned.

"If she had such control over those demons, it would be trouble like before," Gamaunda stated.

"Be wary of her, Sutama. We do not need another sinner." The chief then turned away. "Elder Moyaud, any thoughts on this?"

"A few. The life of this beast was stripped away by those cuts, but its hide and organs remained intact. Its flesh around the wound is shriveled and cold beneath the fur. The witch may possess some new skills, or something worse lingers," the elder summarized.

Cuganwa looked around the room, seeing their concern. Only Deyunca held a scowl as he looked at the animal. The boy began to fidget, tracing his fingers over each knuckle. 'The witch is more dangerous than they said. Is he right?' the boy thought as he glanced at the flustered hunter. 'Why lecture me if she could do so much harm?'

"Any signs of blade-jaws?" Elder Belractu asked.

Sutama shook his head. "Just her ax, a few prints, and crushed grass."

"None from any other beasts?" the elder sighed heavily. "Well, I understand your choices, Sutama. But things may grow tense. May the Great Lord forbid, but trouble seems to be growing out there. You may have to take her life. With any suspicion, you must do it."

"She is trouble!" Deyunca rang out.

Gamaunda rose, bearing fury in his leer Cuganwa had never witnessed till now. The chief gestured to two guards, who lunged for the man. The other hunting leaders and seconds moved away as Deyunca was grabbed and dragged to the chief's feet. Forced to kneel, Gamaunda released a vicious hook, sending the hunting leader's head snapping back. Deyunca's rage still burned as he tried to fight the other guards and stand. "Continue," the chief said, keeping his tone even, almost jubilant.

"She is sin!" Another strike drew blood from his nose and lip, with drops falling to the dirt. "A murderer!" A third strike sounded through the tent. Cuganwa tensed up, not fighting his hands' urge to fidget. "My brother is dead, yet she still breathes." The hunter's words grew into a mumble—a fourth.

Cuganwa's mouth was agape. He looked at the hunter, understanding his anger. Sutama placed a hand on the boy's shoulder. Cuganwa turned to look at his father.

The hunter's lips tightened. 'People are dead because of her,' the boy thought.

"Enough, Gamaunda. The boy must speak now," Elder Yanuma said. Gamaunda stood straight, glaring at Deyunca with each knuckle bearing some blood. The guards released him as the hunter sat on his heels, resting his chin on his chest. "Now, Cuganwa, why did you attack her?"

"I…I thought that is what I was supposed to do," the boy uttered, still shaken from the sudden beating.

"Louder," Sutama instructed.

"I thought I was supposed to. She is dangerous and takes people in the night or steals hunters to kill," the boy went on, reciting the rumors spewed by the village. Deyunca let out a chuckle and turned to the boy wearing a bloodied smile.

"Well, you've picked up the tales nicely, but do you know how he died?" the elder questioned. Her eyes were big like an owl as she waited for a reply.

"I think I do," Cuganwa said.

"Only think? The lessons and laws are to right the sins against us. Don't forget that. Deyunca's brother, To'anu, ran off to kill her and never returned. There is no sin aside from his foolishness. An ambition from his hate and hubris that could've brought danger to your father and others. What if he lived, and she did as well, left vengeful? She could outrun anything and chase down anyone. Her strange stone took those beasts with ease. Imagine her fury turned onto the village just for one man to want his name or position to be greater than others." The elder turned, shooting a glare at Deyunca. Turning back to Cuganwa, she went on, "Don't trust her and don't be tempted by your anger. She may bear a force equal to the storms, which is not something we need to turn on us in this difficult world. We survive working together. She does not and is on her own. Do not disturb that truce, understood?"

"Yes, Elder Yanuma," Cuganwa said.

With a soft chuckle and nod, her smile returned as she sat straight. Deyunca's smile faded, replaced with a narrowed glare.

Gamaunda crouched low, meeting the hunter's eyes. "Anything you care to add?" The worn hunter turned to the man and shook his head. "That's better. We feel for you, but a child shouldn't understand the lesson better than his senior." Gamaunda sat down as the guards returned the hunter to his spot on the carpet. "I think we have only a few things to consider. All of you rest for the next day. After that, some of your parties will come together to gather more resources. We will have to prepare for the coming storm, but first, feast. Celebration for all that you've done should be rewarded. Spend time with your families and share a few of your stories with others. I like the one of a new hunter getting his name, Little Charge-horn." The others chuckled as the boy's eyes widened.

'They already know?' Cuganwa thought.

The chief then continued, "Aside from this council, what are your thoughts, dear elders?"

Elder Belractu spoke first. "We will have to wait further on for the actions of the witch. Keep our distance until we have better understanding of what is happening. The story should give us time away from her and let things settle."

Elder Yanuma then added, "I think she plays with you all. Lonely in her home, she needs something to do and only has the hunters to mess with. Her theft is childish, but do not let that bring any danger to your men, Sutama. Ten years and she's kept her distance. May Lord Kelvert keep that wall whole." Sutama replied with a nod. Elder Moyaud waved his hands as his gaze remained fixed on the ceiling. The man then rose and walked toward his own space. Elder Yanuma shook her head as she and Elder Belractu rose to do the same. As the village aids moved to another room, the guards and Gamaunda escorted the hunters out of the tent as one presented Deyunca with a small bowl containing herbs wrapped in a soft cloth of whip-neck fur. He glared at the smaller man handing him the supplies, but eased his expression as he took up the items.

The hunters all parted as Cuganwa followed his father trudging along in silence as he thought of the witch. A man died trying to attack her because of his ambition. He did the same, thinking it was the right thing to do.

"Father, how did the witch get free?" Cuganwa asked.

Without stopping or hesitating, he replied, "She fled when she was found with those cursed eyes."

"If she hasn't committed any crimes, why leave her out there?"

"So she doesn't have a chance to commit a crime. Remember your lessons, boy. One of the chiefs lost their family from jealousy of the first sinner. Now no chief may have a family to be swayed."

Cuganwa stopped and looked at his father's back with widened eyes. 'He's forced to be alone too?' the boy realized the many training ventures and group meetings in public or studies he saw the man instructing with the elders accompanying him as he led the others. 'There isn't any time,' Cuganwa thought.

"Take your mind off it, Cuganwa. There is much work to be done," Sutama stated. The two continued in silence.

Morning arrived as Cuganwa leaped from his bedroll, tightly rolled it up, and placed it to the side within his living space. He kept quiet as his younger sister slumbered. The boy then pushed past the curtain separating his space from the main room only to find Jogia smiling at him as she fixed some food. Their home was nothing special. It had a large central room held up by poles and the ground and stairs were paved with clay. A fire pit in the center was dug and mortared into the dirt with a port overhead. Three spaces were separated by lines of thick cloth, two for their rooms and the last for storage. On the floor were cushions and rugs of whip-neck fur placed where they normally sat.

With news of a late feast coming that night, only a few pieces of bread, figs, and jerky sat in a wooden bowl in wait for Cuganwa. The boy scarfed down most of his food in large bites causing him to cough. Jogia laughed at his eagerness, but did not try to stop him. knowing he would start making his bow.

"Before you take a single step out of here, pray with me. I want to make sure you have been," Jogia stated. With a final swig, Cuganwa downed the remaining content before gasping for air.

"Thank you, Mother."

"You're welcome but, relax. You act as if you need to chase the bow down. Now, pray with me." Cuganwa laughed as he and his mother fixed themselves to face towards an eastern port in the tent wall. The two recited their prayers in unison before gesturing to the sun's rise.

Cuganwa shuffled to move but stopped for a moment, looking about the room. "Where is father?"

The woman looked back at Cuganwa with a smirk. "He's an early riser. Look outside. The sun grows brighter. Better learn to rise early too, or he will leave you on his next trip."

The boy nodded his head and moved to rise until he felt something push against his side. Caluu was leaning against him with closed eyes. In her daze, she began to mumble the prayer.

"Morning, Caluu but, if you are going to pray, you must do it right," Cuganwa instructed as he moved her to sit properly and performed it once more.

"Are you going to the big tent?" Caluu asked.

"Yes. I have to go," Cuganwa answered.

84

"Well, since you are going that way, you can take Caluu to Elder Yanuma's lessons," Jogia added.

Cuganwa turned to her with pleading eyes. "That bow won't exist until you make it. You can take your sister to the lessons."

"We are on our way," Cuganwa started as the two departed up the steps.

Walking through the village proved tedious as several crowds of people squeezed the two. Everyone was busier than usual as whip-neck drivers rode by with large ration baskets on their sleds. Each one was dropped off at home in preparation for the storm. The two made their way toward the village's western perimeter. They walked along the canal, where many people gathered to wash clothing or collect water. It was filtered by tight barriers of bone to keep out water bites and went under the guard mounds built high enough to peer over the bone wall. The two watched as some of the guards speared any water bites that got in.

The two soon arrived at the dozens of whip-neck pens holding many of the hunters' animals. Caluu began to wave at the animals and their handlers. "Can you get one too?" the girl asked.

Cuganwa widened his eyes before he replied, "Not for many years, Caluu. I would have to trade many things on my own for a whip-neck."

"I wanna ride one," the child moaned as she watched a handler leading a younger whip-neck no taller than a man along with their child riding on its back.

"You will one day," the boy said as he smirked.

After passing the crowds and into the open area, a cluster of young children gathered before Elder Yanuma and another totem. The monument was a half-circular of clay smaller than the one in front of the elder's tent. Polished ivory figures and shapes were embedded in the clay, and each section showed the morning hours where the sun's light would gleam and reflect onto the ground before the afternoon. The first section held a curving sliver of ivory arched toward the sun with engraved lines like spikes jutting to the sky to represent the Great Lord's Light. The next sections illustrated their history with their rise from the river, a dome over the village as the design of curling lines parted over the borderline, the light dispersing, and taking the village. The last few had the light showing in the bodies of people as they hunted animals and rebuilt the village in a larger state along with the witch illustrated with the light missing and eyes larger than the others, and claws for hands reaching out to fight a larger figure with the light symbol and a strange item in their hand pointing to the witch.

The boy held his stare at the would-be witch. It was a new section of ivory not so discolored as the other portions. The witch was nothing as the totem displayed. Cuganwa's lips tightened as he thought back to her image. A normal woman wielding a knife seemed completely removed from the beastly appearance, aside from her speed.

Some of the figures within the totem were being cleaned by a village aid in light brown as the elder greeted villagers leaving their children for the lessons. Other figures and clay tablets standing about the totem represented stories and legends from the tales of hunters fighting against animals and spirits.

As Caluu sat down to listen, Cuganwa made his way to the village center. Men and women rushed about with their supplies in preparation of the night.

'People are getting ready for the feast. I should have plenty of room in the crafter's tent,' he concluded. Cuganwa reached the enormous canopy spanning almost a mile long and wide. Cuganwa winced as a pungent smell wafted his way signing that he was close by. He walked down the stairs, plunging into a wave of heat. Beads of sweat rose on his brow. The boy looked around for someone to direct him failing to notice the thin man leaning against the wall beside a canopy pole.

The man held out a hand, drawing Cuganwa's attention. "What are you doing here?" The man's face was doused in sweat and drenched the front of his tunic.

"I came to make a bow," he replied.

The man narrowed his eyes at him showing his disbelief. "What do you need a bow for?"

Cuganwa turned to show his ivory knife engraved with the charge-horn's head and light of Kelvert. The man gawked him.

"Tsk. I wonder if you can even pull one. Go get water," The man said as he turned away, looking down one of the narrow paths. All around him, villagers worked on different projects. The sounds of pounding, grinding, and hacking was in a chaotic chorus as the village's talent was on full display. Seamstresses, twine weavers, tanners, carvers, butchers, vat attendees, spice and herbalists, whittlers. Blade flinders, pot makers, saddlers, cobblers, and dexters all worked within their small sections of the crafter's tent. The pungent smell grew stronger as two villagers walked down the narrow path carrying a pot suspended by two wooden staves. 'It must be the lacquer,' Cuganwa thought as he held his breath. Every bone, leather, and piece of wood used in the village were dipped into the strange mixture allowing most items to last for years of abuse, even during the storms. Their leather canopies covering the tents were well anchored and braved the razor-sharp sands for a time. Though most animal hides did well to resist the climates, whip-neck fur had its strength due to their thick coats but lost it once the animal's fur was sheered off, and the hide was terrible for leather.

Cuganwa followed the men carrying the pot, knowing he needed to use the vats eventually. With little knowledge of the area, it was his best clue. Several minutes passed as he followed the men to the edge of the canopy. Multiple ports were cut into the ceiling venting out the fumes above dozens of large vats built into the dirt. The men stopped and poured the contents into an empty vat as someone else tended to the kindling in the furnace portion. The lacquer already budding from the heated mortar. As one of the men turned to walk back, the boy caught his attention.

"What can I get to make a bow?" Cuganwa asked.

The man's chin rose as he narrowed his eyes. "Get water." The man then pushed past the boy, leaving Cuganwa confused. 'Why's everyone saying that? What does water have to do with it?' he questioned. A young boy then passed by with a ladle and small pot with a rope around the brim, moving toward one of the other villagers tending to a hide. The boy plunged the ladle into the pot, drew some water, and handed it to the adult. After a quick drink, the man handed over a bundle of leather hide behind him. With a pot in hand, the boy ran off toward the center. Cuganwa followed the child, eventually reaching a walking area where others waited by large urns to gather water. 'Do I have to trade water for information too?' the boy questioned.

Cuganwa sat at the end of a few benches behind others waiting their turn. Other children moved to and from gathering their supplies and returned for another turn to fetch water. With a short wait, Cuganwa walked to another villager manning the urn, who plunged the small pot into the water by a rope, then handed it and the ladle to him. Finally bearing a lead, the boy spent the next few hours gathering all the supplies to fletch his bow. He sat near whittlers learning how to handle the knife as he made large and small holes for medallions and necklaces. Beside him were two large sacks of supplies from knives, wooden staves, sinew, thin pieces of bone good for arrows, porcupine grass, and a small totem of a charge-horn head holding a few yellow beads in its mouth; a small token to ask villagers to help him retrieve the lacquer needed for the bow. Still considered too young, some resources were limited even with his knife. He was drenched in sweat and was permitted to sit by the edge for better ventilation. 'So many are here. No wonder it is so big,' Cuganwa thought. He rarely needed to go to the crafters' tent, for most of those who went were either trained in a talent working for others to produce goods or family members with a single tree. Sutama was only a hunter, while Jogia often cooked for others in trade. Neither had much reason to come to the tent unless for supplies.

"Enough! Go home!" a woman said. Cuganwa looked confused to find the villager Ienka standing before him with her hands on both hips. The woman's eyes danced over the small collection of trinkets he was tasked to bore holes in.

"Oh. Is it time?" the boy thought, considering his task might have a time limit so others could practice as well.

"Only yours," Ienka said with a shake of her head. "The feast is tonight. You will be doing other things to help prepare."

"I still have…" Cuganwa started.

"No. You are a runner for your father. That means there will be tasks to do for the festival. So go," she ordered.

Cuganwa nodded as he handed back the small collection and took his stuff with him. Once he climbed the stairs back into the village space, he was refreshed with a short breeze. The boy crossed through the village until he reached the western totem. In his approach, the pool of children was much smaller as those remaining listened to the elder's story.

Yanuma pointed to a tablet engraved with dozens of structures as she went on, "Even with homes made of stone and towering the mountains, the people explored open waters that stretched beyond their sight." As she continued her tale, Cuganwa found Caluu, and the two left for home.

Ch. 6

Truth and Reality

Cuganwa's stomach protested as he walked back home from running all afternoon. Aiding his father and others, he ran from point to point, delivering messages to villagers for supplies. With the sun starting to set, the lights of three enormous bonfires at the village center became more prominent. People were already beginning to gather as they stuck several slabs of meat on spits hanging from the flames. Baskets of dates and grapes sat on the side. Large urns filled with water and juice sat beside the food, with servers handing out portions. Musicians and singers made their way to the clear spots before performing for early dancers.

The commotion grew quieter as the boy neared his home. Cuganwa ambled on, smiling at the festivities. His legs ached, but he gave them no mind. Soon, his bow would be made, and his training as a full hunter would begin. 'Thank you, Great Lord,' the boy prayed. His gaze turned to the dirt as Nuyani's face entered his mind. In all that he gained, she had none. The elder's lessons repeated in his head.

'Lord Kelvert, please forgive me. I did not know…" Cuganwa started until the unstable steps of Deyunca called his attention. The hunter swayed in his movements, leaning forward. In his hand was a waterskin, but the sweet aroma smelled of liquor. Instead of the usual red and light tan clothing, the hunting leader wore a simple blue set with a green sash. Soothing colors many wore that contrasted the red cage surrounding their lives.

"An-nd what are you sorry for, boy? What does a child need of the Great Lord's mercy?" Deyunca asked as he struggled to walk. Cuganwa said nothing as he narrowed his eyes at the man and tried to walk on. The man stomped forward with widened eyes and cut him off. Both sides of his face were swollen as patches of green from dried ointment covered cuts on his chin, lips, and left eye. "Don't ignore your eldu-der. What are you sorry for?" Cuganwa stayed silent, leaning away from Deyunca. He could not tell what the hunter would do in an inebriated state. "Answer me." His tone was just short of a yell.

"To the witch," Cuganwa admitted.

Deyunca, in turn, leaned back and furrowed his brow. His eyes set on the boy with a burning rage. Cuganwa felt an urge to fidget but closed his fists. "For the witch, boy?" the man held his arm out. "For the demon child? He took my brother, and who knows how many in the dead of night, but you want forgiveness for trying to kill it?" Reeling his head back like a cobra, the man continued to sway, waiting for his answer. Nearing a whisper, he continued, "I thought you were the smart one in your father's lot for even giving it a try. Now you let an excuse like that stop you?"

Cuganwa fixed a glare as he started, "My father seems to get the idea better than you. The elders said…"

"The elders know she is dangerous and think she should be feared!" the man lamented. "The only thing that demon deserves is four parties searching for the den and killing her before she gets another chance." The man raised his head, standing straight and stable as he leaned his head back. Cuganwa stepped forth, readying himself to keep the man balanced. Deyunca instead shot forward, releasing his waterskin to dangle on his wrist, and grabbed Cuganwa's arm with a tight grip. The boy tried to escape as the man's fingers dug into his skin.

"Let go! Why are you…" Cuganwa started.

"Think," the man demanded as he gave Cuganwa a violent shake. "The pain knowing one of your loved ones is dead or taken. How would you feel if the thing snatched away your father, mother, or sister?" The mixture of food and drink wafted into the boy's face as Deyunca stayed only a few inches away, forcing the child to back away. "There are dangers greater than the storm, boy. Did you ever think she didn't like your attempt and would pay you back? She took a charge-horn that could feed dozens. Why not take you too?"

"Let go," the boy said.

"What is going on!" Another voice said. Deyunca righted himself and released Cuganwa. The two looked in the shout's direction, finding Lamoy walking toward them with a bundle of clothing held in one of her arms. The huntress wore a light green dress dotted with a few patterns of blue and violet reaching her ankles. Her gaze fell to Deyunca's reappearing hand. "What was in your hand, Deyunca?"

The man narrowed his eyes at her. Lamoy deftly removed a knife from her sash and presented it as if she were ready to strike. Cuganwa's eyes widened as Deyunca relented, showing both hands were empty. "Perhaps you should calm yourself, Lamoy."

"Or should I say that to you?" Lamoy countered. "The boy looks scared even though he tried to take on the witch? What has Little Charge-horn timid concerns me. So why is he feeling that way?" The woman wore a smile.

"Just giving him a proper education of the world. The boy needs to learn the true threats around him."

"Aww," the woman continued to smile and nodded her head. "The threats around him? Turn around."

"What?" Deyunca asked.

The woman took two steps in a rush, her gaze fixed into a maddened stare. "I said turn." Deyunca moved slowly, stepping away from Cuganwa with arms out and fingers splayed as he made a slow turn until he faced Lamoy. The huntress looked at the man with scrutiny. "Fine. Now leave," Lamoy demanded, keeping her blade at the ready. Deyunca looked at her, gawking. "I don't think I should leave you with someone until your head is clear. Would've thought that beating was enough."

Deyunca fixed a smile as he walked away. "May Lord Kelvert guide you through your trials."

"May a fool learn the brazen die," Lamoy retorted. Deyunca said nothing as he turned about and walked off toward the bonfires. "Idiot." She then turned to Cuganwa. "Now, what was he educating you on?"

"He heard me ask the Great Lord for forgiveness for attacking the witch," Cuganwa admitted.

Lamoy rolled her eyes. "That drew his ire? Of course, it would." She looked back at Cuganwa. "You remember what the elders told you?" The boy nodded his head. "Then that is all that matters. Pray in your room. Keep those thoughts to yourself. He is the most taken, but many share his view."

"Yes, huntress," the boy said.

"Good. Now go back to your business, hunter. This is a time to relieve stress." Cuganwa nodded once more and left for home.

Remaining quiet about the event, Cuganwa readied himself for the festival and left with his family tagging along. He wandered about telling his father about the situation but did not want to ruin their night. As the feast went on, hunters went up one after another to share their feats. Though Cuganwa tried to hide, Iogda and Selsaj smiled as they grabbed both arms and carried him toward the clear circle. He was met with cheers before being left on the edge. Gamaunda stood in wait, ready for him to move forward. 'This is not good," Cuganwa thought as he began to tell his part in hunting the charge-horns. As he looked through the crowd, he tried to avoid his mother's eyes. He mentioned every detail he could remember, as some grew shocked by his mistake and survival. Some of the younger villagers shook their heads in disbelief.

Cuganwa was met with cheers after finishing his part as the others clapped for him. A brief peek toward his left showed his father smiling, trying to hold back his laughter, and his mother forcing her smile with a slow, angry clap. Leaving the circle, Cuganwa heard the two hunters call out, "Little Charg-Horn," leading everyone into a short chant. This only left Cuganwa smiling as he left for another hunter to take the circle. As the feast went on, he left to speak with his friends and eat.

Ch. 7

The Reach of Death

The wind rushed about as the sun's rays passed through the demon gate. Nuyani sat on the sloping ledge staring at a worn Ivory knife bearing a charge-horn's head at the hilt, a chipped edge, and small dark stains on the tip. 'Mother, Lord Kelvert, is this the right thing to do? How am I supposed to protect them?' A tear rolled down her nose and onto the blade. Her attention broke when her core pulsed without command. Taking a deep breath, Nuyani steeled her nerves as she shoved the knife into a sheath and took off toward the village.

Nuyani moved along the brush line, cautiously following the cloud shadows as she grew closer to the village. A quick leap over the water bite river allowed her to reach the outer canal blocked off by a series of bones protruding only a few inches out of the water. Nuyani moved toward the gate, staying out of sight, mindful of any guards looking over the area. "I can do this," she told herself as she pressed her back against the gate. Obscured by shadow, Nuyani could hear only a few water bites linger that made it through the first barrier. She removed a waterskin from her tool strap and released some of the contents into the stream. She repelled the remaining pests using heavy-horns urine but knew time was short as she moved toward the second gate. Nuyani winced as she closed the waterskin and forced her way through the last barrier.

Her heart hammered on remembering her wishful plans to rejoin the village if she could ever hide her eyes years ago. Their glow, ever-present, shone with a soft edge on the water surface. After realizing there was no hiding, she only entertained the idea to pass the time. Swimming through the small canal, Nuyani heard a few groans of whip-necks in the dark. Their pens were close by. Nuyani swam toward the animals to show she was friendly, hoping they would remain silent. Some of the animals leaned down for her to pet them as others continued to sleep or drink water.

"Hi. I'm a friend," she whispered, smiling gleefully as her fingers ran through the soft fur under their chins. It dawned on her how much she missed things not trying to kill her. Nuyani made her way through the canal, keeping her head low as she passed the dozens of homes lining the side, all dedicated to the mounts. The glow of the bonfires could be seen from the edge of the village. Rising from the slow stream, Nuyani stayed low beside the tent. Her body shivered in exposure to the air. She lurked about the tents on the edge, wondering what she was looking for. Her mother's warning and sudden pulse were all that spurred her to come. 'I should leave,' Nuyani told herself. She turned, facing the canal's direction, thinking she was only going mad. Raising a hand to her cheek, she remembered the feeling of the light press, even in delusion. Her fists tightened. The weight of her mother's presence returned. With a deep breath, Nuyani Turned back and released a pulse from her core. She focused on the rapid beats as each wave coursed through the area. Hundreds of small distortions arose before forming into beads of pressure dotting the surface of her internal drum.

Nuyani knelt as if in prayer, focusing more on her sense. Each presence became diverse. Some grew heavy as others swayed and rippled in irregular patterns. Four of the pressures were stronger than the others. Nuyani narrowed her eyes in their direction as she moved toward the group. "Is this what she warned me of? Why are the howlers coming here?" She ran through the area without concern for others until she stopped to see a rectangular pit going only hip deep. Countless stones filled the confines. Nuyani readied her blade for the hidden spirits, her pulse racing until it formed a solid wave. Several white glows then rose from the rubble. The spirits of four men then appeared. They were villagers with soiled clothing covered in red dust. Each of their heads had bloody wounds and gave her bewildered stares. Two of the spirits smiled at her and waved. Nuyani herself eased in her stance, hesitating to wave back. 'Why have you died here?' Nuyani questioned and lowered her arms.

"We built this thinking stone would outlast the storms better than the tents," the eldest man stated. "But we were wrong."

"You can hear my thoughts?" Nuyani asked. The man only gave a wider smile. Nuyani grew curious and tested her theory. 'Are my thoughts opened to you?'

"I don't know what you are saying. It is good to talk to someone, though rare," the villager continued. "Our bodies were taken to burial but, we did not pass on." The man's voice slowly died along with his smile. He looked to the ground. The man then looked back up at Nuyani, releasing a short chuckle. "The one to find us is the witch. What lessons has the Great Lord presented to us?" The man shook his head.

Knowing she could not answer him, Nuyani stared as the others conversed with each other. She could not hear a single word from the other men though the eldest was clearly speaking with them. "Why is this happening?" The burial should free them. Do some spirits remain even after their body is cleansed?' Nuyani wondered what she could do and held out her hand toward the elder villager. She descended a step on the unfinished stairs calling their attention.

"A-are you trying to help us?" the eldest smiled even greater. "Or is this just the fate of a foolish man to be taken for punishment?" Nuyani said nothing waiting for the man to act. The elder held out a transparent hand and grabbed Nuyani's. A smile spread across her face as she moved with instinct. The pulses grew stronger and deeper as the force wrapped around the spirit until his visage became a small transparent marble in her palm. An iridescent flame sat at the center, flickering in all directions. The weight of the presence sat against her drum as if it were a waterskin compared to the small dew of the howlers. Nuyani breathed heavily as she lifted her palm to the sky, and the marble shot to the heavens leaving a brief blue streak. She looked to the sky, only seeing the trail of light fading. When her gaze returned to the others, they were staring back with mouths agape before extending their hands to her. One by one, the trapped spirits were liberated. 'I can move spirits. That means I can free To'anu,' Nuyani thought. A flash of her mother came to her mind. 'I can free you, mother. Is that why…No. She wouldn't send me here to learn to free others, then for her. She said the village is in danger, right?'

"Did you free them?" a voice asked, causing Nuyani to spin around. Before her, a young girl with curious eyes looked at her. "Your eyes look like fire," the child said with a gleeful smile.

'No, I've been seen. But she's not scared. She doesn't know who I am,' Nuyani realized as she sat on the ground. "Yes, they can glow sometimes. Why are you here? Isn't there a party?" Nuyani questioned softly. Even on the village outskirts, she could see the roaring bonfires and hear the softened beat of the drum and strings.

"Yeah, but I was chasing a frog until I saw the lights. They never say anything to me, but you let them out,"

"So why aren't you with your mother?"

"She is talking with my father for a bit. They wanted me to go play with my brother. You're wearing runner things too like my brother. Are you fast?"

"Y-yes, child," Nuyani answered, smiling. "I run a lot."

"I think you're faster than my brother. He's shorter than you. He ran through a snare, and my mother wasn't happy."

Nuyani blinked several times. "Oh. Then I hope he learns better. Well, I must find my own family now. You should return to yours too, all right?"

"But can I show you something?" The child took several anxious looks around and bit her thumb before turning back. Nuyani stiffened as another pair of burning ember lights replaced the dark brown. The girl awaited a gleeful surprise as she smiled. Her joy disappeared, watching as Nuyani showed a look of horror on her face. Another pulse repeatedly beat in the child's direction, slower and softer. "W-what? You have the eyes too. You're the witch but, you're good."

'She knows,' Nuyani started. "Don't show your eyes, little one."

"But you're good. You aren't bad. You helped them. You helped them." The child flailed her arms against her sides as the orange glow left a gleam on the child's tear. "I'm not bad. I help too. I pray too."

"Calm down. You will be all right," Nuyani lied. Her heart raced. "Don't show your eyes to anyone, okay?"

"But, I'm not bad!" the child stomped her foot.

"No. You aren't bad, but you can't show others. They won't understand, you see." The child wiped away some of her tears as she nodded her head. "Good," Nuyani's head spun in search of answers. With another child born with the same curse, Nuyani wondered if she should take the child with her. She dropped the option, remembering howlers were chasing her. If left alone, Nuyani was certain the child would die. 'Lord Kelvert, what am I to do?' the woman thought to herself.

"Hello? Is everything all right?" another voice said. It was Lamoy. The huntress stopped in her tracks as her body visibly shuttered before remaining stiff. Nuyani's heart sunk as she saw the woman recoil at having found two sets of glowing eyes looking her way. 'Loya? Is that you? How did I not sense her?' Nuyani questioned, noticing the child's pulse shortened the reach of her echo.

Recovering from the shock, Lamoy formed a menacing smile as she brandished her knife and dropped the rolled-up clothing. The huntress lunged for Nuyani. "No."

Nuyani grabbed her hands as the blade was held to her throat. The other hand grabbed the loose back end of the hood and hair. "It's not what you think."

The huntress's grip grew tighter as she placed more weight behind the blade, trying to match strength. Through gritted teeth, Lamoy then asked, "And what am I misunderstanding? I've caught you corrupting a child to take away," Lamoy said.

"And who corrupted me, Loya? Please," Nuyani said, invoking an old nickname the two shared. Lamoy froze, holding her grip. Nuyani fought to ignore the pain from her grip. Lamoy was strong. "Things are happening that I can hardly explain or understand myself but, I am not here to cause any harm."

Lamoy loosened her grip keeping the blade against her neck until she stepped out of arm's reach and pulled the child behind her. Her eyes glanced to the side, a sign she would run. Nuyani found it surprising she did not. "Explain," said the huntress.

"I think the Great Lord wants me here to stop… something," Nuyani started. Lamoy furrowed her brow.

"Stop what?" the huntress asked. The young girl stepped back and sat low, trying to make herself smaller. "Caluu? Her?"

"I have nothing to do with her. I swear," Nuyani pleaded.

Lamoy shook her head. "And what exactly are you here to prevent? Nui, this is not the time for one of your schemes."

"I have no schemes. Some sort of wild spirits have been attacking me for the past two nights. I don't know where they come from or why they're after me. But they aren't normal. One even fled toward the Demon Gate. They can kill with a shallow cut."

Lamoy lifted her chin. "And, what does a normal spirit look like?"

Nuyani's voice quivered, "Their last moments. The blow or injury that took them."

"What of To'anu?" Nuyani's brow creased, and she blinked several times to decipher the question. "To'anu! What was his?" The huntress shook her hand. Caluu whimpered.

"Claw marks," Nuyani blurted out. "He chased me on a whip-neck and was taken when a blade-jaw leaped for him and dragged him to the ground. I fled."

"Did you lead it there?" Lamoy asked.

"No. It's not a risk I'd want if one tracked me home. I want to live in peace," Nuyani said.

Lamoy's eyes narrowed. "Do you control those beasts?"

Nuyani shook her head. "That's not something I can do."

"Then why were so many tall horns dead with claws ran through them? Blood-manes or blade-jaws? Your ax was there, so don't deny it," Lamoy pressed.

"The spirits. Howlers. Please, let me show you," Nuyani said, slowly unwrapping the binds on her forearm. "Look." Nuyani turned her arm to face the wary villager revealing four long scars treated by herbs. Lamoy scrutinized the wounds.

"No," the huntress whispered.

"No?" Nuyani repeated.

Lamoy glared at the witch. She was unconvinced until Nuyani moved to the side as blue claws burst from the ground, followed by the malnourished figure. Caluu shrieked and fell back. The pressure against Nuyani's core was heavy. The huntress looked into the spirit's voided eyes as several strands of hair formed a white streak beneath the feathers. Nuyani dived forth, tackling Lamoy to the ground as a second swipe from the specter sailed over them. The witch then turned around, unsheathing her blade, cutting through the specter's neck. Even with a severed head twisting in the air, the howler uttered a desperate cry before its body erupted into blue embers.

"What was that?" Caluu asked.

"That's what I'm looking to fight," Nuyani stated. She looked to the huntress only to find her giving a blank stare into the sky. Nuyani touched the woman's hand, expecting her to recoil. Instead, Lamoy remained frozen. "By the Great Lord." Nuyani then focused her core's pulse until the rapid beats returned to a solid wall. Letting instinct drive her, the echo stretched out, reaching from within her, and channeled through the huntress. Another beat echoed within Lamoy. 'This… power lies in her too?' Nuyani thought. The beat was steady and slow, surrounding the woman's frozen life. 'Is this right?' Nuyani questioned as she allowed her energy to brush against the dull drum. Vibrations soon traveled, multiplying within the ethereal depths as the frozen life swayed and turned about once more.

Lamoy broke from her trance, jumping up as if she were revived from drowning. "What happened? Where's…" She stopped and looked at Nuyani. A look of sorrow formed on the huntress's face only to be replaced with a look of dread. "What have you been going through?" Her body shivered violently, making her words tremble. Despite the cold, the woman broke away and rose to her feet. "What of her?" Lamoy looked to Caluu, expressing the same concern Nuyani felt.

"I can hide my eyes," Caluu admitted sadly as the ember glow faded back to brown.

"I don't understand all this, but…" Nuyani started.

Lamoy held up her hand, stopping her. "I saw a thing I don't understand. Nui, I won't stop you but, I can't help you either." A frown formed on Nuyani's face. "I will take the girl back but, unless you can prove to everyone at once, you will only have people calling each other crazy. Is that the only thing you were after?"

"I don't think so. One came for me yesterday after the first night had three. The spirits think, though. I believe the last was a test. I must check for more," Nuyani replied as she released a pulse throughout the area.

Amongst the hundreds of lives, three weighed on her sense greater than the others. "No. More are here. I have to stop them!"

"What is happening over there?" came another voice. The three looked to find the rising lantern of a guard approaching.

In sharp whispers, Nuyani said. "I must go. Cover your hair. The front has turned white." Nuyani sped off toward the tents. Lamoy retrieved a rag from the bundle of clothing and wrapped it over her head, covering her proud feathers.

The guard was now closer before he asked, "Why are you two out here? Is everything all right?"

"Just making sure the child is safe. She followed a lizard, and I was keeping watch," Lamoy lied.

"What was that screaming?" the man asked.

Lamoy tilted her head toward the fallen hut. "She almost fell in."

Nuyani followed the closest presence, sensing it through the village's northwestern bank, stalking another guard on patrol. The man moved leisurely along, taking a few swigs of water as his torch on the end of a long pole dangled behind him. Nuyani followed close by staying low as she felt the shifting presence move toward the guard. The witch picked up a small rock and tossed it to the man's right just as the specter emerged. Nuyani sprinted a few steps before launching toward the apparition and severing its head as she landed on the embankment. Despite her feet sinking into the dirt, she pushed off with enough force to dive into the darkness as the guard wheeled around, finding blue embers falling. The man backpedaled with his knife raised and brought his torch forward, looking for any signs in the darkness surrounding the tents. Nuyani hid behind one as he turned back to the embankment and found the footprints pressed into the ground. The man gave a double-take before looking toward her direction and searching. He passed by allowing Nuyani to take a different route. Roasted meat and drinks swirled in the air calling for her to stop and take something. She ignored the food while dodging several groups searching for the next presence. The two remaining shifted and turned more rapidly, sometimes growing lighter. They were moving faster as Nuyani felt other pressures rise, then fade. 'By Lord Kelvert's will, no,' Nuyani prayed as she started running. Nuyani was only a dozen steps away when another howler rose behind two villagers alone. The specter swiped at their backs. The villagers screamed in pain as their bodies rapidly shriveled with tight skin wrapping around their bones and fell to the floor. She could feel their life coursing toward the west, not toward the sky like the four she released. Nuyani leaped toward the howler. The apparition turned as she plunged her blade into its chest. In passing through blue flames, she rolled forward, falling into a tent pole and collapsing the side as it snapped. Those inside made a commotion and moved to investigate.

With little time to dwell, Nuyani rose, ignoring the pain in her side, and started toward the last heavy presence making its way to the center of the village. The presence began to surge in its stead. Nuyani's heart pounded with fury, knowing the villagers were in peril. Discretion would only waste time as she ran through the area calling the attention of many. The apparition rose from the ground catching everyone's attention in the area screams sounded off, seeing the ghastly spirit. Nuyani's pulse coursed through her, cutting through the apparition's influence as she drew near.

The life of the villagers soon drifted upward as the lament continued ripping them away. The howlers stopped and turned toward the witch. The specter moved to take off as Nuyani reached the center. It streaked forth with each orb of flame following. Nuyani extended her hand as her energy flared in an orange glow, creating a transparent wall of light erected in a dome over the area. The apparition collided with the light construct as the spheres of life rebounded from the barrier back to the villagers. Others outside of the center covered their eyes from the bright aura. 'You will not leave here,' Nuyani declared as she raked her hand back. The ethereal barrier shrank toward Nuyani, closing in on her foe. Managing to catch the apparition, Nuyani reeled her knife hand back and finished the howler with a slice through its back. The barrier erupted into a blinding light along with the apparition sending white embers everywhere.

Nuyani sheathed her knife and breathed heavily as she staggered by a few tents. Most of those outside the area were trying to fix their eyes from the bright light, while others were soon to arrive. Throbbing pain in her head and limbs made every step excruciating. Dazed and confused, she slipped on a stone, falling to the ground. A coughing fit started as she forced herself to roll over to her side, staring into the stars. Nuyani tried to move her legs, but the feeling faded, leaving only a twitch of her toes.

Her heart sunk as she attempted to move her arms as well. Strength throughout her body dwindled with only her eyes and breathing in her control. 'Not now. I can't move. Why? Great Lord, please. Let me move." With an attempt to call upon her core, the echo constricted, becoming erratic as it traveled through her body. Nuyani winced as her muscles contracted and released painfully. Every tendon threatened to snap under the strain. She left her core alone, losing her last option. Nuyani then saw a figure enter her view. A man knelt by her head and dragged her through the area. Nuyani's head fell low as she saw others gather around those lying on the floor. None were paying attention to them.

"Lord Kelvert sent you to aid us, hasn't he? You wouldn't be here otherwise," the man said.

Nuyani narrowed her eyes, recognizing the voice. They traveled along the northwestern embankment until her captor moved toward the tents and lay her down. Nuyani got a glimpse of the man seeing Odaru as he laid her head back.

"You?" Nuyani's eyes went wide as she remembered the man stuck out in the drylands on his own. The others took him for dead. If she hadn't drawn a few animals away, he would've been. The man leaned down and planted a kiss on her forehead. Nuyani blinked, uncertain how to feel about the gesture.

"Not to be forward but, thank you," the hunter whispered. "I saw you once out there, but I am certain it was you who helped me just like you are now. The Great Lord wants us to work together. I will hide you here. Leave when you can. If you can. May the Great Lord's shine guide you."

'And you,' Nuyani wanted to say along with many other things. Her eyes began to well. The hunter slowly pushed her into the crevice between the tent and stone wall. He turned her head to the sky, ensuring she could breathe. Odaru rose and dusted his clothing as he hobbled away. 'Thank you. Thank you,' she repeated, wishing for a chance to speak.

A few hours passed as Nuyani sat in the cramped space. The feeling in her body's strength slowly returned long before the movement had. Several footprints and loud voices shouted overhead as the guards searched the area for clues. Mention of her tracks in the embankment was repeated several times. When the moons had passed by, Nuyani struggled to climb up. She released a soft pulse from her core, allowing a wave of energy to measure her surroundings. Even in a smaller fraction, pain rose from using the strange core. With the area clear, Nuyani struggled to move quickly as her shaking legs threatened to collapse. 'Great Lord. Mother. Is this the reason for this curse? Must I fight flying dead every night?' She crossed the empty village space reaching the collapsed hunt. Thinking only to hide in the partial stairway, Nuyani found the bundle of clothing sitting alone in the space.

'Lamoy, did you leave this for me?' she wondered. Taking the pack as a sign of good faith. Nuyani made her way through the village and snuck through the canal gates. With everyone preoccupied with the insiders, she ran home unseen.

Ch. 8

Aiming Toward Life

Nuyani lay on the ground staring into the demon lands from the plateau where she left the meat to dry. Several times, blood-manes tried and failed to break the gate. Twice they've struck the side before her, yet she remained aloof to their pestering. 'I did as you asked of me, Mother, but is this all I can do?' Nuyani questioned. She placed her hand on her cheek, remembering her mother's touch. 'You were here but, what do I do now? There is another like me. If more howlers came, how could I stop them all? Great Lord, what was that light?' Nuyani held one hand in the other, inspecting her palm, looking for some secret without succumbing to the pain. 'I know I can go there but, if this goes on every night, either those spirits or the hunters will kill me.' Odaru came to her mind, along with Lamoy and Caluu. "They wouldn't, but they won't be safe."

As she replayed the night's events, the sun's rays peered over the clifftop, slowly bringing light to the demon land. Nuyani turned toward the east and performed her prayer. After raising and lowering her hand, Nuyani turned toward the east and performed her prayer. After raising and lowering her hand, Nuyani recalled the words of Elder Yanuma. Her fables of hunters and guards fighting off beasts. 'I can go anywhere. The west has death, and then the east should have life,' Nuyani thought. As an old fable of tall huts rivaling the mountains and people riding on endless waters as vast as the demon lands. Few could imagine such a thing. She shot up, remembering the Great Lord as a star bringing them to life from the river as the sun did for the brush and grass.

"Then not the east, but the rivers. I will follow them," the witch said, then turned to the west as golden sand glimmered in the sun. 'If death follows, I will bring proof to convince them to move toward life. To survive. Then, I will return, Mother. I will travel the lands for you and free you if the Great Lord wills me the strength.'

Crowing sounded from the side, catching Nuyani's attention. A blood-mane sat atop of an uneven stone watching her. The witch smirked as she stepped to the meat and severed a small portion. The sun-dried most of the ends. Nuyani then turned to the animal and tossed the sliver through the barrier. The animal easily snapped it out of the air, releasing a loud chomp before turning back to the witch.

"Maybe we could share some kindness, neighbor. At least, before we part ways," she said with a smile before heading down the ladder.

Ch. 9

True Threats

Silence gripped the village as Elder Belractu and Moyaud examined those caught in the light during the feast. Eight lives were lost, with bodies shriveled found in their tents. Almost four dozen villagers sat in the center, away from the others. Some bore white streaks in their hair, whether young or old. Dawn grew brighter as many waited for their loved ones, many praying harder than ever. As Cuganwa sat with his sister sleeping in his lap, whispers of the witch passed through many lips. A woman running toward the center and strange beings coming from the earth before turning into blue flames repeated on their breath. Both the young hunter and his siblings were with their friends during the incident but were blinded after hearing the shriek. 'Lord Kelvert, what has happened?' the boy questioned as he felt his stomach turn. The strange hum returned during the night. Cuganwa ignored it, thinking it was just from the drink, he switched with an older villager with curious hands.

Gamaunda approached the elders at work, speaking to one another before walking toward the other villagers. "Everyone, a tragedy has befallen some of our kin during the night. By the Great Lord's will, only so many were harmed as others fell, but still live. We don't know what happened, but we will need everyone to watch for clues or odd natures. Remain where you are until the guards release you. We will find answers," the chief finished before walking off to a handful of his men.

"What do you mean we don't know what happened? Such a thing could only be the witch," someone complained. Cuganwa looked to the side to find Deyunca glaring at the chief and others. His stare hardened, and his breathing was heavy. A shiver ran down the boy's spine as he looked away. From the corner of his eye, he could see the odd hunter rush off but did not dare look his way.

'I don't like him,' Cuganwa thought to himself.

"Cuganwa!" another voice called. The boy looked to his side, seeing Odaru and Sutama waving for him to approach. Cuganwa rose, carrying his sister. "I am glad you are both safe."

"Hello, father. Hello, Odaru. Where is Mother?" the boy questioned as his father ran a hand through his afro and Caluu's hair, making the drowsy child stir only to turn her head in the other direction. Sutama smiled for a moment before straightening himself and wearing the same focused expression as when they hunted.

"Your mother's home but, we have work to do. Take Caluu back. We're helping the guards secure the village, then we're going to hunt with Lamoy's party," Sutama said. "Supplies are still short."

Cuganwa nodded and moved to head back only to find his mother to be standing behind him as well with a glare. "He'll be staying home too," Jogia said. This took everyone aback. Odaru turned and hobbled away with the splint and aid from a walking cane.

"Jogia, this is not the time. We need all the hunters we can get," Sutama said.

"I must help, mother. This is my task too," Cuganwa added.

"No. This is getting dangerous. That stunt of yours was crazy enough. I'm not having you out there with the witch and spirits about. Be a guard," the woman said as she reached for the knife. Cuganwa's brow furrowed as he blocked her hand and lowered Caluu to stand on her own.

"Mother, I have to help. It's my station to do so. Otherwise, not even the guard would accept me. I won't cower when everyone else is working," Cuganwa said as he looked down at his sister. "Caluu, you must go with mother. I have work to do."

Jogia's eyes welled as she clasped both hands together. Sutama stepped forward, placing hands on her shoulders. In a soft tone, he spoke, "We must do this, Jogia. The lives of everyone depend on our efforts. The storms are coming, my love." Jogia nodded her head and lowered it as if a sign of acceptance. Sutama kissed the woman's brow before she and Caluu walked off. Sutama sighed before turning around and waving for Odaru and Cuganwa to follow.

A moment later, the hunters gathered along with dozens of guards before the chief. Gamaunda instructed several parties to search each home for the witch. A tent pole had broken, felling the side in the night, adding suspicion of her hiding. Cuganwa caught a glimpse of Deyunca. The man's gaze, almost trance-like, was fixated on something before him. His jaw was clenched tight as they waited. From enraged to stone-faced, Cuganwa moved, only feeling more uneased by the man. Everyone departed to follow their instructions. Cuganwa moved with several of the other hunters to clear the homes within the southeastern portion of the village. Between checking each home and returning to his father, the boy grew exhausted, running each way. Though he searched for the witch, Cuganwa kept a cautious eye out for Deyunca. His fingers fidgeted.

Cuganwa stopped once he passed a few personal totems built beside the tents. He froze in place, seeing Deyunca standing over a fallen guard with his hand placed over a bloody wound in the man's neck.

"Run," Cuganwa's mind whispered in a sharp, echoing chirp.

"What?" the boy questioned, drawing the hunter's attention.

"Get help! He's been cut, boy!" Deyunca roared. Returning to his senses, Cuganwa did as he was told, running to the first guard about the slain man.

The guard, in turn, went to three others. Within moments, they were informed of the situation and broke off from each other for different tasks. One left to guard Deyunca and help stop the bleeding, another went to retrieve the chief, the third for Elder Yanuma, and the final guard Cuganwa followed, heading to Elder Belractu, who was resting in the village center. The other quarantined villagers moved at ease, while Elder Moyaud examined them again, checking their spirits. When the two approached, the guard pushed Cuganwa forward as Belractu glared at the child.

"And what news brings you two here?" the elder questioned.

"A guard is bleeding from his neck. He needs healing, dear elder," Cuganwa spat out, breathing heavily.

"Take me there," the elder said plainly as he shot up from his seat, maintaining his aloof expression.

Sweat poured from Cuganwa's head as he tore through the village leading the elder back to the eastern side. His lungs burned, and his heart hammered louder than his run through the death snare. A dull hum sat at the center of his stomach once more. Beneath the skin and muscle, it continued without a true, recognizable source. 'Why does this continue to happen?' the boy asked himself only to reach the area with six other guards, the chief, and Elder Yanuma present. Deyunca stood on the sides as another guard pressed wet chunks of herbs into the cut, slowly clotting the wound.

"Move!" Elder Belractu barked with a voice greater than his small frame expressed. The man sprinted past Cuganwa and the village guard toward the fallen man. The man aiding the wounded rose in a rush as Belractu slid in place and pressed his hand onto the wound. His ring's gem glowed with a violet tremble, matching the soft hum the boy felt in his abdomen. "Water. Now." Three of the guards produced their water skins. The elder snatched one free and poured it into the cut, washing away some of the herbs. Elder Belractu then stuck a finger into the wound itself as the ring grew brighter. The humming grew stronger.

The boy then looked to Elder Yanuma, who gave a small nod. Cuganwa did not know what to do as his rasping breaths prevented any speaking. Her eyes lit up a moment as she let out a short chuckle.

"Crafty, child," she muttered before returning a glance to Gamaunda, who rubbed his beard, watching the elder. "Grab Deyunca," she ordered casually. The hunter broke his calm façade, looking bewildered at the elder as two guards lunged for him. Deyunca tried to fight only to find his efforts failing as the guards easily seized his arms and forced him to kneel. Elder Belractu narrowed his eyes at the man before walking off. Yanuma sighed as she shook her head. "Madness curses some in life. I wish some could be better."

Cuganwa was wild-eyed. A hand then rested on his back. The boy turned to find Sutama there wearing a solemn expression. "Father? What's happening?"

"Penance, boy," the hunter answered. "Boldness breeds opportunity for greatness and foolish acts."

"Tell us your story once more, Deyunca," Gamaunda said.

"Fools! The witch pounced on us from the tent side and ran off! She still lurks in the village! The edge broke off when she ran!" the man declared as he looked to the broken ground.

"Yet we believe otherwise," the chief replied.

"The fool is you, Deyunca," Elder Yanuma said as she crouched before him. "I see more than you will ever understand. It's also easy for me to see treachery as blatant as yours. You are not clever. Just a grieving fool."

"Elder, the witch is the culprit!" the hunter proclaimed.

"Where is your hunter's knife?" the elder asked. The hunter went quiet as his jaw quivered. The elder then reached forward, patting his crotch. "I've never known a man to have such a shape." Deyunca's eyes flared, and he attempted to spit. The elder seized his nose, forcing him to cough. "Kill him." The elder moved away, replaced by Gamaunda.

"You'd kill me before finding that demon? Before things are put right?" Deyunca wheezed.

"We leave demons at the gate. One made it in," Gamaunda corrected. Cuganwa shook as he saw the strange stone of his bracelet float. A flat, silver stick rose from the stone.

"Wha…" the boy uttered. Its surface was smoother than polished ivory by even the best craftsmen and gleamed in the early morning sun as it reflected the area around it. It bared a curved point at the top and was longer than Gamaunda's arm. The crystal was fixed at the end of the curved handle, wrapping around the hand. 'What is that?' the boy questioned. Before he could utter a single word, the chief sunk the weapon through the man's chest. Blood dampened the man's tunic and streamed from his mouth as his eyes grew pleading.

"You tried to take one of my men and think I wouldn't take you? That hurt, Deyunca. May your spirit return untainted," the chief said.

Cuganwa's body trembled, and he quickly turned away. Sutama kept his hand on his shoulder. "I know, Cuganwa. But remember the reason we have this role. We served the village. The guards protect it. This isn't a place for selfish gains," Sutama said. His father then turned him toward the others.

The chief had removed the strange blade and cleaned the blood with his sleeve. Gamaunda walked toward Cuganwa and his father while flicking his wrist. The blade sank into the small crystal and returned to his bracelet. 'How is that possible? What kind of blade is that?' the boy questioned.

"There are many gifts Lord Kelvert has given us, young hunter," the man said with a pained smile. "Some don't truly appreciate the things we are given. This only destroys order. Now get ready for your hunt." Gamaunda placed a hand on the boy's shoulder before turning and leading the elder and his men away as they carried Deyunca with them.

'Keeping order, more important than revenge. What else must I learn?' the boy questioned.

Part 2
Cries of the Past

Ch. 10

Pain and Planning

Outside once more, Nuyani sat before the skull with her fingers fidgeting as she looked from her hands to the horizon as the morning light grew brighter. The rasp of wind in the open space was almost as loud as the confines of her home. The witch looked back toward the skull.

'This can work, right? There has to be something. Something beyond these cliffs. If the howlers came from somewhere else, then we should've too,' Nuyani thought to herself. A shiver traveled through her body. A sense of shame wore on her as the idea flew in the eyes of their people's beliefs, the very core of her strength. The lingering questions about the possibilities left a sense of unease stirring within her. 'I have to know. We can survive, right?' She grabbed her left forearm, trying to steel her nerves as she considered the scars running down the limb.

She had been battling an enemy only she could face in the past three nights, and one she doubt would care if the sandstorms blew through the area. Looking to one she understood, Nuyani turned to the half-buried skull in the dirt.

"To'anu. To'anu. Please, I must speak with someone," Nuyani said as she jabbed the skull with a finger. Silence. The witch took a deep breath and released a single beat from her core. The ethereal wave radiated through the area. Nuyani could feel the small beads of life from the shrubs and insects around her on the surface of her core as if they were drops of rain resting on her skin. The heaviest yet was the spirit residing inside the skull. With a clearer sense, Nuyani saw the weight of To'anu's spirit was comparable to a small bowl of water yet condensed to a smaller space. "To'anu, we must speak. I have a plan. I just want your thoughts."

She could feel sloshing about within the confines of the skull. Her brow creased. With a strike of her core, Nuyani released another pulse that coursed from her being and into the skull. Stronger than the last, it forced the spirit to slosh about. "To'anu, listen to me," Nuyani said.

Removing her hand, the top of the skull began to glow white. The pressure shifted against the surface of Nuyani 's core, following the rise of a white flame flying into the air. The light then burst forth as the visage of a man appeared. Nuyani gawked for a moment, focusing on the deceased hunter's expression. The spirit was weeping. Tears trailed from red eyes.

"To'anu…. You cry?" Nuyani asked.

The spirit scowled at her. "Why are you here, witch? Did you not like the new demons you've brought?"

Nuyani glared at To'anu. "I'm not here for games, To'anu. I think I have an answer…" Nuyani stopped as the spirit turned his attention toward the east, facing the village miles away from them. "What's wrong? You've never… I've never seen…"

"My brother, Deyunca, has died…because of you!" To'anu whipped his head around and gave Nuyani a piercing glare.

The woman's stomach twisted. She held a hand on her stomach as her thoughts returned to last night. Several people died despite Nuyani's efforts, as her new abilities allowed her to dispatch the four howlers.

"S-sorry. I couldn't stop them all in time. I barely was able to move around the village…" Nuyani started but was interrupted.

"No. He died this morning," Nuyani froze, staring at the spirit. "His life echoed through Kelvert's land as if it called me. The world seems hollow. I didn't even think I ever noticed such a thing until you came around." Nuyani slowly rose and glared at the man. Her grip on the knife tightened. "If it weren't for you, he wouldn't have tried to rally them…" The spirit fell silent as he looked to the ground.

Nuyani's hand shook. "You blame me for a man's death that was trying to kill me during the closing days to the storm?" To'anu said nothing. "Fools. You and your brother are fools. I hope it does not carry in your blood because it will taint your sons." Nuyani looked to the side, breathing heavily as her own eyes grew red. 'They must blame me for the spirits. But why haven't they tried? No, not now. There's a chance to flee the storms and spirits,' Nuyani thought. She then turned toward To'anu with wide eyes.

"Listen, To'anu. I need your thoughts. There may be a way to keep everyone safe. I think there's land we came from passed the cliffs. If I find proof, we can lead everyone there, and the spirits won't bother us." To'anu looked back at Nuyani through narrowed eyes, remaining silent until he turned away and looked to the east once more. "I've already tried to help and fight even when you murderers tried to come after me." The spirit lowered his head, Nuyani watched his face seeing the corner of his eyes close. "I-I learned one more thing, To'anu. I can free you." This caught the man's attention. Most spirits who lingered in the drylands were kept by heavy guilt preventing them from passing on. Nuyani could never tell what was anchoring him to this land as he stayed within his skull for the past three years. Whether it was his hatred for her, a sense of regret, or worry for his family, it did not matter. She drummed her core, letting the vibrations course through her body and focused into her hand. Nuyani then extended her hand to To'anu.

"To'anu. I can free you." The man's eyes widened as he looked back at her like she had gone crazy. Yet, he began to gawk when the waves emitted from her stirred his form. She said nothing as she waited for the spirit to respond. To'anu said nothing as he turned away. The white light around him brightened and condensed to the same small wisp before descending into the skull. Nuyani sighed. The woman lowered her hand before looking to the east as well.

'Who would want help from the witch?' she first thought before the faces of Odaru, Caluu and Lamoy rose. The three villagers had shown her kindness and were willing to help when she was nearly caught in the village. 'By the Great Lord, I will protect them. I will do what I can, mother,' Nuayni promised as she turned toward the west and sprinted off. Dust clouds trailed behind her rising taller than herself. The brush and sand dunes fell into a blur around her as she made her way toward the demon gate. Within moments, Nuyani crossed dozens of miles through the red lands as she jogged up the gradual stone slope of a cliff nearing the mouth of a cavern. Nuyani made her way toward the ledge and looked onward at the endless desert, the sands glowing gold in the morning sun.

Before, she thought herself a demon dwelling in the same mountains as the other beasts praying every day to Lord Kelvert for the forgiveness of her cursed soul. With the presence of the spirits, she no longer concerned herself with such thoughts remembering the coursing power she held dispatching the first howlers she encountered.

'There must be a better way,' Nuyani thought as she turned and marched toward the tunnel entrance.

As she passed through the tunnel, the soft gray glow of the vine flowers filled the path from above. Once at the end, Nuyani saw the morning sun streamed through the small hole in the eastern cliff wall, barely cutting through the darkness covering the dozens of gray bricked huts at the back of the cavern.

'I have to get everything ready,' Nuyani thought, pushing herself to rush.

She then descended from the shelf to the lower floor and moved to the storage hut adjacent to the shelf. It was even darker within the small home. Nuyani struck her core, releasing a rhythmic beat with distortion on every third or fourth pulse as the energy fed into her eyes. Soft glowing silver outlines of the hut's interior form. Nuyani smiled as she could see the various pots, urns, and baskets revealed to her along with the mortar and bricks.

'I can see better than the first time,' she realized as he moved to the first basket and rummaged through its contents. Filled with random tools and parts, Nuyani pushed aside old pouches, twine other leather works, until she felt for a bundle of tarp. Pulling it out, she then retrieved some twine, an extra pouch, and an ax before ducking out of the small hut. Climbing back onto the taller shelf, she turned to the western wall and stood before the draining indentation. Dried blood remained from the charge-horns along the paths leading to the lip of the ledge where Nuyani placed her urns. She put aside the items before untying one of her pouches.

In retrieving her crystal, Nuyani took a step back and held the stone toward the western wall. In squeezing the clear stone, white lights gleamed from it and trailed along the ground before the charge-horns spilled from their confines and lay on the ground before her. Nuyani narrowed her eyes and held her breath for a moment as the pungent stench of the larger beast wafted toward her once more. Ignoring the odor and rotting hump of the beast. Nuyani went to work cutting into the animal once more. As she cut into the lower sections of the stomach, her eyes glanced at the neck wounds where dozens of arrow shafts protruded.

Loud chops from her ax sounded through the cavern until she severed a large portion and set it on the ground. Retrieving the tarp, she unraveled the piece and placed the meat on it before binding it within the cover. Tying it closed, Nuyani placed the bundled meat to the side. Nuyani retrieved the stone and gripped it once more. The light gleamed over the charge-horns before both carcasses stretched in their forms and poured into a thinning spiral toward the stone. Within seconds, they were gone. Nuyani took a deep breath as the smell of rot slowly eased, and she looked down at the stone for a moment, remembering that she found it when she first entered the cave. She never knew of its origins or found another, but it had been years since she had found out about its ability to carry living things with its light making hunting far easier. She had not yet learned the crystal's limits, wondering if it could house a full heavy-horn or two. Pushing curiosity aside, Nuyani put away the small crystal and rebound the pouch to her tool strap. Collecting the bundle, she started toward the tunnel but stopped.

'Prayer,' Nuyani realized and placed the bundle on the floor.

She turned toward the western wall and climbed to the open space. Though the sun had yet to meet that part of the cliff, Nuyani could not help but pray on the ledge with her mother's spirit visiting in that very space. She glanced toward the west, looking at the expanse of the desert before turning back east. It was all she could do to feel a sense of normalcy. The world's dangers beyond the cliffs were now reaching the drylands, and with the new strength within her. Nuyani needed to prepare. Nuyani's lips curled. 'Is it right to pray now?' she wondered before stopping halfway and rising. She looked out to the desert once more. Her mother called Nuyani's curse the Great Lord's gift yet, doubt lingered.

'I can do this,' Nuyani thought as she stood. Her mind dwelled on a fable searching for proof and safety from the violent spirits. Other than the demon gate, the only opening that remained was one toward the north where a lone river fed into the drylands yet, was teaming with blood-manes and blade-jaws warding off the hunters.

Nuyani made her way down and collected the bundle of meat once more before heading out of the cavern. She raced through the land until she came to the closest river cutting deep into the red earth. She looked into the water seeing the water bites clamoring as usual for a meal as they gathered at the bank, their heads canted to the side just enough to keep swimming as they watched her with black eyes trained on her. As they splashed about, Nuyani kept her core active, releasing thin waves from her core searching for any predators. She could sense the life surrounding the area, but none were heavy enough to draw any worry. Jogging along the riverside, her footing felt unstable as most of the riverbanks were covered in smoothened stones despite their incline.

As she followed the winding river, a death snare patch rising from the bed of stones came into view. Nuyani moved toward a nearby cluster of brush. She measured the twine to match the distance from the shrubs to the vegetation. Nuyani added slack to the twine as she bound one end to the brushes and the other to the bundle of meat. When she was finished, Nuyani made her way toward the vegetation crossing from the red dirt to the stones with cautious steps knowing the network of roots hidden beneath the stones would signal for the death snare to act. Staying only a few paces away from the death snare, Nuyani tossed the meat onto the stones only a step away from the stocks.

Almost immediately, a few of the dreaded fruit on the closest stocks began to swell, doubling in size before they burst, releasing clouds of white powder. Nuyani darted away, moving to the side as not to be downwind.

Knowing of the powder's effects, it was a vegetation most tried to avoid unless trying to burn to grow near the canals. Nuyani waited as the cloud passed by. The rustling sound reached her ears as the serpent-like stock rose from the center. It curled like a snake facing the direction of the bundle. In an instant, it shot forth in a blur opening its six sepals revealing the hundreds of barbs on each resembling fangs. With great accuracy, it struck the bundle taking several of the stones with it in its mouth. The serpent stock then pulled, retreating to the center only to halt when the bundle's twine was taut.

'Good,' Nuyani thought as she started toward one of the stocks. As the stock continued to struggle, the sound of tearing roots made Nuyani freeze as the serpent stock moved further back into the vegetation. Her heart pounded. Nuyani dashed for her objective, pulling out her stone dagger before cutting into one of the stocks. The yellow fruit began to swell, making Nuyani's eyes widen. Water and sap gushed from the stock base with a few slashes as the fruit receded in size. After two more cuts, the stock fell to the side. Nuyani stabbed into its stock and pulled it into the dirt.

After taking the stock, Nuyani plucked several of the fruit and placed them within the spare water skin she had brought. Taking her other water skin, Nuyani began to pour some into the pouch bearing the fruit. The water disappeared almost on contact with the fruit as they steadily grew. Nuyani stopped as the water skin bulged. She wondered if the fruit would burst and held the bag outward as she waited for them to pop. After a moment, she found the fruit was still intact before closing both water skins. She then turned over her hand. Shock colored her face as she saw several barbs stuck to her leather bindings. Her hand had brushed against the viper berries.

'Viper berries fit too well,' Nuyani thought. She used her knife to flick the barbs in between the strands from her leather. Each point in the leather was covered in a wet red paste. 'By the Great Lord, this is the last thing I'd think to end me.'

After collecting the fruit and tossing the stock back into the death snare, Nuyani's brow furrowed. She looked at the serpent stock, which struggled to pull the bundle free. Strolling toward the twine, she looked at the brush finding the first one torn out of the ground as its roots dangled loosely. 'It must be young. It shouldn't struggle this long for something so small,' Nuyani thought.

Looking back at the stock, Nuyni then said, "I think this should be a fair trade."

Grabbing the knife, she cut the tether letting the serpent stock disappear into the depths. After retying both water skins and sheathing the knives. Nuyani then looked toward the northeast, where the other opening into the drylands lay.

'Great Lord, please guide me with your light,' she prayed before sprinting forward and leaping over the wide river toward the northwest.

Ch. 11

Consequences of Choice

As the sky grew brighter, the village became more active. Cuganwa started his second check of their saddle.

"Four tarps, fifteen poles, six ropes, two shovels, four sacks…" the boy mumbled to himself before he paused and looked back toward the village.

While the hunters were going out for a final hunt for supplies, most villagers waited in the center, too afraid to leave for home. Cuganwa could not blame them as everyone recalled the strange figures and the sightings of the witch. Though the others spoke of the witch, Cuganwa's thoughts dwelled on Deyunca's death. Without hesitation, Gamaunda killed him for his betrayal. The boy looked to the ground as his hand started to fidget.

'We serve the village, and the guards protect it. No place for selfish gains,' Cuganwa thought over his father's words. His hands refused to stop shaking, forcing him to ball them into fists to stifle their movement. Cuganwa looked back at the village. He narrowed his sight noticing his mother, and Caluu, talking to Yanuma. As Caluu Clung to their mother's blue and green dress, their mother wore a look of horror as Elder Yanuma spoke. His mother and sister were often quite busy working in the crafter's tent or working with others on another village task.

'Caluu, have you done something?' Cuganwa questioned as he watched them, trying to read their expressions.

The elder finished speaking looked down to the floor as she walked away from Jogia and Caluu. His mother clung to the child even tighter. Cuganwa tightened his fists, and the shaking grew worse.

'What happened?' the boy questioned. 'By the Great Lord's will, are they all right?'

"Cuganwa! Cuganwa!" Odaru called. The boy blinked as he then looked up at his side. He found Odaru looking at him. His brow furrowed as he looked at the boy from the front saddle.

"Yes?" Cuganwa answered.

The senior hunter remained silent as he stared back at the boy for a moment. Odaru then asked, "How many tarps?"

"Four."

"Poles?"

"Fifteen."

"Ropes?"

"Six."

"Shovels?"

"Two."

Odaru paused for a moment as he continued to look at Cuganwa. "Sacks?"

"Four."

Odaru frowned as he looked at Cuganwa. "What's wrong, Cuganwa? You have the numbers, and we need to be ready."

"Sorry, Odaru. I just..." Cuganwa looked back toward the village.

The senior hunter sighed. "Is it because of Deyunca?" The boy closed his mouth.

'Not just Deyunca. The witch and my family. There're problems everywhere,' the boy thought.

"You're not blaming yourself for that, are you?"

"No. No," Cuganwa raised a hand. "I just wasn't ready for that."

Odaru's brow rose in an arch. "Cuganwa, no one would be ready for such a thing. Unless it were their job already. Trust me. Gamaunda has to be, and I don't think the chief wants to."

Cuganwa sighed. "I guess I need to be a better hunter."

Odaru blinked several times. "Cuganwa, being a better hunter has very little to do with being ready for someone's betrayal. That is just something you mustn't allow on its own. Deyunca tried to betray the village. We prepare for animals. By the Great Lord's light, there isn't any reason to halt everyone for a reckless want." Odaru started to right himself in the saddle. "Besides, Little Charge-horn, this hunt should come with some ease as we ride along. I think there are too many of us right now. But this will make things all the faster."

Cuganwa said nothing as he glanced at Odaru's left leg still bound in leather strands for a tourniquet. Despite a broken leg, he was still going. 'Just focus on the village's needs,' the boy thought as he climbed the stirrups of Muga's saddle.

As Cuganwa rose, the whip-neck swung her bulbous head around and began to lick his face. The boy smirked and scratched under her chin at first, only to push her layered bone snout away. The whip-neck stopped only for her large brown eyes to continue focusing on the boy as he climbed. Once Cuganwa reached the top, he sat down on the rear seat and looked about. He and Odaru were placed in the middle of their hunting party's lineup. While Cuganwa's party normally traveled in two parallel lines for their journey, they had to stay in a single file as the left held Lamoy's party, and the right, Deyunca's. Cuganwa avoided looking at many of them as they had faced great grief and embarrassment despite their task. Many avoided facing the other parties. Cuganwa wondered if any of the hunters would direct their attention toward him out of spite or blame him for the man's death. After some time, hunters considered each other brothers. Even, Cuganwa had seen Odaru as more of an uncle.

Before anything could be said, Cuganwa looked out toward the village center once more as Gamaunda spoke to the others. It was easy to see him in a crowd as he wore a red headwrap. Cuganwa's mind flashed to the bracelet as it held the strange flat blade that gleamed like water in the sun.

It was bewildering that such a blade could collapse into that small bead of stone as light shimmered from it. As the boy watched the chief address the village, he saw a family sitting apart from the others as the elders spoke to them. A woman was kneeling with her head low as the younger boys clung to her side.

After a moment, Cuganwa realized that they could be Deyunca's family. The village leader was explaining the situation to the others.

Guards soon came by and escorted the family toward the elders' tent. The village would cremate the body in a special urn and release the ashes into the river where Kelvert first brought them to life. If they wouldn't, the spirit would fester in the body haunting their surroundings, and a new life would not return to the village.

'May his soul return untainted,' the boy thought as the family walked off with the guards to join the other families that lost loved ones that night.

Three more whip-necks started making their way toward the northern gate catching Cuganwa's attention. The hunting leaders, Sutama, Lamoy, and now Bo'ede, Deyunca's second. Today they were in the back of her light brown headwrap covering most of her brow and hair. Bo'ede was a short bald man with a clean-shaven face normally scowling and a mound of muscle. Cuganwa wanted to avoid eye contact with him, seeing a deep red within them.

In a subtle attempt, the boy raised his palm to the sky as he prayed, 'By the Great Lord, may his shine guide Deyunca's spirit.' As if called by the thoughts, Bo'ede looked at the boy, and his expression eased as he gave a nod. Cuganwa hesitated for a moment before doing the same.

Cuganwa's attention then turned to Lamoy as she rode on, keeping a gleeful look about her. At the hunters' meeting with the chief and village elders, she wore her feathers proudly in the front. Noticing their placement, he wondered why she had done so. Even in the few encounters with him in the village, they were always placed in the front.

Lamoy then glanced at Cuganwa, noticing his stare. She looked his way as she announced, "How bold, Little Charge-horn. A hunter for two days, and now you look for a wife?" Cuganwa's eyes went wide as Sutama gave him a look, telling him to be vigilant as the others laughed. The boy straightened in his seat and looked forward. From his periphery, he could see the party of Deyunca also laughing. The tension in their expressions lessened somewhat.

Odaru even chuckled. As the hunting leaders went toward the front, Odaru then asked, "Lamoy, why the change?"

The woman shrugged her shoulders as she answered, "After all this, maybe a little change would be good." Odaru nodded his head. "May the Great Lord's light guide us all."

As the leaders reached the front, the gate was being picked apart by a team of guards unearthing the loose pieces.

In a booming voice, Sutama spoke, "All right we have a simple job to do. Let's get it done before the storm arrives. Let's move."

As the three hunting parties walked parallel, Cuganwa wondered about the passing events. His mother's conversation with the elder, Deyunca's odd behavior, strange cold wounds found on the deceased, and rumors of the witch were all too strange to hear about within two days. 'What's about to happen?' the boy wondered as they made their way into the drylands.

Ch. 12

Beyond the Boundaries

The late morning remained bright as Nuyani cut through the red waste. Taking precaution of meeting any hunters, she went further north toward the cliffs passing several charge-horn sounders and wild whip-neck caravans along the way. As she got closer to the cliffs, she headed toward the east. Nuyani peeked at the cliffs and thrummed her core to ensure none of the blood-manes flew toward her. Even with her speed, she could still be ambushed by the beasts. As time passed, the sun climbed a little higher toward noon as she reached the source of the river before it split into different branches throughout the drylands. Sprinting for nearly an hour, Nuyani looked up toward the sun as she took several deep breaths.

'It should be enough time,' she thought, placing faith in her speed to return to find the lost city, or nothing at all, before the sunset and the others were left alone to defend against the howlers. Turning back toward the waterfall, Nuyani watched as the water descended to the bottom, leaving a thin spray in the process. Stepping forward, she entered the mist, letting it envelop her as the cool spray touch reached her brow. Nuyani gave a deep, relaxed sigh.

A loud trumpet then echoed through the area with a small echo against the cliff. Nuyani snapped toward the source and drew her knife. On the other side of the waterfall stood a heavy-horn. Nuyani blinked at it, seeing how young it was. Though it was still far larger than her, it was only a head or so taller. The beasts were grazers and part of the northeast with wide bodies, thick legs, and short brush-ended tails. Their heads were large with flat faces and fanning ears but, this one was two young as it mustered a threatening façade. The adults had two pairs of tusks, with the lower pair guarding their legs against predators as the top was for combatting each other for territory. Yet the young one before her had smaller tusks no longer tan her arm, and the trunk that would be long enough to sweep the floor and almost as thick with hide to beat approaching predators was just as short.

Nuyani chuckled at the animal as their brown eyes narrowed at her. 'I am no threat to you, young thing, and neither you to me unless you can clear that gap. I can't,' Nuyani thought as she smiled.

Seeing its intimidation did not work, the animal stomped on the ground before leaving toward the planes of tall grass, rejoining its herd. Her eyes were then drawn to the mass of moving red in the distance that messed with her eyes for a moment to make out individual heavy-horns. She could only see two that were battling at the time. Males fighting for supremacy within their parties.

'There's always fighting,' Nuyani thought.

Returning her gaze to the cliffs. A series of shelves, there were two waterfalls with the first easily scaled with so many layers of rocks jutting out, leaving crevices. The runner made her way up the first shelf. As she climbed over the ledge, the roar of the higher waterfall filled the area. Nuyani watched as the mist sailed for a distance before disappearing the further it scattered. The runner was about to climb, but stopped and decided to look to her left. Her ember eyes widened. Nuyani froze at the sight of a curled mound of muscle slumbering on the shelf. It was a blade-jaw. It was twice the size of a man's width and had a short tail no longer than a hand.

Nuyani looked through the area for a good place to hide or stay out of sight. Aside from the higher waterfall, stone pillars were on both sides of the river. Nuyani looked to her side and found the stones at least a dozen paces away. With such a small space on the ledge, she was certain the beast could catch her if it awoke.

'By his shine…' Nuyani thought as she climbed slowly onto the shelf and stalked the stone pillars.

Catching sight of the animal's flickering ears, she failed to notice a loose stone and kicked it forward with a series of soft taps reverberating through the immediate area. Nuyani looked back toward the blade-jaw seeing the creature did not stir. Despite this, she moved in haste, more cautious of her footing as she reached the stone pillars and hid behind one. Squeezing between the first two, Nuyani looked back to find the creature undisturbed. 'Thank you, Lord Kelvert,' Nuyani thought and pressed her head against the stone column. Continuing her journey, Nuyani continued to squeeze through the rest of the pillars until she got to the second shelf and remained cautious of the waterskin on her tool strap.

'I need a way up,' the runner thought as she reached the wall of the next cliff. The crevices of the cliff wall were too shallow for a proper grip making Nuyani pause. Looking back at the adjacent pillar, she moved between them and used her legs and hands to push against the sides, climbing to the next ledge.

Nuyani exhaled as she reached the ledge. 'Why is running easier than climbing?' she wondered as she looked at the next path. There was little space available for Nuyani to walk along as it sloped and wrapped around the cliff wall. Nuyani ambled along with the space to keep her footing. With the roar of the waterfall growing quieter, Nuyani continued down the way and thrummed her core. 'By the Great Lord, I'm glad nothing happened,' She thought to herself. As her core echoed, nothing disturbed the waves as they returned beside the fading pressure of the blade-jaw.

Nuyani then walked into the shadow of the winding ravine. Her eyes trailed over the scaling walls as the wind whipped through the path. Only a few cliffs, and it was already a different world.

'I need a few cooler days like this,' Nuyani thought as she felt her muscles ease.

An air of caution came over her as she looked further down her path, seeing it had an end and the ledge only had enough space for her to cling to the walls if need be. Nuyani then looked to the waters that quickly foamed near the end. Passed the rapids, the water remained clear. She expected the same clamoring water bites to litter the mouth of the river as they did in the drylands. As Nuyani walked on, she had forgotten about the light thrum of her core still ringing as one of the waves grew chaotic. Her eyes widened as a pressure rose on the surface of the ethereal drum.

The runner darted forward just as a cacophony of sounds blared behind her. A loud thud followed by scratching against the stone and a sudden heavy caw were all Nuyani needed to hear, realizing that she was still in the blood-mane's territory as well. She ran forth at a slower pace. The small path made it more of a threat that she may slip and fall into the water. In the first plunge, she would be vulnerable to the blood-mane. The flap of the beast's large wings reached her ears. Nuyani caught movement from the corner of her eye and looked to her left. The animal flew around with its red yawning beak and black eyes trained on her. the feathers of its mane rippling like tall grass.

Nuyani pushed even harder, moving faster within the small space, barely dodging the beast's talons as it crashed into the wall once more. With a flap of its wings, the beast struck her shoulder while she was in mid-step, throwing off her balance. Nuyani flailed as she tried to keep herself upright, but began to lean toward the water. Choosing to drop, Nuyani winced as she landed on her knee. Sacrificing her momentum, she was able to gain some control as she caught the ledge, stopping herself from falling. The loud flaps of the blood-mane's wings signaled its position. Changing her approach, Nuyani pulled her waterskin loose and reached for one of the engorged fruit. The surface was soft and felt fragile, warning that it could burst even in her hand. Without a second thought, she looked toward the beast still righting itself and pitched the fruit at its head.

Her mouth twisted as she silently prayed for it to strike true. The yellow bulb struck the blood-mane in the face bursting instantly as the white powder nearly enveloped the creature entirely. Its wings flapped erratically as it tried to stay airborne. Its mouth and eyes remained wide as the powder caked both. Its pink tongue grew pale before the gagging animal crashed into the side of the cliff and fell into the water. Nuyani breathed heavily as she saw the seizure-induced animal float away.

'Lord Kelvert, I thank y…' Her thoughts trailed off as she could feel new pressures rise on her core. Each of them just appeared without a sense of direction. The river itself seemed to open as yawning jaws opened, revealing a flash of pink before closing on the blood-mane's leg and tearing away some of the flesh. Several more mouths opened in the water and took out chunks of the creature.

'What are you?' she wondered as more of the clearer waters turned, revealing some of the hidden animals chasing the easy meal.

Each of them had dark blue and green scales on top that matched the bottom of the river covering their long bodies. Their eyes had narrowed irises with a dark green and yellow that glimmered in the light. Their wide maws were filled with dozens of teeth.

'I was about to dive in there. How did I not notice them?' Nuyani wondered. She then looked to the other side of the river and found a low riverbank she could easily climb.

Seeing this as her only chance, Nuyani pushed off the cliff wall turning in the air for a dive into the water, and started swimming as the strange river creatures ate the blood-mane. Swimming as hard as she could, Nuyani rushed toward the other embankment and climbed onto the land before starting a jog. Breathing heavily and drenched in water, she felt a chill from the constant gale sweeping through the cliffs. Nuyani looked back at the water seeing strange bumps in the surface that went against the river's flow. Nuyani then focused on her core's pulse, strengthening the next pulse. As the ethereal force coursed over the area, it was met with weaker beats that tried to strengthen itself to match hers, only to collapse and reveal the sudden pressure hidden from her senses.

'How?' Nuyani wondered as she placed a hand on her stomach. She barely understood how the different forces worked, from her own core to the power of life she found in everything that grew. Now a creature before her was using the same pulses to hide its own signs of life. Nuyani then looked back down the ravine hardening her resolve to find their history. With her core radiating beats further, she felt another pressure rise on her core at the top, though it was faint. She followed its direction looking to the cliffs until her gaze fell upon another blood-mane watching her intently. Nuyani took out her knife, wondering if the animal would try to take her. After her near fall and swim, she was not at her best for running. To Nuyani's luck, the animal lay down and rested its head on the ground. Looking to the water, the faint signs of pressure had disappeared, and the bumps on the water's surface were gone.

"Good," Nuyani whispered as she sheathed her knife and started down the riverbank trying to catch her breath.

'At least, they know when to quit,' Nuyani thought to herself as she noticed the soft sand beneath the press of her feet. Despite their coarse texture, they still had a cool touch compared to the drylands.

Keeping her pace to a stroll, Nuyani took notice of the different scenery. The river's flow was gentler now and wider than the narrow section further down the way. The ripples of water remained calm as they allowed the runner to see the bottom. Green plants resembling dishes sat on the surface as slender clumps of leaves rose from the water only to grow limp at the top half. Strange clumps of green foam gathered around each section of the vegetation, with small bugs darting about the area going from one patch to another.

Feeling rested, Nuyani started to jog. A full run was ideal for saving time, yet she found herself continually looking to the vibrant green vegetation growing on the riverside. Her mind, on occasion returning to the green patch wondering if their bright colors were just a trap as well. Her pulses, however, showed that their life was separate and numerous but barely held a fraction of the pressure within the snares. Nuyani wondered if there was a trap, imagining it for small bugs or mice instead. She let the thought pass as her attention then turned to the idea of laying on one of the flat dish-like plants.

"Well, this is a bold little thing," Nuyani said as she looked at the frog. It had a dark blue and gray body resembling stone skin and bulging black eyes with a white center that gleamed in the light. Its back had small blue spots with a few swirling trails like smoke connecting to one another that glowed. The designs glowed in a deep, bright blue as the frog chirped and its body expanded and contracted rapidly.

Nuyani stopped and laughed at the sight of its bulbous body moving so much just from a call. Within a nearby patch of leaves, another frog, with the same colors but dulled, then leaped into the water and swam toward the frog. When it climbed onto the leaf, it placed one of its wide feet on top of the singing frog's face as it continued. The witch smiled for a moment seeing it called a friend, before she returned to her jog. Making her way through the ravine, the vegetation only got thicker as more plants covered the water and some of the riverbank as the roar of rushing water echoed through the hall.

Following the ravine's winding path, the view of another waterfall appeared as the noon sun beamed down into the narrow land. As she grew closer to the waterfall, her eyes fell upon the enormous mountains appearing through the gap. Unlike the cliffs surrounding her, they were gray and white, pointing into the sky as thick clouds surrounded their peak.

'By the Great Lord…I thought the cliffs were the tallest things that existed,' Nuyani thought as she stared at the mountains for a moment before her foot stepped into the water. Nuyani stopped in her place and looked down at her foot submerged beneath a cluster of algae. The runner pulled away and narrowed her eyes as she felt the viscous substance seep between her toes. Her mouth twisted as she tried to kick the algae off her foot. Looking out toward the area, the riverbank ended only to continue on the other side. The water itself split into two rivers. Failing to remove the algae, Nuyani ignored it. She glared at the water and dove in before swimming to the riverbank. Climbing out, Nuyani could only see through a narrow squint of her eyes. Her arms extended from her waist, letting the slime drop from her person.

'I don't want to know what this is,' Nuyani thought as she undid the bindings of her arms and legs.

Nuyani continued to release waves into the surrounding area, only feeling the presence of weaker forces, though she kept the strange beasts hidden in the water in mind. She made her way further toward the opposite cliff in case any decided to walk the riverbank and catch her. With her bindings removed, she began to lace them through her hand to remove the algae.

'What were those things?' Nuyani wondered. 'I don't see how they could hide from me. Well, I found them. I'll name them. I guess if there are hens then, there are blood-manes. So, now with shovel tails, there are these things. They have scales but long bodies. They're not as vicious as water bites, though. They still gather if there is food.' Nuyani paused as she looked at the ground. 'Stalker bites. Water snaps. River Lizards. Big mouths…' As she thought of names, Nuyani continued to clean the leather wrappings.

With the sun shifting, she noticed her shadow's turn. Nuyani then stopped and looked forward. A violet patch of flowers then caught her eye. Leaving her bindings on the riverbank, she rose and approached the patch. Each of them had eight diamond-shaped pedals that folded outward from their base, with the top half colored violet and the inside white. The anthers were contrasted with bright orange and yellow.

One of her mother's favorite colors, Nuyani thought back to her promise to protect the village as she slowly frowned. The same people who tried to kill her, see her as a threat, even hunt her down after she saved the village made every step difficult in knowing that whatever she brought back may never be accepted but, it was the only answer she had compared to sneaking into the village each night to stop them until the storms forced her to stay hidden and the howlers would take their time.

'I will try, mother,' Nuyani thought as she tightened her fist.

Her thoughts trailed off as a dragonfly landed on the same flower she watched. Nuyani looked at the animal's transparent wings as they folded inward before turning away and seeing the area was filled with more flowers of oranges, blues, reds, and yellows. She turned about, stopping only when the sun hit her face. Nuyani let the rays warm her skin as the cool breeze continued to sweep through the ravine.

Only the wind's whisper and the consuming roar of the waterfall filled her ears. Nuyani breathed slowly as she let her mind be at ease. As she drank in the rays, something pricked her left arm. Nuyani's trance was broken as she looked to the side and found a dragonfly had landed on her skin. The runner ignored the curious bug as she focused on the wound the howlers left on her. Aside from the lingering sting, it was a stark reminder of their predicament.

Bringing the wound closer for inspection, she was not safe from the howlers. Nuyani was the only one who could fight them. The dragonfly still lingered on her arm. The runner stared at the insect's large orange and yellow eyes. Caluu then came to mind as she reflected on the previous night. Each of them showed her more kindness and trust than anyone else in years.

'If not for them, I would be dead. Great Lord, please guide me to the answer. I will save them,' Nuyani prayed as she continued running.

As the early afternoon sun hung between the cliffs, Nuyani ran at her normal pace as she left trails of dust taller than herself. With an hour in passing, the ravine had narrowed, and the water grew rapid, its roar echoing against the red walls. Forced closer to the cliff, Nuyani had to slow her run as the riverbank sloped toward the waters. As the path grew too dangerous, Nuyani continued walking as the end came into view.

The opening through the cliff walls seemed odd as the river stopped at the end, draining into a large whirlpool that frothed at the center. Closer to the ravine's end, Nuyani turned her back to the wall and braced the stone with her hand as she took several side steps up a gradual slope to the entrance. Her eyes fell on the whirlpool's center. Nuyani scowled and looked on the stone surface. Without realizing it, even the cliff walls at the end were strange.

"Was it molded?" Nuyani mouthed as she looked at the strange depressions in the stone. Each one had smooth, round ridges heading in a single direction that replaced the parallel crevices in the stone for most of the ravine. It reminded her of the clay urns she shaped. Her heart started to skip as she imagined enormous hands molding the red stone. She struggled to envision someone who could be so large as to shape the mountains. Her thoughts dwelled on the stone's shape as she made her way through the ravine path, baring the same depressions.

'The fable says the mountains opened for us but, I wonder why,' Nuyani thought as she continued running on the stable ground.

Ch. 13

A Hunter's Consequences

Noon had already passed as the party of hunters reached their destination north of the village. As the whip-necks strolled toward a large embankment topped with tall grass, the rear hunters started to unpack their shovels from their saddles. Cuganwa looked on toward the cliffs gawking at their sheer height.

"Cuganwa, we are about to stop. Get ready," Odaru instructed, breaking the boy from his trance.

The boy blinked as he looked down at the senior hunter. "Sorry. What was that?"

"Get the shovel," Odaru repeated. "The others are already starting." The older hunter pointed to the other hunters noting their actions. "We're here to help. Let's not be in the way, all right?"

"Right," Cuganwa answered as he retrieved the shovel from their pack. It was a resin-covered shoulder blade of a charge-horn that was fastened to a branch.

As they neared rising embankment, a few whip-necks climbed onto the higher ground as the others waited by its side. Odaru led Muga to stop by the higher ridge staying close enough to the ground for Cuganwa to step down easily. When the boy did, he followed the other hunters carrying their shovels as they gathered. Once everyone was gathered, they separated into smaller groups and went to different spots in the area. Cuganwa started digging with at least a dozen other hunters in a mixed group.

Another hunter then laid out two tarps on the ground as some of the others worked to pin the corners in place. Cuganwa followed their leads as the hunters tore into the earth piled the dirt onto one of the tarps as more of Lamoy's men came by riding whip-necks to tie ropes to their saddles. In minutes, they already had a hole a few meters wide in and knee-deep. The boy panted as he continued shoveling the dirt.

'I did not expect this to be so difficult,' the boy said as he jabbed at the dirt, trying to loosen the compacted earth.

A few chuckles rose within his group. "Relax, Little Charge-horn. You don't need to keep up with us. Just try to remove as much as you can, and we'll be done soon," one of the hunters commented. Already sweating, Cuganwa gave a quick nod.

"What do you think for your second day, Cuganwa? Not a normal start for a hunter." another hunter said as they shoveled more dirt onto the tarp.

The boy shook his head as he looked back at a thin man with a thick beard reaching down to mid-chest. "I prefer running," he answered, getting a few laughs. Cuganwa's wary eyes then trailed toward the cliffs just beyond the plains. "Do blood-manes bother you?"

"No," the hunter answered plainly. "It's rare for them to approach us. Those demons already live near their game with the heavy-horns. Strong bastards can take some of the young twice our weight in a swoop."

Cuganwa froze, and his eyes looked between the cliffs and the hunter. "If it's that easy, why aren't they after more?"

"Boy, we have arrows," another hunter interjected. "Heavy-horns don't. The day they do, then everything would change." Many of the others laughed, including Cuganwa, as he thought of the heavy beasts wielding an odd bow that matched their stature.

A hunter with a short, pointed beard leered at Cuganwa. Keeping his tone low, the man then asked the boy, "I guess you're more worried about your witch than some bird."

Some of the other hunters gave glances at the man. Cuganwa furrowed his brow, uncertain what the man was trying to say. The hunter continued to look at the boy, only turning away when another hunter stepped into his line of sight, and he looked at the ground. 'I wonder if he's one of Bo'ede's men,' the boy thought as he returned to his digging. Despite everyone being in one place, it did little to help learn who everyone was. The other hunter said nothing to the man before turning away and returning to his own section for digging.

The group remained silent for a moment as they continued their digging. Cuganwa found several roots he hacked through that the others told him to pocket the herbs to make salves. As Cuganwa struggled to unearth a few stones half the size of his head, the others began to mutter to one another. Two hunters began to speak about making a second village within the drylands. Cuganwa smiled, reminded of Iogda and Selsaj, the two hunters working on another dig site weren't the only ones thinking of the same idea.

'The idea's not so rare, then,' Cuganwa thought.

Before long, smaller groups within the party formed as they took on discussions covering their personal lives, fears of the storm growing stronger, the events of the festival, and spirits seeming to return. Even as they spoke, the others were far ahead of Cuganwa as most of the hole they made neared waist-deep. The front and back of his tunic were now drenched in sweat.

'Doing this nearly every day is crazy,' the boy thought as he scanned around the area. None of the others were tired or, if they were, did not show it. Cuganwa took note of their demeanor as they worked. 'They're not even worried about being spotted by the heavy-horns.' A roaming free-rider moved about further away, nearing the line of tall grass. 'The heavy-horns are too tall to hide in the grass. That's why they aren't worried.'

As Cuganwa took a deep breath, Odaru then rode toward his spot. "Cuganwa, would you like some water?"

The boy looked up with wide eyes as sweat trailed from his brow and down to his chin. Cuganwa nodded his head as he rasped, "Yes." Odaru chuckled as he lowered the water skin with a tether. Cuganwa took up the pouch and unfastened the stopper before chugging some of the water down before gasping and replacing the stopper. "Thanks." Cuganwa breathed deeply.

"Take it easy. This is your first dig. You look like you ran here from the village," the hunter said with a chuckle. Some of the others smiled, but mostly remained quiet.

"How's the leg, Odaru?" one of the hunters asked.

The man smiled as he answered, "Thanks to the elder, good enough. Maybe twenty days or so, and it won't be stuck like it is now."

"Good to hear. That fall must've been bad. Did your whip-neck really get that scared?" the man asked.

"It was a large charge-horn. It probably weighed as much as Muga here if I had to guess. But the Great Lord kept us all breathing in the end," Odaru said. The others nodded as they let the wounded hunter leave.

With the day crawling by, the pit they made was nearing Cuganwa's shoulders. More of the hunters started to approach with halved long bones sharpened on both sides and laid them beside the pit.

As Cuganwa continued to shovel, he saw Lamoy approaching with her second following. The two seemed to argue as they approached their spot.

Her voice grew louder as they brought bundles of the same bones with them. "It does not matter."

Her second was an older man with a thin build and short black and gray hair. "You should be resting. Coming out here would only cause trouble. We don't know what those things did to you."

Lamoy narrowed her eyes and dropped the bundle by the pit. "I walk. I breathe. I talk. Until I can't do those things, I help the village first."

The boy looked up. He and several others glanced at the hunting leader, finding her headwrap out of place and the two white streaks running through her hair. Cuganwa halted in his work and stared at the hunting leader. Some of the others noticed the boy was no longer working and followed his gaze to Lamoy.

The huntress turned her sight onto the others who were staring back. Lamoy glanced at the others as she tilted her head forward and brushed her short hair back to display the white strands. "Yes. I saw a spirit. But, before any of you start making excuses for me or try to tell me to leave, the village comes first. And, I still breath," Lamoy stated as she moved on with her second, still trying to convince her to relax.

'She still left the village to lead the hunt. What were those spirits? Did the witch show up too?' Cuganwa questioned as he looked toward the cliffs once more.

They started to remind him of the witch. She had killed the large charge-horn, knocked away an arrow, and now there were rumors of her leading or fighting spirits in the village. He placed a hand on his tarnished tunic, remembering the swift kick she gave him when he lunged at her. Cuganwa thought of his father and elders' words on killing only to lead back to the failed hunter, and his obsession drove him to hurt someone else.

"Keep shoveling, Little Charge-horn. There will be time for questions later. Our time is not endless," a hunter pointed out as he left his shovel on the side and grabbed some of the bones.

"R-right," the boy answered meekly as he continued.

After a few more inches of dirt were removed, the hunters stopped and began to plant the bones into the ground. Cuganwa climbed out of the pit and watched as they created a bed of spikes.

'The way they do things is different from father's group,' the boy thought as he watched the hunters lead the clean tarp over the hole and mark the corners with blue rags. The boy shivered, thinking of what he would expect from the trap they had made. He shook his head, wondering what a large beast would look like falling in. As much as he wanted to ignore the feeling, his hands began to fidget as the carnage still reminded him of Deyunca.

"Move, Cuganwa. There is nothing else for you to do," another hunter instructed.

The boy broke from his thoughts and nodded as he turned and moved toward the other hunters waiting on the ground to the planes.

As questions gathered in his mind, Cuganwa jumped down from the higher ground and climbed up the stirrups of Muga's saddle. Once he reached his seat, Cuganwa looked out into the area watching as two whip-necks rode off into the tall grass.

Ch. 14

Cries of the Past

Nuyani ran along the path, her heart hammering against her chest. She looked with an enthusiastic glee at the area around her. Though she had yet to see anything truly different, the cliff walls had already changed from red to a light brown and still held the same indentations. The dirt beneath her feet had strands of grass and leaves scattered through the area, making it softer than the miles of dirt she usually traversed in the drylands. After an hour had passed, Nuyani reached the end of the path. It opened to an area filled with strange trees with a gradual slope leading the vast sea. Each tree stood straight and had angled layers of dark brown bark wrapped around its trunk with frizzled ends, and at the top were large round fruits with the same dark brown color and just as hairy. Large, vibrant green leaves jutted out in all directions, each one fanning outward with frayed points providing shade. Nuyani looked on toward the horizon. No mountains or other lands were rising in the distance.

"Endless water as vast as the demon lands," Nuyani whispered as she stopped in her tracks and breathed heavily. She held both her arms. "By the Great Lor… Nuyani stopped her phrase finding it strange to say such a name when their origin was from another source.

How could she continue a lie if they were not the origin the elders led them to follow?

'Who is Kelvert?' Nuyani questioned as she looked over the new land. To the right, the land remained bare and free. Looking to the left, her eyes welled as she saw towering structures rising high above the trees. 'It's real.' She covered her mouth. 'Homes that rivaled the height of mountains,' Nuyani remembered from Yanuma's tale.

Several round structures still stood yet, were partially broken. A squared building had a domelike roof with half of it destroyed, and most of the taller portions were surrounded by a wall. Nuyani did not wait as she raced down the slope. Beneath the shade of the canopy, she could see more structures that had fallen and smaller homes large enough to fit a single family. The witch stopped just by one of the fallen buildings. She approached it as it lay half-buried in the sand. Nuyani ran her hand over the beige brickwork tracing the mortar as her brow furrowed.

'What did we run from?' she thought.

A faint pressure then rose and sloshed about on the surface of her core. Nuyani looked to her left, following the source only to find a light blue figure in the visage of a woman running forth. Nuyani's core reverberated, sending pulses through her body as she unsheathed her knife. The specter continued toward her. Nuyani could see the look of fear and worry growing in her eyes until her chest arched forward, her head rose toward the sky, her arms widened outward, and her legs gave out. The witch paused as she watched the spirit collapse to the floor, parts of her sinking through the dirt as if she were never there. The figure disappeared, taking the pressure with it

"W-what?" Nuyani questioned. She then looked ahead as a blue light came into view along with the faint pressure. It was the same woman, the same spirit. "How?"

The spirit emerged from an opening in the wall, running past several small, squared huts as she made her way toward Nuyani. The visitor eased her stance but kept her knife ready. The spirit then collapsed once more in the same manner as the first. Nuyani narrowed her eyes as she studied the spirit and her core. Parts of the woman's face were distorted like twisted smoke. Other parts of her body faded away much like the other spirits she encountered in the drylands. The pressure on her core was already small, but seemed lighter than normal. Even To'anu's presence was stronger. Before she could get a full grasp of the spirit's nature, it disappeared once more. Nuyani let out a pulse once the visage was gone. The sparse energy dispersed, growing faint on her senses. She found it difficult to follow the ethereal force as it flowed and collected once more at the opening where the spirit emerged. Once it was fully reassembled, the spirit emerged once more repeating the same act.

"What caused you to run?" she wondered aloud as she sheathed her blade and slowly walked toward the shadowed path through the outer wall.

Her heart hammered as she felt an enormous weight bear down on her senses, dulling the drum. Yet, she could still feel the presence around her as she entered the hallway. The path had two corridors leading in opposite directions on her side, but both were caved in with rubble covered in webs. The only remaining path was forward. The only lights she could see were some rays parallel showing on the floor and another exit at the far end of the hall. Nuyani tried to ignore the suppressive air around her as she noticed the hall was at least wide enough for her to lie down sideways if she wished. She forced herself to smirk.

A chilling breeze passed through the hall, forcing Nuyani to hug her arms for warmth. Her ember glowing eyes were wide as she watched the countless figures suddenly race down the hall in desperation, most falling before they even reached her. Pain and agony of the life force swirled within the hall.

'I have to keep moving,' she told herself as she ambled through the hall, trying to stay out of the way of the spirits.

As Nuyani made her way down the hall, she reached the first bit of light, finding both sides of the walls lead outside with small pillars baring faded swirling decorations propping up the stone roof. A strange space with a long pool surrounded by a hip-tall wall was on her left. Vines and algae grew from the sides as bugs flew in a cloud over the water. She winced at the sudden overpassing through the open air. There were squared stones on the ground with many shattered and large craters in the dirt. Nuyani squinted at one of the strange formations of brickwork on the other side of the pool. Though the stones arched upward, much of the debris lay within it.

'One of those large huts must've fallen,' Nuyani concluded as she looked on. Many of the stone huts and smaller structures were destroyed completely or had damaged roofs or walls. 'This place. Could I even call it sa…'

The witch stepped backward just as a spirit collapsed in front of her, its visage passing through her body. The spirit's will felt like a single current within the wave energy through her as it brushed her core.

She gasped and gawked as the vision of a hall flooded with fleeing men, women, and children came into view. The person stopped as the body of another fell before her and was trampled in their escape. Before the person could gain their balance, an orange light rose in a glow just before searing pain rose in their back and forced the victim to look toward the arching roof overhead. The person started to fall to their knees. Before they collapsed completely, Nuyani returned to her senses, floundering about as she reached for her back. She could feel the blaze that struck him. She turned away with her back toward another of the spirit in approach without realizing. The spirit ran through her sending another current brushing against her core and transporting her mind into the past. A man pushed two others forward as they bled only for his head to whip forward with a blue glow shining against the nearby pillars. As the first, once the spirit was about to collapse, Nuyani left in the hall with the lingering sensation of cold and pain on the back of her head.

"What is this?" Nuyani said. Sudden attacks that came with such strange pains. She only knew of the howlers to leave a cold mark, but heat. 'Is there another spirit that burns?' she wondered for a moment until the pulse of her core warned her the spirit would soon return. Nuyani ducked out of the way as the blue figure ran by and collapsed.

She looked further ahead, halfway down the hall, falling to their deaths. Nuyani had yet to come in contact with the rest. Still, she quivered. She hugged her arms once more, trying to stop the shaking as she looked out into the other open space. On the left, a paved road with squared beige bricks running down the center. Many of them were shattered as large craters littered the area. Even the rooftops and walls were damaged. Nuyani's breathing grew faster as she looked down at the destruction.

Tightening her grip, she lowered her head and closed her eyes. With a stronger focus on her core, the pulses grew stronger, pushing back waves of pressure surrounding her. She no longer felt the torrent of energy batting her about as her nerves eased. She turned toward the hall, still clutching both arms as she marched onward.

'I am here for a solution, some answer. By Lord Kelvert's… I need a solution,' Nuyani told herself as she was bombarded further with the vision of each passing spirit.

Some were struck with the same strange attacks that were hot or cold. Others were struck with arrows, stabbed with blades, or hit with something blunt to kill them. Nuyani looked down at the ground, finding strange flat sticks along the way with a brownish-red surface. She continued until a spirit that passed by brought on the image of a man clad in a red surcoat and wearing a strange face cover, then thrusting something thin and silver into his gut. Her concentration on the core did well to block out the spirit's pain, but Nuyani was unprepared for the abrupt attack as he had her arms crossed before her, attempting to block. Letting out an audible breath, she continued past the pillars returning to a normal wall and reaching another entrance into a large room with part of the roof caved in, debris piled into the far left corner.

'I don't think I can lead people to this place,' Nuyani thought.

Nuyani's thoughts returned to the four village spirits that lingered in the village. Compared to them, these things are shadows. Do they know they are here? Are they in pain?' she wondered. Her core pulsed several times. Each pulse was stronger than the last as they radiated outward. 'Can I free them? No, I will try.'

Nuyani glared at the ground as she let her entire being become a conduit for the drum as each pulse rose from her. The spirits around her started to move away. She could feel the pressure lightening around her but, it was merely scattered, not gone.

'Concentrate,' she told herself. The last spirits were consolidated into a single point within her grasp. With the energy around her, she was only pushing it away. Trying to shape her will, one of the pulses rising from her being formed into a sphere of blue light over her head. As Nuyani's will shaped the construct, she felt a void blocking out the life force. Letting part of the sphere open, she expected the energy to pour into the construct, giving her something she could exorcise from the area.

'How?' Nuyani wondered as she felt the weight pull away from her, staying beyond her reach. Nuyani relaxed as she looked at the swirling mist of blue light dimly lighting the room's ceiling. She stopped her attempt to free the spirits. Their aimless and repetitive flow seemed to bear some will if they were avoiding her. 'What would keep a spirit to linger in their own death? Do you prefer this place?' To'anu came to mind. 'He at least doesn't trust me because of our history. What's your reason?'

Nuyani first wondered until another presence then weighed on her core. She looked to the side just as a small foot ran through the entrance.

"Hello?" Nuyani called out as she made her way to the entrance only to find another large path with trenches and craters in the ground. The buildings on either side were either caved in or partially collapsed.

She scowled as she saw another spirit through a hole in the wall fight back, only to eventually fall. 'I wish you all peace but, what keeps you here?' she wondered as her eyes fell on another one of the strange brownish red bars lying in the dirt. Nuyani looked about and sent a pulse through the immediate area to find the spirit that disappeared. When nothing arose, she approached the bar and knelt to pick it up by one end. The other dragged against the stone as strong vibrations ran through it and rang with a collision against the stone.

"What is this?"

A feint portion of energy remained within the blade. Nuyani narrowed her eyes at the item. 'It's too shallow for a spirit,' she concluded as she released a pulse to interact with the energy. As the extension of her core reached the hidden life force, Nuyani's senses turned to a quick skirmish as she looked through the eyes of another. Before her was a thin man wearing a white tunic and short trousers suspended by a blue rope tied around her waist, holding different sheaths and tools. He had the same complexion as Nuyani, but wore a mustache in a curled fashion like the chief. He wore a white headwrap, and across his chest was another blue sash empty of any tools or items that gleamed from the sunlight making Nuyani wonder of its purpose. Fury burned in his eyes as he faced off against his opponent. Wielding a spear, the man blocked several attacks from a silver stick before whipping one end around and cracking it against his foe's hand, disarming him.

'What?' Nuyani thought as she watched the man kick her away and saw the fighter spin the silver-colored spearhead around and thrust it into his neck.

Nuyani dropped the item as she brought her hands to her neck. The lingering sting of the spear piercing her flesh remained for a moment. The item dropped released a clang as it hit the ground and sprung up from the same end before the other side did the same. 'What are these weapons?' Nuyani questioned as she released her grip and looked at the item. Hard as stone, yet remained flexible like wood, she wanted to pick up the item once more.

A pressure rose on her core, once again taking her attention away. Nuyani whipped around, finding a figure turning and running around the corner of a building. She stopped for a moment looking between the item and the fleeing figure. Nuyani rose and bolted after the person. 'If they're running, it couldn't be a spirit,' Nuyani thought as she turned the corner.

Nuyani blinked several times as she ran down the narrow alley toward the sea. Already, the figure was down the long path and around the corner. She continued until the path opened to the endless waters. Nuyani froze for a moment as she watched the rolling waves crash against the stone walkway. She looked along the edge seeing some parts stretching further into the ocean with a short end. Nuyani stood straight and cupped her hands over her mouth as she watched the infinite blue. The wind rushed by, carrying the smell of saltwater. Turning to the rest of the walkway, she found more signs of destruction as deep trenches carved through the earth and trailed to the outer wall. Nuyani moved toward some of the debris beside a hole in the building seeing the edge of a curved disk sticking out of the rubble.

Nuyani released a pulse of her core. The wave coursed through most of the area she could see, but only the spirit shadows' faint pressure weighed on her core. The heavier spirit or living person was nowhere to be seen. Nuyani scowled but eased her expression as she turned to the mask. 'If I can't find you, or you don't want to meet, fine. I will learn more with these…pieces,' Nuyani thought as she looked at the strange disk. The little energy it contained made her hesitate as the image of blood flying from the peoples' bodies made her stomach turn. 'Gutting animals was one thing, even a necessity but, this mass murder…' Nuyani's hand trembled as she stepped closer and retrieved the disk. The smaller stones shifted as the item released a grinding ring scraping against the stone.

'Huh. Same material?' she wondered as she freed the disk. Nuyani held both sides in her hands as she looked at the item.

She glared at the piece as she noticed the indentations in the middle matching a pair of lips and nose and small holes aligning with a mouth and eyes. Flipping the item around, she scowled at the mask. Its color tarnished by the years, with a few spots colored green and gray on the surface. Nuyani could feel the remnant energy sloshing about in the facepiece. Taking a heavy breath, she released a beat coursing through into the mask. Once in contact with the energy, she was transported into another person's view. People fled down the alleyway. Nuyani noticed the owner of the figure remove their weapon from the chest of a warrior wearing a white tunic and two blue sashes.

'What?' Nuyani questioned as she noticed the figure's skin was a light blue contrast against the blood spilling down her wrist. She could feel a sense of murderous rage burning in the figure. 'Why were you attacking us? What are you? Did your people become those howlers? Is that why you're attacking us now?'

More questions than answers arose. The waves from the open waters were taller and crashed against the stone path, cutting just above the edge. The figure's feet were swept from beneath her as she fell to the ground. Nuyani's heart skipped as she saw wooden structures smashed against the stone paths branching out into the water. They had leaf-like shapes with the front and backs pointed, and the middle was widened. The belly of the structures was rounded like a bowl, and the tops had different levels with strange trunks rising from the middle and tarps fastened to the straight branches. Though each structure was destroyed, she could tell what they normally looked like from the six or so that were sinking into the water.

Nuyani's attention returned to the figure she followed as they picked up their weapon in the chilling water and struggled to stand. Once the figure did so, one enormous foot stepped into view out in the waters by dozens of paces. Yet the following wave swept onto the path knocking the figure back to the wall and sending one of the destroyed wooden structures propped onto the stone path.

'What is happening?' Nuyani wondered as the figure's sight was obscured by water. Their view cleared only for a large ash-colored branch to slither through the water, trying to wrap around the ankle. As it twisted around the limb, the branch drilled into the stone path as rocks and dirt exploded before the blue figure. The memory ended, and Nuyani dropped the facepiece, letting it clang against the stone

"A branch. Large limbs," Nuyani whispered as she learned forth, propping herself up onto her hands. Her frantic gaze turned to face the direction—a thin young girl wearing a white dress and white headwrap. The woman's eyes fell on the bloodstains formed beneath the headwrap and a few specks of dirt on her face.

'She looks no older than the boy,' Nuyani thought as Cuganwa came to mind. "Hi."

She reached out with a hand in a slow manner. The girl shrunk back, tucking her chin low and bringing her arms closer to her chest, and darting through the opening in the wall. Nuyani's body stiffened as she watched the child flee through the debris as if they weren't there, moving almost as quickly as the howlers. Nuyani rose and ran after her, leaping over piles of debris as she tried to keep the person in view. Too many questions were left unanswered. Nuyani ran through the entrance of the building and out into the main pathway leading to the large stone structures baring the destroyed dome.

The child before ran on the air over many of the trenches on the pathway to the building. The woman followed bounding over the gaps. 'She must be a spirit,' Nuyani thought.

The roads lay in ruin as stone pedestals sitting along the sides bore only shattered statues of busts and the remaining limbs. Nuyani paid them no mind as she felt the gathering life forces swirl around them. In her pursuit, the runner passed through the entrance of the building as the child reached the shadows and disappeared completely.

"What?" Nuyani questioned as she slowed to a walk. She released a pulse from her core, searching for the child's presence. The pressure in the room was pooling through the structure despite the open ceiling. She turned about, trying to find a sign of the girl's presence. "Don't tell me you'll be back at the alleyway, and I have to wait for you to return," Nuyani said.

The woman looked about the area. She stood in a large space with the left half-filled with rubble where the dome was caved in. Her gaze fell upon the faded paintings along the walls as vines grew through the cracks. A mural bordered by elaborate designs showed several men on the wooden structures surrounded by flowing lines Nuyani assumed were the waves. The men faced off against creatures in the waters, each with strange and horrifying shapes of animals she had never seen that were as big or taller than the platform they stood on. One of the creatures had a long gray body with a large eye and several long arms stretching toward the men. The mural ended with the beast lying on the wooden platform and the men celebrating as they faced the opposite direction. A second monster then appeared, this time with several heads and fins like that of a fish running down its back and into the water. The mural ended with a repeat of the last.

The other images were of a ball of thorns, a crab with one of its arms far larger than the other. Several people with silver, blue and red skin, and what Nuyani could connect as a turtle with the head of a long-bodied lizard. Each that stood against the fighters fell and was brought back on the ships. Nuyani looked at their weapons as they wield spears, curved blades, some wielding strange disk-shaped objects covering their torsos, and knives. Nuyani looked closer at the knife-wielding men as each of them had separate designs with white lines around them. Some had blue circles near them and pointed toward the creatures they fought. Some of the knife wielders had the white lines arching over their heads.

The image of the light construct she created at the village center entered her thoughts. Her heart skipped as she nearly formed a smirk. 'Could they be doing what I was?' Am I not the witch?' Nuyani thought as her eyes watered. She followed the mural again, seeing more creatures along the ceiling as an enormous man with a swollen body, strange birds, and from what she could tell, was moving gray land all met the same fate. 'People who hunted on endless water. What were we doing out there? Did we really eat those things?' she wondered as she looked at the enormous man and the blue people in the other picture.

Once she reached the opening in the ceiling, Nuyani broke away and saw the child standing at the back part of the room where another set of pedestals was. These seemed far more important than the others as inscriptions lay on its front and it was made of marble. Yet, like the others, all that remained were the feet of whatever figures used to stand there. Some of the marble pieces ay on the floor beside them, but their finely broken pieces and time had made it impossible for Nuyani to envision what the statue truly looked like.

Before Nuyani could say a single word, the girl's form turned into a white wisp and floated toward a small pile of rubble sitting in the center of the room only a few paces away from the larger stones. The wisp reformed into the child as she sat on the ground, her legs passing through the stone.

'Great, an answer,' Nuyani thought as she slowly walked toward the spirit and sat down in front of her.

The child looked at the woman with senses of curiosity in her ember glowing eyes. Nuyani could not help but, blink finding someone who did not look at her with a sense of disgust or fear. The woman grew a sheepish smile as the child sat closer.

"You can speak to me if you'd like. I'm not a monster," Nuyani stated. The child began to frown as she sat back and shook her head. Blinking several more times, the woman then asked, "You can't talk?" The child shook her head. Nuyani sighed. "I just want to know what happened. Why did we leave? It looks like you were scared away." The girl looked up at Nuyani, her eyes shifting from the floor to her face. "Can you show me?" Nuyani asked. The spirit faced Nuyani completely as her eyes turned red, and tears rose.

The spirit raised a hand and placed a finger onto her forehead. The energy within the spirit flowed through Nuyani's mind. She could feel the shallow pressure washing over her core as her senses changed. Darkness enveloped her sight. Chaotic screams and loud crashes rang in her ears as she was pulled by her arm down one of the stone paths by a man Nuyani assumed was the girl's father. The people of the stone village wore similar attire as they did in the drylands, simple tunic, trousers, and dressed held up by sashes and leather sandals for their feet. People scattered about as bricks dislodged from some of the walls after flashes of light struck them.

Nuyani could feel the child's heart race as another family collided with theirs. The girl fell to the ground as deafening rumbles shook her ears, and dust covered everything before her. The child grew frantic, struggling to stand as she made her way through the dust only to herself alone and near the pool of water. On the other side was the large, rounded structure with both halves intact despite its collapse. The child looked at the end of the tower seeing an enormous glowing bluestone and the structure covered in strange white vines. The stone had a white light rising from its center, only growing dim as the vines slithered about the stone. Once it was completely covered, a full column of the vines ripped through the structure and lifted the stone into the air, sending debris raining down on those trying to flee.

The child raised her arms to shield herself from the debris. As the stones came down, a blue wall then rose over her head, angling toward the pool. The child watched as the wall ripped with the stones striking the surface. She looked about, seeing another fall victim to the debris. She tried to find her father only to find the man beneath several stones as another puff of dust rose between them. Blood trickled from a gash in his head. The girl rushed toward him, trying to pull some of the stones off. Another man brandished one of the strange knives. Unlike a normal blade, it was shaped like a large talon of a beast, even rounded at the base of a blade, and the opposite end had three claws resembling more of a bird's talons.

Nuyani could feel the waves from the stranger as
he released a pulse. Another dome of blue light was
conjured beneath the stones as it slowly grew, sliding the
stones away. The girl brought both hands to her mouth as
she saw her father's mangled legs. As the stranger
continued, her father's eyes widened as he reached out
with a free hand. A pulse exploded from him as the energy
passed the two, and another barrier was erected behind
them. Yellow light gleamed from the rear, making the girl
spin around to find another figure running toward them
with an elaborate staff pointed at them.

'What is that?' Nuyani questioned.

The figure wore a strange gray headpiece with the
same mask. Their body was covered by a long red cloak
worn over their torso and draped from their hip. A single
belt was worn around their waist keeping the surcoat in
place. Beneath that was a strange attire made of woven
rings that gleamed in the sun and fire. The piece covered
half of their arms and legs Nuyani would've wondered if it
were a single piece but, her attention was turned to the
pale peach skin and odd height of the figure that bounded
toward them. His body seemed wide as if he were
scrunched down, and his stout form merely compensated
for his height. The staff's tip had a silver sphere topping it
that began to glow bright yellow. A moment later, another
flame burst from the instrument sailing toward them. The
father strengthened his pulse as the stronger waves
radiated to the barrier. The fire struck against the shield
but was propelled back to the sender. The flame struck the
odd figure only for a third to be released off to the side,
heading toward the stronger aiding them. It hit his
shoulder and he let out a cry of pain as the fire lapped at
his arm. The construct he formed broke, causing the
heavier stones to fall once more onto the man. The girl

cried out as the life in her father's eyes disappeared and grew still. She fell by him and grabbed his arm, shaking his limb.

'Sorry, child,' Nuyani wanted to say.

The other man rose from the ground, the sleeve of his tunic burnt away, revealing his charred shoulder. The girl continued attempting to wake her father but, he remained still. The stranger then rose and wrapped one arm around the child's waist, carrying her away as he ran down the path parallel to the pool. The man yelled to her that they needed to leave. As he did so, the stone wall beside them burst as more ash-colored vines rose from the floor, making the two fall to the ground. The child rolled several times on the ground just as she watched the column of vines wriggle and slither in the air. A bright orb of blue light sailed toward the column and collided with the vegetation. A wall of wind rushed through the area, nearly forcing the child's eyes closed. The vines were ripped apart, with flames burning at the ends.

The child looked to the source of the enormous orb as another was conjured from a second large stone crowned atop of the structures and sailing toward the vines. The sphere continued as the tower fell, with another cluster of vines claiming it. The orb sailed forth, missing its target and going over the roof. A second later, a loud explosion sounded as the ground rumbled, followed by more wind. The child tried to stand once more but sat against the pool wall. Panting as she watched people run about, the girl trembled. Her eyes locked on the stranger who helped her as he rose. He made his way toward her, clutching his burned arm.

'Go child,' Nuyani thought.

The man had to pull the child to her feet and pushed her to move. The girl started slowly blinking several times before she came to her senses and continued running. The child started running toward the center path following the flow of people heading to the larger dome building. Screams filled the air, spurring her forth. Hot tears trailed from her eyes. Her ears deafened and rang with pain from the loud crashes around her. Bodies littered the ground, both friend and foe. Still, she sped on trying to survive.

Before she reached the end of the pool, the girl stopped as something glowing fell before her. She looked to the ground as a thick golden liquid splattered on the floor. The child saw the same cluster of vines were no longer burning and released a strange gold glowing sap. Several drops landed in the area, each larger than a man. She covered herself, expecting the liquid to splash onto her but, found it only sinking into the ground as a large golden ring formed in the stone with strange markings following the curve within the ring. 'What did we leave?' Nuyani found herself asking. The runner's heart was hammering through the vision.

Before the child could make her way around the area within the circle converted into light. A large green hand then rose from the glow of the figure wearing the same strange surcoat and headpiece. This time, the attacker had a shorter curved blade in one hand and a net in the other. Worse, each knot contained barbs. The child shrieked as she backed away from the figure. Without hesitation, the figure looked at the child and threw his net. She froze, watching the snare close in on her until a sudden rush of wind blew from the side, knocking the net away.

The child looked toward the side from where the gate came. Another of the blue sashed men ran forth, wielding one of the talon knives. He pointed the small weapon toward the green figure just before a deep blue orb rose from his hand, growing to the size of his head before it flew toward the green figure. Nuyani felt the strange ripples through the memories of the spirit as the flow of her energy was distorted from each cast.

'These rings…They're strange,' Nuyani thought as she tried to memorize the rhythm projected through the child's memory.

The orb struck the green figure's shoulder sending him off balance for a moment as the blue sashed fighter closed the distance. The green figure stabbed forth, aiming for his opponent's gut. The sashed fighter parried the blade to the side and kicked at the green fighter's leg, trying to force him to fall. Bearing larger muscles, the green figure shrugged the blow off as he turned toward him, following with a backslash of his blade. The sashed man backed away as the green man grabbed his other hand. Raising the short blade, the sashed man grabbed the green figure's arm before kicking up to the enemy's elbow. Thrown off-balance, the two disconnected as the blade came down.

The sashed fighter raised the knife as he yelled, "*Tosgam!* (Fire!)" A flame appeared in the air before sailing toward the green figure's face. Ripples of its energy passed through the area. The projectile then struck and indented the mask. A loud clang sounded amongst the chaos. His head reeled back as blood sprayed onto the ground. The green man's arms dangled to the sides as he dropped his blade and fell over the pool wall submerged into the water.

The man ran to her before the girl could say anything and yanked her to her feet. She was pushed on. She headed down the main path as an entire row of the sashed men headed in the opposite direction with spears at the ready. Water rained down despite the sparse clouds above. As the girl followed many others, the ground before her ripped open as one of the strange slithering branches rose into the air. Buildings and the wall fell apart. It continued as the child leaped over the gap in a desperate bound. Water flooded the path as a sudden shadow trailed over the stones.

A loud crash then sounded from her side. Splinters and boards scattered through the area as the remains of one of the wooden vessels collapsed under its weight. The child pushed on, trying to wade through the water. More ripples passed through her memory, allowing Nuyani to learn from the past. Though she had difficulty walking, the invaders did not. More sap fell from glowing cracks in the flailing limb as the red-clad fighters ran through the destruction.

Nuyani could not tell what she was seeing. There were beings of various sizes and skin colors. The most bizarre were beings with animalistic limbs. Some had normal hands but were covered in fur or scales with claws or hooved feet. The sashed warrior wielded a shield and curved blade while his foe had a net and a short blade. When the man went to stab at her, the woman's legs fused, forming a tail and tripling the length of her body as she slithered back out of the way of the blade. The sashed fighter raised his shield as the woman coiled back with her weapon pointed at his head. She then threw her net forth. With it in mid-flight, she struck in a blur, stabbing into the man's leg. As he wailed and the net enclosed on his limbs, a ring of golden light shined around them before the area within did the same. A moment later, the two fell into the golden void before it disappeared. Other portals appeared as the invaders abducted them. The girl moved on, trying to reach the main building.

She was forced to halt as another strange being cleaved upward with an enormous ax fitting their size. Another of the sashed fighters was split in two and sent flying away. The girl breathed heavily as she watched the figure turn toward her. They were twice the height of any man. Their legs were hooved. Their body covered in black fur. Horns protruded from their massive head, still outfitted with a mask pressed into their brow and cutting into their eyes where dry blood sealed them shut. Its mouth and nose were in the form of a beast. Despite being blind, the being tracked the child's movements. They raised their ax and started to bring it down. She backed away as the large blade made of song stone cracked the earth under its weight. Still, in retreat, she was in range for another attack until a sudden white flash appeared behind the invader. The being turned around, facing another of the sashed fighters as they held a knife and a curved blade.

A bolt launched from the knife with a second yell and coursed toward the large figure. The lightning struck the fur-covered man's mask as their body jittered. They fell to the floor. The fighter sheathed his curved weapon as he moved to the girl and picked her up. He ran with her through the rushing water. The girl then found herself watching another battle taking place above the structures. A man taller than any structure or mountain with his brow cutting into the clouds wielded a curved blade and taloned knife of his own. Wrapped around his waist were several branches leading to a different figure.

'That made us flee?' Nuyani questioned, her body shivering.

The white branches led to a strange figure in a humanoid form but made entirely of wood. The head and torso were covered in a tattered crimson shroud with a hood over the head. An androgynous golden mask covered the face. The towering being had the eye slits open and glowing with a golden light. The tree figure continued its attempts to ensure that larger man as he cleaved through the bindings. He went for a stab at the wood creature's mask. The being backed away their branches, losing much of their reach. Before the man went for another swing, he raised the knife's tip pointed to the clouds. The clouds swirled around the point as lightning danced in their folds. Winds whipped around into a vortex closely descending from above the masked giant. The vortex trapped the branches as large waves rose and spun around the figure, trapping them in the surge. As the clouds and water encased the tree figure, the colossal man raised his blade and swung for a horizontal cleave.

As his hand rose, crossing through the air, a large shadow crossed over the man's body before a sphere, then flew into sight and clamped down on the sword hand, stopping the blow. A fierce gale erupted through the area on impact. The sphere was an enormous mass of pulsing gray flesh bulging out of small sections of its shell. Whether a beak or shell, Nuyani couldn't tell. The clouds and waters stopped swirling around the masked being. Before the large fighter could recover, the masked figure wrapped several branches around his limbs and head.

"Do'alm!" the girl called out.

As the man continued to struggle against branches, the tree being unraveled, showing an enormous heart hidden beneath the cloak. The mask floated forth, ready to cover Do'alm's face. The enormous being turned and outstretched his arms as he shouted in a booming voice. Nuyani noted his eyes were black and deep blue spotted with white, reminding her of the night sky. The entire scene went white before a deafening thunder followed. The child was blind for a moment before her vision cleared. The giant, Do'alm, now collapsed to his knees, sending a tremor through the land as his chest became cavernous as violet flames rose from the inside.

Nuyani could feel her body move as she cupped her mouth. The masked figure released its grasp of the man reassembling its body as it turned toward the mountains. The girl shifted in the warrior's arms as the ground reverberated several times. Approaching the high walls was another giant. A woman with her hands extended outward. Lightning danced between each finger before she fired another blinding bolt. The girl shielded her eyes, blocking some of the light. The flying orb was wounded as the same flames rose from the remaining lower half as it fell to the earth. Given enough time, the masked figure reached for her, wrapping several branches around her limbs. The woman fought against its pull as her entire body started to glow. Her footsteps shook the earth. As the mask floated forward, arching as he listened to the other fighter.

"Kelvert!" the girl called.

'What!' Nuyani thought. 'W-why? Who is he?'

Before her mind was flooded with more questions, a spell ripped through the doors sending splinters through the area. The fighters reeled from the concussive force, but regrouped as the opening gave way. The man named Kelvert then lifted his hand as a large violet construct of a wall appeared in the doorway, blocking several ethereal attacks as more people passed through the barrier. Beyond the rippling light, the girl could see the invaders advancing through the other forces. Both the giants lay on the ground. The gold-sashed fighter then stopped a young boy in passing and handed him his blade. The boy looked at him with pause but accepted the weapon before continuing toward the hallway. Another crash sounded as the roof collapsed and another branch entered the large room. Stones fell as more sap dropped from gleaming cracks in the wood. The child froze as another green figure entered from a portal. Cracking continued to sound, overpowering the screams. More red-clad warriors rose from the portals and headed for the sashed fighters. Stones fell. When the child looked up, her sight was covered in dust before the world went black.

Light returned to Nuyani's sight as she sat in the rubble staring at the young child. The woman's eyes were red. Tears streamed down her face. She breathed heavily as her skin was drenched from a cold sweat. The girl's expression was grimaced as she looked to the ground. Nuyani looked to the child, trying to fathom the pain of the trapped spirit. She diverted her eyes toward the ground as she grew dizzy. The scene played before her was too much. People of different colors, sizes, and beastly parts. Beings even taller than mountains. Strange curses and powers shared by both sides. Her head spun as her body grew hot. Nuyani stomach turned and twisted as she struggled to grasp the spirit's vision. She turned to the side as her stomach heaved. Jerky, nuts, and water fell to the dust as she gagged. Nuyani trembled as the pain rose in

her head. Before she could say anything, she blacked out
and collapsed to the side.

Ch. 15

Weight of Life

Winds whispered to the hunters as they waited on the lower ground. Many of the whip-necks sat on the ground as their riders kept an eye out for any predators. Cuganwa watched as well, seeing nearly a dozen blood-manes fly overhead before leaving toward the mountains.

'So many blood-manes. By his shine, how don't they have the blood-mane symbol?' The boy thought, remembering the emblems engraved into the hilts of their ivory knives.

Cuganwa smirked at the thought until he looked at the ground seeing several ants taking apart a large moth. One of its wings was crushed, keeping the insect grounded and falling prey to the swarm. As the moth beat its remaining wing, a few ants were flung with every flap, only to return later.

"I think we could," someone whispered. The boy then looked back, seeing two hunters conversing.

"A second village? You still think we have the resources or time?" Selsaj asked.

"Why not? The village has grown. Only the training areas don't have huts. Soon we'll grow larger, and moving the gates will take away too much time," Iogda stated.

"All that digging for a second village makes more sense than all the digging it would take to expand what we have?" Selsaj turned with narrowed eyes at Iogda.

Iogda's eyes widened. "If we keep expanding, the huts that are too far out will be exposed to the storms. They'll just be taken away. A second village just makes more sense." His hands flailed about to emphasize his point.

"A wall sounds better than anything else. Why separate? Do you want two chiefs?" Selsaj glared at Iogda.

"No. But why would that be a problem?" Iogda looked at the man, brows pulled tight.

"Same reason there aren't two families in a single hut. No matter how large, they'll fight for space, authority, and resources."

Iogda turned to face Selsaj. "How do you know that? Two villages and two families aren't the same things."

"I've got siblings, and we fight. I've seen families not connected fight. If there are two villages, they will fight. Either for resources or the chief's blade and the elder's rings. There's gotta be something to respect in the other village. People who want to get away from each other will separate, and that's where feuds will get worse. If everyone isn't stuck together to learn to work it out, you just have enemies and sides. A second village won't work."

Iogda stared at Selsaj, silent. "You sure"

"I fought my brother," Selsaj then scratched at his forearm, turning it to Iogda to reveal a long scar going from the middle to his elbow. "Fights can get bad if there isn't a way to work together. Under your glow, I will protect. I will aid my kin."

Cuganwa listened to the senior hunter's words as he turned back to the captured moth. One of the wings was already taken off as the other flapped frantically. He looked at the dark brown circle in the middle of its wings, resembling an eye. The witch then came to the boy's mind making him wonder if she was the same. His father warned the boy never to take a life unless it was a threat but, two men died trying to attack her.

'Is she not a threat now?' the boy wondered. A sudden caw called the boy's attention to the sky. An eager blood-mane circled the area once more.

"Something on your mind, Cuganwa?" Odaru asked.

Before the boy could speak, loud trumpeting rose from the distance. Everyone fell silent as they looked out into the planes. Two whip-necks rode parallel to one another in front of a large adult, heavy-horns charging after them. The rear archers continued to pelt the beast's face with arrows that fell to the floor, unable to pierce its hide. As the hunters continued, the drivers spotted the blue rags on the floor and grew further apart as they led the beast. Cuganwa looked at the hunters' work as his fingers dug into the dirt. His throat grew dry as he watched.

Once the whip-necks passed the markings, the lumbering heavy-horn continued. A thunderous crash and cracking sounded through the area with a distinct trumpet filled with pain instead of rage. Cuganwa's grip tightened as he looked at wallowing clouds of dust, revealing only a hazed silhouette of the animal. Its trumpeting was replaced with whimpering grunts. The other hunters started to move with axes and tarps at the ready.

Cuganwa climbed onto the higher bank as well making his way to the pit. It did not take long for the gentle breeze to carry away the dust, revealing the large red beast stuck within. The boy looked at the mangled animal, trying to remember that it was game like anything else despite its wounds. Its front legs twisted to the side and skewered by the hidden bones acting as spikes. Blood spilled into the dirt. Part of its head stuck out of the other side thanks to its large tusks, only for the left pair to have snapped off, colliding with the pit wall. Its trunk lay limply on the ground. The beast continued to breathe slowly as its large eyes remained half-open, still fighting to live.

"Stay back!" one of Lamoy's hunters commanded. "Until it stops breathing, a flick of its trunk can still send you flying." The hunters watched as its stomach rose and fell with fading strength until it lay still. The hunter then waved to everyone to continue. First were the axes to break through the tough hide as some climbed into the pit to retrieve the fallen tusk. Others placed large water bladders beneath the animal's neck, created new wounds, and collected blood. Cuganwa started thinking back to the ants as he hacked into a layer of muscle around the ribs, blood splattered onto his tunic.

'We collect and hunt together. What hunts us?' the boy wondered as he hacked into the spine of the beast.

They skinned the animal and separated several layers of fat, muscle, and then dozens of ribs. Other hunters took off the heavy-horns legs as others took the trunk. Only an hour or so had passed, and they managed to take most of the animal's remains before burying it to keep the sent of the kill from lingering. Only the blood-manes that witnessed the harvest would stick around to dig up the carcass, biding their time.

"Cuganwa, what's on your mind? You look confused by something," Odaru said.

Cuganwa's brow then furrowed as he looked toward Odaru. "I'm just wondering about the hunts. We take on the other animals in groups but, what hunts us?" Cuganwa asked.

"Hm. You sound like the elders, Little Charge-horn," Odaru stated with a smile. "I don't know. The monsters we have rarely care for us particularly. Maybe the witch."

"I just wonder if she ever really would, or are we just going to attack thinking she would." Odaru furrowed his brow as he looked at the boy. "Deyunca is gone but, he won't be the only one, right?"

The older hunter shrugged his shoulders. "Not likely" Odaru then looked to the ground as he squinted one eye and closed the other. "I think Lord Kelvert has a plan for all of us. It's good to question but, we will know later on. Remember, his light guides us." Odaru looked at Cuganwa with a smile before turning away to pet Muga's neck. The two then waited as the same pair of whip-necks ventured out into the tall grass to lure another heavy-horns.

'Great Lord, why hasn't the witch hunted us? Will that make others still hunt for her?' Cuganwa questioned. As Cuganwa watched the hunters race off into the distance, his thoughts dwelled on the witch's feeling. People have tried to kill her out of fear or anger. 'If I faced that and survived, I think I'd look for revenge. What stops her?'

Ch. 16

Run

Nuyani could feel a strange sense of calm washing over her mind. Her thoughts flooded with sudden visions. The woman's eyes shot open, remembering the chaos that ensued centuries ago. The spirit lay before her, wearing a warm smile. Nuyani sat up. The images of strange people, monsters, and odd powers used even by the defenders of the stone village made her head spin.

"By the Great… How did they travel through the cliffs?" Nuyani wondered. She looked to the spirit. "You've been here for so long." Her eyes began to well. Nuyani held out a hand toward the spirit. The child narrowed her eyes, confused about her reason. Releasing a soft hum, Nuyani's body filled with energy, allowing her to place a hand on her head.

The child's eyes widened and grew red. She launched from her seat, wrapping her small arms around Nuyani's waist and buried her head in her chest. For the first time, the child made a noise, crying as she held on. Nuyani hugged the child to her. Despite her state, the spirit felt as warm as a living being. "What keeps you here? Why haven't you passed?" Nuyani questioned. The child shook her head, still clinging to the runner. "I think I can free you if you'd wish," Nuyani offered.

The girl pulled away, pleading eyes trained on the witch's as the tears ceased. "I can't explain it but, I can free you if you wish. Let you rest," Nuyani said.

She reached out with her hand in offer. The child looked to the woman with an eager stare but stopped. This time, Nuyani furrowed her brow in confusion. The girl then stared and turned to the side behind the runner as if to see something. She followed her gaze finding only the ruins still behind her, and looked back. The spirit was now looking to the ground with a determined look. When she looked up at Nuyani, she seemed saddened, wearing a sense of pain, but smiled before forming into a white wisp and descending into the ground.

Nuyani started rummaging through the rubble and dirt until she found a small ring stone circle she recognized as the child's bracelet. The girl's presence was contained within the item. 'What keeps a spirit lingering in a place like this? Did I offer her something bad?' She wondered before placing the bracelet back on the stone and moving toward the statues. 'Please find some peace, child.'

Nuyani walked away, heading toward the pedestal where only the deities' feet remained. The runner looked back, noting most of the rubble stayed on the right side of the room. The statue sat a good distance away from any stone nearby.

'Do'alm and Do'alc. Were they our gods before lord Kelvert? Are there more?' Nuyani questioned as she moved from the statues and headed toward the tunnel. "Should I still use his name in prayer or the others?" Nuyani whispered. As she passed down the hall, the lingering spirits wailed in her passing as they fell near the remaining blast marks in the stones.

As her hand brushed over the marks accepting the phantom waves of pain, she thought back to the strength that grew in her with every whisper when the howlers first appeared. She remembered each time she ran out into the drylands and thought to stay in wait for a blood-mane or blade-jaw to take her but, something pulled her back to the cave; some strength or source kept the beasts out. Despite everything, it was Kelvert whom she prayed to when wishing for strength, strength that came when she needed it most.

Nuyani looked to the side, seeing another long pool through the pillars as vines and algae claimed the water. She placed a hand on her stomach. 'Should I keep praying to them? Kelvert is a borrowed name?' Her core pulsed steadily as she released the thrum sparsely through the area. Though she wanted to keep her senses sharp, it was hard to focus with the spirits around her.

She strolled down the hall, cautious where she stepped. Her eyes then fell on the pillars, wondering why the hall possessed them. She thought back to the cavern, wondering if it were to keep the air circulating. Nuyani looked forward into the shadowed doorway. Walking through the entrance, she found herself in a dark room with little light passing into her eyes, calling forth the silver outlines. The mortar between the bricks, cracks in the walls, and edges of the doorway all grew distinct in her vision. Nuyani was forced to squint with what light from outside was still visible, grew brighter and painful.

Nuyani sighed. "Every tool has its uses and problems," she said.

She continued looking through the room. There were few stones on the ground, making the area cleaner compared to many of the others she had visited. A back entrance sat on the opposite walls. She looked at the ground and saw several curved pieces. "Is this it?" Nuyani wondered as she marched forward. A pile of the same curved blades sat on the floor. Small silver rings showed in the wall above them. Nuyani picked up one of the items releasing a clang while the point dragged on the floor. The surface of the weapon was covered in dust that Nuyani wiped away. Beneath the dirt, the surface remained reflective, finding no orange, brown, or red spots.

Nuyani smiled as she looked at the weapons. "We can fight them off," Nuyani whispered. She fantasized the image of many villagers swinging the blades at the howlers in defense. Her smile faded as she looked back at the pile. There were at least three dozen weapons on the floor but, even the single one she held still felt a little heavier than her knives. Crossing back over the water would be impossible.

"So close," Nuyani said as she turned the blade over in her hands. She looked at the handle identical to the chief's own weapon. The handle was curved and long enough to fit a single hand. Nuyani found it strange that the weapon still had wood on the handle, expecting it to rot away like other natural portions. She then noticed the outlines of a circle in the hilt's end. As Nuyani released a pulse, she noticed the soft vibrations rising in answer from the circle along with the others.

'What is this?' she wondered, standing and walking toward the back entrance. She saw a smooth, clear jewel embedded in the hilt with a stronger light.

"What?" Nuyani said. Her brow furrowed once more. "This can't be." Her mind trailed back to the chief's weapon, a single encrusted jewel at the end. The chief retrieved the weapon from a stone bracelet. Nuyani then removed the jagged clear crystal from its pouch. Though her stone was rougher and larger than the blade's, it still had the same clouded look to it. She saw through the small stone where wood overlapped the ring stone to shape the handle.

"Do they enter the stones like mine stores food?" Nuyani wondered as she pressed on the small crystal. Silence. The weapon stayed in her hand. None of the shining lights came forth. "Hmm. What else can I do with you?" Her thoughts returned to her chief and to the vision the child shared.

'What…' Nuyani stopped her question as her next pulse rose from her, and the small portion radiating through the stone grew wider and stronger. Nuyani's eyes widened. Keeping her thumb placed on the stone, she willed a single beat to reverberate through her body. The stone's center glowed white. The blade began to twist and pour into the small crystal. The small crystal fell to the ground. 'It's like the crystal but, why can't mine collect anything other than animals?' Nuyani wondered as she retrieved the stone.

The differences between both stones seemed strange. While she required gripping the crystal and directing the light, the smaller one required the strange power. She pushed the questions back for a moment as she repeated the action feeding a pulse into the crystal. Light gleamed from the core, and the blade poured out of the center with the stone fixed into the hilt as it stuck toward the side. Unprepared for its reappearance, the blade fell to the floor, releasing a clang as it hit the earth.

She picked up the blade and stood. Her eyes fell on the polished edge as she saw her eyes show on the smooth surface. Nuyani then repeated several of the slashes she saw in the vision. As she swung the blade about, her brow was furrowed. She could still feel the weight of the spirits lingering in the corridor. The weapons were meant to protect them yet, so many fell. There were far more people there at the time compared to the village.

'If they couldn't defend this place, returning with the village may not be a good idea,' Nuyani realized as she tried to imagine the village guard fighting such monsters. She stopped swinging the weapon and looked at the floor. Her imagination did not conjure a fight but a slaughter. The invaders were strong. Even she began to wonder if any of the villagers would be a match. 'Then we should fight in the village. I don't know if we could return to this place,' Nuyani thought.

She fed a pulse into the stone once more, reducing its size and returning it, and her crystal into the sack. Nuyani turned around only to kick something in the dirt. She recognized the ring stone claws and talon-shaped knife. Her eyes widened as she looked at the weapon. A pulse radiated from her core and into the item. The wave strengthened greatly, reaching nearly three times the initial senses allowed.

"What is this?" Nuyani wondered aloud. She focused her senses through the blade, imagining the odd blue orb the other fighters conjured. The rhythm that radiated from the spirit's memories replayed in the same pattern from her core. The waves rose from her body altogether and formed the orb in the middle of the air. The sapphire lights gleamed in her eyes. Before she could say a single word, a strain rose in her hand as she tried to contain the energy. Her eyes narrowed as she felt the power snap from her body with a strange recoil traversing her core. The blue sphere lit up the dark room and fired as it sailed toward the stone wall. It struck the stone, releasing a loud crack as if the stone was struck with a hammer and light flaring out for a moment. The silver outlines were gone for a moment only to slowly return. "That's it," Nuyani said as she looked at the stone wall. New cracks appeared in the brickwork.

Trembling started to rise in her hand. Nuyani raised the strange knife examining it and her body. A strange prickling rose in her fingers as if blood returned to each digit. The energy returned to her core, stifling the beat and weakening the rising pulses for a moment. Nuyani's mind returned to last night as she managed to create a similar barrier as the fighters to block the howler from fleeing. Her body was wracked with pain and paralysis after each stress of the core.

"It's not hurting. Will it work with the other tricks?" Nuyani wondered as she focused once more on the pulse.

The pulses grew steady once more, rising evenly from her stomach and radiating through her body. Remembering the strength from her muscles, Nuyani willed stronger pulses to radiate. As the waves coursed through her, every muscle grew stronger. Her body felt lighter. She could feel the individual frays in the worn leather resting against her skin and the flowing dust in the air. Yet, her core was not taxed. "How can I do this?" she wondered. Every attempt came to her as second nature, though she was negligent in remembering the pain that often came with the use of the core.

'What else was there?' Nuyani questioned as she remembered the various attacks the fighters launch. Lighting and fire were thrown about like slung stones along with a projectile that looked like blue, white, or clear stones. Some shattered easily colliding with stone as others encased them in a weird, hardened surface. 'A strange world. Let's do something small first,' Nuyani decided.

Raising her hand, she envisioned another light construct. With the others creating them with ease, she wondered how much she may need to work on it. Her core pulsed, releasing a steady stream of energy out toward her hand. Nuyani could feel the energy pool around her limb but not reaching beyond her fingers. Putting more focus on the core, the beats grew deeper as they rose. The energy began to stretch outward, passing her digits.

'A little more,' Nuyani thought as she strengthened the waves.

They reached out almost a foot away. The pulses started to form into a flat surface stopping only of the envisioned shape. A dim blue light rose before as a rectangular construct standing at her height appeared just before her. Nuyani smiled as her grip tightened on the knife. She took a deep breath.

"By his light…" Nuyani started. Her focus broke, and the light construct faded away. "What should I consider? The Great Lord isn't our creator. Is there really any reason to pray to someone else? Do'alm and Do'alc…

I don't know anything about them,' Nuyani concluded. She turned her attention back to her core and attempted the construct once more. With her focus completely on the barrier, the light illuminated the room in its blue glow.

Feeling confident in her ability to wield the barrier, she stopped and looked at the pile of blades lying on the floor. Nuyani placed the weapon on the floor and knelt before the blades. Removing her spare pouch, she took up one of the weapons and collapsed it into the stone. One by one, she filled the pouch with thirty of the weapons.

Scratching then sounded from the hall. Nuyani turned toward the door, wondering if it were just another spirit she had failed to notice. She looked back to the weapons, almost collecting all of them until a constant patter accompanied the scratching. Nuyani looked toward the entrance falling back as a large paw stretched through the doorway. Nuyani released a pulse coursing through the area. The wave collided with an immense pressure resting against her core. The head of a monstrously large blade-jaw poked through the doorway as one of its fangs dragged against the stone floor, leaving a gash in the bricks.

"By the Great Lord!" Nuyani exclaimed as she snatched up the strange knife and scurried through the back entrance.

Crumbling stone sounded behind as she rounded the corner. Her heart leaped as the immediate sounds of scratches against the stone rose at her backside. Nuyani did not wait as she sprinted down the narrow alley. The noise of broken stones signaled the beast was free. Despite her great speed, the patter of the animal's feet grew louder.

'How?' Nuyani wondered as she felt a surge within the pressure. She slid on the ground as claws slashed overhead, scarring the stone.

Her momentum carried her to the end of the wall as she turned the corner with the beast passing by only a few meters. Nuyani swung around as she quickly tied the pouch back onto her tool strap. She fought against the trembling as she looked upon the predator. The blade-jaw stood almost a tall as a whip-neck. Its muscles were tearing through some parts of its skin, showing the red sinew. It growled as it turned to face her. Nuyani could not fight the trembling much longer as she looked into the animal's unblinking, glazed eyes. A large welp the size of her had sat by its shoulder. The flesh grew gray at the base, then gradually into yellow at the top as sickening pus seeped from it. Something was wrong with the beast. Even in hunt, there was a determined glare worn by the animal's, sense of focus. Some signs of life. Yet as it prowled before her, she could only feel as though it were a corpse.

Nuyani raised a hand as she took a step back. The beast launched forth with its maw wide open and claws splayed out. Nuyani dashed to the side out of the animal's reach as it landed. A sense of confidence rose in her as she found her burst of speed quicker than the animal's pounce. Stealing a glance of her surroundings started to diminish that sense of power. The two stood outside the hall with the alignment of pillars. On the opposite side was another long pool. Nuyani sank a little lower in her stance, prepared to dart in any direction. The woman's eyes trailed to the strange blemish as she wondered what infection the beast carried.

The claws slashed at her. Nuyani rose her arms in defense. She conjured a barrier before her as the claws raked against the barrier. Nuyani was pushed back, falling onto her rear but remained protected. Before she could do anything else, the blade-jaw took the initiative and pounced once more. The runner transformed the construct into a dome surrounding her as the claws dug into the light. Waves danced on the construct's surface as if it were water. Nuyani winced, feeling the animal's pressure attempting to pierce her core.

Her face creased further as she called her core to ring forth. The barrier strengthened and expanded, pushing the animal back onto its hind legs. The beast continued to claw at the ethereal defense as it slid away under its expanding radius. Soon the dome stood as tall as the beast pushing it toward the pool. Confidence began to well within her as she pressed on. Her eyes widened when the animal then extended a paw through the barrier, attempting to reach her. The limb stopped at the shoulder and was empty of the repelling energy that flooded through everything.

"What?" she whispered. She fed more power into the construct. It grew larger, backing the animal closer to the pool.

Nuyani stepped forward, moving the dome with her until the infected animal was backed against the small wall. She then conjured a blue sphere and launched the projectiles at the blade-jaw without hesitation. It struck with a loud thwack in the animal's torso. The flesh rippled, showing even its ribs as the beast toppled over the wall and fell into the water with a loud splash. Nuyani did not hesitate as she moved to the wall and reshaped the barrier to fit the entire pool. The beast thrashed about in the water stirring the heavy dirt and algae obscuring her vision of it.

'Just drown. Just drown,' Nuyani thought, waiting for the blade-jaw to give.

Moments passed as she watched the animal continue to thrash about, its fury never tempered. Her breathing grew heavy. The pain and stiffness began to grow in her hands as she held on. She could feel the animal's pressure weakening the rhythm.

"No. H-how?" The creature started pushing against the construct with a paw making the barrier bulge.

Gritting her teeth, Nuyani drew her focus on the wall, demanding it keep its shape. Before her core could respond, the beast broke through the barrier. Shards of the light flew into the air only to fade from sight. Nuyani could still feel them as every piece converted into the ethereal waves and returned to the knife and her core with punishing results. The knife snapped into several pieces absorbing many of the waves, but the few remaining still took their toll. Her hand jittered with pain locking her fingers into claws as her stomach strained and convulsed. The urge to puke rose after the waves struck from the pool wall. The runner fell to her knees, breathing heavily as she watched the blade-jaw emerge from the water drenched the stone.

"How…" Nuyani stuttered. All her thoughts dwelled on the creature's strange behavior. Still alive and moving after sitting in the water for so long.

Worse, she was now hurt, and the knife was destroyed. The pulses rising from her core were erratic and uneven. Her senses were now distorted. Nuyani glared at the creature as she slowly climbed to her feet and backed away.

'You won't take me. None of you demons will have me!,' Nuyani thought as she reached the pillars. Stealing a quick glance, she slipped through the narrow spaces and started down the hall.

Nuyani expected the beast to go around and follow the hall back to her if it cared. She was wrong, then its paw broke through one of the pillars just before reaching the larger room sending new chunks of stone flying. The runner did not wait as she pivoted in place, only for the beast to reach for her, destroying another pillar. A small piece of the debris struck her leg with enough force to offset her running. Nuyani collapsed for a moment as the blade-jaw broke some of the pillars sitting in between, Nuyani tried to release another beat. Pain racked her body as she trembled, nearly forced to sit still.

'What are you doing here? Did you follow me?' Nuyani wanted to ask. If every animal stayed in a special terrain, what was a blade-jaw doing in the abandoned village of stone. Nuyani began to wonder if this was her last moment as its shadow grew larger, blocking out what little light came into the hall.

The flow of the hall changed, growing rapidly, catching the woman's attention. Their flow was uniformed and swirled through the area washing over her core like a tide but, Nuyani remained conscious. The shadow of the beast showed the animal having a fit. Nuyani looked to the side, finding the spirits swirling around the animal's head.

"What?" She then looked back toward the great room entrance as a man wearing a bloodied tunic, with one golden sash over their shoulder and a golden rope around his waist, flew toward her. "Kelvert?"

Before she could utter another word, the energy of the spirit pierced through her core. Nuyani felt as if she were cast in a wave as she blacked out for a moment. Her sight returned only for her to see herself pushing through the other pillars and into a clear area. Despite seeing herself in flight, she was not in control.

"How is this happening?" Nuyani questioned, her heart thrumming.

"Fool! So naïve. You were strong enough," a man's voice echoed in her mind.

"Wait! Are you Kelvert?" Nuyani questioned as she felt the strange flow of energy coursing within her being. A strange chill covered her as the flow stay separate from her senses.

"Never return! This is but a grave." Nuyani watched as her body leaped over another pool and squeezed through the pillars. The sound of collapsing stone resonated behind her. The beast must be pursuing her still. She wanted to turn and see just how close the creature was to capture her. "Never return!" The spirit's voice was stern and commanding. Another set of crashes sounded behind her.

"At least let me control my own body," Nuyani protested. The spirit said nothing as he continued to lead her through another hall.

'Where are we go…' Nuyani found her answer as they came to another hall. The rising pressure of the other spirits sat on her core. Made aware of her core, Nuyani felt as though she could release a single ring and expel the spirit but, she did not. Even the dead were trying to keep her alive.

As they cleared another hall, crashing stones scattered across the floor as the blade-jaw went through the opening made by the fallen structure. The beast panted as excess water poured from its mouth. The spirit in control had her leap to the other side of the pool before looking back. Kelvert then sent several small energy streams rushing toward the core from within. Pulses rang forth in a strange pattern. Nuyani watched as her commandeered body whipped around and rose her hand. The pulses range forth, crossing into the water as a sudden spout rose. The water then hardened into a shape like a spear.

'The attacks,' Nuyani thought, remembering the strange objects all the fighters would use.

The clear spear turned in the air toward the beast and launched like an arrow. The blade-jaw proved to be quicker as it ducked the projectile, which collided with one of the bricks knocking it free of the curved wall. The spirit then turned toward a bit more as the beast bound over the water and conjured a single wall of blue light, sending it forward. The construct collided with the beast midair, causing it to fall into the water.

"Wasteful, fool," the spirit complained as it led her through the pillars and down the hall.

'Wasteful?' Nuyani questioned as she tried to ignore the tightening feeling her stomach. 'Is he complaining about my energy?' She did not dwell on the meaning long as another crash rang through. The passing spirits were gone. Making Nuyani wonder what became of them.

As they ran through the area and crossed the room she first entered, Nuyani felt her control return as the spirit poured from the core. Nearly falling as she staggered a few steps. Nuyani whipped her head, catching a glimpse of the proud fighter before her body dissipated like smoke.

'Thank you,' Nuyani thought.

She continued running up the hill, passing the abandoned stones huts. The loud crash of shattered stone rang from the entrance. Nuyani made it several meters past the homes running into the tree. A second crash then rang, followed by a sudden roar. As the beast's lament reached her ears, her core froze. Cold wrapped around her body, forcing her to fall limp on the ground as her conscience faded.

"Move," her voice echoed, waking her from the sudden stupor. The core rang, breaking through the freeze and dispelling the chill.

Nuyani turned to find the beast looming over her, its maw widened, revealing its teeth. Nuyani held out her hands in defense. A pulse rose from the core, conjuring another barrier between her and the beast. She strained to keep the animal at bay, realizing its greater strength.

She channeled more pulses into her body, strengthening the muscles. It did little to keep the beast away.

Nuyani thought about rolling to the side but knew that would only leave her turned over for the beast to claw at her. She then imagined firing another ball of energy at the beast to take its attention away. Yet, the use of two tricks simultaneously seemed difficult, and her arms were already straining from the animal's weight. The flow of life shifted within the creature, leaving its mouth. As its snout passed through the barrier, Nuyani rolled to the side with what space remained. The beast snapped up several clumps of sand. Making her choice, she released the barrier only to conjure a ball of the orange light within her palm and launched it at the blade-jaw's eyes. It struck with a loud thwack but did little to force the beast back. Nuyani tried to stand. She raised her arms once more and conjured another barrier in reflex as the blade-jaw batted her back to the ground.

She looked at the beast as it took a second attempt to bite at her. Before its head could descend, the flow of spirits swelled in the area. The girl appeared beside the animal and released a shriek as loud and chilling as the howlers. Nuyani's vision grew hazed as she looked at her. Her face was elongated as her chin reached down to her collar. Her eyes shrank to the horrid glints of light amongst a void. Her youthful face was now shriveled with drastic wrinkles.

'No. Are…you turning into one of those things?' Nuyani thought as her fading conscience returned.

"Go!" the child yelled.

As her vision cleared, she could see the spirits encircled the animals once more. It started to grow frantic. Nuyani crawled away from the creature before she was crushed. The animal snapped and clawed at the spirits doing little against them. She looked at the girl finding her face returning to normal, though one of her eyes still looked hollow. She smiled at Nuyani. The woman frowned, knowing she was leaving more spirits to linger, ones she wanted to help but could not.

A fiercer surge of energy rose from the beast's presence. Nuyani's core acted on its own, sending powerful beats echoing through her body. The frigid hold was lessened. Her conscience waned, yet she remained aware. Nuyani fought the gripping confusion as she continued up the hill focusing on her core's strength to enforce her constitution.

Running into the molded ravine, the divots added to her anguish understanding the dangers they fled. The monsters were larger than the buildings people lived in. Beings with the powers to command the clouds, lightning and wind were taken down by a man-shaped tree. There was reason to flee.

The patter of the blade-jaw gaining on her echoed in the ravine. Nuyani ran harder, refusing to look back in fear that the creature would take her. Faster and faster, she pushed herself as the rapids grew louder up ahead. Nuyani felt the pressure grow against her core, signaling that the beast was gaining on her. She glared, seeing the frothing water up ahead. Nuyani angled her approach closer to the wall as she dropped into a slide. The blade-jaw reached out for her as its claws extended further than ever. The animal cut through the leather runner's wear around her hip with a wide swipe, making her shriek in pain. The beast's claw then snagged on one of the pouches as momentum carried the beast toward the whirlpool.

Nuyani looked back in horror as the twine was severed and fell to the floor. She tried to reach for it as it fell on the steeper portion of the stone. As she fell to the ground, it rolled into the rapids. Tears rolled down her cheek. However, time was not on her side as the beast clung desperately to the stone side. Its gaze was still fixed on her.

"By the Great Lord, why?" Nuyani wondered as she stood on the narrow path.

The beast did not bother to climb out, but commit to its daring cling to the side, making its way toward her. Nuyani retreated, running down the path that forced her to move slowly or fall into the water as well. Cursing her blunder, she wondered if she should. Making her way toward the sandy bank. Nuyani started in a full sprint. The blade-jaw was not far behind. Its low growl reverberated against the stone walls as they traveled. Thanks to the winding turns of the ravine, Nuyani kept some distance between her and her pursuer.

'What now?' Nuyani wondered. 'How is there an animal faster than me?' Her mind returned to the larger charge-horn with what seemed to be the same plague. 'A sickness that makes you stronger. No. That's not it.' Nuyani continued to release softer pulses to search the area. As the waves washed over the beast, the pressure sitting on her core seemed strange. It did not contain one but several beads of pressure clustered together, flowing in unison. 'How is that possible?' Nuyani thought of the creature being pregnant but, she had her doubts. 'No, what animal looks for danger if it had a litter?' Some of the beads of pressure shifted and turned within her senses. Thought keeping the same flow, they did not move in the same direction. Her mind returned to the strange yellow blemish on the animal's shoulder. 'What is that disease?'

Her thoughts ceased as she reached the first waterfall. Nuyani darted through the brush and flowers and dived into the algae-covered water. Another splash sound beneath the water signaling that the blade-jaw continued the pursuit. 'It can swim?' Nuyani questioned, seeing how the only available waters contained river bites. There was no way for the beast to become well-practiced on its own. Nuyani swam on, passing the bank, knowing the beast was faster on land. As she allowed the current to carry her away, she could feel her strength fading forcing her to rely on the core.

The water grew faster as she was carried off. Nuyani released several pulses, noting the beast's location and the lack of life around her. Nuyani looked about, seeing the cliff shelves coming into view.

'Those large lizards…' Nuyani remembered as she pulled for the water skin containing the bulbs. To her surprise, none of the yellow fruit had burst. She pulled one free and took out her knife. Stabbing into the bulb beneath the water, the powder burst, spreading as the current washed it away. A flare of pressure rose and dispersed before her, confusing her momentarily.

She then caught sight of a large lizard floating to the water surface, twitching as it went belly up and floated away. Several others fell victim to the cloud while others swam quickly to the river's edges. Nuyani did not wait as she swam on, feeling the looming presence of the blade-jaw growing stronger. Nuyani made her desperate swim to the cliff wall noticing the small ledge she could reach. Reaching for the ledge, she climbed out of the water. Bringing up her feet, she pushed against the wall reaching for the next ledge, and climbed up, finding more space to stand.

Grading claws called her attention. She looked down to find the blade-jaw descending into the water as its slash chipped at the wall. Nuyani started moving down the ledge toward the cliffs. There was little she could do in such a small space. The animal then leaped up and clawed at the wall anchoring to the stone for a moment. Nuyani reached up for a taller ledge as she raised her feet and climbed out of the path of a wild swipe. The beast fell back into the water.

Nuyani breathed heavily as the blade-jaw paddled in the water, waiting for another chance to attack her. Her nerves shook as she looked into the glazed eyes of the animal. Life swirled in its body but, she was certain it was not living. The river itself then opened to a bright pink maw filled with teeth clamping down on the blade-jaw's left foreleg. A smile almost rose on her face thinking the beast would do battle with the large lizard clinging to the limb. Blood darkened the water showing the beast still bled. Another of the lizards appeared, biting at the beast's torso. Flesh was torn from the creature, yet the beast trained its eyes on her.

"Great Lord, what are you?" Nuyani questioned as she lowered her feet.

The beast attempted to climb once more, ignoring its wounds. To her luck, the lizards weighed down the beast keeping her feet out of reach. Nuyani glared as she retrieved another of the yellow fruit. Raising her hand, she threw the yellow bulb down with enough force to make it pop. It struck the blade-jaw square on its snout as the powder scattered over its body and part of the water. The creature's wet fur and flaring nose were caked in the powder. Nuyani watched the creature waiting for it to convulse and grow rigid, left at the mercy of the other predators. Her heart sunk as she watched the animal continue to swim. Her mind returned to the pool as the bubbles stopped rising, and the blade-jaw continued to move.

She continued down the ledge, moving hastily, nearly slipping twice. More of the river lizards started to attack the blade-jaw but did little to stall the monster. Her heart raced, shaking her body as her fingers fumbled on the ledge. She pressed her thoughts, looking for a solution, yet none came to mind. The creature was faster than her. It was unyielding in its pursuit. Worse, it carried some form of infection she worried would take over the drylands if not ended. All she knew was that the creature needed to die, and soon.

The presence of the creature surged, pressing on Nuyani's core. She braced herself, releasing stronger rapid vibrations as she clung to the ledge with a tight grip expecting it to roar again. As the surge of collected energy seemed ready to burst, it settled. Splashing and snarling replaced the lament. Nuyani looked back, finding the blade-jaw covered in bites and surrounded by the bodies of several lizards with claw marks carved through them.

'Why's it reacting now?' Nuyani questioned. Seeing this as her best chance to reach the wider ground, she moved on.

As her ears were filled with the roar of the rapids, Nuyani reached the top of the pillars. She looked for a narrow section to squeeze through in the cluster of hoodoos for easier descent and safety from the animal's reach. Reaching a solid footing, Nuyani found herself on the lower cliff, looking about, curious if it was the same blade-jaw that had faded. As she reached the middle of the cliff's wide space, the pressure then rose drastically.

Nuyani darted to the side as a heavy, gargled roar sounded beside her. The ground shook from a heavy thud. She looked back, seeing the mangled beast riddled with torn flesh as coagulated blood dripped to the ground along with water dripping from its thin coat. Nuyani looked toward the animal's neck seeing a large flap of muscle and sinew dangling. Despite its dead eyes, the beast started to growl as it lowered its body.

'What's wrong?' Nuyani wondered as she looked at the creature.

The animal strolled forth. Nuyani's core remained vibrant, prepared for an attack. Looking to its neck, Nuyani wondered if the light constructs could cut decapitate the beast. Releasing a pulse, she reached toward the animal, imagining the wall appearing at the animal's neck. The ethereal waves radiated toward the space. As if wielding the same sense, the blade-jaw ducked and moved to the side, dodging a wide circular construct of orange light.

'Can it sense things too?' Nuyani wondered as she retracted her hand, willing the construct to return to her.

The blade-jaw lunged for her with a downward swipe. Nuyani backed away to the side, dodging the heavy blow. She spun around. She conjured another wall of light as tall as her but fused to the ground on her other side. Another swipe came from the side and collided with the barrier. Cracks appeared in the earth and on the surface of the light wall's center.

Nuyani's vision doubled before releasing the barrier and ran further from the animal's claws. It tried several times to clamp down on her with both paws, and she barely dodged each of them. She tried to conjure another barrier only for the pulse recoil striking back at the core. Pain radiated through her stomach and canceled out the hum, strengthening her to move. Nuyani fell to one knee as the beast nearly bit her head. Drops from the wet fur tapped the back of her hood as she felt the warm breath envelop her head. Nuyani winced as she tried to stand, her vision returning.

'Fast! What now?' Nuyani wondered.

Her muscles started to ache as she moved about. Her hands trembled. Her wet runner's wear grew constricting. Her breathing grew laboring. Nuyani stared down the blade-jaw and raised her hand as she released a single pulse filling another orb of orange light. Its bright core rivaled a raging fire. The orb sailed forth, striking the animal in its snout. The orb burst exploding the unseen waves through the area. The beast's head went low as its limbs gave, and it fell to the ground. The energy within its body slashed about with a chaotic flow. Nuyani could sense the cluster of pressures coming apart.

'What is in you?' Nuyani questioned as she remembered trying to cut the beast's head off.

She raised her hands, trying to envision the wall of light once more, only for the waves of her previous attack to return, striking the core. Her stomach twisted and clenched, bringing anguish. Nuyani collapsed to the floor, grunting as she tried to power through. Her eyes watered as she tried to watch the beast. The blade-jaw rose, its flow of energy returning to normal. She started to tremble as dead eyes focused on her.

A roar filled the area. Nuyani could feel another pressure sitting on her erratic core. She struggled to turn toward the source finding another blade-jaw leaping from the cliff and flying toward the larger blade-jaw. Snarling and scratching sounded as Nuyani tried to sit up.

'It must be the other male,' she concluded. Most animals avoided battle unless for territory. 'I have to…kill it.'

Nuyani then fumbled with one of her pouches, remembering the last blade she kept with her crystal. The large blade-jaw batted away its smaller foe as it tried to turn toward Nuyani. The runner gawked at the animal as she struggled to retrieve the weapon. Undeterred, the small beast returned and leaped onto the animal's neck. The infected blade-jaw reacted immediately to the attack shaking and jumping about. Nuyani retrieved her weapon and released a small pulse into the crystal. The blade poured from the weapon. She took up the weapon, prepared to engage the animal despite her core.

Nuyani raised a hand to her stomach, noticing the erratic waves were growing steadily. Testing the core, she released an irregular pulse. The wave managed to reach the weapon and corrected itself as it echoed out into the area.

'Good,' Nuyani thought as she ran forward.

The smaller blade-jaw seemed to have experience as it stayed beneath the larger beast. Ever cautious, the beast stood on its hind legs, attempting to find and pounce. Nuyani readied her core, releasing another pulse coursing through the weapon. An orb, the size of her head, hung in the air at the tip of the blade. Nuyani felt the orb pluck free of her control and fly toward the animal. Struck in the head, the blade-jaw nearly fell into the water but stayed upright. The witch then aimed for the ground before the animal's feet, tripping the beast. The smaller blade-jaw bound onto the beast's back and started slashing into it, sending blood spurts onto the ground.

'Right,' Nuyani thought as she readied to send another barrier. The infected animal shot up from the ground, nearly bucking the smaller blade-jaw away as it swung at Nuyani. With the blade in hand, Nuyani could feel a ghostly call leading her movements as he raised her blade hand over her head and aligned the blade with the side of her body, and stepped back. Two of the long claws were severed as they met the weapon's edge. The pieces fell to the floor as gouts of blood fired out. The blade-jaw ignored the injury as it continued to swipe at her with the next paw. She stepped to the left, dodging the descending claws. Nuyani followed with a slash into its front ankle, bringing more blood but doing little to stop the beast.

The beast went for a bite. Nuyani fought the urge to backtrack and created another orb straining her unstable core within its mouth just before its teeth could close on her. The conjured sphere resisted the teeth. Gashes in the teeth and gums rose. Blood spilled to the floor. Nuyani grunted as she tried to keep the animal at bay. She could feel her arms strain, despite the blade stabilizing her core.

Nuyani ducked and rolled away as the teeth clamped shut. Two of the smaller teeth shattered under the beast's force. Like the rest of its wounds, it went unnoticed. The animal then leaped once more, trying to pounce down on the witch but reeled back as it turned to the returning blade-jaw lunging for the creature's neck.

Nuyani pointed the blade toward the ground beside the infected animal. Half the height of the beast, a barrier rose from the ground blocking the animal from retreating. The smaller blade-jaw jumped onto the animal's neck once more, sinking fang and claw into its flesh. The large beast jostled, throwing its smaller foe off. As the animal descended to the ground, the larger blade-jaw spun its paw around swiped at the blade-jaw knocking it toward the river. Nuyani readied herself, expecting the beast to turn for her again.

She gawked at the beast. It turned toward the smaller predator and started after it. Seeing her chance, she attempted to conjure another barrier aiming for its neck. Her face creased as her hand shook. Even with the blade, she could not release another pulse.

'Everything has a limit,' Nuyani thought, watching the larger blade-jaw swipe at its smaller foe, having little luck as it darted around its flank and slashed at its sides. The infected beast was forced to circle constantly protective of its neck. The larger animal then backed into one of the pillars shaking several of them and the one free and leaning against the other pillars. Nuyani looked at the stone columns realizing her options were limited. The witch darted toward the columns as the beasts continued their brawl. Nuyani squeezed through the pillars making her way toward the loosened column. She climbed up a pair of pillars standing on the perimeter of the cluster.

Nuyani pressed her feet against a pillar and propped her back against the other.

Nuyani took a deep breath and released a pulse of her core. The pulses radiated through her body, strengthening her muscles as she grunted, pushing against the pillar. As the animals continued to fight, a crack sounded at the base of the pillars. Small stones scattered along the ground and the pillar started to tilt.

'Just a bit more,' Nuyani thought as a final shove cracked the rest of the stone.

The larger blade-jaw circled with its back to the river. Both it and the smaller beast were preoccupied with each other. Nuyani desperately wrapped her arms and legs backward, clinging to the rear pillar as the other toppled over. The column landed onto the infected blade-jaw as a deafening thud roared through the area. A tremor shook the entire area threatening the other pillars to fall as dust covered the area. The other blade-jaw ran through the dust that obscured Nuyani's sight as the sound of shredding and growling broke the silence.

A smile rose on the runner's face. 'It worked!' she then dropped into the cloud of dust, confident she could land safely from the height.

"Aagh!" she yelled. Nuyani's foot twisted as she landed on a hidden stone.

Nuyani fell back, leaning against the pillar. Pain radiated through her leg. She held her foot and looked at the animals, wondering if they would turn on her. To her relief, the smaller blade-jaw seemed more concerned at ending the infected monster.

'By the Great Lord, this was a close one,' Nuyani thought as she looked to the ledge.

It was time to leave. She released a pulse, strengthening her ankle. The pain barely leaving, Nuyani pressed on. She released a pulse, caution still warning her. Nuyani froze. The pressures remained on her core—both the beast and the smaller beads within it. Nuyani's heart raced. Stones rumbled and tapped behind her. Instincts flared in her mind as she ran toward the ledge.

'Something needs to kill it. By Lord Kelvert's will, it must die. How?' she wondered as she descended the cliffside.

Nuyani ran on as the lone pressure she recognized as the small blade-jaw sailed overhead heading toward the west. Before Nuyani could turn, she felt the returning cluster of pressure weigh against her core. The heavier patter of the beast's feet sounded behind her.

The pain faded. Nuyani ran parallel to the river as the winds rose. The sun sat lower as an orange tint overtook the bright blue.

Nuyani panted as sweat fell. Her legs threatened to give as she ran on, forcing her body to keep moving. Dust clouds rose in her footsteps as tall as her. Her mind blared, 'How?'

Ch. 17

Demon of the Drylands

The caravan made its way along the river. The hunters were elated with a successful hunt, and their sleds were filled with game. Even Bo'ede's men were at ease. Cuganwa, however, looked down at the ground as he clutched his stomach. It felt as though someone was stabbing into his gut. He tried to resist the pain as shallow groans rose from him.

'Great Lord, what is this?' the boy wondered as he leaned over.

Odaru then turned around with a confused look on his face. "Cuganwa, are you all right?" The boy smiled and nodded his head profusely. "Don't lie, Cuganwa. Are you all right?"

"My, my stomach…" he groaned.

Odaru raised his chin. "What did you eat?"

"Ju-ust the jerky and figs," Cuganwa moaned.

"Hmm. Well, that's not good," Odaru said. "Keep your head up or you'll fall over."

Another hunter took notice. "Aye, Little Charge-horn. Are you sick?"

"Stomach's hurting a little," he grunted.

The hunter smirked before reaching into one of his pouches on his tool strap. He then presented a small leather roll fastened closed by twine. He then presented the leather making sure he took notice of the item. Cuganwa looked the man in the eye before the hunter tossed the bound leather to him. Cuganwa struggled to reach out as the pain continued but, he managed to catch it. He unraveled the leather finding dried herb mulch pressed into small nuggets rolling about.

"Chew one and drink some water. It should numb the pain a bit before we reach the village. Just hold out until the elders can see you," the hunter instructed.

Cuganwa did as he was told taking a moment to chew the herb before downing it with water. The pain subsided a few moments later. The boy took a few breaths before he nodded to the other hunter, rebound the herbs, and threw the leather back.

"Better?" the hunter asked.

"A little," the boy said as the pain dulled. "Still there but, I'm fine." The hunter nodded before leading his whip-neck further along.

"Don't worry, Cuganwa. Elder Belractu will see you when we get back. Odd to see you hurt. Did you clean your water skin?" Odaru then asked.

"Yes," the boy answered as he placed a hand on his stomach. He could feel the pain still as his stomach

221

seemed to radiate. 'What is this? I didn't have anything different than usual,' Cuganwa thought. He then remembered the fermented drink he pilfered from the older hunter out of curiosity. 'No, it's been too long,' the boy thought. Some of the other hunters looked at the boy with strange glances. A few of the whispers within earshot mentioned the witch striking him in the stomach. He looked to the others wondering why they were bringing her up. 'They think I'm cursed,' the boy realized as his stomach started to worsen.

"Odaru, your partner is not looking too well," another hunter called.

The older hunter looked back. "Drink some more water, Cuganwa. Try to relax," Odaru instructed.

The boy retrieved his water skin and tried to down some more water. His teeth were clenched tight as his stomach twisted. Pain racked his mind as his grip loosened, nearly dropping the bladder. A strange soundless hum rose from it as the stabbing feeling worsened, pressing into his front before shifting to the side and back. 'What i-is this,' Cuganwa wondered as sweat rose from his brow. He looked down, trying to ease the pain.

The boy then looked up, staring past the heads of several hunters into the northern distance. An oversized silhouette shifted as it steadily grew larger. The driving hunter behind Muga noticed the boy's attention was trained on something else. He looked back, narrowing his eyes to the distance as something approached.

The man's eyes widened as he shouted, "Something's coming from the north!" He began to wave his hand and bow, calling one of the free-riders. Two free-riders approached. One tore off the front to speak with the hunting leaders as the other turned to the back. Cuganwa struggled to keep his head up. It was dangerous to stay still without a real reason. Yet, he felt there would be one coming.

"It's the witch!" came the call from the rear. The others shouted the words as rear archers readied their bows. The caravan continued to move. Cuganwa's attention returned to the pain rising in his stomach, his body shaking.

"Halt!" Came a bellow from the front. Sutama looked to the rear with Bo'ede and Lamoy, turning their mounts to face the approaching figures.

Nuyani raced on, leaping from one side of the river to the other as she conjured small shields to trip the infected blade-jaw. Despite slashes and bites in the mangled beast, it still pursued her. The creature bound over every construct she made, showing no sign of fatigue, unlike Nuyani. Several times, the animal nearly pounced on her. Her vision grew hazed. As she looked at the glistening water as a sign to jump.

'By the Great Lord, just fall. Fall in," Nuyani prayed as she leaped once more, conjured a barrier once more. The beast leaping further than the defense once more. Several pressures rose on the front of her core. Nuyani looked up and blinked several times to clear the haze. Shock covered her face as she saw the caravan of hunters. "Whuh?" is all she could say in exhaustion. 'Why are they out here? The storm will be here any day,' Nuyani thought.

Her mind was split. Bounding over the river repeatedly kept the creature from catching her but, now more lives were at stake. Nuyani grimaced as her grip on the blade tightened. 'The other branch of the river. By the Great Lord, I will lead it there,' Nuyani thought.

The hunters were god smacked by the event. The witch appeared to them carrying another blade, and closed behind was a large blade-jaw that kept up with her. Sutama looked on, his eyes bulging from his head. 'Lord Kelvert, why?' the man thought as he kept his stern demeanor. The hunting leader then removed his bow and readied an arrow as he ordered, "Fire on it."

"On her? Your daughter?" Bo'ede challenged as he grew a stern glare.

"Fire on it!" Sutama glared at the hunter. The others began immediately. "If that demon can make her flee, then what can we do if it turns on us?"

Aim true!" Lamoy added as she loosed an arrow. Bo'ede nodded his head, following suit.

Nuyani gasped for air, feeling her lungs burn from the heat. The animal's straining presence weighed on her, making every breath more labor-intensive. Her body screamed for her to stop. Even her core seemed to tear apart as she continued to use the small gem to steady every pulse. She could only manage to reinforce her strength as she traversed the drylands. This time, her reckless race through the drylands was all she could manage as she crashed through the bushes. A thud sounded beside her. A shiver traveled through the woman's body as she recognized the sounds.

"Arrows," she whispered as the world slowed, her heart raced.

The first missed them both, but the next hundred rained on the area hitting the witch's back, head, and legs with painful taps. Nuyani nearly tripped as her thoughts turned to the cut through her runner's gear. Managing some concentration in the hail of arrows, she conjured a barrier behind her back as the arrows tapped against the ethereal surface, making the image of rain appear in her mind. Tears fell from her eyes, and the shivering started to weaken her run. Behind her, the looming beast was riddled with arrows. Its back resembled more of a patch of stiff grass. It took on more arrows sinking into the flesh and weighing the beast down with its larger size.

The pain grew stronger and unbearable as Cuganwa had both hands pressed onto his stomach, fingers curled as though he were ready to claw the pressure out. The stabbing sensation shifted to his side yet remained deep within him at the center. 'Lord Kelvert, I beg you, please stop this pain,' the boy prayed. His anguish took over sight and sound as he swayed back and forth in the saddle seat, trying to find some comfort.

"Release," the boy's voice echoed in his mind clearer than any other sound. Before he could question if it were his own thoughts or a hallucination, a strange sense burst from his stomach, washing away the stabbing sensation. Cuganwa leaned over, dazed as his fading strength kept him from falling. The boy could feel the grains carried in the wind, the pressures of countless creatures resting on something within his stomach like dewdrops. One other was heavier as if it were a pebble. The sudden feelings twisted his stomach in knots, and Cuganwa began to heave.

Unable to resist, he spewed onto the dirt before blacking out. Without any control, the boy's weight carried him onto the packing portion of their saddle before he slid off and fell to the dirt. Odaru caught a glance at the child as he fell.

"Cuganwa!" the hunter called out. He quickly slapped twice on Muga's neck, catching the animal's attention. "Look," the man ordered. With her long flexible neck, her head slithered to the side to follow Odaru's direction. The animal let out two groans, signaling for a body. "Protect!" Odaru ordered. Muga continued to watch Cuganwa as she backed up standing over him, something

226

other whip-necks did with their young if stampedes or predators were nearby. "Hang on, Cuganwa, Lord Kelvert is at work," the hunter whispered as he measured his draw, angled, and fired, imagining the arrow to skewer the beast.

Nuyani ran on, fighting the tremors hindering her movements. She fought on growing confident as the barrier held the projectiles at bay. 'You're blocking them,' Nuyani repeated. Her speed returned. Slowly the pressures of the hunters faded as a sense of relief strengthened her resolve. A thrum then rang through the area, shaking Nuyani's core. 'What was that?' Nuyani thought. Her senses were fine. More than fine. Her core felt like it was tearing apart, but the sudden wave eased its stress a little.

The blade-jaw also felt the sudden wave and stopped in its tracks. It growled as it looked back toward the caravan. Nuyani stopped as she felt the animal's pressure lessen. Looking back, she did not see the beast. Stopping completely, she turned back to the east, watching as it raced for the hunters.

"No!" Nuyani said as she dashed toward the group. Murderers, cheats, ungrateful. All the words she described the villagers, the hunters, no longer mattered. Their lives were in danger.

"It's coming this way!" the furthest hunter lamented.

"Cut the lines to your sleds! Keep firing and ready the whip-necks!" Sutama bellowed.

The hunters did as they were told, severing the lines to their loads before spacing out. The whip-necks took wide stances as their heads rose to the sky and crashed down on the ground in a chorus rumbling the ground. The blade-jaw ran toward the middle.

Nuyani kept her barrier up, running toward the group as every missed arrow sailed toward her. Pulses radiated from the caravan, reaching her core and steadying each pulse in tandem. Nuyani took notice, but pushed her questions away as the beast grew near. Now the roles were reversed as she sped along, catching up to the blade-jaw.

"Move!" came a call from one of the hunters.

All the whip-necks in the animal's direction cleared to the sides as the hunters continued to fire except for one. Muga continued slamming her head on the ground, attempting to intimidate the beast as Odaru fired in the heat of the moment. They could not turn idly away from the threat. Odaru cursed himself for not using Muga to pick up the child, bringing him back onto the saddle.

Nuyani saw the lone blade-jaw and a body lying on the floor with steady pulses like a heartbeat ringing from them. Pushing herself further, Nuyani ran faster, nearing the beast. Before the beast could attack, the witch pushed her barrier forward and underneath the animal's hind legs. Taken off balance, the blade-jaw flailed before it went into a roll, losing many of the arrows embedded in its back and legs.

Odaru took the reins in hand and kicked Muga's side leading her away. The whip-neck bit into Cuganwa's clothing, dragging him away until they were safely out of the tumbling beast's direct path. Teetering on the edge of the riverbank, the animal scrambled to hold steady. Nuyani strained as her arms and legs screamed for relief. Her core beat on with every strike, feeling like the ethereal drum was tearing itself apart.

The others watched dumbfounded by the scene before them. Stillness gripped their senses as they looked on. Sutama looked at Nuyani, wondering where the blade had come from. His eyes then trailed back to the beast as the strange layer of light formed around its mangled body. Torn chunks of flesh dangled about. Blood dripped from the ghastly wounds in strange thick blobs as they landed in the dirt with soft plops. The hunter's eyes trailed to the blade-jaw's face, seeing the same dead glazed eyes similar to the charge-horn before. Then, he turned to the yellow and gray blemish dangling about on the creature's shoulder as yellow pus seeped from the arrow holes. His breathing grew heavy as his mind struggled to process the event.

'Fall. Fall,' Nuyani thought as she groaned. The beast struggled to stay on balance, shifting to face her instead. But, Nuyani willed the blade to pour energy from its torso up to its chin, keeping the beast in place as it rose on its hind legs exposing its belly. 'Great Lord willing, pleased give me strength for this demon.'

In the blade-jaw's struggle, its leg gave way, slipping off the edge as several rocks and stones fell into the water. Spurred by the sudden development, Nuyani tried harder. Both arms quivered. Then, a thud sounded as an arrow sank into the beast's other leg. Nuyani turned in the direction of the arrows, finding Odaru readying another arrow to fire into the beast. She looked about, seeing the other hunters watching her struggle.

Anger flared in her chest. Her brow creased, blinding her from the pain. "Why are you here! Run!" Nuyani lamented. Her voice boomed more powerful than anyone would expect.

The hunters broke from their stupor. Glares rose in their eyes and they readied their arrows. Nuyani was bewildered as she looked to them, expecting them to fire on her. The sound of the next string pluck made the witch flinch only to find a second arrow fired into the beast's leg.

"Whuh?" she whispered as a chorus of thuds sounded collecting on its limb. Nuyani returned her attention to the animal, refusing to let it right itself. "They're...helping me?"

The beast flailed as it stood on its remaining leg. Its torso arched forward, giving it some balance against her construct. 'Almost,' Nuyani told herself as she watched the remaining ground crumble beanth its foot. Seeing her chance as the arrows continued to fire on the animal's body, Nuyani tried to conjure another barrier against its limb. A small area of orange light shined against the flesh and arrows. Nuyani closed her eyes and tried to force a faster tempo from the ethereal drum. As the wave coursed toward the area, she felt her strength wane. The second barrier fluctuated from the size of her hand to the size of her head. 'No. Just a bit more,' she thought, knowing the beast was close to falling in.

Yet, the pressure of the beast started to change. She could feel the concentrated presence surge and shift. The low growl of the beast reached her ears. Nuyani's eyes shot wide open as one last desperate push only sent her stepping back. The animal then roared as the life energy burst from its body, washing over everyone. Nuyani could feel the wave of power drown her conscience and stifle her core. The pulses stopped. The barrier disappeared. Each hunter, and their steeds, either fell over unconscious or grew lethargic. Nuyani was forced to kneel as her eyes fluttered. Her core resisted the encroaching cold keeping her conscience.

'By the Great Lord...' Nuyani thought. The ground shook as the animal returned to stable ground. 'What can I do?' She looked on, seeing the beast turning away from her.

Her body moved as her heart slammed in her chest. The beast turned to the boy taking a few weakened steps in the process. Nuyani darted for the animal's neck as its jaws widened. She attempted to cleave the animal's head free with a downward slash. The beast leaned away, dodging the cleave by inches before raising a paw and batting Nuyani away. The woman fell to the ground in anguish yet, held onto her blade.

'My boy…' Sutama thought. The hunter lay in the dirt rolled onto his side a few meters away from his unconscious whip-neck. His body awoke as he saw the looming beast approach Cuganwa. 'No, Great Lord. No…' he whispered. Sutama struggled to stand as he saw the witch back on her feet and going for a second attack.

With so much strain, the core's pulses were uneven, half receding backward and disrupting her internal rhythm. Even her borrowed strength started to wane as the pain increased. Nuyani went for a wild swing arching to the sky only for the blade-jaw to lean back, dodging the arch. Nuyani followed with another slash in reverse, keeping the animal from advancing. It dodged the simple attack pulling its head away. 'Not one more step,' she thought, using frantic swings to bar the animal. Each one was sloppy and unmeasured. With most of her strength gone, she let the twist of her body and the weight of her arms carry out her swings. 'What can I do? What is the answer?' Nuyani questioned.

The blade-jaw raised its paw for another strike. Nuyani brought up her arms defensively as a final barrier erected before her. With its claws coming down, it ripped through the barrier with ease. The construct of light shattered into countless pieces. Nuyani's core stopped completely. Her body was racked with pain as she fell to the floor beside the boy. The blade fell from her hand the looming beast opened its mouth. Her eyes widened as she looked at the dirt and bloodstained teeth descended upon her. Another pulse then rose, coursing through the area from Cuganwa. The vibrations met her core, stirring it from a still state.

'We must leave. I can't…' she thought as her core own pulse rose meeting the child's before the combined waves grew stronger together. Nuyani raised her hands just as the teeth closed in. Black lines appeared on the perimeter of her sight before stretching and twisting to the center of her view. The light then poured into the center in thinning lines as a massive black void took over. The world then went black.

"Cuganwa!" Sutama shouted as he started running toward the beast.

The blade-jaw raised his head as loose sand fell from the sides of its torn mouth. No blood. No bodies. Sutama looked to the indented ground seeing both his daughter and son were gone. Rage rose in the hunter as his face creased heavily. He gritted his teeth as his pupils constricted. The blade-jaw looked down at the dirt and sniffed at the area casually. Sutama ran to the side, cutting into its neck with a knife. The beast did not flinch as it continued searching. Blood started to spill down his arm, with most pieces rolling off to the dirt. The others watched the enraged hunter as they revived. The blade-jaw paid no mind to him stepping forward, pushing Sutama away. Off-balance and still affected by the roar, Sutama fell to one knee and dropped his knife. Unwilling to yield, he blindly reached for his weapon and rose to his feet. The animal raised its head and looked to the west. The beast began to walk and lowered its head, ready to run.

Sutama released a blood-curdling scream as he slashed wildly, cleaving through most of the animal's neck. His senses returned when he saw the weapon was not his knife but, the blade Nuyani wielded. The blade-jaw's head dropped down and swiveled open on what little flesh remained revealing the inside of its neck and spine. The body continued to lurch forward as if taking off for a run only to collapse before its first step. A loud thud sounded as the creature fell to the ground, now still.

Sutama fell to his knees, looking at the blade-jaw. Its unrelenting will, spurring it through so many wounds. Normal ones were difficult to escape and kill but, this monster never ceased. 'Lord Kelvert, please guide us with your light. What stirs within the dryland?' he questioned, looking at the giant mass.

The other hunters rose. Many were forced to dismount and retrieve their supplies. Sutama looked past the party to the cliff. 'There. The beast looked to the gate. Hold on, Cuganwa. You will not be taken,' the man vowed as he narrowed his gaze to the cliffs. His grip on the blade tightened.

The hunting leader merely stared back at Bo'ede. "Then we must go." Bo'ede's tone was stern.

"West," Sutama replied as he pointed the blade tip to the other side. "There in the west. We must hurry…"

Lamoy then rose forth. "No, Sutama. We must wait. We'll need council. The elders must know." Sutama narrowed his eyes. "Sutama, please. This isn't the time."

Bo'ede then exploded, "There are too many questions that need answers. Why was your daughter wielding the chief's blade? What was that demon after? Which seemed to be the witch and your son. Your party talks about a new village for size, but that blade gives me another idea about your intentions. Why isn't she dead yet?"

"Enough!" Lamoy said. "Before we start accusing each other of anything, we need to get back to the village. The sun is close to setting."

Sutama and Bo'ede glared at one another. Odaru then rode with Muga behind Sutama. The senior hunter then looked up to his second then back to the others. "Fine. You will take the supplies and game back. We will look for our own."

Lamoy gawked at the man as Bo'ede turned his head to the side, keeping Sutama in his sight. The elder hunter turned to Odaru only to find the hunter falling from his saddle. Odaru grabbed the stirrups of the saddle, swinging in an arch as he cracked Sutama in the jaw. Sutama fell to the ground with full force as Odaru spun on the stirrup. Shock covered their faces.

Odaru stopped his spin. "Forgive me, Sutama, but this is not the best time to be selfish." He turned to the other hunting leaders. "We will look for Cuganwa but, the village comes first."

"Someone has some senses," Bo'ede said as he returned to the others.

Odaru turned to two of his party members. "Tie him to one of the sleds. Take the blade," Odaru ordered as he climbed up the stirrups once more. "We need to keep him bound or he'll fight against…"

Wriggling sounded behind the man. The body of the blade-jaw twitched. All of the whip-necks groaned and backed away, ignoring their drivers. Muga moved and bit onto the extra of Sutama's sleeve and pulled the hunter away. The yellow blemish stretched upward and burst, sending pus flying around the blade-jaw. Loud tapping sounded as several strange worms wriggled from the destroyed blemish. Each of the worms was at least the length of a man's arm and just as thick from what was exposed. Their bodies were in rounded sections of dark brown shells gleaming from the blood and pus within the animal's blemish. Between each joint were small black legs like centipedes sticking from the sides. Their heads were covered in blood-red unblinking eyes that looked like small, polished pebbles. Their mouths were at the center with four sharp pincers surrounding the opening.

"By the Great Lord…" the other hunters repeated as they watched the strange worms wriggle about within the flesh. Their reach never went beyond the body even as one rounded the beast's side, showing more to them buried in the carcass and touching the dirt. It returned to the top, with the others flailing about as their bodies continued to click and tap.

"What are those things?" Bo'ede questioned as he looked to Odaru. The man shook his head. "A charge-horn attacked your party with the same infestation. You didn't see this part."

Odaru leered at the man. "The witch took it," Odaru stated. Bo'ede squinted his eyes. His expression was softer than usual.

"Whatever the case, It's just another reason to speak with the elders," Lamoy interjected. "We need to know what those things are."

"I think their witch is the only one with answers," Bo'ede added.

"What will we do about those worms?" a hunter then asked. Another attempted to fire an arrow at one of the worms. The arrow glanced off its shell and hit the dirt.

"Well, thanks for answering one question," Lamoy chided. "Get a flame and burn the carcass. Dump it in the river afterward."

"Why not bury the creature?" Bo'ede asked, his tone more curious, missing its edge.

"I wonder why the witch had tried sending it into the river. It might be our best answer for these…worms," Lamoy answered.

Shrubs were collected and thrown onto the beast's body along with several small pouches of lard. Staying clear of the worms' reach, they lit a stick on one end and pressed it to the lard. Soon the blaze roared forth, engulfing the body. The hunters waited as the flames consumed the worms too. They wriggled about in the same manner as if the flames were never there. Their bodies bubbled and popped before pieces turned to ash and completely fell apart. After a half-hour, all that remained was a large black mound sitting in the dirt. The hunters started using long poles to scatter much of the ashes before collecting the fallen pieces onto one of the spare tarps. Finding no signs of life, they were confident that none of the worms remained. The hunters dragged the tarp to the edge of the river and dumped the charred remains. A school of water bites clamored for the new meal.

Odaru sat on Muga watching the fish eat, his attention focused on the spine, one of the few bones remaining. Charred portions of the bones had bumps on the surface. The hunter wondered if the shell of the worms melted like resin raising more questions about their nature.

"Odaru!" Lamoy called. The man turned to the huntress as he bit his lower lip and glared at her almost as intensely as Bo'ede would. Lamoy blinked as she studied his expression. "What's wrong?"

"I think that the blade-jaw was dead," Odaru said. Lamoy narrowed her eyes. She looked at him in confusion mulling over his words. She, too, looked at the remaining pieces of ash scattered on the floor. "Strange as it sounds, this is the second beast that didn't die as the others would." He looked at his quiver finding only six or so arrows left. "We didn't see what was inside that charge-horn but, it still came for us despite its wounds. By the Great Lord's light, those worms must be the cause."

Lamoy nodded her head as her eyes grew stern. "We will find an answer. Let's go before night comes."

Ch. 18

Secrets Come to Light

Sutama sat before a burning pyre in the middle of the village. The flames danced in his eyes, watching as if entranced by their glow. He scratched his cheek, raising both hands as they were bound together. The hunter sat alone as a line of guards stood with their backs to him, refusing any who attempted to speak with the man. Jogia and Caluu waited close by with Odaru standing near, trying to reassure the family's worries as they wept. The hunting leader could hear them as his chest ached. He knew he must turn to them, answer to them. Answer to Lord Kelvert. He had lost his eldest daughter, his first wife, and now his son. Other villagers argued with one another about the events. With so many witnesses, many argued he was a hero for fighting the blade-jaw, but cold for leaving his son. Others argued he was a fool for two of his young lost in the drylands and blamed him even for the beast.

The hunting leader said nothing as he waited for the elders and village leaders to speak. He then looked down at his tool strap, finding only his stone knives confiscated and loosened one of the pouches. Sutama undid the knot, closed the bag, and rummaged through the flintstones to retrieve a blue wooden bead. He rolled the beads from beneath his tunic, looking at the hundreds lining the thread. One of every safe journey through the drylands. One for every thankful prayer he had in returning home. His eyes grew red as he dropped the necklace and sighed.

Looking back to the lone bead, he turned it to peer through the opening. "I failed as a father," Sutama told himself as the pain increased.

"I think you should start leading. I failed twice," Sutama stated.

"Tsk. Have more faith," Odaru started. "The Great Lord has a plan for everything. You are giving up too soon."

Sutama blinked several times. "Such strength, old friend. I am certain you're the better hunter."

Odaru shrugged his shoulders. "I learned from a great one. Lord Kelvert willing, Cuganwa will be alive and well."

The older hunter's brow furrowed. "Don't do that, Odaru. Building such a belief can only make the fall harder."

"If it isn't true." The two looked at one another, trading competing stares to drill their point. Sutama's heart started to race. The thought of his boy still breathing made him wish it so as his breathing increased. His back straightened.

"Why? Why do you believe this?" Sutama looked at him.

Odaru smirked, "She hasn't tried anything before, even after To'anu's attempt. Why start now? Why tell us all to run when she pushed that beast into the river, err trying. There seems to be a kindred spirit of Lord Kelvert. Not a witch."

Sutama narrowed his eyes at the man. "Tell me this is more of your belief in the Great Lord and not affection for her."

"Belief, Sutama." Odaru's tone grew stern. "Faith. More things transpiring than just the witch running about."

Sutama's thoughts returned to the news of the worms that burst from the blemish of the blade-jaw. After he was knocked out, they rose and moved about as if searching for something, and another was severed as it was wrapped around the animal's spine. Odaru's eyes then shifted to the side for a moment before two sets of arms wrapped around the man on either side. Jogia buried her head into his shoulder as Caluu did the same. The two wept as they held on. Sutama breathed deeply as he raised his head to the sky. A sense of relief washed over him. He feared his family would reject him for their loss. Sutama moved his hand to sit on Jogia's. Odaru then rose as he turned away from the others and headed toward the rest of the village.

"The Great Lord's light is shining now, Sutama. Have faith," the man said as he hobbled back to the others.

"He is right. This should not have happened," Sutama started.

"No. I believe in Odaru's words. Lord Kelvert's will, that is all we have," Jogia stated as she trembled. "I don't know what else to do but pray."

Sutama rested his head on his wife's. "What will we do? If it weren't for that beast, I don't think the witch would've taken Cuganwa."

"What!" Caluu then called out. Her parents looked at her in surprise.

"The witch took your brother," Sutama explained.

"Then Cuganwa will be back," the girl said. Her red eyes filled with a sense of joy. Her parents then looked at one another before turning back to the child. Sutama looked at his youngest, worried her hope could lead to a harsh reality. "Well, she never bothers you." Caluu lowered her head, recognizing her father's confusion.

"Caluu, my dear, I hope you are right," the hunter said with a weak smile, placing his hand on her cheek. "I should still have hope." Sutama continued to smile but knew even with his return, the village would not treat him the same.

"Do not look so dower, Sutama," someone sounded behind him. The family turned around, finding the village chief and elders standing behind them. In his hand was the curved blade resting against his shoulder. However, on his wrist was the same jewel every chief wore before. Sutama's eyes trailed to the crystal in the leather bracelet gawking at the realization that there were now two blades. "We've worked with you for too long to throw things away with sudden speculation. Cut him free. There will be another caravan."

Jogia and Caluu moved away to let two guards cut Sutama's binds. Free of them, he pulled his family in for another embrace. Parts of his fears lessened as the relief broke his tears free.

Gamaunda then turned away, passing the line of guards as he held up the blades. Many of the shouts and conversations ended or were reduced to murmurs. The chief then raised his other hand. The stone embedded in the leather piece shined with a white glimmer against his palm as before another identical blade poured from it, rising to the sky before Gamaunda closed his hand around the hilt. The other villagers were stunned by the reveal. Suspicion passed through the village of the witch stealing the blade for Sutama to usurp the position. Other theories came that his party wanted to form another village.

The villagers were mixed with several emotions as Gamaunda said, "It seems there is a truth that we must discuss on our history. This blade is from a past we fled long ago. One that has not risen in the three hundred years.

"What is this?" a villager challenged. "We came from water and soil under Kelvert's will. We are the children of the Great Lord. Why are you repeating a fable?"

"Proof of the fable lies in my hand here," the chief said.

Yanuma then stepped forth. She raised her ring to the people pointing the green gem toward them. A bright glow rose from the stone. Emerald lights shot forth onto the ground. Varying shades of green took shape, showing hundreds of stone structures that rose to the sky large crystals floated one several tall structures. A single structure with a dome roof sat in the middle. To one side sat several strange trees topped with wide fanning leaves, the other side containing endless waters that crashed against the stone platform. Some stepped back from the images that the elder displayed.

"We are not from the drylands, but another place that has been long forgotten. There, we were still hunters that traveled the oceans to capture beasts and fight other people from other nations," Yanuma started. Confusion arose in the faces of the villagers. Some looked to one another, trying to find some answer. Never had any elder displayed such abilities. Some were more perplexed by the words of ocean and nations. Two figures then rose above every building carrying the same weapons and strange knives. "Young gods lead us in that old faith to battle and fight but, it ended when something worse came to follow us." The pristine civilization turned into a horror scene as branches and flames rose as people fled from the area. Many of the structures had toppled over or were damaged. The bodies of the gods lying on the ground are still larger than the structures around them.

"You lie!" a villager declared as the image of the enormous, masked figure came into view. "What is that?"

"What made us flee. Creatures and beings beyond our strength drove us into the drylands," Yanuma continued. "There is a world beyond the cliffs that we've survived. And those captured faced a fate worse than death. Even now, some may be in servitude to this monster attacking other people."

"This can't be true," a villager stated. "You're saying people three hundred years ago are still being used

to this day?" The elder shot a look at the man with an
unflinching glare. The villager opened and closed his
mouth several times, thinking the elder was bluffing.

"Who here challenges my knowledge when I've
known so much about you?" Yanuma scanned the crowd.
None stepped forward or spoke up. "There is a history we
have in and beyond these cliffs."

A woman began to weep. "Are you telling us that
Kelvert is a lie?" the villager asked.

"No!" Yanuma turned her palm to the sky as the
green lights shifted into the shape of the drylands
outlining a familiar river and a ball of light one could
mistake for the sun. "When all was lost, we were protected
by the power Kelvert—raised and strengthened by his will
alone. We are the children of Kelvert. There is no one left
tied to the old, failed gods."

"Then what of the blade?" the same man asked.
Yanuma narrowed her eyes at his boisterous attitude, but
saw his questions kept the villagers at ease.

"The blade is but a relic from that life. A useful
weapon for battle," Yanuma explained.

"Then why did the witch have it, and why do we
use one?" the man pressed.

Yanuma's tone grew stern and more assertive as
she addressed the villager. "It would be foolish to leave
such things forgotten. We came to the drylands to survive,
and the blades aid us in fighting true terror. The
witch…may know something worse is coming or is here."
She then looked back to Sutama, staring into his eyes as
hers grew green. The lights changed once more as they

transformed into the large blade-jaw from Sutama's perspective. "Your arrows did nothing to the beast." Whispers began once more. The memories of Sutama looking at the beast and tracking his shot carefully measured to hit the creature and not the witch. His memory shivered as the beast roared with the witch trying to push the creature into the river. It only cleared as his son and Nuyani disappeared before he flailed after the monster, cutting into its neck. He then fell and grabbed the blade instead. Yanuma sighed and closed her eyes. She then turned to another hunter showing the worms that burst from the enormous blade-jaw. Others gasped at the strange creatures.

Gamaunda then spoke, "This is a new threat we may face in the village or the drylands. We must learn what the witch knows and get our answer."

"W-why keep such a secret?" one of the villagers asked. "This is too much to hide. Who were those gods?"

"No!" Yanuma shouted, swinging her hand to her side. Her eyes were wide as she stared at the villager. "There are things you cannot know! Just the names of any of them could call those forces here. We survived and grew under the protection of Lord Kelvert. Otherwise, we would've perished long ago. I hear the screams of everyone who fled and lost loved ones. We survived. Accepted it and be grateful."

Yanuma stepped away as Elder Belractu came forth. "There is little I can add but, learn this. New creatures have come to infect the demons. Even the witch had to flee. Take what you will from that but, the only thing we can do now to survive is to get her word, her knowledge." The elder emphasized his point, raising and lowering his hand in subtle arches. "We must focus on the trouble at hand and answer the important questions. For now, you at least know where things are going." The elder then turned from the group and looked toward the west seeing the fading sun crawl over the edge as violet colored the sky.

Gamaunda then added, "Ten hunters and ten guards will accompany me to the witch's den. We will retrieve Cuganwa and learn of the witch's actions, or we will slay her. We leave tonight."

"What of the storms?" the same man asked.

"The drylands remain surprisingly calm," Elder Moyaud interjected. "The winds are stronger but I see the storm arriving in a few days."

Sutama looked to the dirt as his thoughts replayed on the slain gods and villagers fleeing from their ancient home. 'What were you doing there, Nuyani? Why'd you leave the drylands?'

Gamaunda then nodded his head as he flipped the second blade around and pointed its hilt toward Sutama. The senior hunter raised his chin and glanced at the weapon. The village chief then said, "You must always bring your effort. Redeem yourself. Help us talk to your daughter. Keep the village safe."

Sutama's expression hardened as Caluu looked between Sutama and Gamaunda, gawking at the news. Jogia wrapped her arms around the child. She knew Caluu was upset. The child lowered her head as her face wrinkled. Jogia sat low to the child's height to console her but, Caluu merely started running as she shouted, "Cuganwa is fine! He'll be back!"

Jogia started after her daughter but stopped as she glared at the chief. "Bring "them" home," Jogia said before walking off. Sutama sighed.

"Too many truths, Brother Sutama," Gamaunda stated, keeping formal. He gnashed his teeth as he looked the older hunter in the eye.

"Too many secrets, Chief Gamaunda," Sutama replied.

"It was not my intention to upset her…" Gamaunda started.

"No," Sutama interjected. "She learned now during a stressful time. She would've learned later. She and Cuganwa. But, I just want to get my boy back."

Gamaunda nodded his head before turning to the other guards. "Get the mounts ready with three days' worth of supplies for food and water. We don't know what we will face out there."

As the village moved, several hunters were chosen for the caravan. As the light died over the horizon within the half-hour, the whip-necks were lined at the gate. Sutama sat on his mount, looking at the gate as the sun was dying. He gripped the reins of the whip-neck tightly as the bone gate was picked apart. On his left was a fixed torch lighting the way, and on his right side, the blade sat in his quiver.

"Sutama," someone called. The senior hunter turned to the side, seeing Lamoy. "May the Great Lord's light guide you." The huntress held a hardened stare.

The man nodded before the group rode through the gate.

Ch. 19

Call to the Light

Nuyani awoke in an eternal night as the dark blue sky was not littered with stars or the familiar moons but swirling glowing fogs in varying shapes and sizes. In place of the countless stars she knew were coursing veins of light leading into infinite distances or connecting to the fogs on occasion. The witch began to breathe heavily as her head darted from one side to another, looking for some form of ground. Her eyes bulged as she quivered. No sense of cold or chill assaulted her.

"W-where is this," Nuyani said, finding an echo trailing her voice.

"Be calm, my child," Nuyani's voice echoed in her mind once more. Only this time, each syllable matched with a pulse coursing toward her. This brought her attention to the dull hum traveling through the void.

"P-please. Tell me. Am I dead?" Nuyani asked.

"Far from it, my dear," her borrowed voice continued. "This is the realm of magic or *govtif ved edria*."

"What?"

"More to learn in due time, my child. But first, we must free you from this domain."

"How did I get here? Who are you?" Nuyani said as she looked toward the source of waves rippling through the void.

"I am the one you have prayed to. I am you're Lord Kelvert." Nuyani froze momentarily. "I've brought you and the boy to safety from that beast."

"Beast…" Nuyani repeated in a whisper as a flash of claws, fangs, and bleeding gums rose, reminding her that she was defending Cuganwa and was soon to be killed if not for the black lines engulfing her sight. "Wait! What happened to the animal? Where are the others? A-and Cuga…?" Nuyani then grunted as her rising emotions stirred her strained core. Pain racked her body as every tired muscled ached, and her stomach twisted, forcing Nuyani to dry heave.

"Please remain calm, or it will be difficult for you to leave. You have learned to use my gift well, child. Since the night of the banshees' arrival, you've grown."

"Your gift?" Nuyani repeated as the distraction did little to stifle the pain. The swirling fog she watched then bulged toward her.

"I had to use the strength of you and Cuganwa to bring you through. Unfortunately, with your core so fatigued and his completely new, I could only bring one of you completely through the void. Please, allow me to guide you, my child."

'By the Great Lord's shine…' Nuyani thought as the milk-white, glowing fog-filled her vision. She strained as the sudden waves interacted with her core bringing more pain.

Nuyani struggled to stay awake as her fingers curled, digging into her arms. Pulses burst from the ethereal drum knocking away the surrounding hum as the black lines poured from the periphery and into the center before widening once more. When the pain subsided, Nuyani found herself kneeling on the floor staring out into the desert.

She fell forward, propping herself up with shivering arms. Her breath grew laborious. 'I'm back, Nuyani thought as her sporadic core reacted to the soft pulses emitting from behind her. Nuyani turned to see Cuganwa lying unconscious on the stone floor.

"Other child," Nuyani whispered. "He's here too." Nuyani realized the truth. Their Lord truly came.

"There're two more. I'm related to them both," Nuyani said as she shuttered. I…They live because you protect us." Several pulses rang through the area but at Nuyani's flank. Fatigue wrapped her body, and Nuyani let an arm collapse as she swung around to sit. She looked to the tunnel entrance only to see the faint glow of a blue light showing in the shadows. Before the witch could do anything, her vision became blurred, and her remaining strength failed before she fell unconscious.

Winds howled through the curling cliff face. Cuganwa winced as the small specks of dirt pelted his face stirring him. Waking up, he found himself lying on the ground feeling stiff as he realized he was lying on top of stone. His eyes opened as the memory of the witch and an enormous blade-jaw returned. Sitting up, he looked about only to find a partial night sky over the wide expanse of the drylands toward the east and a twisting ceiling of stone from the cliffs perched atop of a single stone pillar.

"Where…Where am I?" Cuganwa wondered. A gust of wind rasped as it cut around the stone wall, calling his attention. The boy ran toward the corner. His heart pounded away as he saw the orange light glow against the cliff. 'No.' When he reached the end of the path, his gaze fell over the endless sands trailing into the horizon and the sun setting "I-I'm at the demon gate. But, how?" Cuganwa stepped back and turned, ready to run for the east, run for home. He never gathered speed as his foot kicked something heavy yet, giving way. The boy looked down, finding another body lying on the ground. His eyes widened as he looked at the leather-wrapped limbs and tattered runner's attire.

"No," the boy whispered. His body quivered. The person's face was turned away. He padded around the figure until he came into view of Nuyani's face. "No." Cuganwa's heart sunk as he sat on the ground. The stories of the witch taking people away to their deaths ran through his mind. His heartbeat was in his ears as he placed both hands on his head. "By the Great Lord, what happened? Why am I here?"

The boy looked down at Nuyani. 'Y-you're the threat. You're the reason things are going wrong." The boy accused. He looked to his tool sash, seeing that he still had both his stone and ivory knife. Removing the stone knife as he looked at her face. The woman did not stir. Cuganwa gripped the blade in both hands as they shook. "I have to. You're dangerous. Deyunca warned…" the boy paused as he remembered the hunter. He betrayed the village just to try and kill the witch by nearly killing another. The night before, he was almost certain the man would've tried to kill him if not for Lamoy.

"Great Lord, guide me with your light," Cuganwa thought back to the elders and his father, who warned only to take a life if you were in danger. Taking a deep breath, the shaking lessened as he let the blade drop to the ground. "I am still here. I am still breathing. Why? Why did I get taken? Why'd she save me?" He narrowed his eyes at her remembering the beast. Looking to the drylands, the blade-jaw was nowhere to be found. "Did she save me, again?"

"That is one way to see it," the boy's voice echoed in his mind. Cuganwa retrieved the knife and rose to his feet. He held his arms out wide, trying to keep a comfortable space to defend.

"Wh-whuh?" The boy questioned. A strange hum rose from his stomach as palpations passed through the air and struck something deeper beneath the skin. He placed his hand on his stomach, thinking his stomach was turning once more, only to find the soft beat soothing his nerves. Cuganwa lowered the blade as he studied the pulses. They were striking from his flank. The boy turned slightly, finding the source of the strike turning against his stomach as well. When the pulses reached the front of his body, he looked up.

Before the opening to a tunnel, a blue flame floated a meter above the ground. Its light flickering in all directions reminding the boy of a star. Its light danced in the boy's eyes as he gawked at the fire loosening his grip on the blade.

"Are you a trick from her?" the boy questioned.

"I'm merely a guide, child," the boy's voice echoed.

"What do you mea…" Cuganwa stopped. More waves of energy rose from the direction of the flame. His mind came to the memory of the pressure rising in his stomach when the charge-horn was approaching and the temporary relief to his stomach before the blade-jaw arrived.

"I've tried to reach you, child, but my call was not strong enough. Yet, you are here. Thanks to her."

"Who…" the boy started. He paused, wondering if the answer was true. His heart started to race. Another vision then came to the boy. A light looking more like a star above the earth even as day rose. Walls of its light poured through the land blocking a sandstorm as people waited. "Lord Kelvert?"

"Yes, my child."

Releasing a deep breath, the boy looked at the wisp. "What is happening?"

"I am guiding my strongest to saving the village." The boy blinked several times as he reeled back.

"Your strongest?' Cuganwa questioned.

255

"That's right. Those who bear my gifts and receive my call. It was hard to reach you but, you've arrived." Cuganwa froze. His thoughts were read by the flame. The witch lay unconscious.

"I will tell you more, but first, come to safety. We must heal Nuyani, and prepare for the storms." The wisp then flew inside the cave, its light fading into the darkness.

Cuganwa looked down at the unconscious woman back to the tunnel. He sheathed his knife and moved to Nuyani's side, tightening his fists. Rolling her over, the boy looked at her face. All his life, she was the demon to be feared. She scared everyone yet. Now she lied vulnerable to the threats. Injured from some ordeal, appearing as human as anyone else.

"Under your glow, I am protected. Under your glow, I will protect. I will aid my kin. I will aid my home. As day ends, I follow the will of your gleam even through night." Cuganwa recited the morning prayer under his breath as he lifted Nuyani's head, laced his arms underneath hers and grabbed both of his wrists, and moved her to safety.

Part 3

Thrum of the People

Ch. 20

Warning

The hum of another core rose through the dark. Nuyani senses stirred as she slowly recognized the hard ground beneath her and the rasping wind filling the area.

'Whuh?' she wondered as pain shot through her body. Her core continued to receive a foreign hum relieving some of the strain. Awareness returning to her, Nuyani's eyes opened. Her heart raced as she realized it was not her own core at work. She found herself lying on the floor and sat up. Before her sat Cuganwa, looking back with a shocked expression. His hands hovered over her feet, with both palms glowing with blue light. Beside him, a blue wisp the size of a fist floated in the air with occasional rising tendril shooting out in any direction.

The boy smiled before he said, "Hi…"

Nuyani merely replied, scrambling backward until her head struck a stone wall forcing her to stop. Cuganwa's brow furrowed as he looked at her, his mouth agape.

'No. By the Great Lord, I didn't take him?' Nuyani thought. She recognized the cavern as the wind whistled, passing through the parts as shadows lay over

the small huts. Nuyani found herself and her strange
company sitting on the higher shelf where the firepit lay.
Her thoughts were focused only on the boy's eyes as they
were ember in color and glowed like hers. Cuganwa
lowered his hands as the blue light faded from his palms.
Nuyani could sense the ethereal waves soften until the
remainder within him stopped, and his eyes returned to
dark brown. Overhearing tales about her stealing away
hunters to kill in vengeance ran through her mind.
Nuyani's heart raced, pounding in her ears. She had never
taken another life that was not game. 'The villagers.
They'll think the stories are true. They'll come after me.'

     "Relax. I'm just trying to help you," Cuganwa
said, smiling again.

     Nuyani shook her head fervently. "No. No. By
Lord Kelvert's will, I did not mean to take you," the witch
said, tucking her chin and grabbing her head. "I…I was
trying to protect you from the…" Nuyani looked up,
realizing the monstrous blade-jaw was not around. The
last of her memory returned to the creature's jaw
descending on them until the world went black. "W-where
is the blade-jaw?" Nuyani looked about, finding the
cavern remaining quiet.

     "Dead," Nuyani's voice echoed in her own mind.
The woman could feel pulses coursing through the area
much like hers. Yet, they did not rise from the boy but the
flame. Nuyani watched as the sapphire wisp floated
toward her.

     The beats of her heart grew heavy despite her
nerves growing at ease. Nuyani's thoughts ran to one
conclusion. 'Lord Kelvert.'

The wisp then answered, "As you have prayed, *lohtels* (child). The blade-jaw is no more. Sutama killed it with the blade you carried." Nuyani released a deep breath as if a sense of worry had left her.

Cuganwa narrowed his eyes at her. 'Father killed the blade-jaw? You were worried about the village?' the boy questioned.

The wisp then continued, "As the creature was upon you, I pulled you both through *govtif ved edria* to safety as the hunters dealt their blow to the creature. I am ashamed to say that I left them to fate in killing the infested creature when you were desperate to face it." Once more, every syllable she heard, a wave rang from the flame striking Nuyani and Cuganwa's core. Their minds act on their own to produce the sound.

"The blade?" Nuyani replied. She then looked down. Her expression grew somber. The weapons."

'Weapons?' Cuganwa questioned.

"Fear not, Nuyani. Fate has given us more than we needed," the wisp stated. Nuyani's eyes widened as she looked at the wisp.

Her body started to tremble as she tried to understand the circumstance. Danger lurked from every bush, stone, and crevice. Yet, for all her prayers and close calls, the wisp before her claimed to be their lord. A floating flame, no larger than her hand, was their god. "How is this true? Why now? Where were you?" Nuyani's tone became aggressive as she looked at the flame. Cuganwa glared at Nuyani, wondering how she could be so dismissive.

"Your questions are fair. But, I was locked away," the wisp stated.

"What?" Nuyani questioned, glancing at the boy as well. Cuganwa looked to the flame, his expression fixed in a quizzical demeanor.

"Yes. As I've said, fate has given us a true chance, for you both are one of the few who bear my gift. Because you both were together as the blade-jaw attacked, I was able to free myself and save you both with our combined strengths."

"Gifts?" Nuyani questioned. Her breathing calmed and she placed a hand onto her stomach as she listened.

"Exactly," the wisp continued. "Your gifts are stronger *edria* given apart from me to the land. I must explain much despite the little time we have before things grow dangerous. In short, I've reached out to you when I had the strength and direction. The storms that crossed the desert and drylands weakened me and my influence. Before my conscience and power were swept away, I imparted it onto your ancestors, the land, and the animals. I hid within the land only to find the storms had separated me from all that sat within the drylands. The magic around us grew still and weak."

"How did you get out with our help? Why would you need us?" Nuyani questioned, her tone more demanding as she leaned forward.

The wisp floated closer. "You feel the beats and rhythms coursing through you even when you are not trying to use your core, yes?" Nuyani gave a shallow nod. "If it were still, you would die. Imagine the land fed with my power constantly bombarded with forces that could make it still, weakening you with every passing. It was the only place I could go to ensure that I was not destroyed and look after those with my powers remained. With your *edria* in synergy with my own, I could break free, stirring the land's *edria* and move us all to a safer location. I wish I could do more, but, in this state, I am no stronger than either of you." The wisp floated away, ascending toward the fire pit.

"How do I know this is true?" Nuyani asked. Her tone turned gentle yet, still held a sense of doubt.

"I don't ask you to believe me without proof, *edya lohtels* (my child). But, I will show you. I called to you when the banshee came to you that night. I freed you, calling to your strength when she tried to paralyze you." Nuyani blinked several times and looked down at the floor. There was a tinge of guilt weighing on her as the flame listed its efforts. "Give me more time, and I will prove it. Please follow me."

The wisp then floated through the area heading toward the back. The two watched as its light gleamed over the dry stones only to remain stagnant where they could still follow. Cuganwa rose first, glancing at the woman as she collected herself.

'I guess the witch is just as afraid of these things as we are. I used to fear you. But, you fear the wisp. Should I?' the boy wondered. He walked toward the end of the shelf and dropped to the lower floor.

Nuyani got his glance, wondering if the boy was angry with her for some reason. She had faced threat after threat in the drylands, never knowing if it were truly a sin for her survival. Through it all, the sudden words of a strange being claiming to be their god and imparting his power to their people for safety made reality seem warped.

'I don't know if this is real but, this is the closest to the answer I've searched for. I will see where this goes,' Nuyani decided as she rose as well. Taking a step forward, pain shot through her ankle. Nuyani grunted as she collapsed to her knees. 'Damn. It still hurts.' She peered at her foot, finding the swelling was gone. The muffled steps and scrambling then reached her ears as she looked forward. Cuganwa had made his way back up the shelf and headed toward her. 'What?' she questioned as she stared at the approaching hunter.

Stopping just before her, Cuganwa held out a hand. "I always thought of you as fearless as the blade-jaws. What do you need to fear?" the boy questioned as he waited for Nuyani to take his hand.

She looked him in the eyes, paralyzed by the question. Her mind raced. She thought of all the arrows and curses the hunters slung her way as she fought to survive. "I…don't want to be the monster everyone fears. I've been the witch for all this time. I just don't want that to be true."

"Well, now you are another child of Kelvert with his gift, and not the only one," Cuganwa replied.

Nuyani's eyes widened as she looked at the boy, smirking. As inviting as his words were, young Caluu came to mind. 'Does he know?' Nuyani wondered before replying. "Yes. Children of the Great Lord." Nuyani then grasped the boy's hand as he hoisted her up to her feet and wrapped her arm over his shoulders.

Nuyani looked away. "What is wrong?" the boy questioned.

"Nothing," Nuyani answered, resisting the urge to pull away.

"Fine but, let's hurry," Cuganwa said taking the lead.

The two made their way toward the shelf ledge and slowly toward the back. Nuyani attempted to control her core. Distorted waves rose from her center yet, remained shallow as they coursed only as far as her knee before retreating once more. 'Damn, how long will it take you to rest?' Nuyani wondered. She then thought back to the pulse that Cuganwa used as well on her leg. 'How did he do that? There is too much going on. But, if I learn that, then it will be a start.'

"H-how did you do that?" Nuyani started. Cuganwa's head reeled back as he maneuvered the two of them around another hut. "How did you start healing my ankle? I've never learned that."

"Oh," Cuganwa started. "I didn't really learn as much as I just let Lord Kelvert's will guide me. The weird drum in us. It let me repeat his pattern but, I didn't even know it was there until he showed me. I don't even feel the pulses like I did before."

"Really? I don't think I blame you. The first time I was aware of it, the spirits were pressing on my core for me to notice. It was painful," Nuyani stated.

"What were they like?" Cuganwa asked. Nuyani turned toward him with a questioning gaze. "The spirits," he added.

"Oh. Strange forms of death," Nuyani started. Her expression turned into disgust as she recalled their images. "Naked shriveled women with beast-like claws and blue bodies you could see through. They had the strangest faces. Long jaws and their eyes were black with small lights in the middle. Everything around them made you want to run. The air was cold. Their yells freeze you. Their claws make your flesh shrivel."

"Wait. You said their claws make your flesh shrivel?" Cuganwa repeated.

"Yes," Nuyani answered. "On that night, one left cuts on my arm. I was luckier than some tall horns that were nearby."

Cuganwa stopped as he stared at the floor. "The spirits killed those tall horns we found and then that means even the villagers were taken by them," the boy said. He looked toward her. "Then you did stop them from harming the villagers." Nuyani winced at his tone nearly rising to a scream.

"Yes. Yes," Nuyani answered. "Calm down. It was something I had to do. We…must guide one another and help." The boy looked forward with a smile as they rounded the last hut.

"I'm glad to know you were there," the boy said. His doubts faded as he remembered Deyunca. "I guess the monsters aren't always what we are told."

Kelvert floated before the massive wall waiting at head height for the two to approach. Before either could ask why they were going to the back, the wisp touched the stone wall passing halfway through before its pulse coursed through the stone as well. The earthly surface rippled as if it were a puddle before pouring from the center outward. Cuganwa and Nuyani gawked at the display, uncertain how to process such a hard element acting so fluid. The stone surface only stopped to form an arching entrance fitting the same tunnel and traveling further into the cliff. The wisp continued passing through the overgrown vines bearing silver glowing flowers as if they were never there. The two said nothing as they walked on, ducking slightly to pass under the shrubbery. Nuyani was forced to place a hand on the tunnel's sidewall discovering the smooth surface too unnatural not to be manmade as she wondered who lived in the abandoned village.

"I wonder who made this place," Cugnawa stated as if reading her mind. "If no animals are bothering you, then why is no one else here?"

"I think we will find out soon but, I had the same questions," Nuyani replied.

After a few moments, the two reached the end of the tunnel and stretched their backs. Nuyani separated from Cuganwa for a moment and stayed by the wall as she straightened up. Both of their eyes widened as they found Kelvet floating out in the open of an even larger cavern, miles wide and tall. The entire area was like a cylindrical staircase with stairways and ladders carved into the stone walls leading to wider shelves holding countless huts. Pathways leading between structures had moss growing within the mortar or puddles collecting in worn areas. More vines clung to the tops and the ceiling of the area. Nuyani looked toward the top, where the remaining daylight streamed through a large hole in the top that was a perfect circle mirroring the chasm down below. Water streamed from shadow ports far on the other side and streamed down into the center, making Nuyani wonder if the path reached each level. Plenty of moisture was in the air and left a smell of rain lingering in her nose.

Nuyani relaxed, grabbing both of her arms and leaning against the stone wall. 'What happened to these people,' she wondered.

"A fate that may befall the village if we do not act," the wisp answered in her mind. Nuyani froze, not realizing her thoughts were still available to the wisp. "I do not mean to pry but, there are answers. Come to me, and you will find them."

Cuganwa then turned to Nuyani, holding out a hand. Confusion covered her face until she realized he was still helping her. Together they made their way down the worn path seeing the similar stone huts along the way. Pieces of stones on the floor covered in moss also bore deep scars on the surface. Nuyani's mind shot to the blade-jaw that chased her as she froze once more, stopping the two of them.

"What's wrong?" Cuganwa asked. He looked at the stone as well.

"The blade-jaw that chased me. It could scratch stone like this as well," Nuyani answered as she limped on, trying not to halt their movements.

"What?" Cuganwa whispered.

"I went to another village made of stone and bricks. Met a spirit and learned what brought us here. There are monsters and things beyond the cliffs I wonder if we could face," Nuyani stated.

"But, the weapons?" Cuganwa reminded her.

"They were to fight the spirits. The spirits pass through the stones just like Lord Kelvert can. With the storm approaching, I fear for the village," Nuyani admitted. This time Cuganwa hesitated for a moment.

"Then we must find an answer," Cuganwa said, increasing his pace. Nuyani nodded her head and pressed faster as well.

The two walked beyond the huts to the center where a wide space lay in a ring around the chasm. Several small walls standing up to their knees were built in circles, with at least a dozen from what they could tell lining the circular pit's edge. When they reached the small circle Kelvert floated above, the wisp descended through the stone floor. The two looked on, wondering why until they saw the blue light glowing through a man-sized opening in the floor. Cuganwa stepped over the wall, knelt, and popped his head through the hole without hesitation. Below, another room lay with shallow water covering the floor. Kelvert floated beside strange designs in the wall.

"There's something in here," the boy stated as he rose his head. "Lord Kelvert is near a mural. Come on." Cuganwa then maneuvered his feet to meet with footholds in the wall leading down into the area. His feet splashed as he turned around, getting a better picture on the wall. Before focusing on the detail, he felt pressure sitting on his stomach, directing his attention just below the mural. Nuyani followed soon after, hopping with her better foot to reach each indentation as she reached the floor. The water was just above her ankle. She, too, noticed the pressure and spun around, ready for an attack. Cuganwa looked back, hearing the sloshing water, yet he remained calm.

Turning back toward the source, the boy then asked, "Lord Kelvert, what is this place? Whose picture is this?" He looked to the wall seeing different designs carved into the stone surface.

"Tell me what you see," the wisp stated. Nuyani moved forward, eyeing the piece as well. A large silhouette stood on high in the first section of the mural at the left. Only rough circles in the top part resembling eyes told them it was another being of sorts. Vertical striations in the stone with only a few lines separated another section with the silhouette of smaller men fighting it off with what appeared to be blade-jaws, charge-horns, and blood-manes. Another section of striations with a few more lines then showed fewer men standing around. Some with designs lying on the floor and others with odd waving spheres leaving them and heading toward the larger being. Nuyani wondered if that was their life. The next section of the striations and the same wavy spheres rising from their bodies. The furthest section to the right had fewer people and more animals attacking them.

Nuyani shook her head as she looked from one end to the other. She wondered what was happening until she stepped back. At the top of the mural, some of the areas remained rough in straight lines bordering smooth silhouettes of the people and animals.

'This is their home it's showing,' Nuyani thought.

Cuganwa's attention lay on the waving striations that kept growing bigger. He narrowed his eyes at the silhouettes captured within the last. "I-I think these are sandstorms," he said.

Nuyani looked back at the largest section of the waving lines. "You might be right," Nuyani said. "The animals attacked them in their home."

"In here? How?" Cuganwa questioned.

Nuyani turned to face him, her expression somber as she said, "The blade-jaw today was able to scratch stone. It was stronger and larger than any I had ever seen. Worse, it was faster than me."

Cuganwa's eyes widened at the news. He remembered seeing the witch run through the land and parry an arrow with ease. The thought dwelled within his mind as Nuyani turned toward the pressure sitting beneath the mural.

"I cannot recount what took place in this domain as another power dwelled here but, there is one who can if they are willing," Kelvert said as the wisp floated away. "Nuyani, I wish for you to learn more fervently how to use your gifts. Please, meet with him."

"Yes, Great Lord," Nuyani said as she tightened her lips and took a deep breath.

Holding out her hand, Nuyani released a pulse from her core, releasing weak but stable waves coursing through her limb and out toward something small item sitting in the murky waters below them. Within the dirt-covered item, Nuyani could feel it. The sloshing remains of life dwelling within. The bead of pressure weighing on their cores then surged. Nuyani wondered if stirring the spirit had angered it, though she kept her waves too shallow to disturb any life with real force.

Nuyani stopped the pulse of her core. White light started glowing, outlining the item within the water. Several thin swirling lines were revealed in the sudden light before the glow collected into another wisp that floated from the item rising to head height. Nuyani stood straight before backing away and raising her hand to her knife. Cuganwa glanced between her actions and the rising light. Taking precaution, he at least widened his stance, uncertain what would happen next.

The light then burst forth, revealing a man from head to toe standing only up to their hip. Nuyani's eyes widened as she recalled the child spirit's memory of another being of the same height and stout figure attacking her and her father. Stark differences between the two men as the one before Nuyani, Cuganwa, and the wisp had skin as dark as theirs, a wild afro and beard barely giving view to the man's bottom lip. He wore a dark green tunic and lighter green trousers held up by a brown leather belt with the same shining ring stone that Nuyani saw in the fallen village. The man's arms, knees, and legs were covered in ring stone and leather layers. Like all spirits, a bleeding wound appeared just beneath the ring stone and leather on his abdomen, and an outline of white light surrounded his form.

Nuyani relaxed her demeanor. The spirit looked between the two of them and grew a wide grin on his face. *"Ah. Gor men veit. Dwo,"* the spirit said. He waited for a response only to see Nuyani and Cuganwa glancing at one another uncertainly. The spirit's smile faded away as he then looked to the mural. He started to breathe heavily as he ran a hand through his cloud of hair. His eyes grew red.

'If spirits feel this much after death, you can be stuck in your own cage,' Nuyani thought as she remembered both the child spirit and Deyunca staying confined in their areas. 'Can they not move on, or are they waiting for something else?'

The spirit then placed his hands on his hips and looked to the floor. His brow furrowed as his expression hardened.

"Why's he angry now?" Cuganwa whispered.

Nuyani shook her head before saying, "I don't think he remembered. Who or what else was there to call him out? This place is empty."

The man's head then shot up, catching the two off-guard. He glanced at them for a moment before rising and waving for them to approach. "Yolt geig," the man said sternly. Nuyani stole a glance at the wisp.

"He seems to understand the situation. Though with a different language, he may have a solution," the wisp said.

'Language?' the two thought, wondering what the term meant. Nuyani and Cuganwa then approached the spirit as the short man held out both of his hands. The two felt a strange instinct and drummed their cores allowing their energy to surge through their bodies before grabbing the spirit's hands. "*Ne'od mout*," the man said as he bowed his head and let the current of his life surge forth. Nuyani and Cuganwa closed their eyes as they allowed the energy to course forth and swell within them. Their senses disappeared as the world changed to a new setting. The man with several others wielding spears and blades of the same ring stone raced past the shelf and down the tunnel. The silver lights above gleamed against the headwear of the men before him. The group broke free of the path only to witness others fighting against enormous variations of the dryland's worst predators. Each one marred with the same rotting blemishes as the charge-horn and blade-jaw Nuyani encountered.

The battle was strange as the animals acted accordingly to one another. As a large blade-jaw swiped at two men who raised a barrier to block the animal, a blood-mane swept down and struck one of the men from behind, leaving the other to fall as the blade-jaw shattered the man's defense killing him. Nuyani could feel her body shake and her breathing deepened, remembering the visions of the fallen city. Such carnage and onslaught are possible and destined to repeat. However, the spirit and the others were not helpless as they released their own attacks stabbing with spears and blades while casting spells of elements. Clear, white, or blue freezing stones, wind, fire, and even the same energy spheres sored and tore through the various beasts with ease. Many died in the coordinated efforts of the fighters as they continued to battle. The numbers on both sides were too great to count as the chaos continued. The spirits group sprinted down the slope only for a few of the others in front to stop in place, putting them off balance. When the shaking lessened, one of the men rose a barrier and yelled at the others. They all did the same. They could feel the spell activate through the spirit's eyes and the quiver of his energy. A deafening roar then rose as the area shook once more.

The afternoon sun was blanketed in darkness a moment later. Man and beast caught unaware were hidden within the sandstorm.

'This…It flew here already,' Nuyani thought. With the storms reaching her home first before the rest of the drylands, she was accustomed to the early signs of the season. Yet, this was different. No harsh winds steadily growing over time. No cool afternoons. None of the blooming plants lose their flowers of closing into their thick sepals to protect from the coarse sand. Nuyani's thoughts returned to the large silhouette on the mural's left side. 'Something has to be controlling all this.'

The sandstorm then passed within moments. Most of the fighters were gone, with only a few emerging from their conjured defenses. The animals, however, remained relentless. Blood-manes and blade-jaws were susceptible to arrows but, the infected ones returned to battle marred with mortal wounds that would ensure any normal creature would die. Several blade-jaws ran across the land with flaps of flesh dangling in their run, as did the blood-manes whose wings were reduced to the bone. The charge-horns, with their heavy girth, stayed in place and began to run through some of the defending men smashing through their constructs. Screams could be heard from those killed.

The spirits and his crew lowered their defenses as the charging beasts started toward them. Despite downing many of the infected animals, their numbers were overwhelmed, being pushed back into the tunnel. Two more men fell as a charge-horn ran them down and stopped at the entrance. It moved away only for another pair of blade-jaws to enter and charge the men. Desperate to kill, the front warriors fired spells instead of making their defenses. A blade-jaw lost a foreleg only to ignore the wound and pounce on the man killing him. The other blade-jaw bound over the other, surprising the next who chose to conjure a wall instead. The animal then lamented, weakening the warriors for a split moment. It was all the beast needed as it rammed through the barrier and the fighters as well. The man felt a building rage will him forth toward the beasts.

Before he could, a comrade rose and created a barrier around him and before using wind to push him back. Bound in the energy, the man was thrown backward by the gust heading toward the huts. Before he could collect himself, the screams and growls of the others gave all the signs he needed. He looked around the huts wondering if anyone was left. No one was in sight, yet the path to the larger cavern remained open. Understanding why the man ran for the doorway, passing through the arching entrance, and placed his hand on the ground. The path's edges shifted and molded as they crawled to the center. The man watched as darkened figures of the beasts' rounded huts and headed toward him. He continued to feed his own energy into the stone until it closed. The first blade-jaw ran toward him at full speed as the entrance closed. The beast then collided with the wall releasing a loud thud.

The man fell backward, his heart racing as he inspected the stone, wondering if the beasts would break through. Faint screams collected in his ears. The man turned around where the bright light shone at the other end of the tunnel. Fleeting shadows then appeared as the screams seemed to grow louder. A green glow illuminated the entrance. His heart skipped. The man rose and dashed for the other end of the tunnel. Calls for help and yelling grew louder. He emerged from the tunnel and nearly collapsed. Dozens of blood-manes poured through the ceiling hole where a barrier should have been. He watched as the flying beasts plucked many remaining women and children before flying back through the entrance.

Some broke free of the animals' grasps and fell to the floor, injured or dead. Cuganwa shuttered, his pulse wavering and lessening presence.

'You've never seen this,' the fact dawned on Nuyani. 'I wish you hadn't.' Nuyani could feel her own body tremble as well. So much death seemed needless and barbaric, a sin to life and nature. She could feel her stomach turning.

The spirit broke from his trance and started firing what spells he had at the blood-manes. Some that were attacking ignored the wounds she inflicted, continuing their load. A cry then caught his ear on the ground level as a small child tried to stand, his leg twisted. The green glow then surged, calling his attention to the center of the area. The people gathered in a second dome of green light sitting over the giant hole, the light construct creating a floor suspending them in the air. Nuyani and Cuganwa could feel the powerful waves washing through the spirit. The man moved to the child and picked him up before sprinting for the center. He turned away from those airborne, knowing there was little he could do.

He wheezed as he ran with the child clinging desperately to his back. An extra precaution, the man conjured a barrier overhead. Bodies littered the pathway. The beasts spared no one. Each by their claws or dropped by the predators. No bites. Now chewed or severed limbs. Only blood spilled from horrible wounds from falls and claws.

'This…why? What would make anything do such a thing?' the boy questioned. The life of a hunter was simple. Killing was needed to survive. In that, he knew the blood-manes and blade-jaws as demons worthy of respect.

Yet, these creatures bearing the same sickness were murderous and cruel. His strength withered once more as he tried to ignore a pool of blood the man nearly slipped on. The two slowed, yet the man continued as they neared the end of the path reaching the circles. Other people of the stone village leaped into the center of the smaller circles, revealing collected pools of water. They ran on, passing through the green barrier. With greater strength, it was stronger than the ceiling's, preventing any of the blood-manes from entering.

Loud flapping and a caw filled the man's ears as he felt the barrier push down on him. The blood-mane did not bother with plucking him from the earth. No. The beast pounced instead, pinning the two to the floor. The child on his back screamed in pain sandwiched between the defense and the bearded man. Desperate, the man wriggled and freed an arm as the beast snapped at the edges of the barrier, trying to grab hold of him. Blindly casting upward, he released several balls of flame from his hand. The blood-mane screeched as two spells collided with its chest burning the feathers. The beast stood on its rear legs as the flames grew. The man rolled to the side, raising a hand to guard the boy as his other willed the light wall into another shape flatter than a blade leaving a thin line of light in view. He made a pushing motion with his hands, sending the construct forth as it sliced through the head of the blood-mane.

The beast's head fell as the lower feathers continued to burn. The spirit rolled to the side as the body of the blood-mane fell with a thud, and the flames claimed the body. Before he could collect himself, another caw sounded, getting the man's attention as large talons descended upon him. Pushing the child away, a piercing pain in his stomach led to his cry as he was hoisted from the earth. Stuck in the grip of the blood-mane, he found its talons digging into the armor as one pierced his plate. The wind whistled in his ears as he looked toward the ground and grabbed the animal's leg. The ground grew further away. Each home became as small as a bead.

Without a second thought, he placed both hands on the animal's leg and released a flame. His hands departed for a moment as the flames burst from the area. In an instant, the flesh of the leg was burned and feathers singed. The beast ignored the pain as the man dangled by the other end of his armor. With little gripping room to remain, he fell loose from the blood-mane and plummeted to the floor. In a desperate move, the man turned as best he could as he called for the wind aiming for the approaching floor. With some effort, the gust that rose slowed his descent but, the speed was too great as he landed hard on the ground. Still awake, his body ached as the cold floor supported him. He faced the wall of light seeing the people wave to him, hearing their screams for him to move. The young boy he carried sat on the light, yelling for him to help.

The man rolled to his side, finding that he was just beside small rings outlined by the short stone walls. Blood-manes battered the dome of light. As he struggled to move, the pulse rising from the dome grew stronger and faster. Each one passed through him, stirring his core. As the man reached the wall, the green dome became blinding. Shielding his eyes, the pulse then disappeared, leaving only a darker cavern and him alone. His wound continued to hurt as blood streamed down his skin. The blood-manes continued to fly about.

Crawling over the wall, he descended through the hole and fell into the water. He struggled to right himself for a moment before moving to the opposite end of the room and descending toward the bottom. Every kick and twist sent flashes of pain through his body.

'Why is he not blocking it out? Can't you strengthen it?' Nuyani found herself questioning.

He reached the bottom of the well and placed a hand on the stone. Using what little concentration remained, he made a lower brick grow soft like mud and pushed through malleable stone, allowing the water to stream out of the hole. The man then rose to the surface just as a pair of glazed eyes stared at him. He floated in place, wondering what he should do. The beast continued to stare as the water's level fell. The sounds of unearthly caws and scratching sounded on the room's ceiling. They wanted him as well.

The man merely looked back as the blood-mane watched him. He pressed against his wound as the water lowered to the point that he needed to stand. The blood-mane continued to watch. He leaned against the stone wall. A grin came over his face. He slumped down in the water and reached for a necklace. The leather cord was tied to a strange glowing sphere with a weak light at the center, and small, thin pieces of ring stone coiled around it. Nuyani almost mistook it for a soul if not for the single green tint that made it up. The man gripped the small talisman tightly as he released a pulse into it. The trinket replied with a surge of waves that coursed through his body and into his core. The energy rebound and was directed toward the stone wall. Dust and small stones fell away as the mural took form.

The man breathed heavily as he looked back at the opening. The blood-mane was still watching. The man rested his head against the stone and laughed as he looked at the talisman with little else to do. The bead of light was gone with only the coiling ring stone left in place. The world grew faint as he lowered his head and the blood continued to spill. He glanced at the blood-mane. The beast still watching.

The flow of energy ended as Nuyani and Cuganwa could feel the man pull away. With both opening their eyes, Nuyani's lip quivered as she looked at the man. Another inspection showed his hidden talisman beneath his beard. The claw marks on his attire showed the leather beneath it and some of his tunic.

"Th-that's what we are trying to prevent?" Cuganwa asked. His words slurred as he looked away. Nuyani turned to him, thinking he would shiver. His stomach began to heave but, he fought the urge as they stood in the water.

"I'm afraid so," Kelvert spoke. "This is a world I did not have sight of. Another's power dwelled here. Yet, I knew their fate."

"How…Why…They have the same gifts. Why? Why did this happen?" Nuyani questioned, forced to kneel as dread set in.

"They have the same abilities and more knowledge, but not the strength. My gift, too, has allowed you all to do the same and with greater strength. Though, things have not turned out as I had wished. Only a few of you remain."

"Wh-what do you mean, Great Lord?" Cuganwa questioned.

"The village has purged most of those who carry my gift. The stronger *edria* will allow you to do more than normal. I had hoped many of you would grow your strengths together over time. Yet, your fears have led you to this result."

'Fear. It's always because of some fear,' Nuyani thought. She grabbed both of her arms tightly. Her mind recalled to the lessons of Elder Yanuma reciting the story warning of those with eyes of embers. Cursed at birth, becoming demons with sinful powers. The first sinner, a man using his gift for selfish gains and demanding the seat of the chief. "One fool," Nuyani rasped. Cuganwa and the spirit both turned to her. "One fool ruined this." Nuyani's voice grew weak.

"No, we are here for a chance. We can do this. Lord Kelvert has us here for a reason," Cuganwa snapped. Nuyani turned to the boy. "I don't know how hard it was for you but, we need to fight," The boy shook his head, trying to shake away the images of death. "That can't reach the village."

Nuyani's mouth opened though she looked to the floor. 'Should I tell him? His sister is the same as us,' Nuyani considered. 'Our sister.'

A tear fell from her eye. "Fine," Nuyani said as she stood straight. Calling their attention. She then looked to the spirit and held out her hand. The man looked at her through narrowed eyes though he could sense there was no malice. "I want to free you. You didn't think you'd be stuck here? Can I free you?" Nuyani's eyes remained wide yet kind. Her core was vibrant as ever, sending a steady hum through her body. The spirit looked at her for a moment before nodding his head and giving a warm smile.

Before she could say anything, the man grabbed her hand. On his own, his visage gradually disappeared into a white light before condensing into a white wisp the size of a marble. The longer Nuyani looked, the more she could see the strange sphere holding an iridescent light at the core.

'May the Great Lord guide your soul,' Nuyani thought as she raised her palm to the ceiling, and the soul shot upward like a star.

Ch. 21

Hidden Secrets

Nuyani and Cuganwa climbed out of the room and returned to the open area. Both were quieted as they let the gravity of the situation set in. Nuyani now saw the carnage of two civilizations that fell, and more was to come. As she sat on the small stone wall contemplating the dangers they faced, Cuganwa looked about the abandoned huts, a hardened stare on his face. Sifting through the overgrown moss, he found more items of the same ring stone Kelvert corrected as metal. Each one was colored in spots of dark reds, oranges, and browns. As he squatted by the hut entrance, he found another piece of metal in a flattened shape. Recognizing it as a blade, he took up the handle studying its weight. The handle had worn away, leaving only a small slither left. Edges of the metal were jagged, poking into his skin.

Gritting his teeth, the boy raised the blade over his head. Just past his ear, he felt it give way as the flattened wide section of the piece snapped from the thin handle and barely missed the boy's back as the point flipped in its fall and hit the ground. A loud ring came out, echoing through the area. Nuyani, on instinct, shot to her feet and grabbed her knife.

"Cuganwa!" she called out.

"It's nothing!" he called back. "I dropped one of those blades!" Nuyani sighed as she sheathed her knife.

As she stood, she tested her ankle, finding the pain had nearly subsided. Looking toward the opening in the ceiling, the sky still held a vibrant dark red, signaling that night was soon to come.

'There's always another danger,' Nuyani said. As she stood in place, her thoughts dwelled on the final image. The looming figure beyond the sands is the creator of the storms. 'There's a will behind all of this.' A day before, she would've thought herself mad for even thinking something could control the winds but, the animal's behavior and the visions from the child spirit were more than convincing that there were forces greater at work. 'How will I free you?'

"With practice," Nuyani's voice repeated in her mind, followed by an echo. The woman turned toward the wisp suspended in the air. "I will guide you with what power I possess, and once you've learned, you should pursue this goal. But, I warn you. The village must come first. To learn and grow together. Once things are safe, you will have a home to return." Nuyani breathed slowly, trying to relax with the hope of Kelvert's words. "Do you feel rested?" Nuyani nodded. "Good. We should return to the front. I wish to share with you my past before the night is over. You will learn much about the land and your abilities in that time."

The wisp then flew off, leaving a sapphire streak trailing behind as he headed toward the tunnel. Cuganwa noticed and returned to the path. He wore what looked to be one of the armor, chest pieces the fighters wore only tarnished and dawning a few holes. The boy turned, seeing Nuyani make her way back up the path.

"What are we doing now?" Cuganwa questioned.

"We're going back to the front to learn Lord Kelvert's history," Nuyani answered.

Cuganwa raised his chin. "Why not here?"

"I don't know. Maybe he needs to be in a different area," Nuyani answered.

'Great Lord, why do you wish for us to be in the front?' Nuyani questioned, testing if her prayers would reach the wisp.

"The power that lay here is too great and distorting for my abilities. The front is still weaker in comparison and remains safe. There we will be able to reach my latent power without worry of being hindered."

"I see…," Nuyani said, her voice trailing off as she wondered about the different powers before turning to Cuganwa. "Did you hear?" The boy shook his head. "It will be better there than over here for his strength." Nuyani then narrowed her eyes at the boy. "What were you doing, and why are you wearing that thing?"

"Hm? Oh, this is for protection. I wanted to be ready for any of the beasts. It's strange, though."

The boy turned to her. "This place could fit the entire village even if it were five times bigger. Why haven't the animals taken over? I haven't…felt any more *edria* coming from this area. What do you think?" Cuganwa took the chest plate off, finding a few holes in the side closer to the lower gut. Unsatisfied it would protect, he put the strange piece down.

"Maybe a smell then," the boy said, only receiving a shrug in reply. "So, how are you able to run so fast if you only used these gifts a few days ago?" The two were close to the tunnel entrance.

"I was chased by a blade-jaw and got away, thankfully. I didn't even know I could but, my feet were hurting the first time." Nuyani answered. "I wondered why myself, but I think I should wait for Kelvert to answer later."

"Still the others," Cuganwa said. His mind turned to the thought of his father killing a blade-jaw. "None had done so without many arrows and many victims as well. Cuganwa then thought of the witch's actions. Twice she had saved him, yet the village was just as quick to try and kill her as they did the blade-jaw. "What do you think will happen?"

"If the storms don't get us, I'd imagine more infected will come by. Never felt a storm strong enough to shake the ground, though. It's…not right," Nuyani said as she looked toward the ground. The two were forced to do so, ducking beneath the clustering vines overhead. Nuyani then glanced at Cuganwa. "I do have something I must tell you." Cuganwa looked at her, his brows furrowed. "Your sister. She also has our gift," Nuyani said.

The boy looked at Nuyani with wide eyes and knelt on one knee. "It's not something I wanted to keep secrets so, I am telling you now."

"How would you know?" Cuganwa questioned.

"During the festival, she found me. I never noticed her sneak up on me. I talked to her, and she showed me. I was wondering why she wasn't scared. But, she is, and she's looking for an answer. Looking to see she isn't bad," Nuyani said as she sat down. "I haven't attacked or done anything to her, I promise you."

"I know," Cuganwa answered, never changing his expression. "That was before the spirits."

Cuganwa nodded looked to the ground. "Those spirits, infected animals, and that thing across the sands. Let's see what we can do," Cuganwa said as he rose to his feet and walked faster.

Nuyani was surprised by his sudden haste, but knew he was right to hurry. It shocked her when he struck the wall with his fist. ''What's wrong?"

"I-I have to prove that this gift is not a sin," Cuganwa answered.

"What?" Nuyani said, feeling somewhat crossed. "I think I should."

"We both can," the boy shot back, looking at her with a glare and ember burning eyes. "The ember glowing eyes not he. "I think I should."

Nuyani said nothing. She agreed. The two exited the tunnel and walked toward the elevated shelf. There Kelvert waited above the fire pit.

"It seems you both are more than ready for the journey ahead," Kelvert stated as Cuganwa moved to sit by the fire pit. Nuyani first retrieved some timber and flintstones to start a fire.

"Great Lord, you said it was your nature that
weakens you to the being. What is it exactly? What are
you?" Cuganwa questioned. He wore a determined glare.
'How did you grow weak helping us?"

"All good questions, child. The simplest I can
answer is that I am a *haflaj* (angel). I am a being of *edria*,
and this being beyond the sands is an *unflom* (demon), an
opposite to my make," the wisp started.

"Opposites?" Nuyani questioned. "So, for every
lord, there's a monster?" Nuyani wondered, thinking back
to the masked figure and the strange orb of flesh and stone
that flew. She never thought of them as separate.

"No, my child. For every lord, god or deity,
thousands of rival forces are attacking them. Even
amongst each other," Kelvert explained.

"What is your role in this world?" Cuganwa
questioned as Nuyani climbed onto the shelf.

"Your lord. Your protector," Kelvert answered.
The sky, the fire, the earth beneath you have lords who
rule them yet give authority to those with enough power to
protect them." Nuyani's process was slow as she grew
distracted with her questions. "I am *haflaj* and my natural
foe is *unflom*. With my being constructed from *edria*. I am
urged to fight *unflom* who are mostly made of flesh
and *prutosa* (spirit), what you may call life."

"Wait. Does that mean we're *haflaj* as well?"
Nuyani questioned.

"No. Merely *jorno* (elementals). Your abilities are
stronger than normal," Kelvert answered.

Nuyani stopped for a moment realizing her divided attention would not bring the fire forth or give her better answers. "Great Lord, what was your plan?"

"To strengthen the village to what you are today. *Edria* grows in *edvimxarraxalc* (mortals). Not in stagnant beings like myself. At least not without changing my own nature to a consumer. I haven't the will to do such a monstrous thing," Kelvert said.

"Why not?" Cuganwa asked.

"That is the nature of the *unflom*," Kelvert started. Consumes. Take. Devour. Their nature is to grow by what they seize. As a *haflaj*, I grow. *Edria* strengthens with time and practice. And with one wielder, the potential transfers to their young through time, though a slow process. My wish was to grow my power through our people. With time, all of you would possess the same strengths necessary to fight against the *unflom*. Though my efforts did not yield the same results, I had wished for. Still, you live."

"So *unflom* are bad?" Nuyani questioned.

"No. Just another aspect of this reality and two others," Kelvert explained. "There are even *unflom* who've been worshipped and just. The one I attempted to face was far stronger than I had realized." Nuyani turned away and gave the flintstones a good strike creating sparks. An orange glow filled the area accompanying the wisp's soft blue with the timber now burning. "Before we do anything, let's learn to keep the same rhythm."

"Rhythm?" Cuganwa wondered.

"Yes. The pulses emitted from your cores can do more than move from fast to slow. They can also create different patterns that call to the gods themselves and allow you to conjure those elements and other spells at will. Up until now, you had only been using your powers in the rawest form possible."

Nuyani sat beside Cuganwa and looked up to the wisp, "The gods?"

"Others of great power that control the state of existence around you," Kelvert said. Nuyani looked to the floor. There was something strange to know that greater forces existed beyond their lord.

'Rivals?' Nuyani repeated, thinking such a word would imply that their lord could will them to invade others as well. She bit her bottom lip finding distaste in the thought. 'What were we doing before Lord Kelvert guided us?' Nuyani wondered.

"First, learn to match and control the same rhythm," Kelvert ordered. Before either could ask a question, a strong hum from the wisp waves washed over Nuyani and Cuganwa, bringing an elated feeling as it bounced off their cores. The waves were neither intrusive nor hindering. "Notice how strong your thrum, *irboud*, is and try to match mine."

Nuyani did as she was instructed as she focused on the thrum. Within a breath, her core hummed at the same pace the wisp's. As the waves matched, the radius of their reach doubled, coursing further through the area. New senses bombarded her mind as she could feel the rough surface of the stone all around her as if it were against her skin.

"Focus on your objectives and your thoughts, and all that is not needed will fade away," Kelvert said.

Nuyani turned her attention just on the hum itself. With so many vibrant waves releasing and retracing, she noticed the individual rises that made up the ethereal force.

Cuganwa turned his attention to his core, feeling the steady ethereal waves pass through his body yet remaining slower than the powerful hum before. 'I did this earlier. What's wrong?' the boy questioned himself as his thoughts turned to his young sister, mother, and father along with the slain village in the empty cavern. 'I can't let that happen.' Cuganwa returned to his stomach, flexing the muscles only to gain a burning strain forcing him to release his grasp. The boy breathed deeply as he felt his muscles contract from the strain. "To the waters. What am I doing wrong?" the boy questioned, grabbing Nuyani's attention.

"What is it?" she asked.

Cuganwa turned to her but looked at the ground. "I can't get my core to go faster. It's staying the same." Cuganwa was breathing hard, trying to let his stomach rest.

Nuyani looked at the boy seeing his brow was furrowed as he looked at the floor. "What are you thinking about? Try to block it out."

"I-I can't," the boy said as he extended a hand outward. "I've got my family on my mind, and now Caluu is in danger even if the village is safe."

Nuyani shook her head. "No. Block those out for now."

The boy turned to her. "What?" he replied.

"The day I used my own *edria*, I had to block out the dangers and keep my head clear. Focus on the hum. Focus on the feeling, and it will be in your control. Clear your head, or it will escape you," Nuyani stated.

Cuganwa paused for a moment looking at Nuyani in the same stern manner. The boy started to resemble Sutama. He thought back to her words about the howlers. He took a deep breath and closed his eyes with a nod, focusing on the hum. The sensation was ever-present. Yet as he focused on his core, he could feel the waves moving faster. The pulses grew rapid and plentiful. Soon afterward, Cuganwa could feel the other waves emitted by the others start to fade into his own. Another moment and each of the beats were in synch. The gathered waves doubled once more. The energy made his body feel lighter. Each sense was stronger than ever as he felt the grains of sand pelting his skin.

"As I've told, Nuyani. Focus on the thrum itself, and the other senses will fade. Only the important things will remain on your mind," the wisp instructed. Cuganwa did so, focusing and stabilizing his thrum as the rest of the world fell to the side.

"Splendid, you two," the wisp said. "Next, you must focus on a single pulse. See it in your mind and hold on to it." Nuyani did it with ease, thinking of conjuring up a barrier. In the same practice, she kept a segment of the ethereal force locked into one place. Despite being new to the practice, Cuganwa managed to focus on a single pulse keeping the hum slightly larger than his core. "Great. Now feed the rest of the hum into the pulse."

Nuyani did so first. The captured pulse grew stronger, layering over one another. Cuganwa managed the same imagining that her trying to strike a drum at the right time. A short moment later, both had concentrated pulses within themselves.

"Great work. Next, imagine you are stepping into the sphere, like another room," Kelvert said. This baffled the two as their concentration nearly broke.
"*Edria* follows the will of the mind. Your very thoughts take shape and form the world to your whim. Imagine yourselves delving into that very space, and your will shall make it so."

Nuyani imagined entering the strange bubble. It was a small room large enough for her to move comfortably. As her thoughts took shape, she felt her body shiver. Going numb, it felt as if she were separating from something fastened in place. Nuyani fought on continuing to push against the strange binds until she managed to get free. Cuganwa struggled a little with maintaining the ethereal sphere as the bubble shrank in size. Lacking the same experience as Nuyani, he needed more concentration. The corners of the boy's lips curled as his brow furrowed. 'Imagine,' Cuganwa told himself.

His thoughts instead turned to the image of the village canal as the sun's rays gleamed in the water. Cuganwa was much younger than even his little sister. With a sense of glee spurring him on, he leaped into the water. With his mind on the scene, Cuganwa's mind separated from his body, diving into the sphere.

"Yes, excellent. You both are free of your bodies," the wisp said. "Now, try to open your eyes."

Nuyani and Cuganwa did so. The area had changed. The burning fire, bleached bones, and brown stones had all taken on a blue tint. The edges of their sight shook and quivered with the same hum. Her body felt weightless as she looked toward Cuganwa. She could feel her heart skip seeing two of him as one sat facing forward toward the fire in a darker blue tint with his eyes shut, and the other was a ghostly apparition outlined in bright blue and transparent phasing through his body. Nuyani flailed backward. Her hands and feet passed through the stones as she tilted to the side.

"What?" Nuyani questioned as the view of her hand had the same appearance, with bright blues outlining the edges of her body and slightly dimmer blues toward the center. Nuyani was more concerned with her body flipping slowly in the air as her head sank through the stone floor.

"You must calm yourself, Nuyani," Kelvert said. His voice was different. It held a tired rasp that continued to echo, yet it remained sharp as the waves traversed through the strange plane and met with her body. The waves sank no further than the surface of her glowing form, and her waves traveled not through, but along the surface. Cuganwa sat still watching and fighting the urge to laugh himself, knowing that he too could be sent flipping through the air.

"Great Lord, how do I take control of myself?" Nuyani asked as she took another flip. She felt as if she were being turned in water. Her mind returned to the blue void for a moment.

"How indeed?" Kelvert started. Nuyani's face went blank as she looked at the wisp at first. Wondering if their deity found it amusing. To her surprise, the flame had formed into a pulsing sphere with the same bright outline and fading blue light toward the center, and she noticed the surface was transparent. She could see a soul suspended at the core of the blue orb. The surrounding area within held a black mist shifting and turning inside.

"To control yourself, you must direct your body the same way you direct your spells," Kelvert said.

"Whuh?" Nuyani replied both unsure of what Kelvert meant and distracted by its new appearance.

"Guide the pulse as you would a barrier. You will find it easier than raising your hands," Kelvert assured her.

Nuyani tried to relax, fighting her natural urges to right herself using her arms and legs as she focused on her core. With a weightless feeling enveloping her, she could not feel the wind with its small grains of sand or the hard ground. Instead, other waves and pulses radiated with light touches against her skin as if she held her hand against the side of a drum beaten incoherently. As Nuyani twisted in the air, she focused on the back of her head, wanting to counter her slow tumble. The waves of her ethereal body surged to the point and burst out. The wave was too strong. Nuyani's eyes widened as her body instead flipped going forward, and she returned to flailing. The world blurred around her.

'This is weird,' the boy thought as he looked toward Nuyani's physical body in a darker hue. He turned back to her as she worked to control herself with lighter bursts. 'This does sound like the howlers,' Cuganwa thought, remembering Nuyani's words. 'I should try as well,' the boy thought as he concentrated. The rapid pulses were no longer coming from within, but came as a rapid surge running over the surface of his entire body. Each pulse was just as fast and strong as the last. Yet, despite their pace, he could feel every individual ripple making up his being. Cuganwa then looked to one of the pulses and concentrated on it in a curious play. It erupted from his being in a sudden blue orb in all directions. The light then died away, leaving the boy bewildered as to why he did not move.

"You need direction, *edya lohtels* (my child)," Kelvert said. "Though such moves would be an excellent defense."

Nuyani looked at him as she felt the wave. The strength of the ripple was but a fraction compared to her desperate bursts. 'Lighter,' Nuyani told herself, remembering they were weightless. Attempting to copy the strength, Nuyani released a small push from the back of her shoulder, bringing herself upright.

"Uh…Nuyani?" Cuganwa started. His voice trailed with a slight echo as every syllable traveled on the pulses.

"Err…Yes?" she answered, trying to stop herself from moving as she compensated with an opposite thrust.

"Why are you using so many of the beats?" Cuganwa asked.

"I didn't know not to," Nuyani answered as she focused on the pulses, using one at a time to right herself.

The jolting motions turned to gentle nudges allowing her to float in the air.

Cuganwa smiled at Nuyani. "You did it," the boy said.

"Your turn," Nuyani replied. Cuganwa's expression grew blank as he nodded his head and looked to the ground.

After a deep breath, the boy focused on the beats coursing beneath him. Selecting one of the pulses, Cuganwa rose with a light push and floated upward. He looked out around with a gleeful smile. Yet he continued to rise after the initial wave. He started to move his arms and legs as if to brace himself. He continued to climb, nearly reaching the same height as the larger opening in the cliff face.

"Focus, Cuganwa. Come back down," Nuyani said. The boy gave a nod of his head.

He looked toward the ground staring at nothing specific as he singled out another pulse ringing through his head and shoulders before releasing it in a burst. With a countering wave, Cuganwa descended toward the floor.

"Good work," Nuyani said as she watched the boy descend like a feather. Before Nuyani could say anything, a sudden wave sailed by, pushing her away. Nuyani's eyes widened as she then went flipping once more. Getting a knack for the pulses, she immediately righted and looked toward Kelvert.

"Excellent," the orb said. "You both are quick learners."

"How did that happen?" Nuyani questioned.

"It is just a different rhythm," Kelvert said matter-of-factly. "Right now, we match in tempo but, with a different beat or rhythm, you can create an opposing force. Doing as Cuganwa did with a single wave can cancel out most attacks if they match strength but, using multiple beats may be needed at a time." Cuganwa floated toward them, occasionally jerking about as he tried to fight the urge that he might fall over. "Now then. Are you both ready?"

"Just another question, Great Lord," Nuyani started. "Why do you look so different?"

"Ah. I am made of *edria* and have not had a mortal form like you. What you see is the remainder of my being and my soul," Kelvert answered. "As you are human's, you see yourselves in the same form as you live, making your shape. I could mirror that shape but do not wish to do so."

"Really?" Cuganwa asked in surprise. "Why not look this way, Lord Kelvert?"

"Understand that such a thing is needless, and in this realm, there is no one to see me in such a way," Kelvert answered. "Now then, anything else before we move on?"

"Yes. That mist..." Cuganwa said as he gestured with a transparent finger. Nuyani brought up her hand and pushed his down. To her surprise, contact was still possible, though she wondered how much she could pass through stone as if it weren't there. The boy looked between her and the orb before looking to the ground. "Sorry, Lord Kelvert."

"Fret not, lohtels. This is spiritual energy, *prutosa jafcelbe,* the opposite of my being." Nuyani and Cuganwa looked at the orb in surprise. "Remember, all living beings have both. Your bodies just have a third portion in matter. Now let us become one with the land." The two nodded their heads. "Great. Match my tempo, and we will move together."

Kelvert floated closer toward them. Instructing the two, Nuyani and Cuganwa placed their hands on the orb, feeling the vibrations they traveled through his calm visage. The two adjusted their own thrum to match Kelvert. With their bodies in unison, their thrum fused into one. Despite their ethereal state, Nuyani felt as if she were trembling, and her punch could destroy a stone.

"Just stay connected to me," the wisp said.

As they held on, the group descended into the earth. There was a strange resilience in the stone as if they had broken through another barrier humming within the stone of the cavern floor. Its beat seemed different yet so subtle and rapid, Nuyani barely seemed to notice. The group continued. All around them was darkness until specs of bright blue emerged beneath them. Nuyani and Cuganwa looked about as they could see orbs of blue light coming into view the further they plunged. Emerging from the dark was a dim wall of light growing brighter in their descent. The bubbles of blue light grew countless as they continued.

Nuyani and Cuganwa felt that they were going faster with the smaller orbs of light passing them in blurs.

Their hearts pounded as the wall grew near. Fighting fear and instinct, the two clung on to dear faith and the orb. The light was bright as a flame. When the area expanded, the orb struck the surface of the wall of light only to bounce off, ripples revealed only by brighter wrinkles expanded from the impact.

"What?" Nuyani questioned as the collision did not whip the two forward. The group slowly drifted backward. With the wall before them, Cuganwa and Nuyani oriented themselves to facing it as if it were on a horizon. "Why didn't we move forward?"

"We are in unison, child. Resonating together makes us a single constitution and harder to pull apart," the orb answered. "Though we will need more strength."

Cuganwa looked about the area. Amongst the dark, other small orbs of light drifted about. Some bumped into the wall of light before drifting into the opposite direction. Many of the spheres collided with one another, unbound by any force of gravity.

'Are those still as well?' the boy wondered as he eyed a nearby sphere before looking at the surface of his hand. The surface rippled like the heatwaves rising from the drylands but faster. The orbs of light, however, were still. The boy then reached out to a sphere no larger than a pebble. Placed between his first finger and thumb, he held the small orb. It felt solid, as if it were stone.

"Curious child. You're about to learn the next lesson," Kelvert stated.

"Next lesson?" Nuyani questioned as she looked over to the boy seeing the small orb in his grasp. Cuganwa focused on the sphere with his eyes narrowed. The small orb of edria started to soften as the bright edges shook and swayed slowly until they grew faster. Ripples coursed through the orb until it matched the same speed as theirs. "I see. It takes contact to break through," Nuyani said. She then turned to the orb. "But why did you fly into the wall, Lord Kelvert?"

"I like to make a point," Kelvert said plainly. Nuyani and Cuganwa stared at the sphere in silence. "To understand this world, experience is needed. You did not know how edria worked but, here is an example of the two separate forces against one another. One is vast yet completely still as the other is a mere collective resonating at a different pace. Where is the sphere now, Cuganwa?" The boy looked back at his hand, seeing his fingertips in contact but the shifting orb drifting away.

"It passed through. Why…didn't it stay there?" Cuganwa questioned.

"That is a technique for another time. One you would do well to avoid for now," Kelvert stated. "Though my will is guiding you, if you were to collect edria without understanding the change it would inflict on your body, you may live to regret it. You might grow stronger but live longer and pass even family. Some mortals have gone mad from such incidences. So young, a choice as that is not something I would not allow such a thing to happen to you. "Kelvert then guided the group toward the wall of light once more. Slow in their approach, they stopped once in contact, resting against the surface.

"I don't understand," Nuyani started. "Why a lesson in how these things act?"

"Nuyani, did the spirit's vision not show you why? Others may cast the same spells, but the different tempo and rhythm prevent one spell from passing through another's defenses easily. And, I need not warn you about your defenses. If Deyunca and To'anu were to turn and attack others, what would happen with more with my gift? There will be others who will abuse what they have, and there must be others that can counter them."

Cuganwa pulled his lips in thinking of Deyunca. The vengeance-crazed hunter was willing to kill a guard just to send everyone after Nuyani. The boy felt a deep shutter within himself, realizing the danger. His attention then turned to the wall of light. More contrasting ripples rang from the area of contact, stopping only a few meters out in radius. The ripples in the center started to grow faster.

"Together then. Focus on the hum, and we shall pass through," Kelvert instructed. The others did as the orb had asked, finding the waves of their cores resonating at an indistinguishable rate from one another. A larger circle of light formed over the surface until Nuyani could feel the surface budge and become malleable under their contact.

Her eyes widened as the orb first passed through, then hands, and finally their entire bodies. As if passing through slime, Nuyani felt as if the edria they dived into were pulling at her skin.

"I sense a question," Kelvert started. "Remember, this edria is still. We are changing that. If our thrum were any slower, then we would be trapped as I was before." Nuyani took notice of the heavy pull on her construct. The area felt heavy and claustrophobic. Looking about, the area before them was an ongoing plane of light, yet she could feel the edge close to the bordering wall, the darkness, and rocks below the surface. Small orbs were warped and twisted beyond the wall.

Cuganwa then turned to the orb and asked, "Great Lord, what are we to do?"

"You'll help me carry a connection back," Kelvert said.

"Carry?" Nuyani then questioned.

This time there was no answer as the group felt the edria surrounding grow lighter. They were retreating toward the surface of the wall as the twisted orbs shifted on the other side. Yet the light remained all around them. The thrum continued reverberating around them as they moved on, stretching a long column through the darkness. Cuganwa and Nuyani said nothing as they watched the bubbles grow sparse in their passing. The group then rose toward the surface, passing through the firepit.

"Why are we back if we needed to go down to see the memories," Nuyani questioned.

"We are forming a *hafgal* (anchor)," the orb stated. "Here we are closer to your bodies and still connected to the land's edria."

"Why don't you call it yours?" Cuganwa asked.

"I have pulled a mere pale of water from the river. Should I claim I control the river's sway?"

Kelvert answered with a low musing tone to his rasp.

"Oh," Cuganwa replied. "I think I understand."

"Good. Know this, my child, in time, even one being can move a river," Kelvert stated before shifting the group's thrum to a slower pace.

"Well then, this must be a canal," Nuyani said as she looked toward their bodies, still sitting on the floor safe and unmoving.

"Correct. This path will lead us back to the true power but, the portion we hold will allow us to accomplish many things. For now, let us look to the past. Close your eyes and allow the revival of the edria's thrum call to the past," Kelvert instructed. The two did as they let the flow of the edria influence their own energy instead. With such a thin portion, it no longer felt as repressive. Nuyani relaxed her thrum as before, allowing the outside world to influence her mind. As the spirit's energy pushed and pressed to feed her images, edria behaved differently. Through the patterns hummed and pressed against her construct, her own spirit shaped the visions.

The world rippled and shifted around them. With Kelvert in control, the two found themselves soaring through the air from the north over the red cliffs. Nuyani looked to the side and gawked at the enormous crystal flying onward. A deep thrum permeated the area around it. Her thoughts returned to the similar crystals sitting atop of the towers in the vision. 'How are you…*prutosa*,' Nuyani remembered as the faint black clouds barely contrasted the inside of the enormous crystal.

"How are you doing this, Lord Kelvert?" Cuganwa then asked.

As they passed through a cloud, the orb replied, "Every portion of my energy is at my will. As such, even this form of a stone can fly unhindered."

Nuyani looked from the front to the back as she remained on the opposite side of the structure. Kelvert's earthly form was pointed in a spearheaded shape as he raced on. The size of his entirety looked large enough to cover half the village. Looking forward, she saw the approaching break in the cliffs and the sand dunes down below. Through every structure, they were just as transparent as Nuyani and Cuganwa looked. Yet smaller clusters of the same black clouds shifted, wafted, and twisted in areas beyond the walls. Nuyani looked at her body, finding even sparse shades inside her own body, and wondered if Cuganwa's shared the same. As the group sailed toward the southwest, the sand dunes grew dimmer. The outlines became obscure as some of the shadows darkened.

Ahead of them, the light blue clouds had grown darker. Everything in view slowly was devoured by black shadows. Before Nuyani could ask why things were changing, the flying crystal veered to the side as a column of black shadow and fire rushed forth like a tide wide enough to consume the entire crystal. Nuyani could feel her body tremble as whatever they managed to dodge reduced to a thin line before disappearing altogether. Nuyani looked further, only finding a curtain of the black mist coming into view.

"What was that?" Cuganwa then asked.

"That is prutosa in its simplest application," Kelvert replied with an even, controlled tone. Yet, Nuyani could hear a sense of anger hidden in the lord's words.

"Spells can be applied with both forces and are doubly effective against one another."

Before Kelvert uttered another word, the enormous crystal veered toward the opposite side as the group continued toward the darkness. Another column of rushing shadow fired from beyond the veil, almost striking the crystal. Nuyani could feel her form slowing down in the memory as she passed through the column. Her heart raced as she expected herself to die.

A different sense then came over Cuganwa and Nuyani as they looked to the horizon. The mist itself grew darker and raced forth. Their hearts pounded heavily. A stronger thrum rose from the crystal, creating an encompassing orb. The wall of shadow washed over them. The orb and crystal shook violently as it broke through. Nuyani and Cuganwa could feel the thrum slow for a moment before the crystal continued.

"That's prutosa, right?" Cuganwa asked.

"Yes," Kelvert answered as another wall of darkness emerged from the horizon, racing toward them.

"The same things creating the sandstorm?" Nuyani asked.

Once more, Kelvert answered, "Yes."

The dark veil struck the orb. Everything trembled as they passed through. In the collision, the crystal turned slightly and slowed. Before Kelvert's old form could get its bearing, another wall of shadow rushed onward, battering the sphere hard enough to keep the crystal still. As the third wall passed, a fourth rushed on, striking the defense and pushing Kelvert back. The thrum emitted from the crystal weakened. A fifth washed over them, Nuyani and Cuganwa could feel a chill passing through their bodies. The construct then broke as a sixth wall came.

"What? How come it didn't hold?" Cuganwa asked. Nuyani knew the answer. Either the walls were stronger, or Kelvert could not concentrate. Nuyani then looked to the small sphere sitting in the center of the massive crystal.

Kelvert did not answer. She did not expect one, for their deity was reliving such an event. Sharing such a tragedy, Nuyani looked on as another column sailed forth, striking the crystal as it was turned dead center. A chill worse than the blade-jaw's roar or the banshees' touch enwrapped Nuyani. She was certain even her body was shivering from the memory. Even in ethereal form, she forced herself to curl in a ball, looking for some semblance of warmth. Kelvert's old form shook violently, twisted, and flipped as the stream of darkness pushed him back. Licking spurts of shadow parted from the column-like flame tendrils.

Cuganwa looked toward the crystal clenching his fists as if he could brace himself for such an event. The boy looked on toward the horizon shrouded in darkness.

'What kind of demon is this? The world itself is ruled by things stronger?' the boy questioned.

Cracking started to form on the crystal's surface. As the bombardment continued, large chunks of the crystal broke off and fell. Small pieces of Kelvert chipped away as they sailed backward just as fast as they had arrived. The column of shadow began to thin. Kelvert then collided with the side of the stones as another blast of shadow emerged from the horizon. This time, Kelvert created a barrier and blocked the torrent of darkness. Though the large crystal shook under the barrage, it still held. Nuyani and Cuganwa looked at the remainder of Kelvert's form. A tenth of the size, Kelvert was sent back miles beyond the cliffs they passed. Cuganwa looked to the north seeing the faint northern line making up the cliffs and a small gap marking the waterfall.

'This far?' Cuganwa thought as his body shuttered.

The crystal then lowered itself as another stream of the blasts came only for another of Kelvert's defenses deflecting it. Nuyani looked down, seeing several animals similar to tall horns but smaller and shorter horns. They fled the area as the cascading shadows reached the floor. Several animals were caught in their fleeting tendrils as their bodies went limp and souls flew toward the southwest. Kelvert increased the strength of his thrum, reinforcing his defenses as the barrier surrounding them expanded. Reaching the very edges of the drylands, Kelvert sat in place as the beam continued to fire. It stopped only for several large waves of shadow to wash through the land. The walls dissipated on contact with the barriers but, Nuyani noticed the animals below them swept away by the wind and others further west landing in the area with mangled bodies.

More souls flew toward the southwest like shining arrows. Kelvert's thrum increased in speed. Both the shadow and sands stopped but, the pressure continued. Strain met the enormous barrier. Nuyani and Cuganwa could feel the rapid pace growing sporadic in its act. Another blast of shadow rushed forth, tearing through the ethereal defense, striking Kelvert. The crystal shook under the attack as new cracks formed, yet Kelvert no longer broke apart. Instead, the deity released several more thrums toward the surrounding areas controlling his edria and feeding it into the area. The animals and land changed as their bodies were imparted with the strands of edria.

Nuyani and Cuganwa looked to the ground below. Compelled by curiosity, Nuyani flew to the ground watching as several animals grew larger and with thicker coats. Cuganwa realizing he was free to move flew low racing toward the cliffs. He saw the charge-horns, whip-necks, blade-jaws, heavy-horns, and blood-manes all change under Kelvert's influence. Despite the lines of the water bites and shrubs growing thicker to taking on the onslaught of sandstorms.

'They are opposites. That's why it affects him more,' Cuganwa thought as more waves of shadow swept over the land. The animals changed their tactics and withstood the barrage. Some perished but, the numbers of those lost were greatly reduced. 'He didn't create the life but saved it here.'

The boy flew into the cliffs watching through the transparent shape of the stone shifted about with several figures traveling through. Short men wielding strange light sources on poles were waving the lights before them at the front. Cuganwa could feel a faint thrum rising as their light touched the stone, pushing it away as if burning away brush. The people made their way in a quick march toward a natural cavern in the cliffs. In moments relative to Cuganwa, they created their large inner village and moved toward the rest of the cavern, creating an outpost and several other caverns in the cliffs. Before they could go further, Cuganwa watched as a blood-mane was knocked down by a single column of shadow aimed for it and not Kelvert. Another long, slender creature nearly encased in shadow emerged from the sand and struck the blood-mane. The animal's body wriggled and expanded in size in a violent transformation as the creature burrowed into the blood-mane's flesh, swelling the area before the beast stood up and flew over the cliffs.

'Wait. That's like the charge-horn,' Cuganwa said. The blood-mane approached a few other animals, attacking violently as the scratches it left created more solid forms of darkness that eventually grew. One by one, the strange shadows spread to other animals until the cavern played the same way as the spirit's memory. 'There's a sickness spreading through them,' the boy thought as he flew back.

Nuyani watched as the people came through the ravine cutting through the cliffs. Tattered clothing, broken items, and scarce food were carried on their backs as they tried to get through the drylands. They followed Kelvert, whose size drastically shrank as the deity continued feeding energy into the land and some who approached. Nuyani watched as the elders and fighters of the group cast away their metal pieces into the river and turned toward the crystal. Nuyani's brow furrowed as she looked at the pieces. Earrings, bracelets, necklaces, and rings, all bearing markings and figures of the other gods, tossed away to be forgotten. Kelvert started to impart his edria onto them only to reduce further in size with a small handful gaining his power. The crystal then broke apart in the act turning into an enormous flame and instead of feeding some of its power into the three rings.

"Lord Kelvert, why did you give away so much?" Nuyani questioned as she looked at his shrinking form.

"I was being torn apart. The best I could do was protect the life that was around me as my power dwindled," Kelvert stated.

"Why not flee? Why not go somewhere to strengthen your power?" Nuyani asked as her eyes grew hot, wondering if her real body had tears. A fleeting thought made it feel strange that her vibrant ghostly form could still feel such a sensation.

"There is always a hunt for strength, Nuyani. It is a game of survival even your old gods knew and played," Kelvert started. "This was merely the safest place to stay and grow. But as I've said before, haflaj seek out the unflom to fight, and though one seeks death, the other creates life." As Kelvert spoke, the energy stopped separating from the crystal, forming a barrier around the area. The village started to grow. Nuyani watched as souls then descended toward the village. She looked toward the crystal seeing small plumes of darkness appear as the souls flew out of them and to the swollen bellies of women.

"You did create us," Nuyani said.

"No merely guided you as is my nature," Kelvert corrected.

A sense of relief grew in Nuyani as she watched the same lives created then grow and thrive. More black waves passed through the area, and Kelvert's form dwindled further. Nuyani watched as the energy dissipated. Cuganwa then arrived with a stern glare.

"What's wrong?" Nuyani asked.

"There's more to those animals than we realized," Cuganwa said.

"All right. Let's discuss it later. For now, watch," Nuyani said as the history of the village came into view. The waves continued to pass on as Kelvert weakened. Eventually, the deity was merely flame and used the last of his power to the edria stored within the land torn from it. Though many animals wielded the edria, they did not possess the will to use it as their instincts served their needs. Nuyani and Cuganwa shook as they watched the first wave strike the village claiming many in its wake. Many hid under their tents to escape the harsh winds. The two dived toward the land seeing the mass of magic grow still with the passing shrouds of darkness.

Over time, the two witnessed the change of the village's structure as it grew in lower and animal pelts were toughened to withstand the storms. Nuyani watched eagerly as those with orange eyes appeared only looking brighter compared to others in the blue world. The people steadily grew in numbers until the first sinner arrived. With his display of power, he turned against the others and practiced the same abilities Nuyani barely understood as he moved in and out of the world with ease. Cuganwa wondered why Kelvert did not escape then, only to see his abilities were not dependent on the same energy as Nuyani did.

He somehow was separated from the great lord. Yet, it held the same tempo and thrum. Nuyani and Cuganwa watched a desperate chieftain race off on the back of his whip-neck through the terrain, passing heavy-horns and blood-mane territory. Kelvert's small semblance of power sent out energy waves toward the beasts, warding them off. As the chief reached a cliff and climbed to a nearby cave, he found his family in the sinner's clutches. Brazen and fool-hearted, the sinner tried to flee in and out of existence only for the chief to cut him with a slice to the man's leg predicting his movements. The cavern was not empty as the sinner looked to use his powers to control hidden blade-jaws to attack.

Nuyani and Cuganwa shuttered as they watched the chief fail to reach his family as the sinner tried to attack him. Rage filled the chief's actions as he turned and sliced through the sinner's throat. With some power in the blade, he turned to the freed blade-jaws and killed them as well. Cuganwa floated forward to the sinner. His mind flashed back to Deyunca, but he ignored the thought as he watched the man's soul fly from his body, peering through a solid shape in a dark cloak of prutosa.

'He was infested too,' Cuganwa thought.

The man wept for a moment, mourning the loss of his family before carrying his kin out of the cavern and riding back to the village. Nuyani said nothing as she watched with a cold expression. Cuganwa followed her, stealing small glances at her as they traveled on. Once at the village, they hung in the air above the village like clouds watching time slip by. For a fourth time, Nuyani saw a slaughter, a purge of their people with different eyes as the distraught chief declared such abilities to be demonic, no better than the beasts that could kill dozens of men. Nuyani's stomach twisted as she watched. She wanted to retort such thoughts. To change the time and choice. The chief held such secrets as to wield edria much like the warriors they descended from. Yet here, one ability was taboo compared to another. Cuganwa glanced at her fists clenching tightly as she looked onward.

'Damn these beliefs. To the sands with them,' Nuyani thought. She looked at the man as he rapidly aged over time. People gathered to hear the new rhetoric as the chief stepped down to become an elder and another came forth filling the role knowing that he was sacrificing his blood and name for the village's survival. Their demons were gone but no sway would easily be held over the chief who must lead. Nuyani's scowled at the man wanting to hate him, to wish his passing was stuck in the world like other spirits for the lineage of pain and fear that she was born in. The anger would not flare. The hatred did not stick. Even as the passing time claimed him and his body sent to cremation and returned to the river, she could not see a monster. Just a man who lost his family to another whose greed and pride made him that way.

Time continued. Nuyani looked about, recognizing the setting of the villages as the villagers passed by in trailing blurs. She descended to the village as the rushing visages of time seemed to slow gradually. Cuganwa blinked several times as he looked about. Night claimed the sky as the villagers held a festival. The large bonfires were alight.

'Where are you going?' Cugnawa thought, following Nuyani.

Nuyani's disposition changed as she stopped just before the boy's tent. He looked at it, and to her, his eyes widened. The woman grabbed both of her arms and hunched over as if struck by a sudden chill. Cuganwa looked about, wondering what was happening only to focus on the tent, his tent. Time seemed normal as people walked at leisurely paces conversing with one another. Nuyani kept her attention on the tent. The thrum of the world warped and twisted around her as she flew forward.

"I…have another secret, Cuganwa," the woman said as she passed through the tent.

'Secret?' Cuganwa stared on, looking at his home. The boy took a deep breath and sailed through the spaces separated by canvas only to find his home, his space, occupied by a sleeping Nuyani. A younger version of her lying on her sleeping mat. Next to her lay a pile of chips shaved from ivory lying around a knife as a whetstone and carving tools sat by the side. The current Nuyani turned to the other room before the sound of the tent's front flaps could be heard. The soft yet heavy footsteps on the carpet made the boy's eyes narrow.

"Hello, love," came a woman's voice. Cuganwa blinked several times, not recognizing it. His chest rose up and down as he listened to the center space with firelight showing through the entrance.

"Why're you two cooped up in her? Join us. It wouldn't be much of a celebration if my two treasures did not accompany me," Sutama's voice answered after loving laughter from both. Cuganwa's eyes widened as he stared at Nuyani. He could feel his chest pounding like a finale of drums.

"Well, let me wake her, and we will join you, hunting leader," the woman teased.

It was too late as the other Nuyani had awoken with a smile on her face and brighter eyes than the others as her surroundings pulsated. The young girl retrieved the ivory knife and rushed toward the entrance.

"Father," Nuyani called out. Cuganwa was dumbstruck as he flew swifter than the howlers into the other room.

There, his father's eyes bulged from his younger, thinner frame as he pointed to Nuyani.

The young girl halted in her approach as she read his shocked expression. Beside him, another woman resembling Nuyani in all but her hair, attire, and age started to weep as she stood between Sutama and Nuyani.

"Love. Please. We had to hide it. We must…" the woman said.

Her words fell on deaf ears as the man marched forth, changing his expression from shock to pure rage. Cuganwa knew his father to be as devout as any man, even the elders and chief. To find a demon, a corrupted one of blood, stirred many questions and fears in the boy's mind. Cuganwa shook his head as he watched his father's fury rush for Nuyani, grabbing her hair and pulling the ivory knife free of her grasp. Nuyani's mother yelled and pulled at his arm, pleading for the man to release her. Tears welled in Sutama's eyes as he looked at the knife. His face wrinkled with fury as his wife beat his head and back, trying to free Nuyani.

The man tossed the item to the floor and pulled Nuyani away as if she were a mere bundle of clothes. Her mother fell to the floor, calling the man to reason as she crawled to the stairs. Sutama had already pulled her out of his home and into the opening. Nuyani watched as her mother scrounged for the knife she shaved as a gift for her father and ran outside. Cuganwa was breathing heavily. Shock and horror mixed on his face as he clenched his fists. Nuyani said nothing as she sailed by and glanced at him. She flew outside.

Several villagers and guards started toward the man, wondering what madness fell upon him only to see the gleaming ember eyes of his daughter. Their concern transformed into resentment. A young girl they knew for her entire life was now just a demon. Her mother continued to fight as two other villagers grabbed her arms.

The festival stopped. Instruments and songs halted as only the roar of the bonfires and Nuyani's cries could be heard.

"Please! Father! Let go!" Nuyani howled as she tried to pull away from his strong stone grip.

He found a rock large enough to sit in his hand, heavy enough to kill.

"No!" her mother called out, twisting her wrist to cut into the villager's wrist who was trying to hold her left arm and slashed at the other, cutting his cheek. Sutama raised the stone and forced Nuyani to kneel. Cuganwa's breathing grew deeper as he looked at his father, the villagers, Nuyani, her mother. These were the devout people to Lord Kelvert. His father paused, hesitating to deliver the blow, only for her mother to stab into Sutama's shoulder in desperation.

Sutama bellowed in pain as he released Nuyani but not the stone. He whipped around, blinded by his turbulent emotions and striking the woman in her temple. Sutama's eyes widened. He froze, watching his wife fall to the floor and lie still.

"M-Mother?" Young Nuyani whimpered in disbelief as she crawled to her. The woman lied still. Nuyani made her way to her as the village watched silently.

Sutama dropped the stone on the floor and started to kneel as he whispered, "Huloat…"

Nuyani saw him from the corner of her eyes and swung out toward him. They could feel the thrum rippling through the air but, to the others, it was as if she had command of the winds, blowing the man away. Sutama fell to the floor by the sudden force bewildered by the power. The villagers exploded in an uproar, rushing toward her. Young Nuyani protectively reached over her mother, watching as the dozens of hands were silhouetted by the bonfires behind them, creating out-reaching shadows. Before anyone could reach Nuyani, the air bent and warped into a dark void like water draining from a hole. Nuyani and her mother disappeared, leaving only the confused villagers and Sutama on the floor weeping.

'Congratulations, hunting leader,' Nuyani wanted to mouth, wanted to shout. She wanted to hammer the lesson into Cuganwa and show him the pain. She stopped, knowing both he and their sister were all in danger if Sutama was still the same man. With time nearly reaching the current day, the two returned to Lord Kelvert's orb waiting above them.

The group remained silent as they sailed toward the cliffs. Time sped up once more as animals and shrubs below shifted. Once they reached the cavern, Nuyani and Cuganwa returned to their bodies as they ached from the constant use of edria. Cuganwa turned to her with a glare.

"Is that why you saved me? Did you know who I was, sister," Cuganwa chided.

Nuyani glanced at the boy in annoyance as she simply replied, "No. Just thought I'd help a fool who ran through the snare." Cuganwa's glare deepened, expressing his rage as he bared his teeth. The boy's breathing grew harsh as if he were being choked as he moved forward, propped up on his knees and toes. His fists were balled as he began to hammer the floor. Nuyani looked away as the world Cuganwa knew shattered. She drew her lips in as her eyes shined with tears.

"Great Lord, why?" Cuganwa questioned. "Why'd this happen?"

"Survival, child," Kelvert answered.

Cuganwa's head shot up from the floor as he looked at the floating blue flame. His eyes gleamed in ember. "But where were you?" the boy demanded. "We could…"

"Enough!" the wisp commanded. Cugnawa felt his body freeze. Nuyani looked at him and to the blue flame. Controlling them was not something she thought the wisp could do. Cuganwa shuttered, trying to break the freeze. The thrum emitted from his body halted, one Nuyani was not aware it was acted upon. Cuganwa could move as he took several breaths. "I placed my faith in you all as I withered away. I was dying as your ancestors destroyed all that I placed in them, and all my efforts led to you two as the most capable. I see your anger. You fear that this power will turn everyone against you or Young Caluu." Cuganwa was silent, closing his mouth as he looked to the ground. "I could do that but, that merely means that every defense and effort I gave will be for nothing, and the others will die with my strength severed." Cuganwa sat on his heels and looked to the side.

'How do we survive this?' The boy thought as he gripped his knees.

"If you wish to live, then fight. You know the truth now, all truths. Now, will you fight?" Kelvert asked, testing the boy. Nuyani watched.

'Don't give up, Cuganwa,' Nuyani thought.

The boy looked up to the wisp before lowering his head, placing a hand on his heart, and raising his other hand, palm face up. "Please guide me, Great Lord," Cuganwa replied. Nuyani let out a breath, unaware that she had held it.

"Then speak to one another. Share more and learn," Kelvert instructed. "As I wish you to be free, you must fight to do so."

"Yes, Lord Kelvert," Cuganwa replied in a softer tone. He looked to Nuyani, waiting for her to meet his gaze.

Nuyani sensed the boy's attention was turned on her and looked back to him. "What's wrong?" she asked sensing something else disturbed him.

"The sinner. He was infested," Cuganwa claimed.

Nuyani blinked several times before replying, "What do you mean infested?"

Cuganwa looked down at the floor as he tried to find the right words. "You know how the animals attacked the shorter people?" Nuyani nodded her head. "Something is in them. Something without a soul but had the shape of spirit when it entered a blood-mane that fell in the demon lands. The blood-mane grew, and the spot swelled like… like that charge-horn. W-where is that thing?" Nuyani's eyes widened as she retrieved her crystal and directed the lights toward the wall. The pink and gray mass streamed from the stone in a twisting spiral before lying on the floor. Cut chunks exposed to them and rotting smell filling the area.

"What do you mea…" Nuyani started only to stop as her thrum radiated through the carcass. Several new pressures sat on her core. "There's something there now," Nuyani said. Cuganwa felt it as well, and the two stood.

"Caution you two. The enemy may have more abilities than we realize," Kelvert said. The two then turned to the inside of the carcass as the flesh slowly bulged and shifted around the spine. Nuyani removed her knife, a usual act Cuganwa noticed. He copied her actions, trusting her years of survival as they looked at the hulking dead carcass.

"Do you know what it looked like?" Nuyani asked. Cuganwa stole a glance at her. "The thing that was in the animal and the sinner.

"N-No," Cuganwa answered. "Time passed too fast. I only saw it attack the blood-mane before that started attacking others.

"Right," Nuyani rasped. She readied her thrum.

Before anyone could utter another word, the flesh burst, releasing blood as a maw of pincers shot out like a spear thrust toward them. Nuyani reacted with a barrier between them and the strange creatures as she raised her knife. There was little need for the defense as the creature snapped and wriggled several feet from the construct giving Nuyani and Cuganwa a good look at the strange parasite. Clicks and clatter filled the air as the segmented worm wriggled about, trying its best to reach them. Its beady eyes trained on the two. Nuyani shivered. A similar sensation rose from the odd creature as the howlers, an example of a foul perversion of life that made her feel sick. From the corner of her eye, Cuganwa trembled. The same boy who stared down a large charge-horn, and even tried to attack her, was shaking. She knew he had to feel the same terror.

"W-what do we do?" Cuganwa asked.

"It must be destroyed," Kelvert answered, "Its abilities to spread are a poison to the land."

Nuyani looked at the turning flesh as several more lines moved separately from the clattering worm head. Before she could say anything, another of the creatures shot from the corpse's front leg. Nuyani created another barrier despite the first defense already having erected and enclosed the second worm's head in a sphere. Nuyani's construct severed its head. The body went limp as a rope, yet the head continued to click and move.

Nuyani and Cuganwa gawked at the creature in disgust as it continued to move. The shells were filled with a yellow puss much like the blemish on the charge-horn. The two turned to the head as the worms feverishly clattered and moved in the confined space toward them.

Pressure still sat on their cores. Nuyani shook her head. Controlling the sphere, she levitated the wriggling worm head toward the fire. The tenacious creature continued its ill-gotten pursuit of the two as it clicked at them. Nuyani felt cautious of the creature creating a second sphere partially open as the edges cut into one of the pincers. The larger sphere dissipated, leaving the beast's head to dangle. Flames licked at the animal head. Now it noticed the pain and wriggled even faster, attempting to escape the fire. The two shivered as they watched in horror of the severed head managing an ear-piercing screech. When the body stopped moving, Nuyani released her hold on the creature's head, letting it drop into the flames. Cuganwa glanced back at the other worm, still reaching for them unconcerned with the death fallen onto one of its own. The flesh continued to twist and shift, signaling that more were inside the carcass. The boy did not wait, grabbed a stick from the fire pit, and maneuvered around the construct. With a flick of his wrist, he tossed the burning twig into the charge-horn's rib cage.

A flame belched from the gutted creature making Cuganwa fall behind Nuyani's construct. Wide-eyed, they saw the inferno rise only to die out before it towered almost halfway up to the ceiling. The carcass itself burned swiftly. Bone, sinew, and fat fed the fire like a grass field. Cuganwa and Nuyani watched as two more worms burst from the animal's carcass to join in a desperate dance for survival as their flaming bodies scratched at the ground.

Nuyani narrowed her eyes. 'They really are parasites,' she thought, taking note of the worms refusing to leave their host's burning body. Even the river bites were willing to hop and flounder on the round looking for another pool of water in the occasional drought.

The air filled with both the succulent smell of roasted charge-horn and putrid rot. The mixed aroma hit their noses, making the two cover themselves in retreat. 'Can't tell if I should be hungry or disgusted right now,' Cuganwa said.

Nuyani fixed the barrier wall around the beast, realizing it was the best they could do at the time. As the dome enclosed the burning beast, the smoke covered the space hiding the charred creature.

"We eat," Nuyani declared as she lowered her hand from her face. "No sense in going hungry when we could be attacked at any moment." Retrieving her crystal, Nuyani then released the other charge-horn. Knowing better, she released a thrum passing through its body, ensuring it wasn't infested. No disturbances met her call, and Nuyani sighed as she strolled to one of her baskets and retrieved more knives and spicks.

Cuganwa waited by the side as she prepared the food. Curious about his abilities, Cuganwa instead looked toward the dome and tried to replicate the construct. Unlike the others, he found he could follow their instructions but did not like that he needed a guide. Holding his hands out with palms facing one another, he tried to control the thrum once more. As the rapid pulses coursed from his stomach, he tried to guide them through his hands. Remembering the sensation he felt in trying to heal Nuyani's leg, the boy smiled as a blue light shined in both palms.

Ch. 22

Nights of Truth

As the two crescent moons hung in the sky with little more than a sliver remaining in view, Sutama looked at them in worry as the others stoked the fire and readied the camp. His mind fell on Nuyani and Cuganwa. His boy was saved by her and now abducted by her. Or was he saved once more? The man could not tell.

'Great Lord, why is my family plagued with this curse? What reason has it come to us?' the old hunter questioned as he then retrieved the second blade held in a quiver.

Whispers then reached the man's ears from other fires. "He must be planning it. How else did she get the blade?" one man questioned.

"No. He was willing to risk his life for his son and wanted to go alone. He was even ready to give his position to Odaru. He's honest," another defended.

Someone scoffed. "If that's the best reason, then why is the witch still alive? His first wife is dead because of her," another stated far louder than he intended.

Sutama's blood raged on as he shot up from his seat, gripping the quiver tightly as it creased under his grip. The man released the blade, stopped, and turned to face the others.

'To the sands with you,' Sutama thought as he started toward the group. The old hunter halted in his steps when a loud thwack sounded. Selsaj was standing over a guard lying on the ground to everyone's surprise.

"Don't ever talk about such things so casually. People have lived because of his guidance and devotion to the lord. Don't flaunt his trials around for the sake of a laugh," the hunter said as he held his cheek and sat back up.

The others grew quiet as a few looked up to see Sutama standing by. They looked away with a sense of shame. A few shot dirty looks at Selsaj, seeing the young hunter scolding his elder but still correct. Sutama said nothing as he, too, turned from them, his mind plagued with questions. 'Great Lord, what is the reason for this trial? Am I to be judged for Huloat? I will accept that fate but, please spare the boy,' Sutama thought to himself. Sutama pulled the quiver into his lap and pulled out some of the blade, letting the fire and moons light gleam on the polished surface as he caught his reflection.

Footsteps sounded from his side, catching the man's attention. Sutama looked to see Gamaunda approaching him with two small water skins in hand bearing his usual cheerful grin. 'Perhaps a word before we start, "The chief said as he handed one to the hunter. Sutama retrieved the quiver and took up the small water skin nodding back in thanks. "What do you suppose the witch was doing with that blade?" Gamaunda started as he caught his reflection.

The old hunter shook his head as he untied the water skin's thong. "I don't know. Going for heavy-horns is nothing new, but going to wherever that place was to get a blade is beyond me. Lord Kelvert's will, we can find an answer," Sutama replied.

"I don't mean to pry but, why haven't you tried to kill her all these years?" Gamaunda questioned. Sutama froze and looked at him. The chief merely stared back, waiting.

"I couldn't," the hunter stated. "After I…killed Huloat, how could I?" Sutama lowered the water skin. "She looks like her. Sounds like her. Even in the drylands. Nuy…" Sutama paused, realizing how easy it was for him to speak her name. "She…is the last thing alive to remind me of her. I had destroyed that peace. Lord Kelvert has not willed me the conviction to harm her. Every time I have seen her, I thought of an excuse, a reason, to attack when she was already gone. Her eyes hold hatred. She is no threat outside the village."

"She could've been," Gamaunda countered.

"And yet she hasn't," Sutama said, shaking his head.

Gamaunda's stare grew harder. "What do you think keeps her from doing anything?" Sutama looked to the water skin. His lips grew tight as the question rattled in his mind. A moment of silence rose before the man shook his head.

"I don't know," Sutama said, still looking for an answer. His eyes gleamed brighter. The swirling memories brought only pain to the man as he tried to answer the question.

Gamaunda noticed the man's solemn stare into the earth. The chief sighed before he answered, "A devout man must have raised a devout daughter." Sutama's brow rose as he started to turn toward the chief but stopped. His grip tightened on the quiver. He could not accept such a truce, especially when even the others assumed Nuyani was trying to win favor back into the village. Over a decade, the argument was weak to dispute the chief's claim. "By the Great Lord's will, you may have a child more determined to prove she is not a demon and aided you and your party." Sutama looked at the man wondering why the façade. "Let me be more direct." Gamaunda sat closer with his grin disappearing and his tone growing serious. "There are other possibilities. Your daughter is either trying to buy your trust to get back into the village, or she has your trust, and you're using her to take over."

Sutama glared at the chief, the rage returning as his fists shook. The man then stopped as he looked at Gamaunda with a sense of annoyance. "Elder Yanuma would've warned you if I had such thoughts. Why are you testing me?" Sutama asked. He narrowed his eyes at the chief.

"Because I must," Gamaunda stated. "It was no lie, Sutama, that I trust your judgment but, I need to know where your mind is. We are taking on someone more dangerous than any other person alive and probably as dangerous as the beasts that live out here."

Sutama replied, "You think I would turn on the village? By the Great Lord's light, I…"

"I am simply trying to get answers. Nothing has been decided. . Saving your son and apprehending the witch is the best to hope for in this situation but, remember all eyes are on you," Gamaunda pressed. His brow was creased and his tone serious but, they contained his condolences, not spite as others would. "Tell me. Did she go for the sword to create a new village?" Sutama straightened his back and narrowed his eyes as he gawked at the chief. "Yes or no?"

"No. How long is this test, dear chief? I've worked to preserve and keep my men and the village safe," Sutama shot back.

"Not a doubt in my mind but a reason to ask," Gamaunda said. "There are two blades, and you men have talked the most about expanding the village."

"Iogda and Selsaj talk to fill the air and share their thoughts on the trail. Nothing about their comments is meant as a threat," Sutama said.

"Yet, they're one of the few who speak of such things. I do not ask to find criminals, Sutama, but the timing is too close," Gamaunda urged.

Sutama wanted to snap at the man wanted to yell as the rage boiled in him, ready to burst. The old hunter leaned forward, glaring at the chief. "Take only my life if need be, dear chief. By the Great Lord, I am the only thing of sin in this trial. Not my men and not my family," Sutama declared.

"Does that family include the witch?" Gamaunda pressed. Sutama said nothing as the two merely leered at one another.

The shuffle of footsteps sounded behind the two drawing their attention. One of the patrolling guards approached with widened eyes and his hands straining on the shaft of his spear as he looked out into the drylands.

"Yes?" Gamaunda asked, startling the man.

"A-a spirit is close by, Chief Gamaunda," the guard stated.

"What?" the village leader asked as he rose from his seat. "Did you check?"

"Yes. Piut's group harvests this area," Sutama answered.

Gamaunda shook his head and said, "This makes sense." The guard looked toward the chief. "Remember one of the parties had a murder from an affair? We may have found the area." The guard released a breath and lowered his spear as he looked back at the area. "The family cremated his body. By his shine, I wonder why he still lingers."

"W-what do we do?" the guard asked, still shaken by the lingering spirit.

"I will release him, and you will follow me. We are still out in the wilderness. I don't think I'd want to try my luck," the chief said as he flicked his wrist and the curved blade of the village poured from its containment. Before the two trudged off into the brush, Gamaunda then called out, "I don't know what will happen, Sutama. Lord

Kelvert seems to guide you. Just prove it so." The two then set off into the drylands.

Sutama looked back toward the flame. His mind flickered to the night Nuyani fled. Her glowing eyes gleamed like a fire revealing her pain and fear. The rejected gift of a daughter who did little more than work as her mother did as well. The man shook his head, gripping the quiver in his hands. He removed some of the blade, letting it gleam in the fires as another angle of its surface revealed his reflection.

"Great Lord, who is the true sinner?" the old hunter wondered as he gritted his teeth.

Ch. 23

Night Lessons

Nuyani and Cuganwa were already lying down in bedrolls in separate stone huts. With Kelvert acting as an anchor for the well of edria, his bright glow made it harder for either of them to sleep on the high shelf. Nuyani decided to stay away from Cuganwa, still accustomed to living alone for so long. Nuyani lay awake in the hut pressed against the stone wall opposite the entrance with both eyes open. Her thrum was ringing stronger than ever for any threat around her.

'I am a child of the Great Lord. I'm not a demon. I deserve to live,' Nuyani told herself. She looked at her hands, wondering about all the powers and abilities she could use with the Great Lord's gift. His edria made her stronger than normal. 'What am I going to fight with this gift? Will the others still attack?' Worry continued to boil within her as the thoughts of the villagers turning on her and even Lord Kelvert came to mind. She doubted his power until he proved to her with memories only she would have. How would the others? Who would believe a floating blue flame held off the sandstorms long ago. 'I am not a demon…,' she repeated, trying to keep her thoughts at bay as sleep eluded her.

Nuyani's mind instead drifted to the demon lands wondering what dangers lay in such a place. She thought of the walls of the shadow that battered the Great Lord, the streams of darkness that decimated his being, and the black wisps that lay even within his structure. The world of blue was strange. Her mind spun with the knowledge she was given. Life contained both edria and prutosa. There were creatures called unflom, and Kelvert was a haflaj. The parallels wracked in her mind.

'If we traveled in the world of edria, can we do the same for prutosa,' she wondered. Nuyani thought of the possibilities. In seeing Kelvert's memory, she was a construct of pulses in sequence with the others. Thinking of the feelings the spirits gave her, she wondered what she would look like. Her first thoughts came to the image of another howler. She frowned at the thought. Nuyani then thought of the young girl and To'anu. Both wore the marks of their death. She wondered if she could do this living if it would be much of the same.

Curiosity rose in her as she then prayed to Kelvert, releasing her thoughts in concentrated waves toward the wisp, 'Lord Kelvert?'

"Yes, Nuyani?" the wisp said in her voice with a gentle tone and echo.

'I know there is a world for edria but, does that mean there is also one for prutosa, and can one become a spirit without dying?'

There was a pause. "Why yes," the flame answered, elated. "But, is this to see your mother?" A sense of concern and worry hung in the words.

Nuyani's eyes widened. 'I didn't think to ask, Great Lord. But could I, as a spirit?'

Another pause. "There are risks to the other side, Nuyani."

"I do understand, Great Lord, but please. I wish to see her.'

"Nuyani, this is not like the world of edria. The strength you carry will be of your own will and mind. There is little edria can do on that side." Kelvert's borrowed voice grew stern.

'Please, Lord Kelvert. I merely wish to see her just before things grow even more dangerous. In case I...' Nuyani paused, realizing she showed fear despite their deity showing faith in imparting his power to the land.

"I understand your fear, Nuyani. But, this is a place I can do little to aid you in." Nuyani eyes opened wide, "I can take you there, but even more so than ever, you will have to protect yourself."

'Please.'

"Very well."

Before Nuyani could utter another word, she felt a strong thrum course through the area. The waves then condensed within her senses. A strange space became blocked to her thrum as it radiated through the area. Seconds later, a small glowing orb no larger than her stomach passed through the wall. Nuyani blinked as she sat up from her bedroll.

"Let's consider this a lesson then. You must learn to control your spirit. But first, let us free your soul."

She blinked twice before asking, "What do I do?"

"Lie down and rest." Nuyani did as she was told, raising her brow as she watched a sphere of light hover over her. "This will hurt."

Nuyani's body clenched from the warning as the sphere fired downward, leaving a streak of light trailing after. The construct passed through her body, piercing her core and removing her soul. Nuyani felt her mind and body rip away from her flesh as it was held on the vibrant grasp of the wisp. Ghostly pain rang through her as if she were being ripped apart. The initial strike surprised Nuyani but, remembering the pain that came from entering the edria world allowed her to resist as she stayed focused on her surroundings. Once more in Kelvert's hold, she found his abilities boundless as she learned about the world. His visage was suspended in black circles with solid lines that vibrated with his thrum. Wisps of blue flames could be seen in the far distance.

"I...didn't think it'd be like this," Nuyani said, finding an echo to her voice as she looked at her hands. Her body was made of blue once more but in more detail as the outline of her body danced with thread-thin flames and small distortions to the scenery beyond them like heat waves. She could scarcely see them without staring for a moment. Nuyani looked down at the rest of her body, finding the same transparent sphere sitting in place of her stomach and the same size of her core. The iridescent flame within still dancing in all directions.

"This is your soul and how you see yourself," Kelvert explained. His voice rasped once more as it filled the space around her.

The sphere started to move as Nuyani looked about, seeing rapid black waves rising from a source within another wisp of blue fire concentrated in the middle. "Is that Cuganwa?" Nuyani questioned,

"Yes, it is," Kelvert answered. "You've grasped the world quite easily, Nuyani. The souls residing in every living being come from the prutosa world, but unlike edria, souls or *prajialxalc* must stay in a pool or surrounding prutosa. The edria residing within you is holding that pool to house your prajial. Without a container or a way to maintain that collection, the soul would naturally return to the realm. Now let's focus on the next task."

Nuyani furrowed her brow. "What are we doing before we leave?"

"You must learn to move and return along with defending yourself, my child," Kelvert answered. "This is still a place that I have little power in. Both you and I would be at a disadvantage."

"Yes, Great Lord. What's first?" Nuyani asked undeterred.

"First, you must learn to control your movement," Kelvert said. "Then you will learn to separate your mind. This is merely a beginning to the other world. Might be easier to arrive somewhere when you know where to go."

The size of the sphere of edria then increased as it floated above Nuyani. "Try to act or use the protusa as you have magic. Though they are opposites, their use is similar," Kelvert instructed.

Nuyani said nothing as she merely looked to the opposite side of her confines and tried to control her thrum. As if flexing a familiar muscle, Nuyani was propelled forward, yet the feeling was different. To her back, it felt as if she were burning something away as she moved. The sensation of heat rose in her but, never hot enough for discomfort as she floated on. Nuyani looked back and found a trail of blue light following behind her. Forgetting she was inside a small space, Nuyani hit the wall of Kelvert's construct. Small ripples appeared as the point of contact turned almost transparent and weaker than the rest of the dark construct. Once the brief ripples died out, Nuyani felt the wall strengthen in its pulse and pushed her back.

The witch checked her ghostly form, ensuring she would not break apart or turn into embers as the howlers had. "What is following me?" Nuyani questioned as she examined her form. Despite gravity eluding her as it had the other form, she felt there was less of her now.

"Remember, Nuyani, edria comes from a solid state as prutosa jafcelbe (spirit energy) comes from a collection drawn by the soul from the realm of prutosa. One that can also diminish from excess use or outside influences. This is why it is dangerous. Lose too much spirit and your soul will separate and return to its realm where the energy is endless but, your life is gone." Nuyani remained silent as she repeated the warning in her mind. "Try to control your flight once more."

Following Kelvert's orders, Nuyani moved about in the enclosed space to practice her flight. Nuyani spread out her arms as she had seen many birds would and went from the top of the sphere to the bottom and circled the sides. Nuyani could not help but smile as she felt weightless, imagining herself flying high seeing the clouds and sun closer than ever. Nuyani then stopped as she looked at the ghostly trail of spirit lingering behind her. Her smile faded as she thought of the howlers. The spirits had come for her making Nuyani wonder how important her gifts truly were if such beings hadn't come before. Realizing the threat was even more dangerous, Nuyani made sharp turns evading imagined swipes and screams.

'Whatever is out there, I will face it and free you, mother,' Nuyani thought.

Cugawna lay awake in his bedroll. He felt the thrum of Kelvert course through the cavern. He turned, wondering if there was any threat but paused. Nuyani was still, and nothing else accompanied the sudden thrum.

'I'm just anxious,' the boy thought as he sat up.

Looking at his hands, his thoughts trailing back to the day's events. From aiding another hunting party to learning their lord was alive but weakened, the witch they all feared was his sister. Cuganwa ran his fingers through his hair, slowly letting the gnarled strands spring into place. The soft hum of Kelvert and the well seemed to soothe him as his thoughts weighed on his shoulders.

'There must be more I can do,' the boy thought as he focused on Nuyani's constructs. Cuganwa thought those two were the most important to practice with walls of light and guided healing. Taking a deep breath, Cuganwa focused on his core. He could feel the soft hum rising from the ethereal drum at rest. Continuing to concentrate, the boy felt the vibrations grow stronger and faster. Keeping his head clear, Cuganwa envisioned his hands glowing once more. Following his will, the waves grew rapid, coursing through his arms until they reached his hands. Light began to appear in the boy's palms. He smiled. The same repeated patterns were similar to Kelvert's when he guided the boy to heal Nuyani. The waves were rapid but, not all were uniform as nearly every third or fourth wave was larger than the others. His thoughts were cut short as he winced. Cuganwa felt a creak in his leg, finding the bedroll thinner in some areas than others.

The boy pressed his hands onto his leg with a curious grin in place. The vibrations passing from his hands into the limb numbed the creak. After waiting a few seconds, he lifted his leg and tested his knee. The pain was gone.

A wider grin appeared on his face, 'I can't tell if it's healed but, that is much better."

Cuganwa placed his foot on the ground and looked at the wall in Nuyani's general direction. From her story, she had created an orb of light as the shorter people had. Cuganwa placed a hand on his core to remember the spirit's waves that brushed against the ethereal wall.

'Can I remember?" the boy thought as he held up his hand once more and concentrated on the vibrations.

Each wave was strong and uniform as they coursed into his hand. The power collected into a single thrum as a small white sphere of light appeared before his hand. It grew larger by the second until it reached the full span of his hand. Strain then reached his hand as the muscles tightened. Cuganwa winced as his body was forced to release the orb. The edria projectile fired forth like a pitched stone and struck the wall. Small particles of dust rose. Loud crumbling echoed through the cavern. Cuganwa rose to his feet, wondering if his attack would collapse the stone hut. The home proved sturdy as he waited for the dust to clear. Cuganwa stayed silent for a moment, wondering if Nuyani would wake to the sudden noise. Yet, no reply came.

A wide smile now rose on his face. 'Good. I have an attack,' the boy thought. 'Now for that wall,' Cuganwa thought. Repeating the same feed into a single thrum, orange light appeared in his palm and slowly took the shape of a squared wall as it grew. The wall of light was transparent with an orange tint as it remained suspended above the ground. Cuganwa looked at the wall admiring his work as he breathed heavily.

'Great. I can just think of them, and…' the boy looked down and lowered his hand, letting the construct disappear. 'No. She was faster. It was almost an instant,' Cuganwa recalled. Nuyani's constructs appeared several paces away before the worms. His brow furrowed as he thought of the strange creatures bursting from the charge-horn. 'Wonder how many animals those things are infesting now,' Cuganwa thought. 'Doesn't matter. We'll have to deal with that later.' Cuganwa tried to focus his core once more but winced. Taking a deep breath, he blocked out the pain and tried to create another barrier.

"Excellent work," Kelvert said as Nuyani flew. "I believe you have a grasp of this state. Now to learn how to free yourself and return."

"Great Lord, why wasn't that first?" Nuyani questioned.

"You would not know what to free, dear child, or how to return," Kelvert answered her. "I'll take you back to your body. Through the contact of the sphere and her core, she could feel a deadening chill from her body as the thrum was weaker even compared to the first time she used it. The sphere's pulses grew stronger at the top as it compressed downward, injecting Nuyani's soul back into her core. She awoke with a painful chill, making every joint ache a moment later.

Shuttering under the sensation, Nuyani then asked, "Why am I so cold?"

"Your soul was absent, child," Kelvert reminded her. "With it gone, the body is essentially dying?" The woman's eyes widened. "No need to be frightened. The answer to this dilemma will be *prutosa yodseij,* to spirit walk, Nuyani."

"Spirit walk?" she repeated.

"Taking a copy of your conscience and moving as we had in the edria world," Kelvert explained. His tone then grew concerned. "If something were to happen to it, you could be broken or never wake if the control of your conscience is taken. It's merely too vulnerable. Are you certain?"

"Yes," Nuyani declared, not letting a single moment rise for hesitation.

"Good. Your will is strong as well," Kelvert stated. "Now try to turn the thrum inward." Nuyani blinked, scarcely remembering what she had done to do so. The core naturally radiated outward. Remember that the core, the energy moves as you will to try to release a thrum inward and see the shape of your prutosa and prajial."

Nuyani glanced down at her hands, wondering how to do so. Though the pulses coursed through her, he felt as if she were asked to swim backward while facing forward and your back to the sky. Nuyani then looked at her hands as an idea rose in her head. Every discovery she had, Nuyani felt out as she went along. Pressing her palms together, Nuyani sent a thrum coursing through her left and passing into her right. She let the wave rush forth, meeting her core and trying to let it pass through. For a moment, the boundary was passed as she felt the familiar slosh and swirl of life as she felt from those around her. A smile crept on her face but faded as she started to concentrate further. Sending a short pattern of waves coursing through one arm and entering the other, the pulses reached her core passing further with each ring.

'I think I have it,' Nuyani thought as she concentrated on the next thrum, this time sending the wave inward. Her mind envisioned a sphere barrier condensing within her. The opposing forces resisted one another but, Nuyani could feel the ebb and flow of her spirit. The twists, turns and shifting currents were sudden yet familiar.

"Do you feel it?" Kelvert asked her.

"Yes," she replied.

"Good. You will need to see the portions of your prutosa surrounding your soul to prutosa yodseij," Kelvert explained. "Just like before but, to remove a portion and control it with your conscience." Nuyani froze for a moment, thinking of what the wisp had told her. She was to draw from her own spirit and control it. It seemed difficult for her just to see her own soul. To pull sections apart from it seemed daunting. "Give it a try."

Nuyani took a deep breath, her mind dwelling on the thrum traveling through her. Thinking of how she could send the wave, Nuyani sent one of the waves through her core, trying to sever a portion of prutosa. Nuyani grunted as her edria struck her soul. The collision nearly caused her to blackout. Her body swayed forward before tilting back. Kelvert's sphere changed in shape and sailed behind her, propping up her back.

"No. No, child," Kelvert said. "You are to draw from the energy, not to separate it."

Nuyani heard him even in her sudden stupor. "Draw from it? What do you mean?" she questioned.

"Hmm. Perhaps it was too early for you to try this," Kelvert concluded as he removed the sphere from her back.

Nuyani sat up on her own as she looked down at her bedroll. 'I wasn't supposed to take some of the spirit out?' she thought.

"Think of how I return your soul," Kelvert started. "It is not in scooping it out, but to eject it from your core."

Nuyani looked forward, partially understanding what the wisp had meant. With another try, she concentrated on the thrum pushing more waves into her core, focusing on one side of the condensed sphere to remove some of her spirit. As she pressed on, she could feel some of her spirit flowing from the ethereal confines. 'I think I have it,' Nuyani thought. She felt her mind segmenting under the separation as the thrum lessened.

"You are doing well, child," Kelvert started. "If you continued to imagine something different to control it. Another name for your prutosa is a *prajial poljiad,* your soul shadow."

The word rang as clear as her pulse. Envisioning her body moving like a responding shadow, her conscience shifted, transferring from her body to the smaller segment. 'This is…odd,' Nuyani thought as the sense of warmth filled her, almost making up all she could feel. Now in a prutosa form, her edria looked like waving shadows speeding by. Nuyani pressed harder, severing her conscious fragment from the rest of her body. There she looked at her material form, a near statue of darkness with darker waves rising from the center.

"Now for the dangerous part," Kelvert said as his spirit came forth. "Fly with me, and do not linger anywhere without me beside you."

"Yes, Great Lord," Nuyani replied before the two shot toward the southwest. Cuganwa did not see the ethereal form of prutosa Nuyani conjured. Her form merely showed her general blue flame no heavier than a bead on his core as he continued to practice. She smiled as they passed through the sandy area below her. A world of flickering blues contained in solid shadowed shaped surrounded her. Looking to the earth, she could see solid pieces of blue beneath the sands moving about. None of them flickered or danced as her form did. A sense of dread hung over her. Their group was growing sparse, though countless.

"Nuyani," Kelvert called. She looked forward, finding the wisp just ahead by a few feet. His voice distorted in the new realm holding the same rasp and echo, but distant and wavering in strength. With the call of her name came a flow of energy coursing toward her and parting harmlessly around her.

"Yes, Lord Kelvert?" Nuyani answered.

"That is what we face, child," Nuyani looked down to the sands once more. Those creatures are mere copies of the foe we face, a false devourer."

"False?" Nuyani answered.

"Your need to eat and feast to grow stronger is a feat ruled by another god. A trait to aid life in many needs. But, there are pretenders to this role and others."

"Why are unflom trying to take the role of a god? What is the point?"

"The power to survive." Kelvert's tone remained plane as he relayed the answer. "I have told you before that the gods, *wodcojxalc*, seek power along with the titans, angels, and demons. This is for our survival."

"Then, am I a copy for you?" Nuyani grew worried, wondering if his gift was a mere ploy.

"No. Why ask me such a thing, Nuyani? I am here to help and nurture. My nature is to fight such a thing but, that does not mean my wits are so lucid to risk other lives just to grow stronger."

"Sorry," Nuyani looked away, trying to find better words as she felt a sense of fear. Despite the deity's presence, finding out her gift had a purpose was hard to acknowledge from her decade alone in the drylands. "You still carry fear of me, Nuyani?"

"Yes. And questions. After all this time, why hasn't the devourer used the animals as it did before?"

"Look below." Nuyani did as she was told. She did not realize how swift their flight was as clusters of souls sat amongst solid magic pieces came and went. With a sudden glimpse, she could see that the spirits were not solid forms as the others outside the areas. "Even in this land, life thrives. Possibly the reason its focus is not on us entirely."

"Other life. Animals?" Nuyani questioned. The clustered shapes molded together.

"I wonder." His tone was light. "A tale for another time. Look, Nuyani."

A swirling vortex of blue was ahead of the two spirits, like a tornado rising into the sky. Its bottom was fixed to a strange area rounded like a platform yet standing as a single column going into the earth.

"By his shi…" Nuyani stopped as she found her choice of words awkward beside Kelvert. As they approached, Nuyani saw the countless faces of the people and animals stuck in the vortex. Even in an incorporeal form, she could feel a chill run down her spine. Most of the faces wore morose, pained, or sorrowful expressions.

Nuyani and Kelvert stopped at the edge of a ravine. Looking down, there was no end to the rising column. Bringing a hand to her chest, the woman recalled the sense of her mother's spirit when she touched her cheek. The warmth of her spirit trailed to Nuyani as she sensed her mother's spirit.

"Follow your senses," Kelvert urged.

Nuyani did. She felt the familiar warmth coursing toward her guiding her amongst the other currents of prajial and prutosa. 'Mother, please be all right,' Nuyani thought. She sailed forth and passed through the spinning wall of soul. Before her, Nuyani could feel the fleeting waves of spirit gushing from the others. Her brow furrowed as she witnessed souls flying about and colliding with others gathered in a gout of blue flame from a crack in the surface.

"That is how it remains in control," Kelvert stated. Nuyani ignored the cluster as she looked to the spirits.

Though in different forms, she recognized her mother's soul as a different soul struck her.

"Mother!" Nuyani screamed. Huloat's visage appeared as she looked up. A sense of dread rose in her eyes as weathered wrinkles appeared on her face far too deep to reflect her true age. Nuyani's body surged as the flickering edges danced rapidly. Nuyani flew toward them, and her spirit became a self-contained tide. The fleeting spirits turned to stop her revealing their forms as howlers. Nuyani did not care as she barreled through them and collided with the flame knocking the souls free. Men, women, children, and animals all flew desperately in different directions.

"Nuyani?" Huloat rasped. As the life returned to her eyes, her withered form returned to resemble her forties.

Nuyani embraced her mother. "Mother, I have come to free you."

"No. Nuyani, I am bound to this place I cannot…"

"Lord Kelvert is here with us. We can find a way," Nuyani interrupted. The tornado of souls began to spin faster.

Huloat's eyes widened as if filled with life once more as she looked at the floating blue star. Her visage grew stronger, less transparent. The current of her spirit was reinforced as she looked to their lord. A sense of wonder and hope was expressed in her weathered eyes.

The woman then turned back to Nuyani. "Nuyani, listen. I can't go. There is…" Huloat started.

"Mother, please. I can carry you," Nuyani begged, her eyes creasing.

Huloat placed a hand on her cheek. "A storm comes today. Warn the others, my love," her mother said.

Before Nuyani could press the matter, a rushing current rose from beneath them, calling her attention. The howlers started to return and converged on their intruders.

"Nuyani. Protect them. May his shine guide you," the woman said as she smiled at Kelvert.

"We must leave at once," Kelvert urged.

Before the witch could say another word, before the howlers could grab Nuyani, before the gout of flame returned, Huloat's jaw descended far below her collar bone. The woman's eyes sunk in, becoming eerie voids of darkness centered with an iridescent glint. The wrinkles of her face grew deep and monstrous. Nuyani felt her heart sink as her mother's visage was contorted to a howler's, and a surge of her presence made Nuyani's visage quiver. The woman then howled like a banshee, releasing an expanded wall of spirit toward Nuyani. A blue wave raced forth and swept the witch away. Nuyani twisted and turned as if in rapids through the air hurled back toward the wisp.

Nuyani righted herself only to see the gout return, consuming her mother's visage. It was then reduced to her soul. The other specters returned, rounding up many of the souls that fled. The vortex around them spun faster, with the countless souls becoming blurs.

"We must leave, Nuyani," Kelvert called out before his spirit flew forth to surround her, drawing her current to twist and turn as his did, yet never mixing. As a swirling cloud of energy, Kelvert rushed toward the spinning wall. His flow was barely powerful enough to push through, slowing only a small section of the vortex compared to the others.

'No," Nuyani thought as her sight was mixed between rapids of light blue moving in different directions and the details of the large column and swirling souls.

"This is not the time, Nuyani. When you are stronger. Do as she says and save the others first," Kelvert pressed. Nuyani found herself reassembling on the other side of the ravine as the vortex became a single piece varying in off-balanced bulges and gradients of blue.

"Why have her bound?" Nuyani questioned.

"No time to explain," Kelvert fired back. "We must…"

Before the wisp could utter another word, a chorus of screams rang from the vortex. Nuyani raised her arms defensively as a blue wave rose and crossed the ravine. On contact, both Nuyani and Kelvert were ripped apart in the blast. Nuyani then awoke back in her own body. Sweat trailed from her brow as she looked about to find a dark room. Nuyani rose to her feet, lowering herself to ensure she would not hit the ceiling.

'Lord Kelvert?' Nuyani prayed, sending the ethereal waves toward the front.

"I am here, Nuyani," Kelvert answered. "I must apologize, Nuyani. You were not ready to see her."

"What?" Nuyani questioned in an audible whisper, mindful that Cuganwa was still present. "Why am I not ready?"

"If not for Huloat, your mind would've been taken by the devourer, and you would be imprisoned like the others," Kelvert explained. Nuyani stopped in her tracks as she stood outside of the hut's entrance. She leaned with her back against the stone side. "Without knowing any true ways to break free or attack, you would've been taken. Your praijal poljiad would be collected and used to draw more from your prajial, making you weaker every day until death."

Nuyani looked to the floor, seeing her mother's contorted visage that saved her. Nuyani shivered as her thoughts returned to the spirit of the small child in the abandoned village. "W-what happens after death?" She asked. There had to be more to her mistake. Nuyani was certain and wanted to realize an answer.

"Then your soul either is freed or captured, forced to follow the trail of spirit. Your will and mind can be copied that way," Kelvert said. His tone remained soft.

Nuyani sunk to the floor. "Thank you, Great Lord. Thank you, mother."

"You can tell her that later. For now, the storm will approach soon if I recall her words," Kelvert said.

Cuganwa then appeared around the side, catching Nuyani's attention as he looked down at her. Sweat fell from his brow as well. "Is there another secret?" Nuyani shook her head as she told him all that transpired in the night. Cuganwa gawked at her. "Things living in the demon lands. That's not something I thought was possible."

Nuyani smirked as she looked to the floor. "I don't think anyone would. We know too little here."

"And the wave, it's coming from the spirits screaming," Cuganwa repeated.

The witch nodded. "That's why it grows stronger each year. Those who die to it are captured and tortured to follow its will."

"How will the others believe us if it's coming tomorrow?" the boy asked. Nuyani shook her head. "Lord Kelvert?"

"I do not know, child," the wisp answered. "While there is a way to reach their minds and share the visions, there is little chance with so much fear between your powers and the events that came forth."

"Another test of faith," Nuyani said, her tone spiteful as her lips drew into a tight line.

"There should be a way," Cuganwa said, remaining optimistic. Nuyani hid her annoyance at the comment. "They're coming tomorrow, right? There has to be a point to this, or they'd wait."

Nuyani's eyes then widened as she looked toward the floating wisp. "I just remembered something. Lord Kelvert, will the howlers come out tonight?"

"Afterwards," Kelvert answered. "The blast that took our prutosa spread our conscience apart with little to salvage. I imagine the banshee would face a similar fate if they were to leave first. Tonight, the banshee will remain in wait."

Cuganwa smiled. "Can we?"

Nuyani sighed. "A night to rest," she said and forced herself to smile. She then looked up at Cuganwa. "Let's go back to sleep." Her body seemingly growing heavy.

Cuganwa looked at her as she turned. "Can we?"

"We should try," Nuyani said as she continued and returned to her bedroll. Cuganwa did the same thinking of all the information he was given. His heart raced as he wondered what his father would think of each offspring bearing the Great Lord's gift.

'I must get him back to the village,' Nuyani thought. Her mind only danced with the possibility that the hunters would try to kill her. The chances of the boy returning were slim, but it was something better than the life she had led all alone. 'Great Lord, what can I do to stop him from meeting any fate similar to mine, or worse?' Nuyani wondered, even keeping her thoughts from Kelvert as a sense of shame rose. She noticed Cuganwa was completely willing and able to throw himself into the situation. 'He's a little too eager for this. Does he want to prove himself that much?" Nuyani thought of him learning that they were siblings, and her thoughts went to Caluu. 'Is he worried about her?' Nuyani's eyes narrowed. 'What will you do, Sutama?' she questioned. Her mind conjured a scene of a looming man standing over the young child with her eyes glowing ember. 'What will he do?' she questioned, grabbing part of her bedroll in a tight grip. Nuyani then let the thought go as she turned over and went to sleep.

Ch. 24

True Enemies

Dawn broke, and Gamaunda's men were already on their way toward the west. Red, orange, violet, and pink colored the sky as the cold rushed past them, nipping at their skin. Sutama looked to the mountains leading the others through the path. 'Hold on, boy. We'll get you home,' Sutama thought as they crossed from the grasslands into the territory of the charge-horns. Knowing they'd have to take another route through the area, the party turned, heading directly toward the demon gate. Forced to trot through the sand dunes and brush, the group held arrows notched on their strings as they went through the area.

"What do we need to look for?" Gamaunda asked, trying to drive his whip-neck parallel to the hunters.

"For now, just anything of a different color to the brush," Sutama started. "Pink and gray, for the most part, are easier to spot from here." Sutama then glanced to the side and pointed as several humps almost as tall as the shrubs appeared. "They're not able to blend but, the shrubs are tall enough to hide the beasts."

"Sutama, what do you plan on doing once we've arrived?" the chief asked.

"I…will question her. I will ask her why," the old hunter answered.

"That's it?" Gamaunda's archer fired back.

Gamaunda turned back as he demanded, "Let him speak."

"The Great Lord willing, she has never attempted anything. Even after To'anu fell, I believe she will speak to us. She's been gone for so long but, I can't see her harming Cuganwa," Sutama concluded.

"You believe there will be peace if we just ask?" the chief questioned. Sutama looked to the man with a raised brow. "I'm willing to try. No attack on anyone else so far. Why not?"

"But chief, this is the demon. The witch is the one who…" his archer started.

"Who's lived in peace until recent events. All we have are her encounters with large animals and found one with strange worms inside," Gamaunda stated. "We do not have answers, and if asking will bring us the answers we need without bloodshed, then that is the answer I seek."

"This is still the demon," the archer pressed.

Gamaunda pulled on his reins, stopping the whip-neck. "How many could've killed that blade-jaw or the charge-horn? Could you?" The man grew silent. "I don't want to hear another word from you. She's earned an audience at the least. If there is trouble rising in the drylands, she is the one who would know or ask." The man said nothing as he looked away.

"Chief! Towards the south!" a man shouted. Everyone looked to the south to find a man standing alone wearing the usual light brown tunic. Sutama raised a fist, signaling for the group to halt.

As the party stopped, Gamaunda then said, "Send the free-riders." Two of the whip-necks started toward the man.

Sutama narrowed his eyes at the figure, barely making out his face. 'To'anu?' the man thought, remembering the eager hunter from years ago.

As the riders approached, a voice then thundered, "Stay in the cavern!" The man then disappeared as a white light flashed. Each of the whip-necks ignored their masters and slowly moved toward the demon gate.

Sutama and Gamaunda pulled up on their reins trying to control their animals before glancing at each other.

"I think we should move a bit quicker, Sutama," the chief commented. The old hunter agreed and nodded his head.

Nuyani awoke early, sitting up in her bedroll. A scowl was fixed on her face as she realized she was lying inside one of the huts instead of occupying the shelf as she usually would. A part of her wished that everything that transpired was just a dream. The woman rose to her feet and put away the bedroll. Her hand started to quiver as she thought of meeting Sutama once more. Her heart moved a bit faster as she wondered if he would attack, talk, or merely come to collect Cuganwa. Her scowl deepened as she thought of the boy's actions as well.

'He wouldn't keep to himself either,' she thought. Only a day with him, and she had a sense he'd want to prove himself, devote himself as madly as their father would. 'Honest and stubborn,' she found herself comparing the two. Nuyani then took up the roll and walked out of the hut. To her surprise, Cuganwa was exiting his hut as well.

"Morning," Cuganwa said with a friendly yet neutral expression.

"M-morning," Nuyani replied hesitantly. It was the first time she had actually spoken to someone in years without some form of malice.

The two then made their way to the shelf. Cuganwa then said, "I forgot to pray." Nuyani looked toward him.

"Me too," Nuyani said. "Let's start the prayer with Lord Kelvert."

Cuganwa nodded softly and looked to the ground. Nuyani could understand his feelings. The two would be giving a long thank you to their deity as they were present. The subject felt awkward. Passing the front huts, Nuyani took up both bedrolls and tossed them into the stone structures before joining Cuganwa on the shelf.

"Are you both ready?" the wisp asked in a rasped echo in their minds.

"Can we pray?" Cuganwa then asked.

"Why, yes," Kelvert said. His tone sounded surprised. "This will be another experience for you then." Nuyani and Cuganwa glanced at one another. "Please. Carry on."

The two did as they usually would, kneeling to the floor, sharing the same gestures, and reciting the prayer in unison. Within their cores, they could feel their prutosa surge. Their energy twisted and turned in the confines of their cores. As they raised their hands, warmth passed through their bodies. The energy flowed toward the wisp. Kelvert released a thrum, closing a sphere around the energy. The two could feel the wisp's will ring through the air and enclose on the spirit they released. The energy collected around the flame settled within the well.

Nuyani looked at her body, feeling somehow lighter from her core. "What happened?" she asked.

"You're acutely aware of the energy within you now," Kelvert started. "Praying guides your will to those you wish good or harm upon. This sends energy to them. Helping or hindering their will. Remember this."

"Does that mean with every prayer we are killing ourselves?" Nuyani wondered as she thought of the daily routine.

"No. It is naturally replenished by your soul drawing from the other plane," Kelvert answered. "You will not run out of spirit by any normal means."

"Oh. Thank you, Great Lord," Nuyani said. She pressed her efforts to remain respectful of the wisp. She owed Kelvert her life.

"There's a limit to everything," Cuganwa said. "Lord Kelvert, you use edria. What do you do with the energy that is sent to you?"

"I do not have much energy since my entrapment in the land," Kelvert started. "I know little about the source of prutosa sent to me over the years. To my grievance, my best assumption is that the false one has taken it. But worry little about such events. It is time we focused on the hunters arriving soon. Boundaries must be made so room for discussion may bloom."

Nuyani perked up and looked toward the boy as she said, "No using your edria." Cuganwa looked at her in surprise as she leered back. A sense of anger emitted from her. His eyes still had a dark brown to them. "We have to keep them calm before we reveal what we can do."

"I wasn't planning to fight them. Why do you think…" the boy started but grew silent. Lowering his head, he remembered the slaughter of the villagers the same day as the first sinner. Fear still lingered in their people. Cuganwa looked back at her with an intense stare. "Even then, if they attack you, I will fight back."

Nuyani's expression turned to surprise before she laughed. 'A protector, for me?' she thought.

"What?" the boy said.

"Your kindness baffles me," the woman said as she started to smile. "I'm prepared to fight if I must but, I don't know what they will do."

Cuganwa sat back on to his heels. "Neither do I," he replied. The boy then looked up to the wisp. "Lord

Kelvert, is there a way to send a message to them and prove that we are on their side?"

"Not one without scaring a few of them to act irrationally," the wisp answered. "The fear is strong yet. I wager your deeds beforehand have done enough to reach them."

"Then we wait," Nuyani said as she looked toward the cavern entrance and gave a deep breath.

The air whistled in their ears as the sun hung bright in the sky. Half of the men dismounted. Ten were heading for the witch as the others stayed ready for any animals to arrive Gamaunda and Sutama wielded their blades and marched forward, leading the other men toward the slope. Some carried long ropes prepared to bind the witch. The others were prepared to kill her if need be as they pulled slightly on their drawstrings before reaching the slope leading to the tunnel. All were uncertain and on edge.

'Great Lord, what is in store for us?' Sutama questioned as he felt his mind calming. A want, a plead rose in his mind as he moved ahead. The weapon in his hand seemed almost pointless as they entered the tunnel. Darkness covered them before it was replaced by the warm silver glow above their heads. The men looked up, some even resorting to pointing their arrows at the glowing flowers. Sutama and Gamaunda kept their attention ahead as they held their weapons at point.

Cuganwa and Nuyani stood behind the firepit as the footsteps echoed through the stone hall. Nuyani's breathing became heavy as the pressure on her core was not the only thing weighing on her as she fought the trembling on her hands. She licked her lips and started to glare as she watched the first leather shoe pass through the darkness.

Gamaunda and Sutama passed through as Kelvert's blue glow gleamed on their weapons. Sutama kept a stern expression as he normally would but blinked seeing his son still breathing and seemingly well. The other guards and hunters came in with their bows ready as the men approached. Each man glared at the pair and stole glances at the floating blue flame above the fire pit. Nuyani fought the urge to step back. She wanted to hide more than anything else. Her thoughts on the dangers of the banshee and storms disappeared. The violent spirits brought death with a touch, yet the man before her made her hands shake.

"Hello, Nuyani. We've come for the boy and to ask you a few questions," Gamaunda started. His voice was friendly enough but, Nuyani could sense a façade about him. She glanced at the man, not recognizing him with a curled mustache.

She glanced at Sutama. 'Why aren't you the one speaking?' she questioned, trying to fight the fear.

"We just came for a few answers," Gamaunda said.

"I have answers. But, tell the others to leave," Nuyani said, fighting her urge to shiver. She could feel their prutosa start to twist and turn to make her feel uneasy.

"Cuganwa," Sutama finally spoke. "Are you well?"

"Yes, father," he answered. "There is more we must tell you."

"We?" Gamaunda questioned, raising a brow.

"Yes. Strange…worms are appearing in the drylands, and we know how," Nuyani said. "Just want to speak. I will stay here."

"She's the one who made them," someone whispered.

Nuyani glared as she looked toward the others. "I haven't made anything. I just live here," she replied. "Monsters are coming to the drylands."

"All right," Gamaunda said as he straightened up and lowered his weapon. "Then you'd be willing to come with us, right?"

Nuyani's eyes widened. "No!" she shot back. "I've no reason to… Listen. A storm is coming." Nuyani stopped herself, reminding herself that worse things were to come.

"What's the storm have to do with this? If you truly cared, you'd come," the belligerent commented.

"Quiet," the chief commented. "We just want answers."

Nuyani could feel the same guard's spirit twist and surge faster within him. "Tonight! The storm will reach us."

"No. Today," Kelvert chimed in. "My children, it moves faster!"

"Her flame speaks!" the guard shouted before pulling back his notched arrow and releasing it. Nuyani retrieved a knife from her hilt and parried the projectile. The others soon joined, seeing her weapon, and fired. Nuyani conjured a wall between her and the men before blocking the projectiles. Cuganwa looked as though he was ready to join, only for Nuyani to push him away.

"Ceased this at once!" Kelvert rasped. Nuyani and Cuganwa could feel the wisp attempting to cast spells with the edria, but the energy trembled fiercely, growing unstable as it tried to expand. Kelvert's thrum revealed the low hum of the cavern. Its pattern was softer but constant and distorting.

Gamaunda ran forth as the barrage of arrows ceased. His speed caught Nuyani off guard as he closed the distance. The man swung his blade into her construct. The barrier bent toward her once struck before shattering. Nuyani's eyes bulged as she felt the recoil of her magic return like a strike to her stomach. Clutching her gut, she struggled to back away before another swing could be made. Instead, Gamaunda raised his blade to stop the others.

His men did not respond as they released more arrows. Nuyani fought against the pain and conjured another barrier between her and the others as she rolled off the shelf. She glanced at the man, wondering if he would advance once more.

"Wait!" Cuganwa shouted and raised a hand. Two of the closest archers rushed Cuganwa and pulled him toward the exit. "Wait! Let go! There's a storm coming! Listen!" His shouts were in vain as the others continued to fire their arrows.

Nuyani fell back toward the huts as the others came by. A thrum rang from the wisp. Walls of light were conjured around several men, including Gamaunda and Sutama. "Cease at once!" the wisp shouted. The demand went ignored as the two blade wielders slashed at the barrier. The air reverberated as Kelvert fought against the resisting edria of the cavern. The walls bellowed before shattering.

Nuyani's eyes widened as she sensed the energy ripple and recoiled back toward the wisp. 'Even you, Kelvert?' she thought as she dodged more arrows. 'No. He's doing something else.'

She fell back as the archers closed in, freed from the constructs. The first archer that acted was much more eager than the others as he rounded another hut toward her left. Nuyani's speed proved the better as she lifted her hand and instinctively released a spell orb. The attack sailed forth before he could draw his arrow. The energy struck his arm, resounding in a loud crack as his arm

shifted backward. He screamed and fell to the floor, his
arm hanging limply. He dropped his bow and grabbed the
loose limb to hold it still. Other archers came forth to
cover their fallen brother. Nuyani parried a few arrows
and dodged the others.

'What can I do?' she wondered. Nuyani weaved
through several of the huts trying to put space between her
and the others. Gritting her teeth, she tried to find room,
tried to find a peaceful answer. Once an archer was found
in her path, he watched with cold a glare not fitting his
shaking figure as he drew his bow. Nuyani glared at him
and thrust her palm forward. An orange light sailed forth,
growing in size. It flew toward the man as he released his
arrow. The small missile fell away as the construct
collided with the archer. Keeping control of her strength,
the man was sent back only a few feet, making him
stumble.

Nuyani darted around pushing and shoving the
men to fall, careful not to harm any of them and avoiding
Sutama and Gamaunda. When she found most of the men
were grounded, she hopped onto one of the huts shouting,
"Listen to me!" Her voice boomed, vibrating through the
cavern. She looked about at the shocked eyes of the men
seeing her standing above them. Sutama looked at her
with a strange expression she could not accept. Regret nor
guilt, neither befit the man that changed the course of her
life. Not the idea of the religious man she knew. The tip of
his blade remained pointed to the floor. Nuyani focused on
him as he slowly approached. "There is trouble. Please.
Just listen."

The old hunter stopped just before the hut staring
at Nuyani. The others did not move, waiting for their
chance to act. Nuyani felt the urge to shake once more as

she looked at him. As she opened her mouth, she heard footsteps patter on the floor. Nuyani turned and raised her arms as she created another construct. Gamaunda ran toward her and, in a single leap, was rising toward her with his blade ready, coated with a vibrant thrum. Unlike the others, she could not feel the pressure of his soul. With ease, the man swung at Nuyani shattering her defense. The recoil paralyzed her with pain as she fell to the floor before Sutama.

As the village chief took her place atop the hut, he breathed deeply and looked toward Sutama. "Well? What is your choice, Sutama?" the hunter asked as Nuyani struggled to stand. The pain of several days returned to her.

"I…" Sutama said as he looked at his blade.

"Just listen!" Cuganwa suddenly shouted, emerging from the tunnel and creating a barrier between the two. "Nuyani! Help!" The boy's eyes met hers. What was once brown now glowed ember. As his thrum rang through the area, she could see the patterns of his core sending images from his mind. A blood-mane came, infested like the other beasts. Nuyani rose as Gamaunda landed before her.

"The Great Lord guides m… Your men outside are being attacked," Nuyani said.

"What?" the chief questioned.

Sutama stepped forward. "Prove it," he growled, presenting the blade to her. Gamaunda turned to the man with wide eyes and gripped the blade even tighter, thinking of severing his hand.

"Kill her!" a shout came in a long groan.

"Silence!" the chief roared. He then looked to Nuyani with a wide smile. "Prove it." His tone changed to a friendly challenge.

Nuyani gawked at the two in surprise but grabbed the blade and ran off as she followed Cuganwa out of the cavern. As the tunnel's shadow enveloped them, she released a thrum. Kelvert's struggle distorted her pulse slightly, but she could still sense them. Dozens of small pressures in different clusters, all moving about in separate groups. As they raced past the silver glow and into the bright sun, the image of the shorter fighters came to Nuyani's mind. Warriors fought against the infested beasts as the storm came forth.

'By the Great Lord's will, I have speed,' she thought. 'It won't be the same.'

The other half of the men were fighting two of their whip-necks that had grown abnormally large. Some men had already been crushed by their wild swings as the remaining three fought beside their riders. An infested blood-mane started its dive toward a party of hunters. With the blade in hand, Nuyani focused her conjuring and created a dome over the men. Stopped short, the blood-mane's claws struck her barrier, forcing the beast to right itself in the air. Nuyani ran forth and closed her fist, inverting the dome into a sphere around the beast. Nuyani could feel the prutosa surging within it. Doubling the thrum fed into the construct, she was ready as the blood-mane released a blood-curdling caw through the area.

The construct rippled violently yet, held. The other men looked back at Nuyani with looks of shock.

Nuyani did not look toward them as Selsaj amongst the men expressed relief. The sphere condensed, closing until it stopped only large enough to contain the animal's head and the yellow blemish sticking from its chest. Nuyani pulled on the construct keeping the beast off balance. The blood-mane cawed as it was forced to the ground and tried to pull away. The surge of spirit within the beast resisted the strengthening pulse of the construct as Nuyani attempted to decapitate the beast.

"Protect the others!" Nuyani ordered Cuganwa as she ran for the beast.

She followed the examples of the chief's and fed her energy into the blade. The silver edge held an orange tint that extended a hand's length further. Closing the distance, Nuyani willed her construct to pull toward her forcing the larger beast to expose its neck more. Holding the blade overheard, Nuyani slashed downward, cleaving through the animal's neck, the coat of edria passing through the construct with ease.

The animal's head fell, revealing the rotten insides of its neck and a familiar shell weeping yellow pus. Dumbstruck, the men rose and began to approach Nuyani and the blood-mane.

She looked toward them. "Getaway!" she snapped. Nuyani released the first barrier and created another wide enough to cover the three men in front and push them back. The remaining worms then emerged, clawing and clicking in the air toward her. Nuyani backed away and created smaller spheres around their heads, decapitating them. A few slashes bisecting the heads of each worm stopped their movements. Their pressure against her core was gone. Sensing the other men would attack, Nuyani created another barrier and pushed toward the group sending the construct to knock them down. As they toppled over, she looked away and ran toward the riders guiding their whip-necks to circle another that was infested.

Three bodies lay on the ground. 'This has to stop,' Nuyani commented as she ran between some of the riders and created a barrier around its front legs. As if sensing her intentions, the larger whip-neck raised its legs, attempting to dodge but, whip-necks were not the most graceful of animals as her construct appeared and severed the front hooves. The animals did not respond as they landed and stood on the severed limbs. Nuyani stepped back as she looked at the animal's faded brown eyes and the large gash in its neck.

"By the Great Lord," she whispered.

The whip-neck raised its head and shifted its weight to swing from the side. Shooting both of her hands out, Nuyani created a barrier around its head and did her best to hold it in place. The animal struggled to move, flailing its front legs as coagulated blood spilled forth. Nuyani then shifted the construct and cut the creature's neck completely. The body then fell. Nuyani stepped toward it and released a thrum. The wave passed through the carcass. Only the fading pressure left but, she could feel branching sections in the animal's body.

"They breed that quickly?" Nuyani thought before she turned to see the hunters and guards on their whip-necks ready to fire. "W-wait! Everyone lives!" Nuyani said, holding out her hands, trying to stop the others from attacking. "Please. Go to the cavern."

Some of the hunters trained their eyes on her. Others looked toward the whip-neck and back at the cavern. "Where are the others?" one of the men shouted as he narrowed his eyes and pulled on his bow.

"They're in the cave, and they're alive," Nuyani explained, trying her best to remain nonthreatening. It did not help that she had killed two animals within moments of each other. "Please," she said and created a barrier covering herself. 'Just listen,' she thought. The man glared as his chest rose and fell. Lifting his chin, Nuyani expected him to fire at her, despite the barrier.

"Come this way!" a sudden shout came. Everyone looked, even Nuyani, finding Gamaunda shouting at the others. The chief looked at the carnage around them.

Two of the infested beasts were dead, as were three men and one whip-neck were on the run toward the east. Cuganwa stood with some of the others and their whip-necks.

"Come to the cavern!" Gamaunda shouted. Some of his men left the cavern. Nuyani sighed and gave a weak smile, relieved from their presence.

"Nuyani, move!" Kelvert ordered. His demand was intense as his thrum rang through the area.

Looking to the demon gate, she shuttered as a clouded brown line rose on the horizon. A sudden pressure weighed on her core. Her breathing grew heavy as she felt the grip of the approaching storm tighten. 'How?' Nuyani thought as she looked on. The clouds grew larger as the rushing wind swept her hood back, revealing her tangled hair. 'G-Great Lord? How?'

"Together! Match Cuganwa and make a barrier," the wisp instructed.

Nuyani followed the instructions sensing Cuganwa's pattern and matching it. The boy could feel the flow of energy as he guarded the others. Letting their thrum resonate, his barrier's size increased and turned blue. Nuyani conjured her defense with the same sapphire light as he covered the others. Kelvert followed their lead, matching their thrum and using the well as another barrier rose, erupting from the cavern in a bright dome standing just over the cliffs.

Shadows were cast as the wind roared deafeningly. Gamaunda and the others wondered what was happening as they saw the walls pass through them. The other men looked on dumbstruck at the rushing sands. Before any of them could say a thing, the ground trembled violently. Even with their thrum reinforced together, along with the well, Nuyani tensed every muscle. The whip-necks splayed their legs outward as the shaking worsened. Others lost their footing as small stones sailed by. In a single rush, the sandstorm stood over the cliffs and struck the risen land enough to make everything tremble in its wake as sands coursed over the domes. A body of one of the hunters struck the transparent wall, and Nuyani looked away as the sand-ridden gale pinned him in place. Cloth and flesh were stripped away in moments as blood became caked with grains of sand and trailed upward and to the sides. The others looked in horror only as they approached Nuyani's sides.

"What's happening, witch?" one sneered. Selsaj, who somehow managed to join the other party, then struck him in the side, earning him a confused look, which he returned with a glare.

"There was a storm coming. We barely learned about it and wanted to warn you all," Nuyani said. Her tone weakened as the corpse was carried upward by the wind only to move upward as all that remained were the man's bones. "There's more out there," Nuyani said.

"All right, then what now?" the first man asked in a calmer tone. She could still hear the aggravation in his voice. Nuyani looked forward, seeing only the dark clouds of sand around them. Her barrier was their only source of light.

'Lord Kelvert?' Nuyani prayed. Her thrum barely passed through the area as the prutosa powering the storm was thick and suffocating. Through their shared connection, Nuyani was able to connect her thoughts.

"They must carry you," Kelvert replied. A sinking feeling rose in Nuyani. It was hard enough for her even to allow Cuganwa to be around her, but to be carried by the others made her want to squirm. The hatred in her had dampened, but it was still too soon for her to have any comfort.

Nuyani closed her eyes and gritted her teeth as she maintained her stance. With such a large barrier, she needed to concentrate on its hold as much as possible. The other men approached with the whip-necks. The two saw Nuyani's face reading her disdain.

"Well? What must we do?" Selsaj asked in a kinder tone.

"Carry me to the cavern," Nuyani hissed through her teeth.

"What?" the hunter asked, baffled.

Nuyani then snapped, "We can't hold these walls forever. Carry me to the cave."

The two looked at one another and back at their party. A sense of disdain came over them as they did what they could. Nuyani shuttered when one of the men touched her arm, making the barrier waver for a moment, but Nuyani's concentration held. In lifting her, two men grabbed both arms, careful not to bend them in fear of breaking her control. A third took up her legs. Taking on their strange march, the group made their way toward the cliff wall and followed it along the way. They stayed silent as the winds whipped around them.

Cuganwa's arms strained under the pressure. Cramping started to set in. 'No. I will hold,' the boy thought as he pushed himself and the others carried him toward the entrance. His fingers curled as he grunted. The men carrying him gawked for a moment. He could see their fear. "We will make it," the boy declared.

As they moved on, they saw the overlapping barriers of the groups before reaching the stone slope. As the two groups converged, some led the whip-necks in first as they squeezed through the tunnel. Nuyani and the others gradually reached the shelf where the others waited.

"Release your barriers. You are safe now," Kelvert said.

Cuganwa and Nuyani released their holds. Sighing in relief as the strain ended. The boy nearly collapsed to the floor as his muscles strained. Nuyani's breath was more in control as she glanced at Cuganwa and felt a sense of pride seeing him power through the same pain.

"This is what we needed," Kelvert said in an audible rasp.

The others turned to the flame with wide eyes. Nuyani found some of the others staring at them. "Don't get any ideas," she growled and tightened her grip on the blade.

Gamaunda shook his head as he let his own blade recede into its crystal. "We just wonder what fate has brought us."

Nuyani tried to control herself but, she felt her body quiver. There were now others in her home, others who first sought to kill or capture her. Now they were unfortunate guests. She sighed and retorted, "The Great Lord's light guides us."

Gamaunda looked up at the blue flame suspended over the ground. "Oh, I think he does," the man said.

Sutama moved to the boy's side. "Are you hurt?" he asked as he reached out with a hand.

Cuganwa stopped his father's hand from reaching his face as he replied in gasps, "I… know what happened." He glared at the man in anger.

"What exactly?" Sutama asked as he lowered his hand. The man continued to stare, seeing the glowing ember eyes of his son. "Great Lord's will, this is not what we…were?"

"This is what you used to wield," Kelvert chimed in. The man turned to the flame. "Imparted my power on to you all in the times that passed it may grow and face the forces that took the people of this cavern." Some looked about to the empty huts. "There is a force beyond these cliffs that wields the storm. If you wish to know, I can show you."

The others looked at one another hesitantly as some tended to the whip-necks leading them to the smaller spaces between the huts. Sutama glanced at his son seeing his eyes return to the orange glow before slowly fading to their usual dark brown. "I must know the purpose of this," the man growled as he stood and looked to the flame. "Show me."

"I as well," Gamaunda added.

"Wait. Chief, is this wise?" one of the men asked as he looked at Nuyani, still unsure whether they could trust her. Nuyani narrowed her eyes and stared back at him.

The chief turned to him and shook his head. "Look at where we are. Others are already dead outside, and she…" the man gestured to Nuyani and Cuganwa with a finger. "These two took it down. We know too little. We are trapped! The storm is here, and their spells have us breathing." His subordinate stood silently. Gamaunda looked from him to the others inviting protest. His tone grew low. "Get settled in and wait for answers. Respect her home, and don't try anything."

A reply came in a resolute nod as his subordinate backed away, joining the others. Nuyani said nothing as she stood and moved toward the hut she stayed in the night prior. 'Great Lord, I…want to be alone,' Nuyani said to the wisp.

Answering only in her mind, he replied, "Very well. Take your time."

Once inside, she conjured a barrier around the structure and sat against the back wall. The storms finally came. Proof of her innocents was shown. Despite all that transpired, she did not want it.

Ch. 25

Difference Between

Demon and Devotion

Cuganwa watched as Sutama and Gamaunda sat by the firepit. Their eyes were fixed on blank stares at the wall of the cavern. Kelvert's thrum kept them entranced. The boy sighed as he looked at the leaders and back at the other men. Some looked back at him with glares. Cuganwa felt a sense of unease as some returned to their rations, whispering amongst themselves. He turned to the front of the cavern, where two more guards stood on either side. They shared occasional and brief glances at the boy.

Sitting alone on the shelf, Cuganwa tightened his fists as he looked at the village chief. 'This is how you feel, Nuyani? We just saved them,' the boy thought, wondering if the others would try to attack him. 'Will this convince you?' The boy looked to the ground thinking of the village. His sister, mother, and others were facing the storm stronger than ever. His hands shook as he wondered what their fate was.

"Cuganwa," Nuyani's voice echoed in his mind. His eyes widened for the moment then eased.

'How are you doing this?' The boy questioned as a prayer.

"Just copy what Lord Kelvert does," she answered. "Use the pulses to speak. Don't bother the others, though."

With his own thrum increasing, he tried to do so as he said, "Hello?" He could hear the echo in his voice as the word traveled on the radiating pulses.

"Good. I can hear you," Nuyani said. Her tone turned serious. "We're going to the village."

"What," the boy questioned.

"Like we did to get the well. We'll use our edria and go there."

"And then what?"

"Protect them. Help them. Something. I don't know." Nuyani's tone grew frustrated, "I want to do something, even learn what the storm is doing out there. At least, we can know then."

"All right," Cuganwa answered enthusiastically. "I want to know too. Are you coming out?"

"N-no." Nuyani's voice was hesitant. "Anyways, do you remember how to leave your body?"

Cuganwa paused for a moment. "I think I do." He was not as certain.

"Well, just try to follow my lead." Nuyani cleared her head and let her core race, sending waves throughout her body. Once the waves moved fast enough to resemble a solid state, she separated the ethereal form and entered the form. Though her conscience separated, she did not feel the same tearing from her body as before. 'Good,' she thought as she looked at the rippling edges of her hands. "Do you get it?"

"Yeah," the boy replied as he did the same. He had some difficulty as the strain of the barrier he made still left lingering pain. "Within a moment, the world shifted to blue, leaving everyone in a dark shift as they walked about. The boy's eyes widened as he saw the sphere of Kelvert doubled in size and vibrant as it struck the cores of his father and the chief. The barrier Kelvert erected was wide and large, encompassing most of the area. Beyond the barrier, random black streams trailed across the sky, occasionally thickening with the unconcentrated energy. The boy then looked to the side and saw Nuyani floating by as two men passed through her legs. Nuyani floated away, careful not to strike their cores.

"Ready?" Nuyani asked.

"Yeah," the boy answered as he noticed the men approach him and look at his body. The boy was stuck in a trance of his own. Cuganwa ignored them as he floated toward Nuyani.

"How are you feeling?" she then asked.

The boy blinked and looked at her. "Fine, I guess."

Nuyani gave a hard nod. "All right then. We'll go to the village. I felt other pressures that were more concentrated than the others. I think the howlers are back."

"Howlers," the boy whispered as his eyes shifted about, trying to remember.

"Don't worry about remembering. You will know if you see them. Pray to Lord Kelvert, we don't," Nuyani stated before rising and flying off through the stone wall. Cuganwa looked back at his father but flew after her.

The two passed through the barrier and were almost swept away by the black current surrounding them. Tumbling toward the east, Nuyani called out to Cuganwa. Quickly their thrum resonated, bolstering their strengths. The two then emitted more pulses from their constructs, repelling the waves around them. The occasional swell of prutosa nudged them about, but they remained fairly stable.

"This was stronger than I thought it would be," Nuyani said. Cuganwa nodded at her. Her gaze then fell to the ground seeing the countless lives below them.

Nuyani descended to the floor, followed by Cuganwa. A group of charge-horns was closest. They watched as some of the larger beasts laid down, facing the brunt of the storm as others dug into the ground. The darker shade of their bodies made it difficult for Nuyani to see the gradual cuts littering their hides. Cuganwa's heart gave a skip as they watched the sounder struggle yet, hold on. The two looked at one another before flying east. The water bites shined through the earth as they approached the river. The animals behaved differently than she expected. Despite the tons of sand flying about, the water bites collected at the surface and swam in long parallel rows up and down the river. Stopping just below the water surface, they saw the clusters of sand collecting at the top but never large enough to collect before the ravenous animals broke them down.

"Even these creatures serve the drylands," Nuyani commented.

'We have to clean the canals after the storms. Wonder if they do us a favor,' Cuganwa thought before flying off to the village.

The two continued to sail on. Through the sections of land, they found animals bearing with the stronger blast but surviving, nonetheless. They reached the familiar shape of the village. The wide and high standing bone gate had the western section destroyed and the high mounds greatly worn down by the winds. Cuganwa flew even faster, with waves nearly pushing Nuyani away and disrupting the synchronization. Nuyani instead met his pace and raced after him. The damage worsened the closer they came. The spear-like poles of the broken gate were left as debris strewn about the village, some skewering unfortunate villagers. Most of the homes were destroyed as the canopy and tents were gone, and those who remained within the low areas lay flat on the floor to let as much wind pass by as possible. Cuganwa flew past many of the home dugouts and reached his home. His heart raced as he watched his sister and mother huddled together against the wall. He held out his hands, looking between Nuyani and the others.

Grabbing his shoulder, Nuyani got his attention, seeing that she was looking at something else. The boy looked further to the north seeing the forms of two dark shadows flying about from one dugout to another.

"What are…" Cuganwa started.

"Howlers," Nuyani answered. "This is what I feared." The pressure of a soul then swelled on their forms before growing lighter as the ethereal marble sailed toward the demon lands. "We have to stop them." Nuyani then flew forth toward the specter in a black-flamed form. Where hollowed eyes were was now an open space merely showing the world behind the violent spirit.

Nuyani held out a hand and fired a spell orb toward the specter. The spirit slithered to the side, dodging the projectile before flying toward her. With her opponent closing in, she created a barrier before her with the encroaching opening pointed toward the specter. The howler flew in and was captured. A sigh of relief came to her remembering the spirit she faced seeming more tactical than her sisters'. Nuyani clutched her fist, compressing her barrier around the specter. The spirit thrashed about the confines.

'Will this not kill them?' Nuyani questioned. She then thought back to her encounters with the other howlers and Gamaunda's weapon tearing away barriers. 'They have to be torn,' Nuyani thought for a moment as she held out her hand. She envisioned her fingers like the claws of the specters. Each finger grew thin and elongated to three times the length. Nuyani approached the barrier and swiped at the sphere. Her claws passed through the construct and tore the spirit into several pieces. The barrier widened from the sudden burst of energy no longer being concentrated. She relinquished the barrier releasing the energy to the winds.

"That's what I'll do," Cuganwa growled as he felt the pressure of another apparition that was close by.

Nuyani looked to see him flying toward a spirit. An urge to fly after him rose within her, a protective side that seemed to be instinctive but, she stopped and watched. With fury rising, Cuganwa flew toward the specter and held out his hands. Nuyani expected claws as she had done, only for him to conjure a thin line of magic and shape it into a curved blade much like the chief's. Nuyani saw him charge with reckless abandon toward the specter. The howler charged toward him as well with a hand raised to swipe. Cuganwa stayed lower than the apparition and swung with incredible speed, cleaving through the specter before her arm could descend.

Black embers scattered around the area before the winds carried the prutosa away. The boy looked about, searching with both his eyes and the weight against his core. Cuganwa looked and saw another of the spirits. Without hesitation, he charged for her. Nuyani looked on and saw him cleave the specter in two.

'A fighter like the others,' Nuyani thought as she recalled the other's vision.

As the boy focused on the remaining spirits, Nuyani released a searching thrum, passing through the area. She could feel the energy of the others. Some had cores with a strong vibrance matching hers. The cores of others were weaker yet, seemed capable of using even the simpler spells she knew. Nuyani joined the fight and few after one of the few remaining specters. She created knives finding comfort in the chosen weapon and slashing through them.

Cuganwa made quick work of the spirits. Even with six slain, he was prepared for the next spirit. When the battle was over and the heaviest pressures no longer plagued his senses, the boy looked to see Nuyani hovering over his home. The boy flew back to her, wondering what Nuyani had planned. Pulses radiated from Nuyani's form as she pressed her forehead to Caluu's, who reacted as if the contact were physical.

"Caluu, can you hear me?" Nuyani said as the words rang.

"Nui?" the child replied as the sands howled and the girl winced. "Where are you?"

"We are here in thought. We've come to hel.."

"You're my sister!" the girl's mind rang. Nuyani's thoughts were cut short as a new mix of emotions came forth. "D-did you know?"

"Only when you told me who Cuganwa was. But he, and your father and Sutama are safe. And I'm here to keep you safe, too," Nuyani said.

"H-how?" the child asked.

"Just follow the rhythm you feel in your heart, okay," Nuyani said.

Caluu then said replied, "But…" She trembled as she clutched tighter to Jogia.

Cuganwa then came forth and placed a hand on Caluu's head. He met the thrum as he said, "Caluu."

"Cuganwa!" the girl said in a mental shout, nearly blocking their thoughts.

'Is that another trick I should learn?' Nuyani wondered for a moment as she gathered herself.

"Yes, Caluu. But there isn't time. Just do as we do, and you will protect mom and yourself, all right?" Cuganwa urged.

"A-alright," Caluu said sheepishly.

Nuyani then released a pulse radiating from her hand and coursing through Caluu until it reached her core. The child's eyes went wide and glowed as she discovered her own magic. Nuyani let her edria reverberate to her sister's core. As the thrum radiated from the child's body, Caluu's thrum burst from her core rapidly and vibrant as she copied the humming rhythm of the witch. A sphere rose from her center until it encased both her and Jogia. The shadows that surrounded them moved away. The loose ends of their clothing and strands of hair were no longer at the whim of the gale. Jogia looked around, noticing the wind had stopped berating them.

"Good, Caluu. Do this for as long as you can," Nuyani said.

"I will try," the child said as she squirmed in Jogia's arms.

"Nuyani, can we get the others to do the same?" Cuganwa said. Nuyani looked to Cuganwa with shock.

"Do it," she replied. Cuganwa reached a hand to his mother, trying to calm her first to the sudden surprise before trying to reach her core. A few seconds passed, and Nuyani could feel the coursing edria resonate between mother and daughter as the sphere expanded and pushed against the shroud around them. When Cuganwa was confident their construct would hold, he backed away from them.

"She says thank you," the boy said as he looked at the two. A few scars and tears in their clothing caught his attention. Cuganwa clenched his fists. Nuyani moved to his side catching his attention.

"We must help the others too," Nuyani urged. Cuganwa nodded his head. The two then flew and conversed with the other survivors to create barriers. Nuyani found much resistance at first, and many even tried to blame her for the storm's strength, but the constant wind and sands proved useful for convincing a few stubborn minds to try their hands at least protecting themselves. Minutes had passed, and the village soon turned into a field of orange domes as the winds sailed overhead.

Cuganwa flew to the whip-neck pins and found the animals fairing far better than he expected. Though the closest to the banks still had injuries from the razor-sharp wind. The boy did the same as he did with the others and tried to attune with the edria of the animals. In connecting with the whip-necks, Cuganwa froze as he could feel a deeper thrum rising from their entire bodies. From the ends of their fur to the muscle beneath, it was as if the animals were made entirely of edria.

'The Great Lord imparted his power to the land,' Cuganwa reminded himself. As the beasts followed his will and created barriers, all the same, even connecting with one another as if guided by their reins to do so.

Cuganwa smiled as he floated away from them. The whip-necks continued to hold the barriers as the boy wondered if there was a way to guide them to other villagers in need. He kept the thought in place as he flew to more huts to try and save them.

Nuyani move swiftly, finding many people were more than capable of creating suitable constructs but never knew how. As she continued, Nuyani eventually traveled to the fallen main hut of the village elders. Drawing closer, Nuyani saw the elders and a few village aids sitting against the wall. She rushed to them and tried to press a hand on Yanuma's when Moyaud reached out and grabbed her wrist. The witch was shocked by the sudden movement as the man looked her directly in the eye, a widened smile and awe worn on his face. Nuyani froze, not certain how to read the expression. The soft pulses of his ring radiated through him and toward the other elders. Yanuma and Belractu looked at Nuyani as well, each of them using their rings' abilities in tandem. Tears formed in Yanuma's eyes as she looked into Nuyani's recent memories. Moyaud's sight allowed her to see the other defenses erected through the village. Moyaud released his hold on Nuyani and held the same hand upward in a gesture similar to the morning prayer. Nuyani remained speechless as she felt a sudden wave of pressure separate from the shroud of prutosa bombarding her that seemed less intrusive. Unsure of the effort, Nuyani moved away from them, and Belractu placed a hand on Yanuma's shoulder, who was covering her mouth.

Making her way to the next group of people, Nuyani could feel a strange current of spirit racing against the direction of the false devourer's. 'What is this?' Nuyani questioned. 'Are they praying?' Nuyani wondered as many channels encircled her then trailed off into the drylands. Seeing the energy was not hindering her, she continued to aid the village.

Through sunken eyes, he witnessed the spirits' attacks and the enormous monster behind the storms. 'Huloat,' Sutama uttered. She was gone by his hand alone. To see that his efforts were unfounded brought a wave of guilt to the old hunter. Lord Kelvert fed his power to the land. Another people unrelated to them fled because of the horrors of the drylands. As the memory of the land slowly came to the present, the two witnessed Nuyani's efforts as she stopped the spirits that came to her home and at the village. Sutama shuttered once he saw his youngest approach the witch looking for an answer. 'No. I will not make this mistake twice,' the man said, reinforcing his thoughts. As the visions continued, the image of Nuyani rushing through and discovering her new skills came by, and a feeling of awe washed over him as he witnessed his second dragged Nuyani to safety. His breathing grew heavier as he looked on.

'Great Lord, how have I been so wrong?' the man questioned. He paused for a moment, recalling all that was taught in the village. 'We must change this.'

The visions ended, and the two men finally moved after an hour had passed. Sutama blinked, feeling the sting of his eyes. It was difficult to stand as the weight of his body returned. The old hunter looked to the side only to find his son sitting near them in his own trance. The man shook his head.

Turning to Kelvert, Sutama then asked. Great Lord…" The others turned to the man with shocked looks, some with disdain, others of discovery as they looked at the floating flame as well. "What can I do for my children? What can I do to protect them?"

"Love them," the wisp answered, carrying a mixture of voices present. Everyone could hear the wisp. "This world is harsh, and the growth of the village means you will see forces beyond these cliffs, both friendly and hostile. It is best to prepare for such matters. Grow together. Live and survive as you've had before. Accept what they can provide and learn from the others."

Sutama looked to his son seeing his eyes shining like embers once more. "Yes, Great Lord," the man answered as he sat down once more.

Gamaunda then spoke up," There is much we must learn in this situation, men! The witch is no demon. It if weren't for Sutama staying his hand and Nuyani's efforts, things could've been worse at this time."

"This has to be a trick," Vu'olag snapped. Gamaunda wore his smile as he looked to see it was the same guard who disobeyed him and had his arm broken by her spell. He moved about slowly with his limb strapped to his side by an extra rag. The man strolled forward from the back of the cavern.

"What were you doing back there?" the chief questioned.

"Searching for blade-jaws," the man stated simply. The others turned to him. "We know these

demons can do so. We have to be ready." Some shook
their heads and glared at the man.

"You moron," one of the men said.

"No!" the guard shouted back and pointed at the
others. "These are demons. The witch takes men and kills
them."

"Vu'olag..." Gamaunda called, catching the
man's attention. "Don't make this about your son. We
were wrong." The guard's face contorted with rage as he
pulled a knife from its sheath and lowered himself as if
ready to attack.

The others readied themselves for the attack, but
then Vu'olag stopped and dropped his knife. His eyes
grew red as he crouched low and covered his head with
his free arm. The man groaned as others approached and
collected the blade. No one said anything as they led him
to the circle away from the others.

Sutama rose and glanced at his son. 'I have to do
better,' the man said as he thought of Caluu.

"Sutama," Gamaunda called. The hunter looked to
the chief. "Come with me. We should talk." Descending
from the shelf, the two then made their way toward the
back where some of the whip-necks lay. Two guards were
there seeing to the animals. "Go look after Cuganwa. He's
in a trance. Make sure he is safe." One was Selsaj as he
passed by Sutama, silently glancing at him. The hunting
leader did not look back; his eyes revealed his thoughts
were more concerned with other matters. As the two left,
the chief went up to one of the steads and petted the
animal as it turned toward him and licked the man's hand.

"I never thought things were so different from what we were told."

"Neither did I," Sutama said, a sense of defeat in his voice. "Why are we here?"

"Because of you," the chief answered as he continued to pet the animal's head before leaning against it. "Your children found Lord Kelvert. Your child found another blade. Your devotion has led you to accept the flame and, I cannot see your choices as wrong. I'd think you a fool if it weren't for the other accounts that took place in the drylands."

"But, why are we speaking alone?" the hunter asked.

"I need advice. The elders are not her but, you have the wisest word still," Gamaunda said and folded his arms. "What would you do? With all that we were shown, what would you do?"

"Stop the killing of any children with the eyes. End the witch tales or tell the truth completely, even our fault," Sutama said plainly.

"The children are a given. But, the tales are a better choice?" the chief questioned.

"Yes. Whomever those people were fled and had powers compared to Nuyani. The others saw how she took on the animals…" Sutama started.

"No. Why is this choice better?" Gamaunda's stare grew more intense.

"Will we exile every child just for them to come back angered and resentful? That will create your other village if you wish." Sutama argued. "Is this to test if I'm a fool?" 'I wonder if the village still stands,' the man thought as another sound of crumbling stone reminded them that this storm was still present.

"Good point," Gamaunda said as he looked to the floor wearing an almost cheerful look.

"Why do you ask?" Sutama narrowed his eyes.

Gamaunda looked back at the man. "I need help if the elders disagree with my current choice." Sutama blinked and raised his chin. "I want to allow those with the Great Lord's gift to continue living in the village and gain the strength Lord Kelvert intended for us."

A sinking feeling rose in the old hunter. "Is this for you to have a family as well?" Sutama asked. His eyes were still narrowed. 'Are you after Nuyani?'

"No, this position as chief should not be weakened," Gamaunda answered.

"What are you after then?" Sutama asked, his tone growing aggressive.

"Survival of the village. A thinking, planning village that doesn't have men attacking one another just because they have fears and superstitions instead of actual proof that someone is a threat." Gamaunda nearly started shouting as he looked to the ground shaking his head. His tone quieted. "That massacre for us and the people who were here, we could be next if we don't plan. We have information, and we have to think."

"The village has already seen Nuyani's actions," Sutama said as he held out a hand.

"That may not be enough. Even Vu'olag still sees her as a demon because of his own children," Gamaunda explained.

Sutama looked at him with a hard glare. "How many others have children with orange eyes?"

"Many," the man said simply as he continued. "There are many things I wish to change. I doubt this will be any different in what we are seeking."

"If what the Great Lord says is true, his power grows with every generation. Is it already here?" Sutama questioned.

"I can't tell. Based on what we were shown, I wouldn't be surprised," Gamaunda said. "Either way, another concern I have is with the people who were once here. Where did they go, and where were those animals taking them?" Sutama sighed and shook his head. "Well. Let's just see what Nuyani knows once she comes out. I still want to ask why she went through the northern ravine."

"Proof," Sutama said.

"Proof?" the chief repeated.

Sutama gave him a plane stare. "If there were anything else to do to win favor or just be heard, I would go for proof."

The chief looked at the floor and smiled as he said, "I wonder why the elders still passed down that story. Maybe when desperation comes, someone will find a way.”

“Was there anything else?” Sutama then asked.

“How the village fairs right now,” Gamaunda said. “Let’s pray for them and see.”

The two then returned to the front, finding both Cuganwa and Nuyani present on the shelf as the others prayed to Kelvert. Nuyani wore a look of disdain as she healed Vu’olag, who seemed to share the same sentiment. The two said nothing after her palm stopped glowing and walked away. Nuyani stopped once she saw Sutama. Her stare then hardened as she approached him.

“There are a few things we need to talk about,” Nuyani said. Cuganwa walked up behind them. “It’s about the village.

Ch. 26
Storms and Souls

Everyone remained quiet as they listened to Nuyani and Cuganwa explain the village's situation. The storm proved fierce and had ripped most of the tents away, leaving everyone exposed to the storm. Worse as Nuyani feared, howlers were prowling during the storm. In an effort to protect them, Nuyani and Cuganwa used the edria of the village to create barriers to protect themselves. Some of the men were awe-struck at the news. Others moved to Kelvert's side to witness the same visions the others had seen. A few men gathered the courage to explore the rear tunnel and see the hidden settlement.

"We may have a day before they are too tired to keep their walls active," Nuyani said. "After that, they may be attacked again by the howlers or…" Nuyani shrugged.

"Well, this makes things easier if everything works out," Gamaunda commented. This drew Nuyani and Cuganwa's attention. "Your actions already proved you were never a threat to us. Were they aware of you two, or were you making the barriers without them knowing?"

Nuyani blinked as she looked at the man. "It's not something you can be discrete in. We had to convince them to let us help." Cuganwa nodded his head. "Even in the storm, the village…" She blinked slowly. "Besides that, they are safe for now but, I don't know how long this storm will last."

"The first came and went in moments when it shook everything. This one might be the same," Cuganwa suggested.

Nuyani pursed her lips, considering it. "I don't know but, we will need an answer soon." She then stepped to Sutama and held out the rounded crystal containing the second blade.

"What's this?" Sutama asked.

"It's yours," she stated plainly.

The man blinked at her. "Will you not need it?"

"No. I have my gift and knives. You might," Nuyani said as she conjured an orb in her other hand and changed the shape to a similar sword. Bewildered stares fell on the ethereal blade. Its shape, like the curved sword, remained solid, yet its entirety danced with a shifting blue flame, leaving a sapphire gleam on her clothing and eyes. "I don't think I can cut as well without focus but, I learn more each day. Like how many have power like me in the village." Nuyani then looked to the chief, bearing an accusative glare and tone.

"Many may have a talent but not the knowledge to wield it," the chief stated. "Perhaps you can change that?"

Nuyani's eyes widened as she backed away. "I can't. I don't…know," she said plainly.

"Nuyani?" Cuganwa questioned.

"Helping with survival is one thing but, I am not a part of the village," she declared. "You have a teacher." Pointing at Cuganwa, Nuyani could see some of the other men agreed with her choice.

"It might as well be done, Nuyani," Gamaunda said.

"No!" Nuyani snapped as she glared at the man. "I am the witch. I am the one you all wanted to kill days ago. I was stuck out here. My mother and the Great Lord warned me of the spirits that came to the village." Sutama and Gamaunda exchanged a glance, remembering the vision of the past as the banshees attacked the festival. "You have your teacher, and Lord Kelvert is back. After all this, I will save my mother," Nuyani said.

"Where will we go?" Gamaunda pressed, still trying to convince her. "The village is destroyed, according to you both."

"Take the large cavern for all I care. I won't be here long after," Nuyani said. She then walked past the others returning to the hut and erecting a barrier.

"Nuyani," Kelvert's familiar echo then called. "Not to pry but, why shun them away?"

"Great Lord, I wish to understand how I could stay," Nuyani started. I lived, and she died protecting me. The village lives because of her. When she is being attacked and tormented out there, without rest, and came to me, how can I leave her and just accept the village? I have to free her."

"I see," Kelvert replied. "Take your rest, Nuyani. There may be an answer."

Cuganwa then approached Sutama with a solemn look on his face. Anger and confusion battled in him as his questions welled up in him.

"Say it, Cuganwa," Sutama said in a gentle tone and breathing heavily. It was odd to see his stoic demeanor now vulnerable, yet there was little either would expect.

"I just wanted to know why you never told us about her," the boy said. "With the other carving, I always thought it was grandfather."

The man looked to the side as he then answered in a low growl," I never spoke on it because there was nothing I could say. I thought I lost them both and was cursed. You and your mother were a second chance after proving my faith to the others. This was the way things were done."

"And now?" Cuganwa pressed.

"I will protect you, your sister, and your mother with all I can," Sutama said.

"Does that include Nuyani," the boy added.

Sutama shook his head. "That is up to her. Our home is open to her if she wishes. Though she will reject it. But, what about you, Cuganwa?"

"I…" Cuganwa looked to the ground. "I understand why, and I don't blame you, father. I think she would be better here than me."

"Lord Kelvert guides us," another man chimed in. The others looked at him. "Well, how else did you two learn your tricks if the Great Lord didn't teach you?"

"Nuyani practiced with different skills. I just copied her when I could," the boy admitted.

"Whatever. Let's eat until they have an answer," another man said as he retreated to the group circle.

With a single word, the boy found himself famished. He wondered if he should speak with Nuyani. Sutama then started toward the circle. He stopped and looked at Cuganwa.

"Join us," Sutama said. His tone was more inviting. Cuganwa hesitated and looked at the others. Some still held their suspicions, but a few still waved him over.

As the boy sat down in a spot, he looked in the direction of Nuyani's hut. He then asked, "What about, Nuyani?"

The others looked at one another. Sutama then said, "Let her be. She has her own way of life here. If she chooses to join us, I will not turn her away." Cuganwa looked at his father, seeing his gaze grow long and distant at the words. The words seemed long buried, even rehearsed. The others glanced at him with looks of worry and a few in contempt.

The boy glared at the others. "What do you have against her? We, she saved you. Why do you still see her as evil?"

"Because we aren't ready," Vu'olag said. Cuganwa looked at the man who was testing his repaired arm. "She saved you and us, but we don't know what she is capable of. Remember the first sinner,"

"The first sinner was infested with one of the worms," Cuganwa shot back.

"Boy, was his mind and eyes so taken over that his body doubled in size and kept going on after every fatal blow?" the guard asked. Cuganwa was quiet. "This is still a mystery to you too. I know you've seen many things but, that's why we are cautious."

"This is a mystery to us all," Sutama added.

Vu'olag leered at the old hunter. "No disrespect to you, Sutama, but you, siding for your daughter is not a surprise. We just wanted to know if there was a way to justify it. In my mind, there is but, I still doubt her."

"Your thoughts. Not ours," Selsaj added. "We get that she is a threat but, so far, we're alive because of her. Let it rest."

"And what am I supposed to let rest?" It's too convenient in my eye," Vu'olag said. He narrowed his eyes and looked at the others with an air of self-importance. "She killed the first infested animal. She found another blade, proof that we are from some other place and not from the Great Lord." The man then held out his arms and looked toward the wisp. "And in place of the shining light that guarded our people, we have a ball of fire no larger than my head."

Cuganwa narrowed his eyes at the man as his annoyance built. Confusion, then surprise, were expressed on the boy's face as Kelvert's subtle thrum ended catching his attention. He then turned to the wisp. Sutama looked at him and then to the wisp. A moment later, the ground shook once more. Distant rumbling echoed through the hall, reverberating the stone. The others then looked toward the wisp shock covering their faces.

"What's going on!" Nuyani yelled, running out of the hut with her knives drawn.

"Ah, I have your attention now," Kelvert said audibly in a mixture of their voices. Vu'olag lowered his hands as some of the others began praying. "This is what my power prevents, child. This is what I've prevented for years before I lost power I imparted onto your ancestors and was imprisoned in the land. Now, I return with my gift amongst only a few who survived."

'Lord Kelvert. Please, he's the only fool amongst us,' she prayed as the loud crumbling continued. Kelvert's booming voice drowned out any sound she could make.

"Worry not, Nuyani," Kelvert said in her voice echoing alone in her mind. "This is merely a show of force. They must learn." Her mind was put to rest as she kept herself from sighing. It was easy for her to hold her look of worry with the sound of crashing stones still echoing in the distance.

Kelvert continued to speak to the others. "You've tested my patience, so I will test your faith. If all before you is false, if the lives lost are mere illusions, then look upon the visions and walk into the sands. You will find your answer. Or be silent. Doubts such as yours have allowed the village to remain vulnerable. You name one as the first sinner, yet many slaughtered the innocent. I question you. Act or be silent."

Vu'olag said nothing as he turned away from the wisp, looking to the ground before them. As ordered, he was silent. Kelvert's thrum returned as the sounds of stones falling and shaking of the cavern ceased. One of the other men slapped Vu'olag's shoulder, gaining his attention as the two stared at one another, expressing their annoyance.

'That's one way to deal with him,' Nuyani thought as she considered tossing him out of the cavern and into the winds. A part of her detested the man greatly after realizing how much destruction befell the village.

Her ears perked up as she felt a pressure shift and twist in place against the flank of her core. Nuyani turned to see what was happening only to find a wry smile of one of the men eying her backside. Mindful of her runner's wear torn in several places, she felt heat rising to her face as she twisted around to face the man and guard her back. Nuyani realized that her status as the witch was now diminishing in the eyes of others, and to a few, she was merely a woman.

She retreated around one of the huts breaking sight from the man continuing until she reached the shelf. Nuyani looked on seeing Gamaunda in quiet prayer beneath the wisp. To some small degree, she was not surprised knowing the importance of his role as chief. Those who qualified in the village had to have such dedication.

"All leaders must be disciplined," Nuyani whispered as she looked from the chief to Sutama. She blinked and pulled her head back as she saw the man approach her. A low thrum rang from him, making Nuyani wonder how much even the chief knew of edria.

His towering figure and strong presence, however, he seemed smaller than before. Sutama strolled over to her with his hands behind his back. Nuyani took a step back and clenched her fists. "Yes?" she asked.

Sutama stopped just a pace before her and looked at Nuyani with a raised chin. "You saw Huloat on the other side," the hunter started.

Her eyes flared with rage Nuyani barely controlled as she shot back, "No." she pointed at the man. "No. You cannot say her name to me."

"Fine. I won't but, I only seek to find a way to see her, Nuyani."

She shivered and held her glare. 'I don't want you using my name either,' she wanted to snap back.

"The visions of what you've faced in the demon land. I wish to see her. Is there a way?" Sutama asked.

Her rage boiled within her and her fists shook "Why?" she sneered.

"To give what peace I can. To apologize for being a foolish man," Sutama's voice started to crack. He recovered and continued. "Even if it is but a moment, I wish to see her. I will seek to atone." Sutama held a stern glare.

Nuyani's thrum passed through the man, and she could feel the sway and stir of his spirit. The current rushing within the bead of pressure was stronger than many others present, even her own. Nuyani sighed. 'Lord Kelvert said that spirit requires a strong will to maintain,' Nuyani thought. Her jaw tightened as she admitted to herself only the maddened devotion of the old hunter was something she had to respect. Whatever lay in his heart, he remained devout. Nuyani continued, "I think we can. There is a way to do so but, it will be dangerous."

"Clever, child," Kelvert rang in their minds.

"Great Lord, do you think it will work?" Nuyani questioned.

"It just might," the wisp answered.

"What plan is this?" Sutama questioned.

Nuyani turned to him and answered, "We're going to stop the storm." The declaration earned her the attention of everyone within earshot. Gamaunda smirked as he kept to his prayer.

Moments later, Nuyani had retrieved the bedrolls and placed them on the shelf. Sutama stood by, waiting for Nuyani's preparations for their trip to the demon lands. With both rolls laid out, Nuyani took a seat on the first and waved to the other for Sutama to sit.

"This has a risk. Do you remember what Lord Kelvert showed you?" she asked as the old hunter took a seat.

"Yes. This exposes our mind and conscience to be more vulnerable, even for the Great Lord," Sutama recalled.

"Yes. Your will is strong," Nuyani started. 'Even more than my own to see my mother.' Nuyani questioned, trying to decipher the difference in their spirits. "This will push us through with the rest of the prutosa Lord Kelvert has collected."

"Why has it not been used before?" Sutama asked, looking to the wisp.

"We couldn't," Kelvert said simply. "Edria makes up my body, and containing prutosa before now was not possible. As I was trapped within the lands, little of the prayers you've sent could reach me. Now things have turned in our favor, and the prayers of the village have returned in strength. My make does little to aid with such a force still. I would expand and need to balance my spells differently."

"The two energies do better with a normal body," Nuyani said. "But they cancel each other."

"I see. And what will be our part in this?" Sutama replied.

Nuyani straightened her back, trying to strengthen her conviction as she said, "I will guide our spirits there with Lord Kelvert's prutosa, and we will disrupt their flow with our own."

"Why do you believe this'll work?" Sutama asked.

Nuyani almost glared at him for asking a question that could seed doubt but, the flow of his spirit showed no sign of wavering. "Prutosa needs a certain amount of energy to use, and edria uses more endurance. With more prutosa, we wield a strong current to push our way through. And this storm will cost a lot of energy."

"Then let's begin," Sutama said as he moved to lie down.

'You're prepared,' Nuyani said with a mixture of shock and relief.

Nuyani did the same lying down on her bedroll. Closing her eyes, she concentrated on her thrum and used a pulse to eject some of her spirit as her conscience split into the black cloud. Nuyani then waited as Kelvert brought a large edria sphere containing prutosa. She passed through the sphere and waited as her spirit started to turn and twist the still pool of energy. It was strange as the wishes and prayers of the village rose in her mind in small whispers. The people praying to Kelvert for a single day reached the great lord. It was odd to Nuyani as it seemed even some of the whispers were for Nuyani herself and Cuganwa.

Nuyani felt as though her body was on fire as she looked at her form with the same flickering outline. The others watched as her blue form, no larger than a hand, flew over Sutama and entered his stomach. Approaching his core, Nuyani thought she would have to pry some of his spirit out of the sphere. With ease, she reached for a small portion of Sutama's spirit and pulled with a long flickering blue line trailing from the rest of his spirit.

Despite being made of the same energy, on contact, Sutama's spirit was as different as their real bodies. The energy twisted and streamed differently than her own, never mixing. Once enough energy was pulled from his core, Nuyani floated out of the man's stomach leading his spirit to take shape. Sutama blinked as he looked around, the sensation of his body peeling away seeming strange as he looked back at his form. The world sat in dark blues and blacks aside from the souls sitting in spheres of darkness within each person's body.

The others looked on in surprise, wondering how she could grow smaller and remove another's spirit. Before anyone could say a thing to them, the two looked as though they were conversing before they disappeared, leaving only a sudden flint. Their bodies remained still on the bedrolls, sound asleep.

'May his shine guide you,' Cuganwa prayed.

"Cuganwa," The chief then called.

"Yes, dear chief?" the boy replied as he turned to face the man.

"They will be busy looking for answers but, I saw your sister form a weapon with her edria," Gamaunda started. There lay a strange warmth at the boy's core hearing Nuyani referred to as his sister. He could not explain it, but both were serving the Great Lord despite their beginnings. "I think it would be wise for you to take on a little practice then." Gamaunda then flicked his wrist, presenting the blade of the drylands. Cuganwa felt a shiver run through him as the deaths of the first sinner and Deyunca came to mind. "Learn to wield a weapon well, and you'll be more capable for any situation." Cuganwa nodded his head as the chief flipped the blade around in his hand and held it out by the hilt toward Cuganwa.

"Shouldn't he use his own edria?" one of the others commented.

"It won't matter if he doesn't have a weight to draw an idea from. Otherwise, the techniques will matter little," the chief commented.

Cuganwa gawked at the blade gleaming in Kelvert's glow. Holding a major symbol of the village was nothing he'd ever imagine doing, even if he did not have Kelvert's gift. "So let's see you try some steps." Cuganwa gave an eager nod before mirroring a fighting stance Gamaunda took with his right foot back, his right hand having a palm face the floor, and his left hand held out and angled as though he were holding the weapon.

"Ready," Cuganwa said.

'This seems faster,' Nuyani thought as she and Sutama coursed through the air, passing familiar clusters of life. She never thought about her sense of the unique ebb of her mother's soul reaching out to her like soft waves rushing toward her more chaotic compared to sensing another's edria instead.

"What should I expect?" Sutama asked.

"Just pain," Nuyani stated. "Many people and animals had been captured and beaten to this demon's will. It's hurting her soul." 'This was your fault,' Nuyani thought as she clenched a fist. The trip was brief as the two stopped just on the ravine's edge. Something compelled her to halt just for a moment—the same black stage beyond the jagged ring of cliffs. Sutama looked into the abyss below.

"Why have we stopped? Do you think we will fall?" Sutama questioned as his eyes fixed on the vortex of blues spinning before them.

"N-no," Nuyani answered. "This is just different." Nuyani looked to the spirits. The weight of others depending on her actions started to hinder her choices. Their failure would do more harm than good and could even be worse if they were trapped.

"Are you ready?" Sutama asked kindly.

"Yes," Nuyani answered.

Nuyani then took the man's hand and focused past her fears and doubt before the two shot forth. With the tide of spirit behind her, Nuyani pierced through the vortex sending other spirits loose as a ripple passed through the remainder of the vortex as if it were the surface of the water. Sutama looked about as the current of his spirit became faster. The two looked about until they saw the gout of flame rising from the crack. Sutama could feel the ebb of Huloat's soul.

Sutama started toward the gout of flame and ignored the rushing tendrils of spirit surrounding them as if in a trance. Nuyani took to the defense, moving in a spiral around the flame and her father to create a torrent of spirit surrounding them. Banshees howled and bombarded the current, trying to weaken the shifting tide. Nuyani halted, floating higher than her father and the flame as she maintained the barrier. She narrowed her eyes as the process was different from wielding magic. While the strike of her core created a constant and all-encompassing barrier, the use of prutosa seemed more like the constant threading and pushing of the prutosa. As Nuyani felt the flow slow with each bombardment, she grew desperate.

Seeing one of the specters closing in, Nuyani thought only to strike the banshee down. Following her command, the prutosa formed a sickle-like wave following the spin of the current and struck the banshee. Nuyani expected embers and a cleaved head floating away. Instead, the spirit dissipated into smoke, with some streams collecting into the sickle and adding to Nuyani's pool. Along with the spirit's assimilation, she could feel a small tether from the being leading to another soul scattered within the wall of spirits.

'That's what the lord meant,' Nuyani thought as she felt an instinct tugging at the back of her mind to draw the soul in. 'No,' Nuyani declared as she focused her thoughts on the only reason they were there, stopping the sandstorms. More sickles arched from the twisting waves of her will, cleaving through more and more of the spirits.

Sutama approached the flame reaching for his wife. As his hand plunged into the inferno, it tried to push through his visage only to twist around his ghostly limb and give way. The hunter could feel the ebb of her calling to him. "Huloat," the man uttered as his spirit peeled away the flame creating a space for the soul. The transparent bead with the iridescent flame was then encased in his wife's visage, yet in a wrinkled and tattered image. Huloat opened her tired eyes with some effort as the wrinkles faded, gradually returning her to a lively form. "My dear," Sutama croaked as he placed a hand on her cheek.

"You came for me?" Huloat said in surprise, her voice tired and in a rasp.

The man pulled her in, embracing her as tightly as he could. "Forgive me, love," Sutama said. "I did not know. I will trade with you."

"No. I love you. I understand. Live for her," Huloat said as she looked to Nuyani. Her soft smile deepened. "Live for the others."

A sudden thrum rose from beneath the stage. Nuyani looked back, seeing the fire split into multiple long tendrils diverted by the hunter's will as he and Huloat were together. The souls closest to the thinned sections of the flame escaped firing off into the distance. Below them, the crack in the black stage had flickering embers of shadow rising into view. 'The flame uses prutosa and magic,' Nuyani wondered as she looked to her parents. Despite the years of hatred, this one moment of closure brought her anger to a simmer. Her mother then turned to her in full, pulling away from Sutama.

"To me, Little Flower," Huloat said. Nuyani was uncertain but did as she was told. Another thrum, even stronger than the first, rang through the area. Nuyani raced to their side. "Through the crack! Quickly."

Nuyani did not wait as she wielded as much of the torrent into a spiral entering the opening. The black flames were pushed down. The blue glow of the prutosa was alight beneath the platform revealing dozens of the symbols Nuyani had never seen before. The one with the flame spewing out was seen in a black silhouette imprinted on her mind. 'Seal,' Nuyani read in her mind. Before she could do anything else, the black flames rose once more, piercing through the glow. It erupted from the crack as Huloat pushed Nuyani aside. Fire engulfed her mother and the other souls still lingering. Her visage returned to the small clear marble holding the starlike flame. Nuyani looked on stunned, wanting to break her mother free. Fleeting lines of black swirled around the souls.

Sutama's attention was on the approaching threat of the banshees. The wall of souls no longer spun about, merely drifting in the air. As one banshee neared Nuyani, Sutama stepped between the two and struck the being with ease. Nuyani's attention was regained as she looked at the other opponents. 'We must leave,' Nuyani thought as she felt the surge of prutosa swelled around her. To Nuyani's surprise, she had not expended all the energy at once. With a final push, she and Sutama forced their way past the other spirits and wall of drifting souls. Sailing through the land, the two escaped from the area.

The two were not safe even out of the confines of the slowed vortex. Waves rippled through the land, shaking the air around them. Nuyani let the coursing prutosa swerve and twist under the influence as they dodged a beam of prutosa within meters spinning around it like a curved leaf fallen prey to the wind. The first column ended. Nuyani veered to the side with only a short moment to decipher the blast's aim. As they sailed through the area, Nuyani caught glimpses of different shapes in the ground glowing blue in a dark area she expected to only be sand and rock.

A large cluster of blue beads caught Nuyani's eye. 'What are they doing there?' Nuyani wondered in a fleeting thought as they flew by. The large ebb and blasts then stopped. Nuyani looked back into the dark horizon, sensing nothing in approach. Instead of thinking as to why, they sailed on counting their blessings.

On arrival at the cavern, they saw the large dome of dark edria covering the cliffs, with a few boulders falling, revealing the dark ethereal wall. The thrum rang from it, still rippling their visage, but the two passed through the defense unhindered. The two entered their bodies and leaped up from the bedrolls.

Nuyani immediately looked to Kelvert. "Has it stopped?"

"Splendid work. It will," the wisp answered. "Soon, the prutosa will be expended, and the storm will stop. It will be safe to leave. However, I do not know how long. It might be long enough for the others to retreat to the cavern." Everyone stopped as they looked at the wisp.

"It's going to stop?" one man asked as he looked at the others. Vu'olag looked at them with bewildered eyes. The man started to tear for the first time since she met him.

"You've brought miracles, Nuyani." Gamaunda started. "But, how will we bring nearly twelve hundred people through the drylands safely? I know the first trek was desperate but, I'd rather not leave our people exposed to more danger."

"What do you have in mind?" Nuyani asked.

"Just wondering how you traveled here. Can you repeat it?" Gamaunda asked. Nuyani froze for a moment as she looked at the ground. She had never done the feat on command. "Is it possible?"

"I don't know. My only goals each time were to get away, and the second was with the Great Lord and Cuganwa's help. Trying it on my own was never something I thought of," Nuyani explained. She then turned to the wisp. "Lord Kelvert, is this something I can learn to do in time."

"No. Each leap through the govtif ved edria requires you to use too much energy that will leave you drained. Your power grows but, the risk with the remaining enemies is too great," Kelvert warned.

Nuyani then felt for the small crystal in her pouch. "I wonder if this thing could help us travel," Nuyani thought aloud. Gamaunda looked, wondering if it was the same stone that allowed her to carry so much weight.

"Nuyani, that stone," Kelvert started. She looked up at the wisp. "How did you come about that stone?"

"I found it here in the cavern when I was trying to hide the first night," Nuyani answered.

Nuyani blinked turned toward the back wall. Releasing a pulse from her core, she fed the energy into the stone. The stone radiated with a white light at the center. Small rays pointed from the core toward the back wall. The light projected a wide circle on the wall. White lights outlined the circle with a deep-sea of dark blue, and various lighter lines trailed endlessly in the void. Nuyani blinked as a half-smile appeared on her face.

"This may work,'" Kelvert said in an elated whisper.

"Great Lord, what is this?" the chief then asked.

"This is a portal to the *govtif ved edria* (realm of magic)," the wisp explained. "I brought Nuyani through this realm with some difficulty. But that stone, it will allow greater access to the world if we connect the two points."

Nuyani then ended the pulse and turned to the wisp offering the stone. "Then this is a part of you," she said. Gamaunda looked at Nuyani with a smirk. "Will this add to your strength?" Only a pause filled the air. The others turned to the wisp wondering why Kelvert had grown silent. "Lord Kelvert?"

"You may keep it," the wisp replied in a gently yet proud voice. "Amongst all your efforts, it has served you well." Nuyani's fingers curled around the stone as she held it close to her heart.

'I had more than one gift from the Great Lord,' Nuyani thought to herself.

"No!" the wisp said. Calling everyone's attention. "More of those strange devourers have made their way into the drylands. The storm will end soon. Nuyani, race to the village and protect the others as soon as you can.!"

"Yes, Great Lord," she replied immediately.

Moments later, Nuyani paced back and forth on the shelf, releasing thrum after thrum studying the flow of energy passing through the area. Her nerves were getting the best of her as she waited. She attempted to create portals a few times but only reached into the void. She even thought of using Cuganwa's help but, both waited, not wanting the gale of wind and sand to funnel through the portal.

Nuyani looked over to the others. Gamaunda spoke with the others seeing how they would transport as many people as they could to the cavern. Cuganwa spoke with the others telling them of the whip-necks huddled together and the amount of debris that lay around the area. Speaking together, the men made plans. An hour passed as Nuyani continued to wait by the entrance tapping her foot on the ground. On occasion, the others would climb onto the shelf and pray to Kelvert.

"Nuyani," Gamaunda then called. She looked at the man. "Perhaps you should rest, even for a little." Nuyani raised her brow in response. "You'll be running the whole way to face more infested. Just rest for a moment." The man's expression changed to a sincere one as he relaxed.

With a heavy sigh, her shoulders sunk low. Nuyani had not realized how stiff her body was. She then answered, "You're right."

With that, the man smiled and dropped to the lower floor as she sat on the edge. Nuyani wondered what was happening as she felt for her heart. The sense of danger and fear still lingered, but not from the men present.

'It's been less than a day, and I'm letting my guard down. By his shine, am I that foolish?' Nuyani wondered.

Speaking only to Nuyani, Kelvert then replied, "Little to call foolish when everyone seeks the same outcome, dear child. You look to survive and save others. They wish to do the same."

'Great Lord, I still feel uneasy around them but, is this better?' she thought.

"Consider it temporary before it can become permanent," the wisp stated. "There is more that can be done to earn each other's trust."

'I-I understand,' Nuyani said as she waited.

Cuganwa looked at her, wondering what he should do. 'If I could run as fast as her,' the boy thought as he looked to the ground.

Sutama sat beside him and noticed his creased brow and focus lay elsewhere, "What's on your mind, Cuganwa?" he asked in a low tone.

The boy turned to him. "I just wish I could help her as well. I'm not as fast," he explained.

"You won't need to be," Gamaunda then said on the other side of their circle. The two turned to the chief. "You're able to fight spirits like her. Even a little control of your powers will defend us against the infested animals. The man's smile was warming as he finished, "You'll be a great help in the fight when we get more sleds." Cuganwa nodded his head in compliance as his father placed a hand on his shoulder.

'How are you this cheerful?' the boy wondered.

419

Ch. 27

Infestation

More time passed as the cavern grew silent. The wind continued to howl from outside. Nuyani sat facing the tunnel. Spurred by her constant pulses of her core, she could sense the waning energy outside. The howls then died down into sharp whistles, then silence.

"Go," Kelvert commanded. Nuyani leaped up from the floor and tore through the tunnel.

Her thrum provided context to the outside world as most of the life she sensed seemed normal and swaying. Yet others seemed solid in structure, never swaying in their presence, only a weight against her core. Nuyani pushed the thought aside as she ran to her limit through the drylands, the clouds she raised created a small dust storm with each step. Even passing over the wide gaps of the rivers with little effort. Minutes later, she reached the tall grass and followed the hunting trail. She knew at such speeds, striking a small stone or stick facing the wrong direction could cripple her greatly. The lands seemed a mess as most of the grass at the southern had been flattened toward the east. Random bodies of blade-jaws and blood-manes were found. Even a small charge-horn welp lied randomly in the grass.

'The storm. By the Great Lord, may it be over,' Nuyani thought as she passed through the tall grass and reached more of the drylands. What she remembered as the white gates contrasting the red dirt and green shrubs was now gone, with only a few pieces of the gate remaining. If not for the river and dug-out canal leading through the rising bank, Nuyani would've missed the village. As she approached the rising land, her thrum revealed several weights dot the surface of her core. 'No. They're already coming here,' Nuyani realized.

When she reached the top of the compacted bank, Nuyani peered down into the lower area. Most of the tents were gone. Those that remained were tattered and ripped. Poles were ripped from the ground. The village was worst off on a second view. Yet, life remained. Several of the people seemed unconscious from using their edria for the first time. Others moved about weakly as they scrounged for supplies.

Fueled by desperation, Nuyani's voice was amplified as she shouted. "Gather together!"

People froze and looked at her with surprise but moved on command. Nuyani felt a sense of shock seeing the people listen to her order. She descended to the gathering party, realizing the larger village was nearly halved after the storm.

Yanuma stepped forward. The elder's hair was ragged as dirt covered her face and soiled her green clothing. "By his shine, Nuyani. Why have you come alone?" Some of the others looked to the runner warily.

"The others are on their way. I am here to guard you," Nuyani said as she looked back toward the bank.

"Wh…" Yanuma started.

Nuyani interrupted. "Infested animals are heading this way. I will try to stop them but, all must listen to me." Yanuma's expression hardened as she looked at Nuyani. Many others looked to her. "Take up any poles, spears, or arrows. Keep the animals at a distance, and I will stop them."

Immediately, the people did as she said. Taking arms with any long item they could. Nuyani looked to the bank sensing the animals close by. She then felt a hand grab her wrist. Nuyani looked to the side to find Yanuma covering her mouth as her glowing green eyes shed more tears.

"The storm…" she started. "The Great Lord…"

Nuyani tore her arm away as the elder sand to her knees. This was not the time as the animals grew near. The witch still felt apprehensive toward the elders as they continued the stories spurring others to wish for her death. Even with the misunderstanding cleared, the burn lingered.

With a glance back, she could see a fraction of an enormous ring of spear-bearing men and women holding the perimeter as the young, old, and injured stayed in the center. Nuyani turned back just as the ground trembled. Others did as well. A chorus of flapping wings, snarls, and grunts radiated over the side. Several pressures then shot ahead. Nuyani took in a sharp breath and raised her hands as she released a powerful thrum from her core. A larger wall of orange light appeared above her head, wide enough to blanket even a heavy-horns and one or two whip-necks.

The people looked to the sky. Several blood-manes roared over the bank just to collide with the wall. Nuyani grunted as the opposing energies met, threatening to dampen her thrum. Holding strong, Nuyani willed her construct to fold on the beasts before splitting them into spheres, encasing their heads to decapitate each beast. The bodies fell to the earth with hard thuds. Taking a deep breath to calm her racing heart, Nuyani's gaze fell back to the bank as blade-jaws then appeared. A quiver came to her hand but, she ignored the sensation and focused on the animals.

Raging pulses shot from her core as she created a large construct with an arching slope resembling a curling ocean wave. The animals slid into the construct stopping on the bottom of the light flushed with the ground. There were three of the beasts. As Nuyani rolled the construct forward, a blade-jaw on the further left escaped as the others were compressed. Nuyani saw the animal running toward her. With a sudden twist of her wrist and swing of her hand, the large construct shrank into spheres once more and ripped off the heads of the infested before launching into the remaining blade-jaw.

The sudden projectiles drilled through the animal's flesh with ease as the first orb carved through half of its snout and the other through the center of its neck. Slain, the beast fell into a slide stopping only a few paces away from her. Nuyani turned away, feeling the beast's energy dissipate as more came over the horizon. Grounding herself, Nuyani began to fire spell orbs as she sensed more blade-jaws, blood-manes, and charge-horns rushing down the slope. Some fell into the half-buried canal. The group of people fell back, letting her continue the defense as the animals pressed forth.

The smaller animals fell to the spheres but, the charge-horns proved sturdier. As one of the lumbering monsters came close to her flank, Nuyani thrust out a hand in reflex, creating a construct in a spear shape. The ethereal polearm skewered the beast with ease as it passed through the head and into the hump. As the animal tumbled over, Nuyani stepped to the side, letting it fall, and dropping her hands to both sides as she took a deep breath. Her run left her sweating, and every spell took more of her endurance, straining her muscles.

Nuyani's mind went blank for a moment failing to notice an approaching blade-jaw. The enormous feline raised a paw with extended claws. Nuyani looked to the side guarding with her arm as she made another light construct big enough to cover her body. The beast struck, shattering her barrier and sending her to the floor. Nuyani's core grew chaotic as her thoughts grew disoriented. Nuyani looked to the beast, barely conscious as its jaw descended on her. She tried to force the erratic beat to follow her will but, it was too slow to respond.

Shunk. Nuyani heard a sound as a growl followed. She looked to the animal as blood dripped from a spear wound going through its head. Nuyani did not hesitate as she willed another light into an arching blade and cut through the animal's neck. As its body slumped over, Nuyani conjured a second wall causing the carcass to slide away. Looking back as she tried to stand, Nuyani saw Odaru waving for her to retreat to the group. Her legs shivered under her weight but, she pushed on and stood.

Taking a moment to read her core, Nuyani counted the scattered beads of pressure. Only six were left but, that did not make the situation any easier. Taking several breaths to clear her head, Nuyani felt a surge amongst three of them. She looked to see two blade-jaws and a blood-mane lowering their bodies.

Her eyes widened, recognizing the behavior and crouching. Instinctively, the thrum of her core vibrated event faster. Their heads rose. Their maws widened. Their roars drowned out all sound in the area. Their spirits rippled through the area, causing many of the people to collapse. Nuyani felt her core shake but resisted the paralyzing cold as she staggered forward. Her face contorted from the effort as she raised her hand, struggling to keep steady. She released several strong spell orbs toward the animals hoping to strike at least one. To her luck, a sphere struck one of the blade-jaws in the head, knocking it to the floor as blood seeped from the gash.

The others continued their strange howl. The disorientation lessened only a little, but gave her clarity to the other villagers whose souls were fleeing from the area. 'The other beasts," Nuyani remembered as she focused on her thrum, letting the waves reverberate faster until they became a solid wall blocking out all influence of the roars. Nuyani removed a knife in instinct and charged for the beasts. With a lunging stab at the first, she buried the blade in its neck. Her edria extended further into its body like a spear and struck the worm hidden around the spine. The beast fell.

The next blade-jaw stopped its lament and lowered its head to face her. Nuyani raised her hand to the beast and fired another spell orb. It jumped over the projectile with ease. It closed in on the woman with claws extended only to meet with another construct bisecting it in the air and falling to opposite sides. Nuyani then watched as three remaining blood-manes swept over their heads, giving fatal bites and claws, even lifting villagers in the air only to drop them. The people screamed as they tried to dodge their talons.

Nuyani could feel her body screaming in pain as she lifted her arms and released more spell orbs. The projectiles sailed through the air, striking two blood-manes as they swept across the floor. The third, however, caught someone instead.

"No!" came a shout from amongst the chaos as little Caluu was clutched in the beast's talons and climbed into the air.

Pain and fatigue disappeared from Nuyani's muscles. Whether it was their blood connection or the fact that they shared the same gifts from the Great Lord, possibly even both, Nuyani felt the world lift her as the black lines came into view. The void streamed in the center only to be replaced by a closer image of Caluu and the blood-mane. She found herself airborne and reached out to the child. Caluu looked to Nuyani with a terrified expression. Willing her own energy, Caluu's edria resonated with Nuyani's, allowing the two of them to create a barrier covering them both. The construct severed the animal's talons as the two plummeted. "I have you. Don't worry," Nuyani said as they clung together. Covering their eyes, their cores rang in unison and moved even faster, strengthening the construct. The barrier expanded, nearly doubling in size as they were about to strike the ground. The barrier did little to stop the fall as Nuyani slammed into the ground first. Releasing a hard grunt, she nearly fell unconscious as the usual fatigue and pain returned. Little Caluu lay on her stomach, dazed.

'By the Great Lord, you are safe,' she thought.

The beat of wings in the air then called her attention. At the corner of her eye, she saw the beast closing in. Her head in a fog, and her core stifled, she was now easy prey to the blood-mane. Nuyani struggled to turn, rolling Caluu away as the beast closed in. A sudden caw rang out to Nuyani's surprise, and she saw another blood-mane appear and grab at the wings of its larger counterpart.

"What?" Nuyani wondered as the two enormous beasts clung together and fell into a spiral slamming to the floor with reverberating thuds carried through the dirt.

Others watched as the two continued to scratch and claw at one another. The smaller blood-mane retreated only when a worm shot out from the rotting wound hidden in its neck. The creature lashed out, reaching desperately. With some of her strength returning, Nuyani fired another sphere of edria at it. The projectile struck its shoulder, carving away some of the flesh but, the orb dissipated almost immediately on contact. It seemed like enough as the blood-mane stumbled on its footing. A wounded shoulder and missing foot made the creature stumble despite its tenacity.

Fatigue quickly enwrapped the witch as her head tilted backward, growing heavier. Even wounded, the strange creatures lying inside the blood-mane carcass were too large a threat to leave unattended.

'By the Great Lord, how do we stop it now?' she questioned, now wishing she had taken up her father's offer of the second blade.

The worm continued to pilot the blood-mane into attacking. 'What do I…' Nuyani's thoughts grew quieter as her vision started to change as she saw the scene of a larger hand reaching out to a blade-jaw staring at her. She could feel the flutter of spirit. 'What?' Nuyani mouthed. The vision faded. With the sudden stir in her soul, her senses started to grow acute to the spirit of others around her. The most chaotic was the smaller blood-mane. Whether she understood the flow of its spirit or general demeanor, Nuyani saw the animal's determination to win. Desperate to find a solution, Nuyani broke her conscience free of her body.

Now a blue spirit, Nuyani could feel some of her fatigue fading away. However, the flow of her spirit seemed slower and weaker than usual. She let the fear go and flew toward the smaller blood-mane. Entering its body, she met with the creature's soul. With a simple brush with the animal's spirit, Nuyani gave her thoughts of the other animal falling into the river. With a fierce beat of its wings, it seemed the blood-mane understood as it rose in the air. The infested beast failed to reach its foe despite several jumps and lunges into the air.

The blood-mane continued to backpedal until it flapped its wings, lifting into the air. It sailed up the bank leading the infested. The corrupted animal tried to fly after them only for its damaged wings to give it some lift, yet it failed back down.

Taking this chance, the blood-mane flew in a circle dodging the mandibles of the protruding worm and sinking its talons into the beast's wing on the opposite side. The villagers looked stunned at the beasts in battle. Lamoy then emerged from the crowd armed with her ax and ran toward the larger blood-mane. Nuyani looked to the side as she watched her old friend raise the ax over her head and chop into the beast's left hindleg, cleaving halfway through. The worm flailed about, almost striking the huntress, but she guarded the blow with her ax. On collision, she was knocked away, tumbling down the slope.

The smaller blood-mane gained more momentum dragging the infested over the rest of the compact bank. Clicking and flapping sounded amongst several splashes in the water. The sounds quieted as only a single blood-mane flew away a moment later. Nuyani could feel the collected spirit within the blood-mane release with each devouring bite.

The villagers looked around, searching for any other infested animals. The area was clear. Nuyani sent several thrums through the desolated village finding only the frantic, scared and tired souls of everyone around her. Caluu then awoke and looked at Nuyani. The girl's eyes widened as she looked at Nuyani, who could only manage a frail smile before blacking out.

Sutama breathed heavily as he gripped the reins of his whip-neck. As a flickering shadow appeared above him, the hunter blindly swung with his blade cleaving through the leg of a blood-mane. He then pressed his hand onto the neck of his stead and released what little control of edria he understood into the animal. The whip-neck responded in kind as its head whipped around and bludgeoned the animal, making it crash to the floor in a heap of dirt. Cuganwa saw the animal was down and released a spell orb at the beast's head. The beak and eyes exploded into chunks of pounded flesh. The boy looked about, watching for the approaching beasts as a handful of blood-manes and blade-jaws remained.

Charge-horns were a part of the infested group but proved to be the easiest targets after leaving the cavern. As Cuganwa created another orb decapitating a blade-jaw, another shadow loomed over him. The boy turned around as a blood-mane was closing in. Selsaj, riding as an archer on an adjacent whip-neck fed edria into his arrow as he took aim and shot at the animal's limb. The talons and feathers burst apart as the edria imbued projectile struck the animal. The short lessons by Kelvert and Gamaunda served well in batting away the infested. A blade-jaw dashed forth, closing on the archer only for Cuganwa to create a wall a few feet before Selsaj. The barrier broke from the beast's lunge but slowed the animal enough to keep the hunter safe.

Cuganwa's hand quivered from the pain, but he drove on and used his other hand, releasing another orb and striking the beast in the head. With the others and Cuganwa wielding edria, they diminished their pursuers down to one blood-mane. Though larger, the beast stayed far behind, where it safely dodged arrows and spells with ease. The beast blinked for a moment as if studying the predicament. The others started to cheer as its head turned away.

Cuganwa gritted his teeth as he gripped the handholds of the rear saddle seat. 'No,' the boy thought as he forced his hand through the loop, securing him to the seat and closing his eyes. He took his edria form and flew toward the blood-mane. The creature sped faster, surprising Cuganwa as he could feel the rising pressure sitting against his being. 'What are you doing?' The boy wondered. Not certain he wished to know, Cuganwa fired another orb at the beast as he created another sword in the other hand. The beast craned its head back as the flow of prutosa within it surged. Spirit then burst from the creature knocking away the orb and even Cuganwa as he remained disoriented. When he righted himself, the blood-mane was a small dot heading north.

A fearful thought crept in the boy as he wondered if the creatures were learning to cast spells as well. Cuganwa was starting to feel the strain on his body as pain radiated through him. The boy then returned, waking as he started to curse.

Sutama looked back at him, surprised by the outburst. "Easy, Cuganwa. What happened?"

The boy looked with wide eyes to his father. "It knocked me away," he answered. The two held their gaze as Sutama realized that things would become worse.

"Then be grateful and pray, Little Charge-horn!" Gamaunda shouted. "Today, it flees. Today we breathe. The village breaths." The others felt rallied as they continued racing through the drylands.

"Prepare my child," Kelvert said in the boy's mind. "You have done well today but, we must always prepare." Cuganwa let the words sink in as he looked to the north. The blood-mane was out of sight, and its pressure was gone.

Ch. 28

To the Witch's Den

The group continued toward the east. Sunlight waned over the horizon as they started to set up camp. Once everyone was ready and resting, Cuganwa projected his conscience again and flew toward the village. As night began to take hold, he saw the mass of the remaining villagers marching through the darkness led by two of the elders. As they shuffled onward, Cuganwa could see Nuyani lying on the back of a saddle unconscious. Guards watched over her as they continued toward the west.

Cuganwa gawked at the march. 'They're keeping her safe. They accepted her,' the boy thought.

Seeing fewer people than before, he raced through the crowds looking for Jogia and Caluu. His mother carried the young girl who was fast asleep as well. "By his shine," Cuganwa said with a sigh. Torches were raised as the village's largest caravan followed the path.

With everyone heading toward their camp with at least a day's journey, Cuganwa turned and flew back toward the camp. Cuganwa found his father placing a water skin beside him along with a wrap of jerky and a few nuts.

The boy then awoke, surprising his father as he blurted out, "The village is heading this way!"

"Wait. Really?" a distant voice asked, calling everyone's attention.

Cuganwa turned to the rest with wide glowing eyes. "Yes. They'll be here in a half a day, maybe. Everyone is coming," the boy continued.

Before the cheers could start, one of the men asked, "How many?"

Cuganwa's glees subsided at the tone of the guard. His mouth quivered before he answered, 'Just over half." Some of the others lowered their heads at the news. Cuganwa could see the fear in their hearts. Fortune smiled in his favor but, that still left the others.

"No. Do not sulk," Gamaunda ordered. "We must remember Lord Kelvert lead us to an outcome where anyone is walking here after this storm. There is reason to mourn. Do it when everyone is safe." The expression of the others hardened though a glint from the fire did reveal a tear on some of their faces.

Cool winds rasped in her ears as the familiar cushion of her bedroll lay against her skin. A strange sound stirred her slumber. The sound of soft voices and whispers. 'Voices? Where am I?' Nuyani thought as she sprung to a low crouch flipping the loose corner of her bedroll away. Nuyani reached for her knives, finding them gone. The secured straps and bands protecting her arms and legs were gone. Even her hair was not only free from its hood but was combed. Nuyani looked down, finding her attire in a loose light tan dress instead of her usual dark red runner's wear. She hugged her body as if trying to cover herself.

"By the Great Lord," she rasped through gritted teeth. She looked about, finding her familiar surroundings in a stone hut.

"Splendid. You're awake," a gentle voice called from the entrance. Nuyani looked, seeing Yanuma present in a tattered green dress and bearing several scars covered in salves and wraps.

Nuyani glared at the elder and created a barrier. The construct exploded from her in a dome colliding with the stone structure with a loud thud reverberating through the cavern. Bits of dust shot from the loose cracks in the stone. The elder looked at Nuyani in bewilderment.

"Calm yourself, child. You're home," the elder said in a soft voice.

"Don't mess with me!" Nuyani snapped, fully aware of her surroundings. She could feel the presence of everyone's souls and the thrum of not just Kelvert and Cuganwa but many others in the larger cavern. "You've kept such a secret. Is every elder of fables so conceited to keep our history as a lie? Will you cover up this one too?"

"Don't question me when it comes to secrets, child," the elder said in a commanding voice as she straightened herself to look taller and narrowed her eyes at

Nuyani. "Hate me all you want. It was kept hidden because of the consequences that came with it. Seafarers that hunted monsters to gain more power and even attacked other civilizations. Tell me how it isn't fair for us to be attacked the same way."

Nuyani scowled at the woman. "Ah. Silence means the wilds haven't taken your senses. So does remembering the fables, to begin with."

Nuyani ignored the compliment sensing a rouse in the elder's words. "Then what happens next?"

"Unless you plan to be the first two-legged turtle, come see what the village can offer in atonement for our ignorance," Yanuma challenged. "We have a generation to train. Your brother is already hard at work."

Nuyani blinked several times. Though she knew Cuganwa was family, the words were still alien. "So, you aren't planning to kill anyone with glowing eyes?" Nuyani finally asked.

"Not unless they've sinned." The elder gave Nuyani a hard look. Nuyani kept her glare. "Follow me and see what your efforts prevented from being lost."

Nuyani did follow behind the elder as she walked on. Other women wearing the server's garb and the usual guards were scattered amongst the small huts. Approaching the front shelf, Nuyani saw her stuff cleared from the fire pit as dozens of small children and a few adults sat in prayer. Even with closed eyes, Nuyani could see the small slivers of light peeking through their eyelid.

"Great Lord?" Nuyani asked in a fearful tone drawing the elder's attention.

"Do not worry, Nuyani. I have merely masked their presence to let you sleep," the wisp stated. The thrum ended, releasing a bombardment of thrums that coursed through the area. "I am sharing some of your experiences with the others for them to learn."

"Wait. How long have I been asleep?" Nuyani asked.

"A day or two," Elder Yanuma answered. Nuyani looked back at her in surprise. "The day you stopped those beasts from killing all of us, we fled here." The elder looked to the ground. "I guess with disaster, any refuge is better than the one where you are most exposed."

Nuyani said nothing as she kept her expression clear. "Well, I'm happy to see things may change."

"Really?" the elder asked in a challenging tone. "To be sure, let me introduce you to someone."

Nuyani gave a quizzical glare to the elder as the two made their way past the servers and headed toward the rear tunnel. The vines and glowing flowers were trimmed back, allowing the two to stand and walk straight. Nuyani looked up into the vegetation, missing the strange rain-like scent that subtly sat on the moist air. Now it was replaced with a different scent, the collected smell of hardworking people and animals condensed into a small space. Her nose twitched as the two made their way down the tunnel. Yanuma noticed Nuyani's discomfort and released a sigh as they finished their trek and entered the larger cavern.

Nuyani looked around, seeing the area full of life once more. People moved about doing what work they could in their new settings. On a second shelf in the far side, Nuyani could see the whip-necks corralled in a space where the vines were overgrown. The waterways were clear, letting the water stream through the stone canals and feed the wells near the center. Many of the men worked to break down and reassemble several huts into larger spaces to fit themselves as others collected the rusted metal into it challenging to set up in the new environment.

Some of the villagers in passing greeted with, "The light brought you." The elder waved back with a smile. Making their way to the center, Nuyani saw a group of women standing together.

"Jogia, I have a visitor!" Yanuma called out in a loving tone.

A woman then appeared from the group and wore a look of shock and amazement before rushing toward them. The woman looked straight at Nuyani, making her feel uneasy. Jogia grew a smile as she placed a hand on Nuyani's shoulders. Her eyes glistened with tears before the woman went in for an embrace. Nuyani's eyes widened for a moment until the thrum of her core resonated with Jogia's.

"You're Caluu's mother," Nuyani said.

The woman pulled away, only to kiss Nuyani's forehead, surprising her. "Thank you," the woman strained. "Caluu and the others, they have your example. We don't have to fear." Jogia tried to fight the flow of tears surging forth. Nuyani blinked several times, realizing what she meant as the group of women behind her had the same expressions with red eyes and tears of joy.

"Y-you're welcome. The Great Lord guides us all," Nuyani said.

"Bu his light bright you," Jogia said and released Nuyani. The others whispered the same quote and performed the prayer gesture with their hands. Nuyani was touched by the gesture, but felt a strange well at her core. She noticed the flow of prutosa leaving their bodies and entering her core.

Nuyani blinked with her eyes widening. 'Are they actually praying to me?' she wondered. Nuyani felt an assuring hand touch her arm and saw Yanuma giving her a concerned look. Despite not liking the elder, she did calm down, merely thanking the others before they left.

"Every mother there has a child saved thanks to you," Yanuma said once they were out of earshot.

Nuyani stopped in place, catching the elder off guard. Yanuma turned around to see burning ember eyes begin to tear. "My mother is gone because of all this. Thank the Great Lord and her, not me." Nuyani's lips went taut. "I still have something I must do."

"Going to the demon lands to free her soul?" Yanuma asked. Nuyani narrowed her eyes. "Her warning saved us all. I didn't get that from our last contact, just the first time. Hate me if you wish but, you've done plenty for the people. I just wish for you to teach us more, then you can go anywhere you wish without worry."

"I'm not that free," Nuyani said to the elder. "There's a demon out there that is trying to kill us and take our souls. Aside from me wanting to save my mother's soul. I have to go."

"Then why not teach as much as you know before you leave? You'll have safety here and allies to protect you." Yanuma gave a large smile. Nuyani looked at the elder with a stern expression and gave a slight nod. Yanuma chuckled. "You almost look like your father." Nuyani's eyes widened at the comment. "Come now. Let's go back to the front and speak with Gamaunda."

Returning to the smaller cavern, they approached the healing elder, teaching some others how to perform basic healing routines for cuts and burns and salves to mix. Nuyani saw many of the village guards and some of the servers taking on the task.

Elder Belractu then looked up at the two and straightened his back as he waved for another villager in server garb to take over for the lesson. Belractu approached the women, wearing a rare smile as he turned to Nuyani and said, "His light brought you." Nuyani felt a bit odd seeing a village leader acknowledge and thank her. "If you're able to heal and mend bones as well as I can, then there is a lesson that all can learn."

Nuyani felt a lot calmer in Belractu's presence. Compared to Elder Yanuma, he did not have an air of mystery or secrets around him. "Thank you," Nuyani started. "Why are you teaching so many now?"

The elder's smile disappeared as he looked at Nuyani with a tilted head. He then said, "You've seemed to forget that few have Kelvert's gift. So all of them can learn to mend as Lord Kelvert taught Cuganwa."

"I see," Nuyani replied. 'Is this all just about the convenience they have with the others?" Nuyani questioned.

His face saddened, revealing a fatigued man. Belractu had only a few recent scars he healed while in the cavern. "There were many that were lost in this storm. Comfort or not. We owe you our thanks. The Great Lord, you and Cuganwa," Belractu said.

The elder then nodded, returning to his stoic demeanor, and returned to the others to continue their lessons. Nuyani and Yanuma then made their way down the first tunnel and outside. Once there, they saw a group of men crowding around Gamaunda as they discussed the infested animals. Cuganwa and Sutama stood close by. They planned to collect more supplies and their dead. Knowing how the worms spread through wounds, their ritual of cremating the dead became even more important. The woman approached the group, receiving a few head turns leading morning prayer gestures. Nuyani's hand twitched in response to their motion.

Nuyani froze a few times, still feeling uncomfortable around so many people. She forced a weak smile to those who gave the gesture before looking on toward the chief. 'Well, they aren't knives or arrows,' she told herself as she watched Gamaunda use small stones and pebbles to replicate the image of his plan. Looking at the arrangement, there were nearly twenty stones in pairs along the middles, with a dozen single stones surrounding the parallel formation. The man then used a spare stick to point to the center pair.

"Cuganwa will be here. Look for any animals and slow them down. Only then can we kill them in time," Gamaunda stated. The others looked on, studying the terrain. "From what we've learned with the Great Lord's return, these worms may infest us as well but, we think more than animals do, making an infested human more dangerous." Nuyani's eyes widened as she then saw the chief open his hand and reveal an orb of blue light no larger than a pebble. His eyes weren't glowing as hers did. His thrum was weaker than her own. "We will need to be ready. Let us learn from the past."

"Hm. You taught him and the others a thing or two," Yanuma commented.

"There's little that I've taught. Only what was shown to me or something I picked up," Nuyani stated.

The elder turned to her. "We've only told him how to channel his will with the blade," the elder started. "Learning how to do it on our own isn't something even the elders know. But, that's a trick we must look into."

"Ah. Priestess. Elder Yanuma. Please join us," Gamaunda said.

"Priestess…" Nuyani whispered, feeling a mixture of emotions from the word. Yanuma's history told them that priests and priestesses were once a part of the village as well when Kelvert was initially blocking the storms, but the positions were renounced once the Great Lord had left.

"Nuyani. If you would join us on the expedition, we would be even safer than before. A lot of supplies will need recovering," Gamaunda started. "It will be safer for us all."

"I…will join you then," Nuyani said.

The chief nodded and continued. "With the priestess aiding us, we can have her watch the rear. Her abilities would cover any vulnerabilities we have," Gamaunda continued. Each person after was listed for their position. Once the process was done, the group dispersed. The village leader then turned to Nuyani and Yanuma, wearing his usual warm smile. "Morning, you two." The chief then started to look Nuyani up and down, noting the change in her attire. Though not offended, Nuyani shrank away. Whether desired or not, she was not used to such looks. "A good look for you," the chief said.

"Thank you," Yanuma whispered.

Nuyani felt compelled as her ears grew hot. She then repeated, "Th-thank you."

"And good morning to you, Gamaunda," Yanuma added. "Tell me. What do you think is out there?"

The man's smile faded as he answered, "there are still things we need to learn about this storm and the worms. Aside from that, Elder Moyaud is missing. Whether he's alive or not, we must find his body or the ring." Nuyani caught Yanuma with wide eyes. Even she had not realized the elder was missing.

"How long has everyone been here?" Nuyani questioned.

"Half a day at most," the chief replied. "There are still matters we need to attend to. Food and wood." The man then turned to Nuyani. "How did you manage your supplies?"

"I always ran to the trees for wood. Food is a bit easier if you follow the river. There's plenty of nuts and fruits. But, after this last storm, I don't know what'll be left."

Gamaunda nodded his head. "We will see," he replied.

"Yes but, Moyaud is missing. What will we do if we cannot find him?" the elder asked.

"Keep going," Gamaunda said as he shook his head. The dismissive words left with a tinge of pain in his tone. "His insight, and yours, guides us, but we will have to either find other means or go on without."

"If he isn't found," Yanuma emphasized.

"Yes, elder. If he isn't," Gamaunda continued. "The best thing to consider is that he is merely missing and that we have you and elder Belractu."

Yanuma looked down. Nuyani looked at the elder, surprised to see her joyful smile gone and revealing frailty. The elder then shook her head and looked up at Gamaunda. "We will have to find that later. Right now, we must speak as a group," Yanuma said. "Right now, we must discuss another matter with the village."

A moment later, Nuyani found herself sitting with the elders and Gamaunda in a hut with several layers of tarp lying over the entrance and window to keep the sound to themselves.

"No!" Nuyani bellowed. The others looked at her in surprise.

"Why not? Is this not what you wished for? To be a part of the village?"

Gamaunda look disappointed as he added, "This is a chance to lead us to be stronger."

Nuyani glared at the man. She then shot back, "Mistakes or not, if you want a priestess or priest, make one from the village. I'm not looking to be worshipped."

"Yet you are. The Great Lord spoke to you. And through you, the village still lives," Yanuma pointed out.

"You have survived everything and thrived here and are the best leader for this," Gamaunda added.

"If anything, the journey you've taken and abilities you've learned all point to the same lessons that we've taught, or rolls we've played," Belractu added. "You see through three worlds more than Moyaud. You can heal. Even use the power of others to do the same. You can see memories and speak with your e-edria."

'They are learning more,' Nuyani thought.

"For all we know, you may even learn to share them. Lord Kelvert has told us how you controlled the blood-mane against the corrupted one."

"Not to correct the Great Lord but, that wasn't control. I asked for help," Nuyani corrected.

"Well, we're glad it did," Yanuma commented, taking a deep breath.

"Why do you need a priestess?" Nuyani questioned.

"There's little guidance in the village as of now and faith," Gamaunda said plainly. "It may fracture."

"Fracture?" Nuyani questioned, narrowing her eyes.

"Our lessons and history have made everyone question their faith in our leadership," Belractu said. "To stay together, the village needs you. Your family values and Kelvert's guidance are the best examples for the village." Nuyani looked to the elder. It had only been five, or so days, and they were pairing her back with Sutama and two children she barely knew. Nuyani knew what it meant, but her years alone felt like they would never end. Something made Nuyani pull away. "If we don't come together now, what will happen if we are fighting each other, and the next storm brings more beasts?"

'I won't let another storm rise,' Nuyani thought as she wore a determined glare staring at the floor.

"Just consider it this way. You've proven our ignorance to the Great Lord's gift and can correct this so no one will forget the true meaning. You are an example of what the village should strive for. You will never be alone," Gamaunda said in a soft tone.

Nuyani glanced at the man then returned her gaze to the ground. "Just give me a few days. I need to think."

Yanuma narrowed her eyes. "What else is there to worry about, Nuyani?" she questioned.

Nuyani looked the elder in the eye and replied, "Two days ago, I was the witch. Any other man or woman would kill me on sight. I've seen the hatred. Even the sinner influenced the end of those with the gift after only a single day of tragedy leading to the death of others. No. I will wait. I will try to accept you all but, I was the one first cast out." Nuyani did not wait for a rebuttal as she left the hut.

Returning to the same hut where she awoke, Nuyani sat on the floor and hugged her legs. With her thrum, she could feel the presence of everyone nearby. Gritting her teeth, Nuyani only felt the urge to hide and get away from her now crowded home. She grabbed at the loose ends of her dress, cursing that she was left vulnerable to others. Wanting her runner's wear, Nuyani ripped part of her dress, not realizing it was nowhere near as durable. Letting out an audible grunt, she turned to the bedroll and lay down.

Ch. 29

Witch or Priestess

A few days had passed, and most villagers had settled into the larger cavern. As Nuyani exited her hut, she was left relatively alone by the others at night. She looked down at the side of the hut where several gifts, figures, and items were given to her as a strange tribute. It was odd to Nuyani to receive so many thanks and prayers from others. With her awareness of the energy, it was hard not to notice and used to keep her up at night. Luckily the ethereal forces at her command seemed to be very versatile as she was able to separate a sliver of her own edria and layered it within an ivory talisman with a fox carving. She left the prutosa stored within. As Nuyani moved toward the front shelf, she saw a few guards standing around villagers in prayer.

The area had changed, though Nuyani was not certain it was unwelcomed. The indented firepit had an obelisk that allowed it to stand below Kelvert. Nuyani climbed onto the shelf, forgetting the new stairs in place for everyone, but never forgetting the shifting eyes of men and boys that seemed to always aim for her backside. As she sat down at a mat and joined the prayer, others greeted her and moved on.

"How do you feel, Nuyani?" Kelvert then whispered in an echoed voice of hers.

'Strange, Great Lord,' Nuyani replied. 'I am grateful but, things are quiet. It is odd.'

"What is it you wish?" the wisp asked.

"I want to keep them safe but free my mother too," Nuyani said.

"Then you must do so," Kelvert said. "A leaf moves with the river Nuyani but, fish swim up and down its tide. Move forward and prepare them for the time you must leave."

Nuyani looked to the ground as she thought of Kelvert's words. "Thank you, Great Lord."

As Nuyani rose and remembered but ignored the stairs, she then caught sight of Caluu and Cuganwa. She had not seen the two for days as her role as priestess came with an assortment of responsibilities she did not expect.

The young child rushed forward with arms out as she shouted, "Nui! Morning!" Other adults disappointed the child as the front was seen as a temple of sorts. Nuyani did not care as she lifted the child and hugged her tight. Strangely, Nuyani trying to save her allowed the two to save each other. Though Nuyani never said it, she counted it twice. "Morning Caluu. Morning Cuganwa. How are you both?" Nuyani said with a warm smile and a whisper.

"Morning. We are fine. How's being the priestess?" Cuganwa asked.

"It's different. Did you come to pray?" Nuyani asked.

"Yes," Caluu said with enthusiasm.

Nuyani chuckled as she left the child stand and waited for her siblings to pray. As Nuyani watched, she felt the thrum of Kelvert expand. The wisp's thrum expanded further, converting the edria of the cavern. Nuyani felt a sense of guilt seeing the shorter people slowly become erased. Though, she knew they had escaped. When her siblings were done with their prayer, they all walked to the rear tunnel and greeted others along the way. Nuyani's smile and waves were genuine, but her hand would occasionally twitch, reaching for a knife that was not there. Cuganwa noticed as well, wondering if there was something else he could do.

'Nuyani, are you all right?' the boy said, releasing concentrated waves toward Nuyani so no others could hear their conversation.

The priestess answered, 'I don't know. I feel safer, but empty. I hope all will be well. What are you doing for today?'

'Taking your lessons for the other guards,' Cuganwa answered.

'Oh. I see,' Nuyani thought as her mind trailed to her dread teaching the others. Though more women joined the hunting detail Nuyani could only guess were motivated by her, there were still too many people around her. As if instinctive, she managed to dampen and hide the thrum of her core and ebb of her soul from others. Teaching this with other basic senses, pulses and strengths

449

proved draining. The odd part for Nuyani was learning that the edria fed to them by the Kelvert had different effects for those with the wisp's gift. While she was able to run faster, others had stronger traits in adapting edria in constructs, were stronger naturally than others, or could command animals synchronizing their thrum with others'. All facets she had to learn on her own. It was strange to her that running was the one trait she had best. Nuyani did find it comforting when she found children in the hall conjuring small constructs of lizards and frogs mimicking their behaviors as if they were living.

'Don't copy worms,' Nuyani thought and confused Cuganwa for a moment until he saw the small figures.

'What will you teach now?' the boy then asked.

'I don't know,' Nuyani answered. 'Most of what I learned everyone picked up in two days. I might just have new guards to teach.'

'Why are you going?' Nuyani asked.

'I need to know more in general. The caravan will be dangerous. So, if you have anything new…' Cuganwa began.

'Cuganwa, you know as much as me. Not worth your time,' the priestess said.

'Well, I think it'd be good as a priest,' the boy said as he looked forward. The two then exited the tunnel entering the cavern filled with the village. Many of the huts on the lowest level were broken down and made into larger homes with the roofs bearing leather tarps or wool blankets instead of an overhanging wall. On the other side, others had found another sealed tunnel much larger than the front, which they used to move the whip-necks in and out of. Even other supplies such as good clay and stones were found in use. Though the people beforehand lived here, the villager collected any metal pieces they had and threw them into the larger pit. No one wanted to have such keepsakes around.

Many other obelisks were erected from stone and dirt at crossing paths for prayer and sharing stories. Nuyani could see Yanuma working with a large party of people to build another crafting hut as masonry workers created stations at a proper size once they could get the area up and running. The two passed through the area where fewer people and homes had yet to be broken down and moved to the rear tunnel. They watched as a roaming party of men entered another branching tunnel as they made their way out. There were dozens along this one path and possibly more on the other levels as networks cut through the cliffs. Everyone feared if the infested, even regular animals, would use the paths to get into the village.

The three eventually made it outside, where a group of people crowded around a pair of villagers in a fight. Thrums rang out as Nuyani saw one orb fire forth and collide with the head of a man with his head reeling back. Small spurts of blood and spit flew up as he fell to the floor.

"Stop!" Nuyani called aloud as they moved closer. It was Selsaj lying on the floor. Before him was another guard who had Kelvert's gift. Nuyani narrowed her eyes at the man. Only days with a new ability and others abused what it could do. "Leave it to practice." She then conjured a barrier between them before lowering down to Selsaj, helping the hunter stand. As he held his nose, the orange glow of his fingers was a sign he was healing his bloodied nose and split lip.

"Sorry, priestess. He just needed to learn the difference," the other man said.

"There's an enemy to bludgeon out there. Not here," she replied. The man said nothing as he backed away and gave Selsaj a wry smile.

"What's going on?" Cuganwa asked.

"He wanted to prove we were nothing just because Kelvert taught us how to see the past," Selsaj answered. Cuganwa looked at the man. Many others saw Selsaj and the others with respect for sparing Nuyani and having a hand in their survival. Others saw it as a chance to tear them down.

'I must be getting attached,' she thought. Nuyani started the lessons knowing there would be more to the issue. Two hours later, most had left with only Nuyani, Cuganwa, Caluu, and Selsaj remaining. Nuyani stopped the hunter. She had noticed the rhythm of his thrum was often thrown array when he tried to do too many things.

"Selsaj, try to do only two things one at a time but faster," Nuyani said. Selsaj looked confused by her. "Look. I don't know what you can do fully, but you tried to sense, hide, conjure and fire spells all at once. Even I can't do all that." Selsaj nodded his head. "Try to sense, then attack, sense, block, sense, conjure. The less you work too many things, the easier it will be on your mind and body."

"Yes, priestess," Selsaj answered as his eyes lit up to the routine. It worked well. Though Nuyani constantly used her thrum to know where everything was, she hardly tried to juggle too many things at once. The hunter walked off, his expression seeming deep in thought.

Later, as the sun sat at noon, a caravan quickly moved through the drylands. The whip-necks moved faster than ever as the edria within them nearly doubled their speed. Nuyani wondered if the beasts could catch her as well, though she mostly used her speed naturally. As she looked to the rear with the winds whipping by, a sense of comfort wore on her. Others road with some discomfort as the speed of their mounts was not something they were used to. 'What is out there?' Nuyani wondered, looking past the cliffs now as nothing but small barriers. She wanted to tell the others she planned to leave. Nuyani didn't know how to say it to Caluu and Cuganwa. She wasn't certain if they knew.

As another hour passed, the caravan reached the ruins of the village. To their shock, the bodies were gone. Nearly half of the people had died dropped, clawed, skewered, or taken by the sands. They were all gone. The party descended the slope and made a circle at the center. As the others assembled the sleds, Nuyani moved toward the largest section where the animal carcasses remained. No footprints, clothing, or blood trails gave a single clue to the deceased's whereabouts. Nuyani sat on the ground for a moment, and Cuganwa stood close by. She projected her conscience through her edria form and started to scour the area for its memory, a trick she learned while continuing to pray at Kelvert's side. What she did not expect was the memory to be hazed or erased. The turning of time with blue shadows and figures remained as black clouds covered the area. Only up to the death of the last infested blood-mane dragged into the nearby river remained to be seen.

Nuyani returned to her body. "There's no memory," she said as she looked to Cuganwa. The boy sighed, rubbed his face, and ran a hand through his afro. Biting his lip, he started to shake his head.

"This is just another mystery," Cuganwa moaned as he looked to Gamaunda and started walking.

Nuyani looked to the cliffs and eastern end. "Where would they go?" she questioned. "She remembered then that the infested took the bodies of the shorter people as well. "Where were they taken?" Dread set in as Nuyani thought to herself, 'I have to leave the drylands.'

As the party returned with food and supplies, it was clear the task would take several trips. Nuyani attempted to use her crystal but found its opening blocked. Even with the party linking together their edria, it only opened to govtif ved edria. It was a strange sign of good fate as the party saw a blood-mane dive for a young charge-horn killing it and eating. During the remaining days, Nuyani brought the guards who knew how to conjure blades into the lessens and worked diligently to improve everyone's abilities.

"Are you all right?" Cuganwa asked. She turned to face him. "What is wrong? You've committed to the role more and more. We haven't seen you at prayer."

"Sorry, Cuganwa. I just fear…a new enemy," Nuyani said. The boy thought the same as he remembered the blood-mane releasing a wave of spirit to repel him. "Things are different every time we look."

"What are you expecting next?" Cuganwa questioned.

"Us," Nuyani said.

Later that evening, Nuyani sat with the elders, Gamaunda, and to her surprise Sutama. The old hunter was different. With so many days apart, it was strange to see the man thinner than usual and wearing blue in his attire instead of red.

"Well, I think the obvious is made clear," Gamaunda said. He smiled at the others.

"Great," Nuyani started. "You can help everyone." This took the others aback for a moment, thinking she either wouldn't care or insult him as the seer of the elders. Nuyani looked to the others. "What? This will be needed. I fear something else may come."

"Nuyani, what troubles you?" Yanuma questioned.

"The bodies are all gone meaning the worms or animals may have taken them. What will those gifted and infested do? It worries me," Nuyani stated.

"Well, isn't that why you're the priestess?" Gamaunda commented with a smile. "These things are bound to happen but, it is you who has aided us this far."

"But what say you, Sutama?" Belractu asked.

"Keep searching the tunnels. There're more caverns and chambers than we ever realized. Perhaps the other people still live in their own dwellings. By the Great Lord, we can only hope they have an answer to our predicaments as well."

Gamaunuda nodded his head. "There are several parties already in search but, I think we will need search leaders as much as we need hunting leaders," the chief stated. He then looked to Nuyani. "What do you think of the villagers you've trained? Do you think any of them deserve leadership?"

Nuyani narrowed her eyes and looked to the ground as faces appeared in her mind. "I can see a few. None are too skilled but, they can hold their own," Nuyani admitted.

"Good. Let's have something made as a sign for the leader of these new groups. That will mark the best to lead in your classes," Yanuma suggested. The priestess nodded in agreement before moving they moved on to supplies. The speed and strength of the whip-necks made hunting simple.

Once the meeting was over, Nuyani found herself wandering toward the stables for the animals built into the cliffside. Despite the free space within the caverns, it was a bit much to expect such large animals would feel comfortable inside all day. As Nuyani rounded the corner of a raised tent, Odaru tended to Muga. No longer on a limp, the hunter stood on his own as if the injury had never occurred. She paused for a moment sensing several pulses radiating from the hunter. Muga blinked, and her eyes shifted to her, catching Odaru's attention.

"Hello, Dear Priestess," the man said with the same warm smile. "How are you this evening?" Odaru turned to her, revealing a long leather cord with six blue beads hanging freely next to them.

"Hello, Odaru," Nuyani said. "I'm fine. Just on a walk to clear my head." Muga groaned and craned her head over to the priestess. Nuyani placed a hand on her head and started to scratch under her chin as well.

"What's the matter?" Odaru asked as he crossed his arms.

Nuyani held Muga for a moment as she thought of her answer. "I fear the enemy is coming and creating new ways to attack us. Would you fix the problems as they come, knowing they'd get worse, or would you go to the source even if you don't know how to fix it?"

"Ah. To the point," Odaru said. "The source is the bigger issue. Soon, the growing problems will become just as unsolvable as the source." Nuyani stared at the man staying quiet. "You know that, don't you?" Nuyani sighed and stepped to the side. "What're you planning?"

"To stop the source, of course," Nuyani stated. "I just don't know what I'm leaving." Nuyani never realized it would happen but, she was becoming happy. The love, admiration, acknowledgment of the village all came to fruition. Even her responsibilities to the others gave her a sense of purpose beyond survival.

Odaru approached the priestess and smiled. "You know what you must do. Just remember that what makes it all the more precious. The Great Lord guides you." Nuyani was swift as she leaned forward and embraced the hunter placing a soft kiss on his cheek. The wise hunting was now at a loss for words.

"I think you deserve thanks as well," Nuyani said. "I don't think my family would be as well off without a great friend."

This deepened Odaru's smile. Nuyani then made her way toward the entrance as she moved with haste.

"Careful hunting leader. You've been captured already," Lamoy declared from the stable. The huntress moved to the man's side and hung an arm around him.

"I have my moon," Odaru stated before the two kissed.

The next morning, Nuyani had given a small list of items for the village aids to acquire. The others looked worried as many of the items were herbs and tools for scavenging and hunting. In her next few drills, Nuyani challenged the others to find her in the drylands while remaining hidden from her. Hunters vs. the priestess. With two days, and fatigue, Nuyani had captured most of the guards and villagers, with only a handful finding her first. To Nuyani's surprise, she found Selsaj to be an effective hunter with his senses. When the small set of bracelets with green beads arrived, she did not hesitate to hand one to Selsaj. As the next few hunting trials went underway, the bracelets were handed out and not without scrutiny as some tried to demand their position. Even in a new location and new leadership, villagers still yearned for positions of power and favor. Her denial of favorites only spawned half-true rumors of Nuyani looking to leave, the wilds calling her to flee the village. It only made her wonder who knew of her plans and why they cared to belittle her efforts. As time passed, Nuyani grew confident in the villagers she trained. The hunting continued without issue aside from the usual dangers. It was time to leave.

The following day, Nuyani left her hut wearing runner's wear along with a tool strap with her usual assortment of items as two stone knives sat in their sheaths and a third made of ivory with a single fox surrounded by Kelvert's light carved into the hilt. After her usual prayers, Nuyani moved to the front with many eyes following her movements. Nuyani walked through the tunnel and made her way to the curling roof near the demon gate. She looked at the stone seeing the powerful scars in the rockface she never expected to see. Nuyani tightened her leather-bound fist.

"You've called, priestess?" Sutama then said. Nuyani turned around, showing her welling eyes.

"Yes, f-father," she said with a stutter. "I have. I need to show you something."

Two of the guards at the slope looked to see the two moving their way and down the area. They watched as the elder and priestess walked along the dirt to a nearby fissure. Nuyani breathed deeply as she stopped at the edge. A small cluster of purple flowers still grew as a small stream trickled through despite the winds. Sutama looked at her.

"This is where I had to bury her," Nuyani said. "I don't know if she was taken because she wasn't cremated, but I did the only thing I could." Sutama looked to Nuyani and back to the flowers. "I blame…blamed you for so long, but I don't know if I can't blame myself."

This time the old hunter started to shed tears. "Why have you shown me now?"

"Because you will promise me…" Nuyani declared as she spun to face him. "Promise me you will send prayers and wishes to her so that she is not alone. Promise me she will know your wishes and gratitude and that you will do for Caluu, Cuganwa, and Jogia what we lost all these years."

Sutama stepped forward, placing hands on her shoulders. "I promise." As he removed his hands, he undid the knot of a bracelet on his wrist. Nuyani looked at the item, recognizing the small crystal housing the blade she brought to the drylands. Lifting her hand and placing it in her palm, the man said, "I will pray for you both. I will be there for Caluu no differently now than in the future, Lord Kelvert willing." As the man departed, Nuyani put the bracelet on. She then turned to the west, facing the opening of the cliffs. Lifting her talisman of the fox, she prayed, releasing as much of the prutosa as she could to her mother, hoping some power would break any hold on her soul.

Nuyani then started to run east, a final goodbye as she reached a dirt mound with a brush missing its flowers and growing through the left eye socket of a skull.

"You're still here," Nuyani said as she felt the soft bead of pressure begin to surge. To'anu's visage appeared in the light of dawn as he looked with a proud smile.

"Didn't know I could serve in death. I must be blessed by the Great Lord," To'anu claimed.

Nuyani wore a serious expression on her face as she looked at the spirit. "You could meet Lord Kelvert and your family."

The man smiled. "No. I have been here long enough. There is more shame that I've brought than glory I could gain. I just warn you…," To'anu's glare turned serious. "Do not take spirits lightly. Even I was able to do something once I learned more of the world."

Nuyani nodded and revealed a small spade, a sack filled with lard and bramble, along with some flintstones. To'anu was speechless as he watched the witch present her hand. Her core radiated with strong, steady beats reverberating to her hand until a soft glow rose in her palm. Silently the soul said nothing as he took up her hand. The pulses radiated outward, collecting the soul as it concentrated into the palm of her hand. Nuyani then repeated the morning prayer gesture raising her palm to the sky as the soul fired like a star into what remained of the night sky free of the dangers to life and spirit in the drylands. After taking a moment to dig up the bones, Nuyani placed them in the sack of lard and bramble before lighting the bag with a spark. The fire climbed to hip height.

Nuyani waited as she let the flame consume the bag, and the ashes remained. Taking all that remained, she poured the ashes into the river where the water bites nipped at the pieces. 'Be free, hunter and at peace,' Nuyani thought.

Turning to the west, Nuyani had one thought as she took another breath and focused her thrum. Pulses hummed through her entire body until every part of her was elated. Nuyani continued until it felt as if she were lighter than air. Black lines started to form at the perimeter of her vision before engulfing her sight. Another light appeared at the center, rushing forth only to be replaced with the golden sand under the morning sun's rays. Nuyani looked back, seeing the cliff gap. She managed to leap through space on her own but felt lost as she left the lands. Releasing a deep breath, Nuyani turned only to hear a sudden thud in the dirt.

Nuyani looked at the sand, only to see an arrow fired into the ground with an item attached to the shaft. The woman looked back and saw two guards at odds. One shouting and staring at her with his bow in hand. The other tried to stop him as he pulled on the man's tunic. Nuyani's thrum strengthened her sight as she could see the redness of his eyes and spit flying from his mouth. Nuyani looked to the arrow, retrieving the ivory talisman connected to the shaft. It bared the image of a fox on it, but unlike the polished surface of the piece, a jagged flaking line was cut through the neck.

She looked back at the man. 'There will always be someone who feels betrayed,' Nuyani thought as she placed the item in her free pouch next to the crystal, flintstones, and herbs, before walking on toward the west.

The end